GENESIS

FIRST COLONY - BOOK ONE

KEN LOZITO

ACOUSTICAL BOOKS LLC

Published by Acoustical Books, LLC

KenLozito.com

Cover design by Jeff Brown

ISBN: 978-1-945223-12-9

1

THE FREIGHTER WAITED for clearance to make its final approach to Chronos Station while Connor Gates and his squad hid in a shipping container in the vast belly of the vessel. Connor glanced at his men. They were the most famous squad that no one outside the NA Command had ever heard of. Officially they didn't exist. For hundreds of years, black ops military platoons had celebrated a long tradition of working in the shadows, and their effectiveness was measured by the undetected execution of their missions. Even within the shadowy confines of black ops, Connor's Ghosts were a bit of a legend. When failure was not an option, it was the Ghosts who were given the toughest missions. Connor had been the CO of the Ghosts for ten years—not even a blip in the prolonged lifetimes of people in this day and age.

"We're patched in, Colonel," Sawyer said.

Connor used his implants to access the open comms channel on the bridge.

"Freighter JEC 2701, hold your approach while we validate the codes for your ship," the harbormaster said.

"Copy. We'll hold the approach," the freighter's helmsman replied.

A sub-screen appeared on Connor's heads-up display that showed the ship's codes being matched up with the records being transferred from the lunar shipping yards.

The station comms channel was muted by someone on the freighter's bridge, and Connor heard the helmsman speaking.

"Captain, with as many deliveries as we make to this station, you'd think they'd give us a warmer welcome," said the helmsman.

"They're following standard protocol," said the captain.

"Yeah, but targeting us with their weapons systems every time we come here is a bit much. It's not like we're part of the Syndicate or anything," said the helmsman.

"And here I thought you couldn't wait for some shore leave on a luxurious seventh-generation deep-space station," said the captain.

Connor muted the comms channels and clenched his teeth at the mention of the Syndicate. He'd been hunting them for the past five years, patiently working his way closer to the vast crime family that had the power to challenge the nation-states of old.

The soldier next to Connor checked his weapon while he waited. "If they only knew the head of the Syndicate had taken up residence on this station," Major Kasey Douglass said.

Kasey had been Connor's second in command for almost as long as he'd been hunting the Syndicate.

"Only if our intel is good. Remember Sandy Springs?" Connor asked.

Kasey nodded. "Kinda hard to forget that crapstorm of an op."

"This is the right place. I know it. A civilian space station that has weapons capabilities to defend itself from attack matches his MO," Connor said.

"You still think the entire Syndicate is run by just one person?"

"It is," Connor said.

"But we don't have a name for this guy," Kasey said.

"We have his location. He's smart. Even if we'd come here with combat shuttles under stealth, we would have run the risk of alerting him. And even though the Sandy Springs op was a disaster, we learned a lot," Connor said.

"Yeah, not to trust the chain of command in our own org. We're completely off the reservation with this. No backup," Kasey said.

"Had to be this way. I couldn't risk the mission becoming compromised. Besides, it's not like we're breaking any rules. I do have authority to conduct this mission," Connor said.

"I won't argue about authority, but this is a civilian station— and not just any civilian station. This is Chronos. Only the most affluent dignitaries, ambassadors, and heads of corporations use this place as their go-to spot. If we have an incident here, it could hurt us. We should report the op to COMCENT," Kasey said.

Connor regarded Kasey for a moment. The major was doing his job, voicing his concerns to his commanding officer. "Your concerns are noted, but this is still a comms blackout op. COMCENT will be notified after the op is complete, Major," Connor replied.

"Of course, Colonel," Kasey said and let the matter drop.

They all knew why they were there. The Syndicate had a significant research and development operation that did not abide by the Earth's R&D accords, freely testing anything and everything on human subjects regardless of sex, age, or ethnic origin. Some of the research stations they'd shut down throughout the solar system still gave him nightmares as he recalled cross-species genetic experimentation that created horrific monsters that were set loose to test how well their experiments had worked. The Syndicate had become the NA Command's highest priority, but the real work fell into black ops command channels. The Syndicate was among the most ruthless organizations in history.

They had little regard for human life and operated above the law. The fact that they'd set up operations at a place like Chronos Station was a testament to their practices in maximizing collateral damage.

The harbormaster cleared the freighter to dock, and within the hour the large freighter was being guided to its docking slip. The Ghosts waited in silent anticipation. Once the ship docked, they could move under the cover of offloading activities. No one would suspect that one of the shipping containers carried an infiltration force.

"Wil, are you in the station's systems yet?" Connor asked.

Wil Reisman waved his hands around, working through an interface that only he could see. "I'm in but only with transit access. We can get schematics and access the maglev transport, but I'm not in the secure Mosi system, Colonel."

"Good. Those systems are closely monitored. I don't want them tipped off to our presence," Connor said.

"I've uploaded the station's schematics to our suit computers," Reisman said.

Connor brought up the schematics, and his suit computer showed a one hundred percent match for what they had on record. He inputted the latest intelligence overlay, and a path highlighted to a destination called Rabbit's Foot.

"Send coded message to Bravo Squad. The op is a go," Connor said.

The ship's status showed that it was docked and the automated loaders would begin offloading the shipping containers to the station. Connor glanced at Tiegan, waiting for his tech ops specialist to give them the go-ahead.

Large lifts came for the priority pallets first, and Connor felt himself shift to zero gravity until their shipping container was brought within the station's gravitational field. He engaged his combat suit's camo-mode, which rendered them invisible to anyone watching, as well as to the station's sensors. The secure latch of the shipping container's door popped open and Connor pushed his way out, dropping down sixty meters to the ground. His combat suit absorbed the shock of his landing, and he quickly moved to the side while the rest of the squad came down and took up positions on the space dock.

The space dock was a massive open area through which all ship traffic to the station was routed. Freighters like the one they'd stowed away on docked in a designated area away from civilian transports.

"Contact," Denton said.

Connor looked over and saw a standard Bosheir Security Mech patrolling the dock. The large mech could either be piloted by a person or engaged in patrol mode, allowing the mech's AI or pilot to remotely operate the machine. Large cannons gleamed on the mech's metallic forearms, and its head swiveled in their direction.

"Hold. It's a T-series 10-01 and can't detect us," Reisman said.

Connor waited. Samson had the mech in his sights, his heavy rocket launcher ready to go if needed, but the mech turned away from them and stalked off.

The Ghosts headed in the direction the mech had gone, watching as work drones went about unloading the shipping containers after transfer off the ship. The heavily armed soldiers systematically moved forward two by two, with the first group clearing the area before the next group came up and took point. Most of them were armed with a third generation M32 pulse rifle with grenade launcher. The compact firearm packed quite a punch for its size and was ideal for close-quarters combat.

The few actual dockworkers in the area didn't notice them as they made their way across the docks and entered one of the large freight elevators.

"Reisman, we need those markings," Connor said.

His intelligence officer worked through the options on his holo-interface while Connor kept a careful watch on the elevator's progress toward one of Chronos Station's many common areas. An empty elevator would certainly be noticed by the local security office.

"Okay, time to blend in with the locals," Reisman said. He gestured with his hand as if flinging something at his squad mates. Within moments their combat suits produced a realistic-looking hologram of someone who lived on the station.

Samson growled. "Come on, man. You turned me into a pregnant woman."

The others grinned. Connor glanced down at his own combat suit and saw that Reisman had assigned him the hologram of Chronos Station security force personnel—black armor and a helmet that only showed his jawline underneath the visor.

"That's the way it goes, Samson. This time you drew the short straw. Congratulations! You're about eight months pregnant," Reisman said.

Samson turned toward Hank. "What are you laughing at? You got stuck with the grandma this time."

Connor glanced around at all of them to be sure there were no abnormalities in anyone's hologram. "Alright, by the numbers. Check each other out," Connor said.

The disguises were preconfigured for operations that brought them among civilians, and they used forms that put the casual onlooker off guard. Not many people would look twice at a pregnant woman or an elderly couple.

Connor checked Kasey, whose outward appearance resembled a morbidly obese man. Maintaining the hologram was taxing on their combat suit computers and couldn't be sustained for more than a few hours.

The elevator doors opened and the Ghosts exited. They followed a few corridors and were ushered through a security checkpoint. They didn't carry any heavy ordnance, and the scanners wouldn't be able to detect the ceramic composite that made up their combat suits. They did, however, need to store their weapons so they couldn't be detected.

The squad divided as they made their way across an expansive common area. Chronos Station sported blue skies and a parklike setting for its patrons. Though Connor couldn't smell the air, he imagined it was as fresh as if he were standing on a forested pathway back on Earth. Chronos Station was among the largest in the solar system and was restricted to the more affluent population. There was enough space for everyone and hardly any crowds, so the risk of someone accidentally brushing past the hologram and actually bumping into them was almost nonexistent.

The Ghosts converged on the platform for the maglev trains. Maglev trains didn't make any noise, and the top-of-the-line inertia dampeners gave no indication that they were traveling nearly five hundred kilometers an hour. The train cars were luxurious, and Connor noticed a few squad members glance longingly toward the food stations. Being topside on an op was a rare treat. Usually, they traveled through the bowels of a location and stayed out of sight, but there was no doubt the Syndicate would have ample security monitors watching all those entry points. Connor was wagering that their unorthodox approach would get them close enough to where the head of the Syndicate kept himself that their surprise attack would make escape all but impossible.

A flickering of light caught Connor's eye and he turned toward it. Samson's hologram was slipping, and Connor's mouth tightened. No one else on the train seemed to have noticed, so Connor walked over and gestured for Kasey to follow him. They were joined by two of the others as they circled around Samson. Reisman went over to Samson and swore.

Connor glanced behind him and saw Reisman working on Samson's combat suit. The hologram was nowhere to be seen. Perfect. He just wanted this to run smoothly, and having a damn suit processor fail on them wasn't that.

Kasey cleared his throat, and Connor turned back around. A small boy was looking at him, and his gaze narrowed suspiciously.

Connor waved. "Hello there, Citizen," he said, using the deepest official voice he could muster.

The boy's eyes widened and he backed away a few steps. Then he turned around and darted over to his family.

"Check this out," Kasey said, gesturing toward the wallscreen.

The image of a massive spaceship under construction at the Martian shipyards was displayed and a commentator began to speak:

The Ark—humanity's valiant effort to reach beyond the confines of our solar system to establish the first interstellar colony out among the stars. We're now just weeks away from the Ark's christening, Earth's first interstellar colony ship will begin the longest journey ever embarked upon by mankind—a journey that began over a hundred years ago in 2105 when the star XPA6 was first observed among a group that held our best hope of an Earth-sized planet. Probes were sent out to see if any of these stars could support life as we experience it here on Earth. In 2182 we finally got our answer and the Ark program was born. Now, in 2217, three hundred thousand people will embark on a journey that will take eighty-four years to complete...

Connor stopped listening and glanced at the info-terminal beneath the wallscreen. The train was approaching their stop. "You have twenty-five seconds to get it fixed," he whispered.

The boy returned with a teenage girl who was probably his older sister, followed by his parents. The boy was gesturing toward them.

Connor stopped himself from shaking his head. He hadn't come all this way to be pestered by an overprivileged eleven-year-old brat. Connor faced them and put as much stern into his stance as he could while the others stood poised to knock out the family with stunners if they became a problem.

Just look away, kid, Connor pleaded in his mind.

The train came to a stop and Connor felt someone tap his shoulder.

"I'm feeling much better now. Thank you," Samson said, but his voice sounded like that of a woman.

"I'm glad to hear it," Connor replied.

The boy rubbed the back of his head as if he wasn't quite sure what he'd seen while his father ushered him off the train. Connor motioned for his squad to wait a few seconds and then they exited the train as well.

"Commander, I bypassed a bad processor branch, but the hologram's gonna overload it if we can't find cover in a few minutes," Reisman said.

"Understood," Connor replied.

They quickly left the platform and headed toward a nearby service tunnel. His nav computer noted the change in their path and updated the time-to-destination on his helmet's heads-up display.

With Reisman close behind, Samson went ahead to the maintenance tunnels, where they overrode the locking mechanism and went inside. They locked the door behind them and Connor hoped the unauthorized access hadn't been detected. One by one they disengaged the holograms and their combat suits returned to a deep gunmetal-gray color.

Connor retrieved his M32 from his storage compartment and the others did the same. Now was the time for speed, so they blazed a path through the maintenance tunnels that were normally frequented by maintenance bots. The bots hardly registered that they were in the tunnel with them, most likely due to the bots' rudimentary recognition systems determining

the Ghosts' combat suits were just more bots on maintenance
duty.

The Syndicate's stronghold was in the middle level of the
station toward the interior. This was the part of the station that
would be least vulnerable to attack. Connor had studied the
station's schematics and knew all the ins and outs for this section.
He'd seen enough military installations to recognize the design,
even with the lavish furnishings. According to the schematics,
they were on the premises of a luxurious hotel.

They came to a stop outside a maintenance door. Connor was
certain it was being monitored, so he gestured for Reisman.

The tech specialist moved forward. "Nothing to see here. Just
another lowly maintenance bot trudging along," Reisman
muttered.

The door retracted into the ceiling, and the Ghosts went
through to a nearby station where two guards were posted. The
guards glanced over toward the open door, and when no
maintenance bot came through, one of them went over to
investigate.

The guard peered through the door and activated his comlink.
"Central, we have a maintenance door open on Deck 19, but no bot
has come through. Do you have any bots on sensors?"

The guard stepped through the doorway. The door shut, and
he turned and banged at it from the other side.

Connor engaged the charge they'd placed and the banging
stopped. The Ghosts then waited while the second guard came
out of the station to investigate. As he stepped away, Connor fired
a stunner dart into the guard's exposed neck, the shock of which
caused the guard to drop to the ground, unconscious.

"Station 19, do you copy?"

Connor glanced at Reisman, who nodded that he was okay to
speak.

"We're here, Central. That door is shut now and won't open.

We'll need to schedule a repair crew to come check it out," Connor said. The hacked signal disguised his voice based on the speech patterns recorded from when the guard had spoken earlier.

"Confirm. Repair crew will be sent out. Carry on."

The comlink signal deactivated, and Connor looked at Reisman. "Good work," he said and looked over at Kasey. "Any word from Bravo Squad?"

Kasey shook his head. "Negative, sir."

"Alright, we go on. You're cleared to only engage hostiles, so if you don't see a weapon, we can't use ours. Clear?" Connor said.

The squad replied that they understood.

"Okay, Samson, you're on point with Jefferson and Oslo," Connor said. "Reisman, you're with me. Kasey, you're with the others."

Samson was six feet eight inches tall and a bear of man. Connor had seen him fire a T49 assault rifle in each hand while maintaining accuracy.

Samson led them forward, and Jefferson covered him. Oslo was just behind. The trio moved forward on point, and the rest of the squad followed in pairs. They left the maintenance tunnels behind and made their way through the lower levels of the hotel, stopping at a service elevator and waiting while Reisman overrode the controls so they could get to the sixtieth floor.

Reisman stopped what he was doing and looked at Connor. "Special access required, even to put in the floor number. If I override it, they'll likely detect it."

Connor's brows pulled together in thought. "What about the fifty-ninth floor? Can you get us close?"

Reisman checked. "Ah, there it is. Fifty-eighth floor is still under construction."

"Perfect," Connor said.

Reisman punched in the new destination and the service elevator began its ascent. Connor would have preferred to break the squads up into six-man teams lest one of them got pinned down, but he chose speed over caution for this op. He checked the comms status for Bravo Squad, which was being led by Denton, but there was nothing. He had doubled up for this op, breaking their platoon into two squads. They had separate ships and approach vectors, but even with comms blackout there still should have been at least an encoded check-in. Connor frowned and felt the hairs on the back of his neck stand on end—a feeling he'd get when an op was about to go south.

The service elevator stopped and the Ghosts readied their weapons. When the doors pulled apart, a dark, half-finished floor could be seen beyond. Samson checked his corner while Jefferson checked the other. Both men ducked out of the elevator with two more Ghosts behind them. The rest of them followed, and Connor scanned the area ahead. There were large stacks of construction materials amid offline machinery. Connor narrowed his gaze and switched to enhanced view, cycling through different bands until the area came alive with soldiers wearing combat suits just like theirs.

"Take cover!" Connor cried and lunged behind the nearest construction vehicle.

The rest of the Ghosts scattered toward cover as the Syndicate soldiers opened fire. The head of the Syndicate had known they were coming for them. This whole op had been a trap.

2

_____

BLISTERING weapons fire tore into the machine Connor hid behind. The Ghosts were seasoned professionals who were at home on any battlefield, whether on a ship, on a space station, or in the jungles of South America. They spread out and took cover, returning fire while they evaluated the battlefield.

Connor set his ammo to frag grenades, stuck his M32 rifle around the corner, and saw where two enemy soldiers huddled behind a stack of metal beams. He angled the rifle up and his targeting computer identified the proper angle. Connor fired a grenade.

The Syndicate was down two soldiers.

Samson unleashed his T49 at full auto, and Jefferson did the same. Connor moved to the other end of the machinery he was using for cover, and Kasey came to his side. Across from them was a crane. He needed to get over to it so he could flank their attackers.

"I'll cover you," Kasey said and brought up his pulse rifle.

Connor sprinted across amidst a hailstorm of deadly fire from Syndicate mercenaries while Kasey provided covering fire as promised. Connor felt several shots glance off his armor as he slammed into the crane and circled around, flanking the four-man firing team that kept Kasey pinned. Connor aimed and fired his M32, taking out two Syndicate soldiers, then ducked back behind the crane as the remaining two soldiers fired their weapons at him and Kasey seized the opportunity to take them out.

Connor opened a storage compartment in the leg of his suit and pulled out two drone spheres, flinging them up into the air and activating them. The drones split apart. One zoomed directly over the enemy while the other went across the battlefield. The active drones sent data back to Connor's combat suit.

"This was a trap, but I think we got here sooner than they expected," Kasey said.

"We'll continue to flank them and stay out of the choke points," Connor said.

He sent his orders over the secure comlink and the Ghosts moved forward. The Syndicate soldiers were likely ex-military, and their tactics might have worked on a different platoon.

"Jefferson's down," Oslo shouted.

"I'm coming," Malarkey said over the comlink.

Connor watched as his medic hugged the ground and crawled toward Jefferson. Samson bellowed as he provided covering fire. Connor and Kasey continued up the side, using massive metal girders for cover. They'd flanked the soldiers that had Samson and others pinned down, and the two groups ping-ponged the Syndicate soldiers. Agility was essential for blazing through the battlefield.

Malarkey opened a comlink to Connor. "Jefferson's gone, sir. They hit him with something that ate through his armor—"

Malarkey stopped speaking and started screaming.

"Commander, Malarkey and Woods are down," Sawyer said.

Connor swore, hating what he was about to do. "Bring out the NESS and avoid Malarkey and Woods."

The nano-robotic explosive seeker swarm, NESS, was a last-resort weapon that could level the whole floor. Oslo pulled out a metal canister and keyed in the activation code on the panel, then hurled the canister past the Syndicate soldiers and tumbled away. A weaponized nano-robotic swarm burst from the canister.

"I've sent the clean-and-sweep protocol, sir," Kasey said.

There was a bright flash, and the bodies of their fallen soldiers disintegrated. There could be no trace of the Ghosts having been here. Connor heard Samson growl as he kept firing his weapon at full auto. There were more reinforcements bolstering the Syndicate ranks.

"Damn it! Where is the NESS?" Connor demanded.

"Online now, sir. It'll be in position in twenty seconds," Tiegan replied.

The NESS interface came online, and as commanding officer, Connor had to be the one to authorize its use. But the Syndicate soldiers had stopped firing their weapons, so Connor brought up the drone feeds. A woman stood in the middle of an open area and stared defiantly at the drones.

Connor sent out the cease-fire signal to his team.

"The fabled Ghost Platoon. I must admit I'm impressed with your performance. You did much better than that other team," the woman said.

Connor ignored the bait and stayed behind cover. "Then you know it's hopeless. We've got you. The Syndicate is finished," he said and peeked around the corner.

The woman looked to be in her mid-forties and wore a blue business suit, but due to the possibility of prolonging, there was no way for Connor to tell how old she was. She could have been anywhere from a hundred to two hundred years old, and there wasn't an ounce of fear in her cold gaze hidden under a mask of amusement.

"Did you really think that if you came here and destroyed this place the Syndicate would just disappear? That I have no contingency plans?"

"I'd call it a good start. I'll find whoever your successor is and take them out as well. You see, your operations at Sandy Springs got the attention of some pretty powerful people, and I'm authorized to take you out," Connor said.

The minimum time required for the NESS to move the pieces into position was twenty seconds, but this conversation was allowing it to probe deeper into the structure of the building.

The woman smiled. "Tell me, Connor, which R&D company do you think came up with the NESS?"

Kasey glanced at him and Connor's eyes widened. She knew his name.

"Are you saying you invented the NESS?" Connor asked.

He stayed focused but also kept wondering how the hell this bitch knew his name.

"Connor Gates, rank colonel, commanding officer of the Ghosts Special Forces Platoon in service of the North American Union Alliance. Believe me when I tell you that there isn't a member of your platoon we don't have detailed files on," the woman said.

Connor took a shot, aiming a foot above the woman's head. The woman's form wavered for a moment and the hologram vanished. In her place was a large mech that dropped its stealth field.

"You know an awful lot about me," Connor said.

"Indeed we do. You can call me RJ," the same woman's voice said from the mech's speakers.

"Okay, RJ, you must know there's no way you're walking out of here alive," Connor said.

RJ laughed. "You've been at a disadvantage since you started hunting the Syndicate because your small mind cannot grasp what the Syndicate actually is. We're everywhere. There isn't a part of your world that isn't touched by us."

"I think you have an over-bloated sense of self-worth, pretty common in megalomaniacs. I've taken a few down in my career, and I'm ready to add you to the list," Connor said.

He brought the NESS interface up on his suit computers and was about to activate the device. The rest of the Ghosts continued to identify targets and escape routes.

"I wouldn't do that if I were you," RJ said.

"You're not me," Connor replied.

"If you engage the NESS, you'll destroy this entire station, not just this floor as you were expecting. I know the rules of engagement, Colonel, and your authorization to take me out doesn't include the wholesale slaughter of millions of people," RJ said.

The NESS they'd brought with them didn't have anywhere near the ordnance to destroy the station.

"Some might consider the price worth it," Connor bluffed.

"Your military record says otherwise."

"If you were willing to destroy this station, you would have done it already, unless we really did catch you off guard and you're stalling for time," Connor said.

He opened up a comlink to Reisman. "Can you confirm what she's saying?"

"I've been trying since she first mentioned it, sir. I've got nothing. The NESS has been deployed and has converged on the support structure of this floor."

"Why don't you come out from where you're hiding?" RJ said. "I've ordered my forces not to fire on you."

Connor shook his head. "You'll have to forgive me if I don't take your word for it."

He checked the status of the other Ghosts. They'd all lined up shots on the large mech. If he gave the order, that mech would be taken out in seconds.

"You're still trying to figure out whether I'm telling you the truth. I will admit you've been a thorn in my side for longer than most. I'll tell you what. I know your tech specialist is trying to determine whether my threat to the station is real or not. I'll save him the trouble," RJ said.

Connor glanced over at Reisman and his eyes became as wide as saucers. "There's a NESS deployed station wide. It's on every level!"

Connor's gut clenched. They were in a stalemate. His mind raced, trying to find some way he could achieve their objective and not lose the station. The NESS required specialized encrypted protocols that couldn't be copied. Reisman was good, but no one could break it. RJ's thumb was on the trigger to take out the entire station.

"We walk away and—" Connor began.

"Not quite as ruthless as your reputation says you are. You're the first person in a hundred years to be in my presence and able to inflict physical harm, and the thought of killing millions of people shatters your resolve? This encounter hasn't been as illuminating as I'd hoped it would be," RJ said.

The large mech took several steps back.

"Why? Because I won't play your game?" Connor asked.

The mech stopped. "You've been playing my game, Colonel, for the past five years. Granted, your presence here denotes a hole in our security that will soon be rectified."

"Sir, the NESS field is being activated," Reisman said.

"What are you doing! I already said I'd let you go," Connor shouted.

He came out from cover and pointed his weapon at the head of the Syndicate. The mech kept moving backward and Connor fired his weapon. "Is that all this was? A way for you to test your security?"

"Goodbye, Colonel. We won't be meeting again," RJ said.

Syndicate troops resumed firing on them and Connor scrambled behind cover. He emptied his mag of frag grenades, laying fiery waste to the Syndicate troops, and then pulled back toward Reisman.

"Can you block the signal?" Connor asked.

Reisman shook his head. "According to this, the signal was sent before we even got to the station. It's been on a timer . . ." His voice trailed off as if he couldn't believe what he was seeing.

Connor tried to access the station's systems, looking for a way to signal the evacuation protocols.

"Sir, we need to fall back," Kasey said.

Connor glanced the way RJ had gone.

"There's a way out if we go this way," Kasey said.

Connor looked where Kasey was gesturing. The path lay in the opposite direction. This whole thing had been staged, and the worst part was that RJ wanted them to escape. Connor turned back toward where the Syndicate forces had retreated and screamed.

Kasey grabbed him and spun him around, putting his head inches from Connor's own. "Listen to me. You found her once. If we get out of here, we can find her again."

Kasey let go of him, and Connor looked at Reisman. "Try and signal the evacuation using any protocols you can find. Use anything to signal that something is wrong with the station."

Connor gave the order for them to retreat, and the acid taste of bile crept up his throat. They quickly made their way to the edge of the floor as the NESS triggered the explosions, stemming from the far side of Chronos Station.

"Combat shuttle en route," Kasey informed them.

Samson placed breaching explosives on the outer walls of the station. Once they detonated, a containment field would become active that would prevent the atmosphere from escaping, but the field wouldn't prevent them from leaving.

"We can wait to be picked up. Use your suit jets to get clear of the station and head toward the rendezvous point marked on your heads-up display," Connor said.

The Ghosts leaped out of the gaping hole, and Connor waited for them to go. He kept glancing at the Chronos Station info terminal feed, which showed the number of residences numbered in the millions. Powerless to stop the destruction, Connor felt the crushing weight of the soon-to-be-dead pressing in on him. With one last glance at the station's interior, he leaped away from Chronos Station.

3

THE COMBAT SHUTTLE'S autopilot homed in on their beacons and found the remains of the Ghosts. They'd never heard from Bravo Squad. The NESS detonated on Chronos Station, having used its advanced targeting artificial intelligence to position all the pieces at the weakest points. Something as large as a space station that was home to millions of people would have taken weeks for the NESS to deploy. When the NESS went active, there were fiery explosions that were instantly expunged by the fire suppression systems of the station. What killed all the people was the collapse of the station's superstructure, which overwhelmed any redundancy systems in place.

"Anything show up on the scanners?" Connor asked.

He'd hoped there would be some evidence of a ship leaving, but a debris field as massive as Chronos Station had overwhelmed the combat shuttle scanners.

"Negative, Commander," Reisman said.

Connor nodded, having expected as much despite his fool's hope for a break. The remaining Ghosts lined the shuttle, looking as shocked as he felt. Connor had to address them.

"Men," Connor said, "we've lost some of our own today—Jefferson, Malarkey, Oslo, Denton . . ." Connor went on to list all twelve members of Bravo Squad, and each name was like a punch to the throat. "I want you all to know—and this is on the record—that I take full responsibility for what happened. I've punched in the coordinates for the shuttle to return to COMCENT."

"With all due respect, sir, that's bullshit," Samson said.

"The Syndicate laid a trap for us. We were there. There was no way they were going to let us go without blowing the station," Reisman said.

Connor fixed them all with a stern glare. "My op. My objective. My command. My responsibility."

The Ghosts looked at him with mixed expressions.

Kasey cleared his throat. "Why don't we take a few minutes to calm down and then decide our next steps?"

"The decision has been made. You'll get a new CO and they'll likely promote you, Kasey," Connor said.

Kasey was about to respond when klaxon alarms signaled a target lock on their shuttle.

Reisman raced back to the shuttle's cockpit.

"Sir, the Battleship Carrier *Indianapolis* is two hundred thousand kilometers from our starboard bow. They're hailing us," Reisman said.

"Open a channel," Connor said.

"Combat Shuttle *Trident*, you're to change your heading to the following coordinates. Failure to comply will be considered an act of aggression that will be dealt with swiftly. *Indianapolis* out."

"They've sent us an intercept course," Reisman said.

Connor reviewed the coordinates. "Follow it," he said. They couldn't outrun a Barracuda-class battleship carrier. He glanced at Kasey. "What do you make of this?"

Kasey looked at the coordinates and frowned. "They don't want us coming in through the main hangar."

"Who's the CO of the *Indianapolis*?" Connor asked.

"We're locked out, sir. Once I put in the new coordinates, they took control of the shuttle's navigation systems and everything else," Reisman said, thrusting his hands in the air helplessly.

"*After* the new coordinates were entered?" Connor asked.

"Affirmative, sir," Reisman said.

Kasey leaned over. "What do you think it means?"

"I think it was a test, but without knowing who's in command, there's no way for us to know for sure," Connor replied.

Kasey frowned and gestured for Connor to step aside so the others couldn't hear them. "They're all thinking it, so I've got to say it."

Connor's brows pushed forward. "Captain."

"Not now. I'm speaking to you as a friend. I can't let you take the fall for this," Kasey said.

"You objected to this whole op because of the civilian presence. I wouldn't listen," Connor said and shushed Kasey as he began to speak. "I appreciate what you're trying to do, but I made the call and this is my burden to bear."

Kasey glared at him.

"Uh, sir, they're guiding us to a small cargo bay on the port side," Reisman said.

"Acknowledged," Connor replied.

The combat shuttle quickly closed in on the battleship carrier, and Connor glanced out the shuttle's windows. He'd begun his military career serving aboard a carrier like this. The NA Alliance Space Navy was a mix of the military branches of old, with each performing their specialized tasks. He'd first been recruited into the special forces and then into the Ghosts. Black ops had been his home for much of his career, so it was fitting that it was all coming to an end on a ship like this.

As the combat shuttle was remotely guided in, Connor started to make his way toward the rear of the shuttle but stopped as Kasey spoke.

"Officer on deck," Kasey bellowed and stood at attention.

The rest of the Ghosts came to their feet and saluted Connor, and although he wasn't one for emotions, his throat thickened at the gesture. They'd bled together, and some of them had died along the way. Connor returned the salute and headed for the back of the shuttle where the hatch was. The shuttle came to a stop and the rear doors opened. Connor expected to be greeted by a company of troops ordered to take them all into custody. Instead, there was only the *Indianapolis's* executive officer, along with five soldiers.

Connor stepped off the shuttle and saluted the XO, who was an older man, appearing to be a bit out of breath. The soldiers kept checking the area and hardly paid any attention at all to the Ghosts.

"Colonel Gates?" the XO asked.

"Yes, sir."

"I'm Captain Tung Yep. We don't have much time. If you and your team will please follow me," the captain said.

Captain Tung Yep didn't wait for a reply and turned around, walking away. Connor jogged to catch up with him.

"Are you the commanding officer of this ship, sir?" Connor asked.

"No," Captain Tung Yep said. "My orders are to retrieve you and your team and escort you to cargo bay D97. I don't have time for questions."

Connor didn't press the captain for any more information since he doubted he'd get anything useful. The rest of the Ghosts followed him. They'd been allowed to keep their weapons, so they weren't being taken into custody for the moment.

"Captain, I'm prepared to make a full report regarding the events on Chronos Station," Connor said.

Captain Tung Yep was leading them through a series of darkened corridors whose ambient lighting came on when their presence was detected.

"Stop right there, Colonel. Not another word," Captain Tung Yep said. "I can't know anything else about who you are other than to confirm your identity and then deliver you into someone else's custody. If you tell me anything about the events that have transpired in the last twenty-four hours, it will be considered an act of treason and I'll be forced to take you and your men into custody while an official investigation is launched."

Connor nodded, finally understanding why the captain didn't want to hear what he had to say. He'd been involved in enough missions that fell into the military "gray area" to recognize when the rules were being bent, but he had no idea who his mysterious benefactor was.

Captain Tung Yep came to a stop in front of a pair of wide doors. He gave his authorization and the door opened to a dimly lit room beyond.

"Colonel, this is where I leave you," the captain said, and then he and his five-soldier escort disappeared down a nearby corridor.

For a moment, Connor hovered in the doorway. The cavernous room beyond was some sort of storage area.

"Step inside, Colonel Gates," a voice called from inside.

The voice sounded wizened, carrying a tough rasp to it as if the owner of the voice had been in command longer than Connor had been alive.

Connor stepped inside and was quickly followed by the rest of the Ghosts. A few of them whispered to each other.

"You can leave your weapons in the containers to the side," the voice said.

Connor saw the faint outline of a man standing just outside the lighted area.

Connor frowned. "Of course. Right after you step into the light."

"You always were a stubborn pain in the ass, Gates. Can't you just do as you're told?"

An old man stepped into the light. Four thick gold bars rested on his sleeves.

"Admiral, sir," Connor said and stood at attention.

The Ghosts instantly followed Connor's example.

Fleet Admiral Mitch Wilkinson stepped before Connor and regarded him for a moment. "You know, if you'd joined the space navy and transferred under my command when I asked you to all those years ago, you'd have avoided this mess," the admiral said. "At ease."

Knowing better than to question the orders of a flag officer, Connor's squad went over to the storage containers and stowed their weapons. Kasey took Connor's M32 from him.

"You know me, sir. I learned from the best," Connor said.

He hadn't seen Wilkinson in almost twenty years. Wilkinson had served with Connor's father.

Admiral Wilkinson looked over at the Ghosts. "Combat suits too," he said and gestured for Connor to do the same.

Connor went over to his team and engaged the shutdown protocols for his combat suit. The armored unit split down the chest and opened. Connor stepped out and immediately became aware of his lack of personal hygiene over the last thirty-six hours.

"Come on back. I'm sure you're nice and ripe, but it's certainly not going to kill me," Admiral Wilkinson said.

Connor went back over to the admiral. "I'm sure you didn't just happen to be in the neighborhood, sir."

"No, you're right about that. The destruction of Chronos Station is going to have swift repercussions. It's only a matter of time before a scapegoat is targeted."

"How would anyone even know we were involved?" Connor asked.

"You think the Syndicate is beyond releasing the names of you and your team to the public?"

Connor went cold. If working in black ops had taught him anything it was that keeping your identity secret was paramount—both for your protection and that of your loved ones.

"There's no way the alliance military will condone the actions that led to the station being destroyed. You'll be branded terrorists, hunted down, tossed in jail, and probably executed for treason."

Connor felt heat rush to his face. It was like explosions were going off in his head. An image of his son, Sean, came to the forefront of his mind. The last time he'd seen him he'd been three years old, and that had been eight years ago. He glanced over at his team. They were all in danger. Some of them had families.

"Now before you do anything stupid, you and what remains of your team need to follow me," Admiral Wilkinson said.

4

CONNOR FOLLOWED ADMIRAL WILKINSON. More lights came on, revealing a massive warehouse filled with storage containers that were marked with a golden sunburst.

"Recognize it?" Wilkinson asked.

Connor shook his head. "No, sir."

The admiral nodded. "Never mind that. Why don't you tell me what really happened on Chronos Station."

Connor followed the admiral through a maze of storage containers all marked with the golden sunburst. He filled Wilkinson in on the op, figuring at this point he had nothing to lose. It was a break in protocol, but all black ops teams accepted the fact that there might be a time when COMCENT needed to disavow all knowledge of them and the operation they were part of. Flag officers like Admiral Wilkinson were privy to knowledge that most others wouldn't be. It came with the job. Connor broke down his recent activities in his hunt for the Syndicate—from the pieces of intelligence they'd gathered that put them on the path to Chronos Station to getting inside and storming the Syndicate stronghold.

They reached the edge of the warehouse, where there were several rooms, and Connor recognized a mobile medical unit setup. The people inside wore blue uniforms with a gold caduceus on the shoulders. One of the men walked over to them.

"We're ready for them, sir," the man said. He was of Asian ancestry, but he spoke as if he'd grown up south of the Mason-Dixon line.

"Connor, this is Lieutenant Kim. He needs to do a quick check of you and your men," Wilkinson said.

Connor frowned. "We're not due for med checks. What's this all about?"

"Just a precaution. I'll be across the hall, waiting for you," Wilkinson said and entered an office.

"Shouldn't keep the old man waiting, sir," Lieutenant Kim said and gestured to the room.

Connor nodded for his squad to go inside and then followed. Doctor Kim pulled him out of the line to go first, saying the admiral had specified that Connor be checked first. Connor followed the doctor to one of the exam tables and granted access to his biochip. Within moments, all his medical history appeared on the doctor's mobile holoscreen. Lieutenant Kim flipped through the history and noted Connor's vital signs, which confirmed his excellent health. The doctor brought up a secondary screen that looked to have information about Connor's physiology. The information on the screen went by so quickly that Connor couldn't read it. A panel hissed opened from the bottom of a cabinet, and cold vapor licked the edges. Lieutenant Kim reached inside and pulled out a medical injection gun. Inside the small tank was blue liquid.

"What's that, Doc?" Connor asked.

"It's a booster shot for your nanites. Your records showed you were out of date."

The doctor came over and pressed the metal tip against the

side of Connor's neck, squeezing the trigger and pushing the actuator forward, forcing the cocktail of blue liquid past his skin.

"You're all set. We'll check out the rest of your team, but the admiral's waiting for you," Lieutenant Kim said.

Connor rubbed his neck and glanced over at Kasey and the others. In response, Kasey jutted his chin up once with a slight raise of his brows. It was something he'd always done to let Connor know everything was fine.

Connor looked at the rest of the team calmly awaiting their turn to be checked by the doctors. More than a few looked over in his direction. He'd been their CO for years and they'd been through hell together, and yet today he felt he'd let them down. He kept going over the events that had led to the standoff with the head of the Syndicate. He doubted RJ was even her name. And was the person behind the voice even a woman? In hindsight, he kept thinking that instead of hunting his prey, he'd been led by the nose. He left the room and stood out in the hall. His breath quickened and he balled his hands into fists.

Connor heard slow footsteps from across the hall, and Admiral Wilkinson's steely-eyed gaze regarded him. There was neither judgment nor compassion in Wilkinson's slate-blue eyes—just an acknowledgment shared by those who were in command. Lives were always on the line, and today, lives had been lost. A lot of them.

Wilkinson waved him inside the office. News feeds showed on the wallscreen.

"Have you heard about this?" Wilkinson asked and gestured toward the screen.

Connor looked over and the feed showed a commentator on a ship in one of Earth's oceans.

"We've studied almost every square kilometer of our solar system, built colonies on Mars and Venus and space stations among the outer planets, and we're still making discoveries back home. We're only scratching the surface of the secrets in our own oceans," Wilkinson said.

Connor glanced at the screen again and then back at the admiral. "Permission to speak freely, sir."

"Granted."

"Why did you bring us here?"

Wilkinson waved his hand and the news feed stopped. He then gestured for Connor to sit down while he took his own seat.

"There're no two ways about it. You're in the shit. As deep as one can go. Before we go into all that, what were your future plans?"

Connor's mouth hung open. "My future plans? Millions of people are dead and you want to ask me about future plans?"

"I had my intelligence analyst pull your records from the shuttle. They sent me the information you intended to file in your report. A mass-destruction NESS was deployed throughout Chronos Station. The NESS was brought online and activated, causing catastrophic destruction to the station. Nowhere does this report say it was you who detonated the thing, and I know a team like yours doesn't bring enough ordnance to destroy an entire space station," Wilkinson said.

"She used the transponder codes from our own NESS so when the salvage teams go through the wreckage, all fingers will be pointed at me and my team," Connor said.

"You think you're the first person to get kicked in the balls?"

"I don't know how you can equate me getting kicked in the balls with millions of people dying. If I had the bitch in my sights right now, I'd pull the trigger, no hesitation," Connor said.

Admiral Wilkinson sucked in a deep breath. "I need to know who you have left on Earth."

"Why do you want to know?"

Wilkinson let out a bitter laugh. "Stubborn right to the end. Your father was the same way. You're so angry you can hardly see straight and realize that I'm trying to help you. If you have anyone on Earth who's important to you, I need to know so they can be protected."

Connor swallowed hard. "Alyssa, my ex, and our son, Sean."

"I need more than names. I need last known locations. When was the last time you spoke to them?"

Connor's mind raced as he tried to think of the last time he'd seen his son. "It's been a few years," he said, his own voice sounding rough.

"How old is Sean now?"

Connor frowned. "He'd be eleven years old now."

A deep pang crushed Connor's chest. The primal need to protect his son that only showed itself in the quiet moments between missions pushed its way to the forefront of his mind.

"You haven't seen your son in years?" Wilkinson asked, unable to keep the disbelief from his voice.

"He needed a father who was going to be there for him, not someone who was away on deployment eleven months out of the year . . ."

Wilkinson shook his head. "A boy deserves to have a father in his life, even if that father is married to the mission."

Connor's vision swam as if he were looking down a long tunnel. A spike of adrenaline pushed the darkness back and he felt as if he were sinking into the chair. "What have you done to me?"

Connor looked toward the door where his team was and surged to his feet. He took a step and stumbled to the floor.

The admiral knelt down beside him. "Try to relax."

"The doctor didn't give me a booster shot," Connor said, his words slurring as if he were drunk on too much whiskey.

He tried to crawl, but his arms and legs wouldn't move. The last thing that registered in his mind was the southern drawl of Lieutenant Kim speaking.

Admiral Wilkinson rose to his feet and looked down at the unconscious form of Connor Gates. He'd promised David that he'd look after his son, which had been all but impossible with Connor choosing to join the special forces.

"It took them all a while to go down," Doctor Kim said and waved for his staff to come in and retrieve Connor.

"To be expected. The Ghosts would no doubt all have been using the latest implants and nanite technology that aren't available anywhere else," Wilkinson said. "Your staff . . . have they been briefed?"

"Of course, sir, as you specified. We were never here and none of this happened," Lieutenant Kim said. "But can I ask you a question, sir?"

"Go ahead."

"I just don't understand why."

Wilkinson sighed and regarded the doctor. "I've served the NA Alliance for a long time. Life for the cause, but sometimes the laws and procedures we fight to protect aren't good enough to effectively judge our soldiers. The Ghosts deserved better than what they were going to get."

"I don't understand. Are you so certain they would have been implicated, much less convicted of a crime?"

"The Syndicate has a lot of influence, and I'm unwilling to take the chance, not when I have a debt to pay."

Stasis tubes were being lined up in the hallway.

"Sir, what happens to them now?" Lieutenant Kim asked.

"You and your staff have done a great service, but your task is done," Wilkinson said.

The lieutenant's eyes widened, and Wilkinson was once again

struck by a doctor's sense of entitlement. "We can't just leave them here. They need to be monitored . . ." The lieutenant's voice trailed off as a squad of soldiers without rank or insignia marched down the hallway.

"They'll be taken care of, I promise," Wilkinson said.

The mobile medical unit left them, and Wilkinson made a mental note to have them watched to be sure they kept their mouths shut.

One of the soldiers approached. "We're here to transport the cargo, sir."

"One minute," Wilkinson said, and the soldier stepped to the side.

Wilkinson reached into his pocket and withdrew a data storage stick. He walked over to Connor's stasis tube and opened the access panel, glancing at the stick that held the recorded message he'd hastily done while Connor was in with the doctors. After a moment he shoved it inside and closed the panel. He'd done all he could.

Wilkinson turned around. "Daniels," he said, "take these containers to the Ark Project and mark them for transfer to permanent storage. At no time are these containers to be out of your care until they're permanently stowed. Is that clear?"

"Absolutely, sir. We'll report back to you when it's finished," Daniels said.

Wilkinson knew the soldier could be trusted, but he still had a lot of favors to call in to make this work. He would have liked to have done more. Lord knows Connor deserved better than this, and he hoped that one day Connor would forgive him for what was about to happen. But . . . better to ask forgiveness than permission.

"Carry on," Wilkinson said and returned to the small office.

"Ship's log," Wilkinson said. The ship's computer chimed, indicating the log was open. "*Indianapolis* was the first ship to find the wreckage of Chronos Station. Preliminary scans indicate there were no survivors or ships detected nearby. We'll be conducting an investigation and reporting our findings.

"Computer, package the log and beam a transmission back to COMCENT."

5

CONNOR FELT something tugging him from a deep sleep. The more awake he became, the more he became aware of the tingling pain he felt in his hands and feet. It felt as if his eyes were pinned down by steel weights and refused all his attempts to open them. There was something hard in his throat. He heard the sound of muffled voices speaking but couldn't understand them. Connor tried to cough, and his throat muscles worked to expel the hard rod that was in his mouth. He raised his hands, but someone held him down. The tube in his throat was yanked out. He winced and coughed weakly, spitting out a foul-tasting liquid as someone helped roll him to his side.

"Give yourself a few moments to adjust. We've just pulled you from stasis," a woman's voice said.

Connor couldn't tell if he was just having a really bad dream or if he'd awakened to a nightmare where he was trapped in his own body, unable to move.

"Can he answer questions yet?" a man's voice shrilled.

Though Connor couldn't open his eyes, the man's tone grated on his nerves.

"Not yet, Dr. Baker. He's only just come around," the woman said.

Connor heard someone stomp across the floor.

"I don't know how this could have happened. Dr. Peter Faulkner, the eminent planetary scientist, was supposed to be in his pod. That's not him," the man said.

Sounds of footsteps stomped closer to Connor.

"Hey, can you hear me? We need to know your name."

"Doctor, please. He just needs a few minutes for the stasis drugs to wear off. We've got revival protocols to follow. Perhaps you should step outside."

"Don't get snippy with me, Kara."

"Of course, Dr. Baker," Kara said.

Connor was gently rolled onto his back, and the bed he was in started to rise. It was hard to think. He pushed his eyes open, and it was like trying to see through thick syrup. Connor squeezed his eyes shut and moaned. Someone pressed a cool wet towel on his face and wiped the gooey substance from his eyes. Connor opened them and saw a young woman looking down at him. She smiled.

"Take it easy and give the revival cocktail some time to work. You're likely to feel a bit off until it starts to kick in," Kara said.

Connor cleared his throat. Everything about his body felt wrong.

"Drink this. It will help," Kara said and put a straw in his mouth.

Connor sucked down the liquid, which contained a faint trace of cinnamon. He drank a few mouthfuls and coughed because his throat refused to work properly. A thin man with beady eyes glared at him.

"Do you know where you are?"

"Doctor—" Kara began.

Dr. Baker swung his beady eyes toward the woman. "Thank

you, Kara. I'll take it from here. I'm sure you have other patients to check on."

Kara glanced at Connor regretfully. "I'll be just outside," she said and left the room.

Dr. Baker walked to the side of the bed, snapping his fingers in front of Connor's face and then by his ears. He shined a bright light in Connor's face. Connor tried to raise his arm, and the doctor glanced down.

"Motor control and response to stimuli are normal," Dr. Baker said. He leaned down. "So I know you can hear me. I don't know who the hell you are, but you'd better start answering questions."

"What are you talking about?" Connor said, his voice sounding gravelly in his own ears.

"This is taking too long," Dr. Baker said and crossed the room. He pulled a syringe from a container and filled it with clear liquid from a vial.

Connor tried to wave the doctor off, but he was too weak.

"Now, this will sting a little," Dr. Baker said and jabbed the thick needle into Connor's thigh.

White fiery pain shot through his system as if there were lightning burning through his veins. Connor screamed and grabbed the doctor by his shirt, pulling him in. Dr. Baker's eyes widened, and Connor growled as he shoved the doctor across the room. Whatever the doctor had given him had made him able to move, so Connor stood up as the doctor turned around. He limped over and grabbed the doctor, pulling him off balance while driving his knee into the doctor's chest.

"I'm sick of doctors sticking me with stuff, asshole," Connor said.

He shoved the stunned doctor into the wall, and the beady-eyed tyrant collapsed to the floor.

Connor became aware of a sharp pain in his thigh and saw

that the syringe was still in his leg. He yanked it out and clutched it like a knife. "Let's see how you like being stuck."

Connor charged across the room, fist raised, but the door to the room opened and someone tackled him to the floor. Strong hands grabbed his arm, and he let go of the syringe. A man in a blue uniform tried to pin Connor down, but Connor twisted around and punched the guy in the stomach multiple times, then drove his palm up into the man's face. The man fell off him and Connor was on his feet instantly. There were screams coming from the hallway, and a wave of dizziness washed over him. Something hit him in the back, and a jolt of electricity brought Connor to his knees. He collapsed forward and his cheek slapped against the floor. A small amount of drool escaped his mouth and he groaned.

"What's going on here?" someone asked with the voice of authority.

"I'm sorry, Dr. Quinn. I left him alone with Dr. Baker and then I heard shouting coming from the room," Kara said.

"Alright. Let's get him up in that bed. Get the restraints on him," Dr. Quinn said.

Connor felt himself being lifted and taken back to his bed. Metallic straps raced across his body, securing him in place. He lay there, knowing the effects of the stunner used on him would only last for a short while. He watched as they carried Dr. Baker out and felt a small bit of satisfaction when he saw blood dripping down the doctor's face from a shallow gash on his forehead. He was really starting to hate doctors. Connor closed his eyes and drifted off to sleep.

Later on, Connor woke up again. He was alone in the room and the metallic restraints were still wrapped around his body so he couldn't move. The door opened and an older woman walked in, her long brown hair pulled back. She regarded him like a mother would a misbehaving child.

"You're awake. Have you calmed down?"

Connor nodded. He didn't know how long he'd slept, but he felt more refreshed than he had before.

"Good. I'm Ashley Quinn, head medical doctor on the Ark."

Great. Another damn doctor. "As long as you don't go sticking me with any needles, we'll get along fine," Connor said.

Ashley's lips curved. "Dr. Baker's bedside manner leaves much to be desired. I'm sorry about that."

"You can say that again," Connor replied.

He tried to stretch, but the restraints kept him in place.

"I'll make you a deal. I won't stick you with any needles unless you give me the okay, and I'll even let you out of those restraints if you promise not to attack anyone else. Deal?" Ashley said.

Connor nodded.

Ashley pressed her lips together. "I need to hear you say it."

Connor blew out a breath. "I promise. Why are you treating me like a child?"

"Vocalization of a promise has a higher success rate," Ashley said.

She tapped a few commands into her tablet computer and the metallic restraints retracted back into the bed.

Connor raised his arms and stretched, letting out a large yawn followed by a sigh. He hated being tied down. He glanced at the doctor. She was a handsome woman, and her confident gaze held none of the telltale signs of inexperience, despite her outward appearance. A wedding ring gleamed from her left hand.

"Where am I?" Connor asked.

"That's the real question, isn't it? I'm afraid it's going to take a bit of explaining," Ashley said and regarded him for a moment. "You look like you could stand stretching your legs a bit. Would you like to take a short walk?"

Connor looked down at his appearance. He had on a white close-knit unitard that strained against his muscles.

Ashley turned around and opened a cabinet door, pulling out some clothes, along with a pair of slippers, and tossing them on the bed. "I'll step outside while you get dressed. Then we can talk about where we are. And I'd like to find out more about you and what you remember."

Dr. Quinn turned and left the room. Connor glanced at the door as it shut and sighed. He pulled off the unitard and took a quick sniff. A musky scent assaulted his nostrils, and he flung the unitard into a container marked for laundry. He really wanted to take a shower and wash, but there was no bathroom in the room. He put on the gray shirt and sweatpants Dr. Quinn had found. The synthetic cotton felt soft against his skin. He slipped his feet into the slippers and headed for the door.

Connor stepped out into a long hallway where people were walking about from room to room. All of them were wearing some kind of blue uniform with a golden sunburst patch on the shoulder. He frowned, trying to remember where he'd seen that symbol before, but the vague memory remained stubbornly out of reach. To his left were two men with shock-sticks on their belts. The looks they gave him were neither challenging nor relenting.

"My office is up this way on the left," Dr. Quinn said.

Connor glanced at the two men and raised his eyebrows.

"You did cause quite a ruckus when they woke you up. Tim and Theo are here just in case," Dr. Quinn said.

Connor nodded, and they started walking down the hallway. He glanced inside some of the rooms and they all had stasis pods in them. None of the rooms had windows, so he couldn't use that to determine where he was. Connor found that the more he walked, the less stiff he became.

"I can have lunch brought up if you're hungry," Dr. Quinn said.

Connor frowned. "Why are you trying to be nice to me? It's not that I don't appreciate it, but . . ."

"I've found that common courtesy can go a long way, and I think we've gotten off on the wrong foot," Dr. Quinn said.

She opened a door to an office with a wide desk. Behind the desk was a window, but it was grayed out, so he couldn't see outside.

"Have a seat," she said and told Tim and Theo to wait outside.

Connor sat down in one of the plush chairs on the opposite side of the desk. Dr. Quinn sat down on the business side and opened up an info terminal.

"Okay, is this where the interrogation begins, Dr. Quinn?" Connor asked.

"No need to be so formal. You can call me Ashley if you want," she said and seemed to consider him for a moment. "If I had to guess, I'd say you've served in the military."

Connor didn't reply.

"I need to ask you a couple of questions before we get to explaining where we are. First, can you tell me the year?" Ashley asked.

"It's 2217," Connor said.

Ashley noted his answer. "Will you tell me your name?"

"Gates, Connor."

"So you *are* in the military," Ashley said.

"I'm not at liberty to say, ma'am."

Ashley smiled. "Ma'am. That's one I don't hear too often anymore," she said and entered his name into the info terminal. She waited a moment and then glanced at him. "It says here that you were NA Alliance Special Forces and you were killed in action."

Connor frowned and his gaze narrowed.

"Here, look," Ashley said and tapped a few commands in so a holoscreen appeared over the desk for him to see.

Connor's eyes widened. He was looking at his own service

record, which was supposed to be sealed since he was black ops and the CO of the Ghosts.

Ashley pulled a data stick out from a drawer in her desk. "We found this in the storage unit of your pod for personal effects. Any idea what's on it? We tried to have a look, but it seems encoded for you."

Connor took the data stick from Ashley and looked at it. "I've never seen this before."

"It's fine. One of the side effects of long-term stasis is that sometimes your memory takes a little while to catch up."

"Long term? How long have I been in stasis?" Connor asked.

"We'll get to that, I promise," Ashley said.

"How about we get to it now? How long have I been in stasis?"

Ashley pressed her lips together. "It's been a while, but—"

Connor rose to his feet. "I want a straight answer right now."

He glanced at the information on the screen. "You shouldn't have access to that information. *I* don't even have access to it, which means you must be part of the NA Alliance Intelligence, high up in the chain of command. My commanding officer is Colonel Benjamin Crouse of the seventy-third brigade—" Connor stopped speaking. The image of an older man with gunmetal-gray hair appeared in his mind as if he were standing over him.

"You've just remembered something, haven't you?" Ashley asked.

"Admiral Wilkinson," Connor said.

Ashley entered the name in the search bar. "Admiral Mitch Wilkinson, CO of the Battleship Carrier *Indianapolis* from the years 2197 through 2220 . . . shit," she said.

"Twenty-two twenty! What the hell are you talking about? Have I been in stasis for three damn years?"

"Connor, please calm down. I'll tell you everything you want to know. Please, just sit down," Ashley said.

The door to her office opened and Tim stuck his beefy head in. Connor's breath came in gasps.

Three years in stasis. Fuck!

Tim and Theo hovered in the doorway.

"Connor, look at me. Never mind them. It's just you and me," Ashley said.

Connor swung his gaze toward her. "How long have I been in stasis?"

Ashley swallowed. "Two hundred years."

Connor frowned and tilted his head to the side as if he hadn't heard her. "Two hundred years? Is that what you said?"

Ashley held her hand up imploringly. "I know this is a lot to take in. You've been in stasis for two hundred years and eight months."

Connor couldn't catch his breath, and he clamped his hand down on the chair. Small sparkles of light flashed in his vision as he fought to remain conscious. He glanced at Ashley. "Please tell me this is some kind of joke."

"I wish it were a joke, but you've been in stasis for two hundred years like the rest of us," Ashley said.

Connor had spent a bulk of his career reading people and had a sense of whether he was being lied to or not. Everything in his gut told him Ashley was telling the truth.

"You've been in stasis for two hundred years too?" Connor asked.

Ashley nodded.

Connor started laughing and looked back at Tim and Theo hovering in the doorway. "You almost had me going. Did Wilkinson put you up to this?"

Ashley frowned. "No, I already told you I wasn't lying."

Connor craned his neck to see if anyone was behind Tim and Theo. "Is Kasey out there? Or Reisman?"

He took a step toward the door and Tim held up his hand.

"Clear window," Ashley said.

Connor turned around and looked out the window, which displayed a view of the black canopy of space on one side and a blue planet on the other. Instinctively, his eyes searched for the continents he expected to see, but the land masses were all out of place. A fuzzy area at the bottom of the window cleared last. Surrounding the planet were several distinct rings that resembled a vast expanse of highway made of light.

Connor slowly walked toward the window and gazed at the alien world. He turned toward Ashley, his mouth wide open.

"We're sixty light-years from Earth. The astronomers have an alpha-numeric designation for the star system, if you'd like to know it," Ashley said.

Connor looked back out the wide window. Off to the side and in the distance was a large cigar-shaped ship.

"What ship is that?" Connor asked.

"That's the *Galileo*. It's a seed ship, and it's been here for twenty-five years," Ashley said.

Connor brought his hands up to his head and raked them through his short hair. He couldn't stop looking out the window, but at the same time he couldn't believe what he was seeing. He felt his knees go weak and he leaned against the wall. Connor closed his eyes and felt like he was going to be sick.

Ashley came to his side and put her hand on his shoulder. "Just breathe. Everything is going to be fine."

Connor's mouth went dry and he couldn't catch his breath. He looked over at the door, where Tim and Theo looked back at him sympathetically. Connor gulped some air and sprinted toward the door. Tim and Theo drew back in surprise as Connor tucked his shoulder in and barreled through them. The two men went down like bowling pins and Connor darted off, running down the hallway. There was shouting behind him, but he hardly heard it. He had to keep moving. This must be a mistake or maybe some psychological form of interrogation. The Syndicate was known for their ruthless interrogation techniques. They could have put this whole sham together, but to what purpose? The Ghosts were an effective special ops team, but they didn't harbor any specific intelligence the Syndicate couldn't get through other means.

Connor ran down the long white hallway. He glanced inside some of the rooms as he passed, and the ones with windows all showed an Earth-like planet with rings around it.

Two hundred years!

Connor rounded a corner and kept going. This hallway had people in it.

"Get out of the way!" Connor shouted.

The people in the hallway scrambled out of reach. He glanced behind and saw a group of men chasing him, all armed with stun batons. He had to find a way out of there. If this was a ship, there must be a hangar, or if he was locked away in some secret facility then there must be a communications array he could use to send a signal out to COMCENT. They would dispatch a team to pick him up. Were Kasey and the other Ghosts here?

The hallway opened into a small atrium with large windows. The alien planet was outside, and Connor stopped running. Nearby, a mother stood holding a child in her arms while the child pointed out the window.

"Is that our new home?" the child asked in an awestruck voice.

The mother smiled and nodded. "It sure is. That's our new home. We'll get to go down to the surface soon."

Connor gasped and his gaze darted around, looking for some way to escape.

"There he is!"

Connor spun around as a group of men closed in on him.

The leader put his stun baton back on his belt and held out his hands. "I know you're scared. I'm here to help you. Just come back with us."

"Stay away from me," Connor said.

The child started to cry as the mother and child ran away from him.

"Just stay back," Connor said.

"Alright, I'm staying back. Just calm down, buddy. You got a name?"

Connor looked at the man and took the measure of the other men. They held the stun batons like they knew how to use them. Connor took a step toward one.

"We'll use the stunners if we have to. Don't make us."

With five men facing him, they thought they had the advantage. Connor had faced worse odds. He darted in, taking one of them by surprise, then clamped down on the man's wrist and swung the stunner toward the other man closing in on them. Connor dragged the man around while twisting his wrist. He took the stunner and jammed it into the man's side.

Two down.

Connor heard a stunner being swung through the air and ducked out of the way. He rolled forward and came to his feet, swinging his own stunner at the man, and the glowing tip smacked against his face.

Three down.

The remaining two men kept their distance.

"There's nowhere for you to go."

Behind the men was a hallway that led out of the atrium. "Get out of the way," Connor said.

"It's not gonna happen."

"You can't stop me," Connor said.

"Maybe not," said the man, and he looked behind Connor, "but she can."

Connor spun around to find Ashley Quinn standing there. She

gave him a disapproving look as she jabbed a stunner into his stomach.

Connor felt hot pain spread from his middle as he sank to the floor.

"I thought you said you wouldn't be any trouble," Ashley said.

No words would come as the darkness closed in.

6

CONNOR WOKE up strapped to the bed again. He shook his head and sighed. Dr. Quinn entered the room and stared down at him with a quizzical brow raised. He assumed that Ashley was a mother because only mothers could pack so much disapproval into an expression. Connor glanced down at his arm to see an IV plugged into his vein.

"I have you on a mild sedative," Ashley said.

He felt a bit calmer, but that meant he was off his guard.

"You still don't believe what I told you," Ashley said.

Connor pressed his lips together and shook his head. "Just go ahead and do what you're going to do."

Ashley tilted her head to the side with a slightly bemused expression. "What is it you think I'm going to do to you?"

"I don't know. You tell me."

Ashley shook her head. "Well, I had to stick you with a needle to hook up the IV bag, so I broke my promise. But you were unconscious and unable to put up much of a fight."

Connor looked away at the wall.

"I had no idea you military types were so mistrusting. What is it you did in the military?"

"Don't you already know? You have my records."

"Yeah, but they didn't make much sense to me. I'd much rather hear about it from you. Anyway, there were a lot of references to something called the Syndicate," Ashley said.

"Are you really going to tell me you're not part of the Syndicate?"

Ashley laughed as if the idea were the most absurd thing she'd ever heard. "You make it sound so sinister, but no, I'm not part of any syndicate."

"Sure," Connor said.

"You've looked out the window of my office and you were in the atrium. You saw the planet," Ashley said.

"I saw an image of a planet. For all I know, you put that image up there to fool me."

"Why on Earth would I do something like that?"

"To keep me off balance and lull me into a sense of confidence so I'll give you information," Connor said.

"I think you give me too much credit, but since we're talking, do you know how you came to be in a stasis pod in the first place?" Ashley asked.

Connor's thoughts screeched to a halt and he frowned, unable to remember.

"The pod that you were in was supposed to be occupied by Dr. Peter Faulkner. He's a planetary scientist whose help we really could use right about now and a close personal friend of Dr. Baker's. The man you beat up," Ashley said.

"I think we can both agree he had it coming," Connor replied.

"Some would agree. But given the circumstances, I think we all could be given a bit of leniency for some of our behaviors. You know, like running around the Ark like a madman, scaring a child and his mother half to death. That sort of thing," Ashley said.

Connor thought about it for a moment. Why would the Syndicate go through all that trouble? Could they be trying to brainwash him?

"Someone really did a number on you. I can see you still don't believe me," Ashley said.

She grabbed her tablet computer and typed some things in, reading the screen for a few moments and then looking up at him. "Counterintelligence and counterinsurgency. You've been trained not to take anything at face value."

Connor shrugged as best he could from within his restraints.

"No response to that? Okay. Have you heard of the Ark program?" Ashley asked.

Connor frowned in thought. A wall seemed to give way in his mind and the floodgates holding back his memories opened. Within moments he remembered Admiral Wilkinson drugging him, and he looked at Ashley in alarm. Could she be telling him the truth?

"You've just remembered something else, haven't you?" Ashley said, peering at him intently. She came closer to the bed. "I wish you would just trust me. I'm telling you the truth."

There was a knock at the door. Ashley walked over and opened it.

"I heard someone finally knocked Baker on his ass and I just wanted to thank them in person."

"Lenora, please. That's not very professional."

A woman with brilliantly blue eyes and long auburn hair walked in. She looked at Connor and then at the straps but didn't seem surprised.

"Another one not taking the news very well," she said.

Ashley stood next to her. "Lenora Bishop, this is Connor Gates. I'm afraid his being here is something of a surprise to everyone, including Connor."

Lenora glanced at Ashley, and her big blue eyes widened when she looked back at him. Her full lips made a circle, and Connor found himself fixated on Lenora's beautiful face.

"Oh my god, I'm so . . . wow," Lenora said. "I can't believe it. How the hell could this have happened? I thought all the pods were vetted before entering storage on the Ark."

Ashley shrugged. "Evidently something slipped through the vetting process."

Lenora looked back at Connor. "You're just gonna have to deal with it. We slept for two hundred years, and like it or not, you're gonna be part of humanity's first interstellar colony."

The edges of Connor's lips curved upward. "We'll see."

Lenora leaned in and looked at him intently. "Oh, you're a stubborn one."

"I've been called worse."

"I'll bet," Lenora said.

"What do you do here?" Connor asked.

"Well, everyone does a little bit of everything, but my specialty is archaeology," Lenora said.

Connor glanced at Ashley, who gave him a nod. "Why would they bring an archaeologist on an interstellar colony mission?"

"Are you kidding me? Why wouldn't they? We had no idea what we were going to find. All the probe sent back was that the conditions were within Earth norms, so humans could survive here. And in the end, we didn't end up anywhere near where we were supposed to go. So you ask why bring an archaeologist on a colony mission? And the answer is to get the answers to the tough questions," Lenora said.

Connor smiled and found himself enjoying the sound of her voice. "Like what?" he asked.

"Just wait until you get down to the surface. We've found remnants of an alien civilization. And I'm not talking about evidence of parasitic life. I'm talking about a species that built something. A whole civilization," Lenora said.

"So there are aliens on this planet?"

Lenora frowned. "Technically, yes. They're just not the ones we found ruins for. We're still looking. Anyway, I have to go. It was nice to meet you, and I do hope to see you on the surface someday."

Lenora left the room and Connor watched her go.

"Lenora has a lot of energy," Ashley said.

"She certainly does," Connor said.

Ashley regarded him for a moment. "You still don't believe it, do you? Not fully. Okay, let's try this again. I'll take the restraints off and you need to cooperate. I'm not sure what the long-term effects are of repeated stunning, and I don't want to go look it up."

The straps retracted and Connor was free. He didn't know what to think.

"Come on, let's go," Ashley said.

"Where to now? Another window for me to look out of?"

"I'd like to introduce you to my husband, Tobias," Ashley said.

Connor decided to cooperate. He'd tried running and it had landed him right back in restraints. If this was the Syndicate trying to brainwash him, he figured he'd see how far they were willing to go.

"Sounds good. I can't wait to meet him," Connor said.

———

7

CONNOR FOLLOWED Ashley out of the room and saw Tim and Theo waiting outside.

"Gentlemen," Connor said in greeting.

He expected a warning look or some indication that the two men wanted some kind of payback for what he'd done to them, but there wasn't anything.

"Feeling better?" Tim asked.

Connor glanced at Ashley and then back at the two men. "Worlds. Hey listen, about before..."

Theo smiled, revealing a great big set of pearly whites in contrast to his dark skin. "Looking forward to next time. There's a pickup football game on the surface. You might want to think about joining up."

"I'll think about it," Connor said.

The Syndicate was pulling out all the stops to convince him he was shanghaied on a ship that was some sixty light-years from Earth, so Connor dutifully followed as Ashley led him through a series of hallways with no shortage of people busy doing a number of tasks.

"Are you taking me to the bridge?" Connor asked.

"Goodness no. The Ark is the biggest ship we've ever built. No, I'm taking you to one of the hangar decks nearby," Ashley said.

If they were taking him to a real hangar deck, they couldn't be too concerned with him escaping. "Is your husband a doctor too?"

"No, Tobias is the governor of the colony," Ashley said.

"Governor? Really?"

Ashley ignored his dubious tone. "Of course. Can't set up a colony without some kind of government. Once we're established, we'll hold elections and stuff, but that won't be until everyone is awakened and the colony is established on the surface of the planet."

Connor let out a slight chuckle.

"I know you're having doubts. I can't even imagine what this must be like for you. Just try to keep an open mind, okay?" Ashley said.

She led him through a series of doors that ended in a command center. There were multiple rows of workstations about with teams working. There were also windows on the far side of the command center that overlooked a massive hangar bay.

Connor stopped in his tracks, his mouth agape. He looked around, taking a few steps forward. Throughout his career he had been conditioned to take in information and adapt as needed, but nothing had prepared him for this. If this was the Syndicate trying to brainwash him, he felt like it was beginning to work.

Ashley waited patiently for him with a knowing smile. "Come on, I want you to meet Tobias. He's in the conference room over here."

Connor glanced back at his escorts, Tim and Theo, and they gave him encouraging nods.

"You could have warned me," Connor said.

Tim grinned. "And ruin the surprise? You wouldn't have believed us anyway."

Connor followed Ashley across the command center and into a conference room. In the middle of the room was a long table that had a holoscreen outlined in translucent amber lines to give it definition. An older man with salt-and-pepper-colored hair stood in front of it. Next to him were three younger men, not much more than boys.

"Tobias," Ashley called as they approached.

Tobias was sipping coffee from a mug and turned at her call. He hastily put his mug down and stuck out his hand. "Hi there, I'm Tobias Quinn."

Connor shook the proffered hand and introduced himself.

Tobias gestured toward each of the young men in turn. "This is Noah and Lars, and this is my son, Sean."

Connor blanched at the mention of Sean.

Tobias glanced at his wife. "Did I say something wrong?"

"No," Connor said. "I have a son named Sean."

Tobias's expression became somber. "I'm so sorry."

Connor clamped down on his emotions, but his heart was thumping like a rabbit. He needed to keep it together. "It's not your fault," Connor said and looked at the three young men. "Nice to meet you."

They returned the sentiment in kind.

"Could you guys give us a few minutes?" Tobias said to the young men, then turned back to Connor. "I bet you could use a drink."

Connor looked at him. "Yeah, I think that would be good."

Tobias walked over to the side and pulled out a metal container. He grabbed a couple of glasses and poured two fingers of dark amber liquid into each.

Tobias handed a glass to his wife and then to Connor. "Kentucky bourbon. A little taste of home," Tobias said.

Connor downed the bourbon in one swallow, and it blazed a

path down his throat. Warmth spread across his chest as he felt the alcohol immediately start to do its thing.

"I'd offer you another, but then I'd start getting that look from my wife. You know, that look that tells you you're heading into trouble," Tobias said.

"Careful now," Ashley warned and gave Connor a wink.

"Okay, let's get to it," Tobias said. "You were found in Peter Faulkner's pod and you have no recollection of how you got there. Judging by your reaction to being on the Ark, I feel it's safe to say that you had nothing to do with being stowed away. Sound fair to you?"

Connor put his cup down on the table. "I didn't sneak aboard this ship. In fact, I'd only heard of the Ark a few days . . . well, let's just say recently."

Tobias nodded. "What's the last thing you remember?"

"I'm not at liberty . . ." Connor's voice trailed off and he frowned. "I'm not sure if any of that matters anymore."

"Sam, can you bring up anything we have about Connor Gates?" Tobias asked.

"Of course. One moment," a generic male's voice said through speakers on the ceiling.

"Sam is our artificial intelligence for data reference and research, both of which are crucial to us building a life here," Tobias said.

Connor's service record appeared on the holoscreen. As he read through it, words at the bottom of the screen appeared in bold red lettering like a punch to his gut.

"KIA - DV. Guilty of the destruction of Chronos Station and the deaths of . . ." Tobias read aloud and looked at Connor.

"Five million people," Connor finished.

He stepped closer to the holoscreen and read through the report on Chronos Station. Connor felt like acid was gathering in his stomach. The report painted Connor and the Ghosts as an elite military outfit that had gone rogue.

"What does DV mean?" Ashley asked.

"Disavowed. It means the NA Alliance Congressional Council separated themselves from me when our operation to bring down the Syndicate went bad," Connor said.

He looked at Ashley and Tobias, who both waited for him to continue.

"My team and I were on Chronos Station, but it was the Syndicate and not my team that caused the destruction," Connor said.

He told them about his hunt for the Syndicate and how it had led them to Chronos Station and the Syndicate's leader.

"So someone stashed you aboard the Ark," Tobias said.

"Evidently," Connor said.

Ashley walked over and handed him the data stick. "I think those answers could be on here," she said.

"Where'd that come from?" Tobias asked.

"It was in the storage compartment for his pod," Ashley said.

Connor looked down at the black data stick. "Is there somewhere I can look at what's on here?"

Tobias regarded him for a moment. "Yes, right here. Ordinarily I'd offer you a bit of privacy, but I think we all need to be on the same page regarding how you got here. Wouldn't you agree?"

"I don't have anything to hide," Connor said.

Tobias gestured for him to put the data stick into the analysis tray. The tray glowed, and a liquid metal probe came out of a small panel. Small bolts of electricity leaped to the stick. The liquid metal formed a receptacle, and the data stick plugged inside. A command window appeared on the holoscreen:

VOICE PRINT ID - NAME - RANK - BRANCH

"Connor Gates, Colonel, North American Alliance Military, Special Forces."

VERIFIED.

Admiral Mitch Wilkinson's face appeared on a video log file that opened automatically. Connor glanced at the date on the file and noted that it was from the year 2217. He started the video.

"Connor, by now you must be twenty-five light-years from Earth and have figured out that it was I who put you on the Ark. I'll do what I can for the rest of the Ghosts. I'm not sure whether I can get them on the Ark, but rest assured that I'll see to it that they're safe. I imagine you're quite angry and confused. Well, that can't be helped, and by the time you get this it will be over eighty years into the future. Even with prolonged life spans, I'll be dead and gone by then.

"I imagine you'll have a few choice words about what I did to you, but I couldn't stand by and watch the son of my dear friend get thrown to the lions for a crime he didn't commit. I had to act and couldn't wait for confirmation of what the NA Alliance and the Syndicate would do. We had a special delivery to make for the Ark program, and its special nature required that it be carried out under military control. You were going to be made the scapegoat for the destruction of Chronos Station. Hell, you probably already knew that part before you even saw this message. Seems strange to me that you'll view these events as if reading from the historical records, but for you it'll feel like it was yesterday. I'm sorry for that, but as I said, it couldn't be helped.

"I know you intended to reconnect with your son and possibly your wife. That won't happen now, and I know you'll hate having the choice taken from you. I'll watch over Sean for you, and he'll know his father was a hero and not the terrorist that will no doubt be portrayed by the news outlets." Wilkinson looked away from the camera as Connor heard his own voice. Wilkinson switched off the video.

There were so many emotions vying for attention that Connor felt numb. He *had* wanted to reconnect with Sean and had always assumed there would be time. If this journey had taken the Ark two hundred years, Sean would now be an old man. Connor couldn't even send him a message to tell him he was still alive and that he loved him.

"Sam, are there any records for Sean or Alyssa Gates?" Connor asked.

"Apologies, but I have no records of either of them," the AI said.

"They might have had to change their identities," Ashley said.

Ashley had a point. If the Syndicate was hunting for him, they could have targeted his family in hopes that it would bring him out of hiding.

"I'll never know," Connor said, swallowing hard.

"We can keep looking through the records. I'll make sure you have the access you need to do so," Tobias said.

Connor wanted to thank them, but he couldn't muster up the effort. His mind was reeling from what Wilkinson had done.

"Wilkinson was a flag officer. He'd have had the resources to get you aboard the Ark and he'd also have been able to protect your family," Tobias said.

"I hope so, for their sakes," Connor said and rested his hands on his hips. His mind was racing so much it felt like there was pressure building inside his ears.

"Perhaps you need some rest. Give yourself some time—" Ashley began.

"No," Connor said. "I need . . . something to do. I need to move around." He glanced at Tobias. "I need a job."

Tobias nodded. "Your case is a rather unique situation. There are always transports going down to the colony. Perhaps if I have someone give you a tour there and I follow up with you in a few days we can discuss things like next steps."

"I appreciate it. I have another question, if you don't mind," Connor said.

"You're entitled to as many as you want," Tobias said.

"Wilkinson said the rest of my team might be aboard the Ark somewhere. Is there any way we can find them?"

Tobias's eyes widened and he blew out a breath. "We have three hundred thousand colonists, most of whom are still in stasis. I can have some of my people look into it, see if there was any evidence of tampering with Peter Faulkner's pod, which could point us to other pods. That will take some time. Alternatively, we'll know when we bring the other colonists out of stasis."

"When will that be?" Connor asked.

"I think that kind of question will be best answered if I tell you about the Ark program itself. I trust you know that we're not where we'd planned on being and our journey took about a hundred years longer than anticipated," Tobias said.

Connor nodded.

Tobias gestured for Connor to sit down, and Tobias joined him.

"I have to step away for a few minutes. Be back in a bit," Ashley said.

Connor watched her leave and looked back at Tobias.

"The Ark program. There are hours of vids you could watch, but I'll give you a quick rundown," Tobias said and brought up a small holo-interface so he could control the screen. A star map appeared. "This is the Earth and our star system, and over here, roughly twenty-five light-years away, is where we were supposed to go."

The star map expanded, showing a line from Earth to another star with the designation HD-Alpha-2. "We sent a probe there and some other places about two hundred years ago, looking for a place we could send the first interstellar colony. The information sent back about the planets surrounding HD-Alpha-2 was the most promising. It was time for the next stage of the ongoing project—securing funding and convincing the general public that an interstellar colony was something we could achieve. We received overwhelming support. The original plans called for a colony of five thousand. Instead, we had millions of people who wanted to be a part of the Ark. We eventually settled on three hundred thousand souls."

"So you built a big ship and just set off toward this star system?" Connor asked.

"Not quite that simple. The Ark was one massive ship, but it was also made up of smaller ships that we could use once we got to our destination. There was also a seed ship that went ahead of us," Tobias said.

Connor glanced around. "What ship are we on?"

"This is the Ark. The seed ship had no human presence aboard. It was completely run by machines and thus could travel at much faster speeds than the Ark. The seed ship was to get here first and start running experiments and studying our future home. This way, when we finally arrived we could hit the ground running," Tobias said.

Connor studied the star map and nodded. "I'm with you so far. What went wrong?"

"Nothing went wrong," Tobias said.

Connor pressed his lips together in a thoughtful frown. "You didn't arrive at HD-Alpha-2, so something had to have gone wrong."

"Sam, show us our current position in relation to Earth," Tobias said.

The view of the star map expanded out farther and showed a course change and a distance of sixty light-years from Earth. There were glowing points along the track the Ark had taken to the star system they were currently at.

"What are those glowing points?" Connor asked.

"Good question. In basic terms, they're communications buoys we dropped along our path here. They allowed the ship to send and receive data bursts back from Earth. This way, if there were advancements in technology that would be useful to us, they were packaged and sent to us," Tobias said.

"So you dropped these comms buoys and they just send and receive data? How do they hold their position? What happens if a few of them get damaged? Wouldn't the whole thing just break down?" Connor asked.

"The buoys do more than just send and receive data. There are redundancies in place by design. They keep track of their neighboring buoys so when a new one is added, it lets the others know that another link in the chain has been added. If some are damaged or have become inoperable, the nearest buoys will shift position and try to contact the next buoy up the chain. This will continue until communication is reestablished. It's important to remember that we're talking about communication in interstellar terms. The data bursts, while faster than any ship we have, can't go faster than the speed of light," Tobias said.

Connor poured himself a cup of coffee and took a sip while he considered what Tobias had said. "So if we're sixty light-years from Earth, at the very minimum any message sent from Earth today would take sixty years to reach us here."

"Exactly. We've had communications from Earth, but they're quite old, and we receive the messages, or info-dumps, a piece at a time. Only when it's completed can we see what's in the message," Tobias said.

"I'm with you so far," Connor said and peered at the spot on the map where the Ark had changed course.

"Approximately twenty years into our journey, the ship's computers received a major update from Space Command Central. This update contained a new course heading, as well as updated protocols for the ship's systems to follow," Tobias said.

"Did they say why?"

Tobias frowned and looked to be deciding how he should say

what he was about to say. "We're still piecing together what happened. We think they might have learned something about our destination and decided that the best recourse was to redirect us to another star system."

Connor considered this. He'd been on ops where the chain of command had updated their objectives, and what seemed random to a new recruit made sense later on. The Ark program wasn't a military operation though.

"What could they have found that would make them send us to a star system they knew so little about?" Connor asked.

"Well, they knew we had the seed ship so wherever they sent us we wouldn't be completely in the dark once we reached our destination. There could have been advancements in deep space observation that led them to do this, or something could have gone terribly wrong with HD-Alpha-2," Tobias said.

"How is it that we didn't run out of resources along the way?" Connor asked.

"Another good question. In terms of power, we have plenty. The Ark has multiple fusion reactors aboard that will eventually be brought to the planet's surface," Tobias said.

"Yeah, but you need materials to build the comms buoys, for instance. Even if you had a surplus of materials, it couldn't have been enough for almost triple the amount you thought you'd need," Connor said.

"Our tech platforms include onboard robotic fabricators. Once we deviated from our original course, the seed ship would have identified things such as asteroids that would be viable candidates for the Ark's use. Once we were within the vicinity of one, our own robotic workforce would use the same retrieval techniques we used to mine the asteroid field beyond the orbit of Mars. They'd bring the specimens close and extract the resources we needed," Tobias said.

"I didn't know so much automation had been part of the design for the Ark," Connor said.

"There were a lot of people involved. The intent for the colony was to be self-sufficient, so we needed the capacity to gather the materials we'd need to build our new home," Tobias said.

"I understand that part. But the automation involved in keeping this ship going for a hundred and twenty years beyond what it was designed for is something else entirely. We're lucky to even be alive," Connor said.

"Well, we made it, certainly. But as you said, we're operating outside of the original design specifications. Systems did wear out, and when we first woke up there was a lot for us to do to get where we are today," Tobias said.

"How many people are awake?"

"About twenty thousand. Most are on the surface of the planet. We can't just wake everyone at once or we'll have severe shortages of things like food and water. The people on the surface are setting up farms and living spaces. Each group contributes in preparation for the next. That part hasn't changed, even if the landscape has," Tobias said.

"When Ashley first showed me the planet, I thought it was fake," Connor said.

Tobias brought up a three-dimensional image of the planet. "Now that we know more about you, I can understand why you'd think that."

Tobias bridged his fingers together in front of his chest. "I'm very sorry for what happened to you, Connor," Tobias said. "I can't imagine what you must be thinking right now. It's going to take you some time to adjust. Have a look around the colony. There's no shortage of things that need to be done, problems that need to be solved. Think about where you'd fit in here. In essence, this is a second chance for you should you choose to see it that way."

Connor had more questions about the colony and the events

that had led the Ark here. At times during his conversation with Tobias, he felt as if his mind were spinning. He didn't know what to think or how to feel. Perhaps a tour of the colony would help.

The mere thought of his wife and son were enough to thicken his throat. He hadn't seen them in years, but he'd always assumed there would be time to reconnect with them. He wondered what had happened to the other Ghosts. Were they here, frozen in stasis? Or had they lived out their lives quietly thanks to Wilkinson? Connor might never know all the answers to those questions, but he intended to find out as much as he could.

The door to the conference room opened, and Ashley Quinn walked back in. Tobias came to his feet and Connor followed suit.

Ashley came over to them and spoke to Connor. "There's a transport leaving for the planet. Lars, Noah, and our son, Sean, are going down."

"Oh, Lars is going too. That's good," Tobias said. "Lars Mallory is the son of Franklin Mallory, who's our head of security. If you're up for going down to the surface, I think checking in with Franklin would be good. He can set you up with a couple of tour guides over the next few days."

Connor nodded. "I just want to thank you both. I really don't know what to say. I think going down to the planet is a good idea."

Ashley smiled. "Good, I'm glad. Lars is just outside the door. Once you get down there you'll be set up with some clothes, and there's a colony initiation program to help familiarize you with . . . everything. I'll be coming down planet-side tomorrow and I'll find you."

———————

CONNOR LEFT THE ROOM, and Ashley let the door close before facing her husband.

"Well, what do you think?" she asked.

"I meant what I said. I can't imagine what this must be like for him, and at the same time I'm wondering if there are any more people in the same boat as him," Tobias said.

"We can initiate a search, but we really won't know until we open up each stasis pod and look inside. Did you tell him everything about the messages from Earth?"

"I think he has enough on his mind right now. We don't even fully understand what they mean," Tobias said.

"We've been here six months and we still don't fully understand why they changed course. I never would have thought such a massive override was possible," Ashley said.

"Do you think there is a psychological profile on him somewhere? Each person who was part of the Ark program had to go through a selection process, and despite what information we were able to retrieve on Connor, so far it's minuscule compared with our other colonists," Tobias said.

"I'll look, and Franklin will be evaluating him to be sure Connor's not a danger to himself or others," Ashley said.

Tobias eyed her for a moment. "You like him, don't you?"

Ashley smiled. "Yes."

"He reminds you of John, doesn't he?"

Ashley looked away. "A little bit. My brother was military for life."

"Connor is special forces. We know that much at least. There's almost no mention of the Ghosts he referred to, so he must have been part of some black ops group. Those groups generally don't include the nice guys."

"Given some of the local wildlife on the planet, that may be a good thing," Ashley said.

"Has there been another attack?"

Ashley shook her head. "No. They would have told you if there was. It'll be interesting to see what Connor thinks of our new home."

"Ever the mother of us all. Okay, let's get back to work," Tobias said.

Ashley kissed him on the cheek.

"Will I see you for dinner tonight?" Tobias asked.

"Only if you're very lucky," Ashley said, grinning, and they left the conference room.

8

As CONNOR LEFT the conference room, he had the feeling that Ashley and Tobias needed to discuss a few things, probably about him. Taken at face value, Tobias and Ashley seemed like genuinely good people. They had a job to do, regardless of the circumstances of his own unanticipated presence on the Ark.

Connor needed to get away and welcomed the opportunity to get some fresh air. Even before the Ghosts' last mission, it had been a while since he'd been planet-side on Earth. A deep pang seized his chest and he felt his throat thicken as he thought about Wilkinson's last message. The admiral must have recorded it while Connor had been with the doctors, which meant that there must not have been a lot of time for Wilkinson to throw all this together. The more Connor thought about it, the more he wanted to know about the circumstances that had led the Battleship Carrier *Indianapolis* to intercept their combat shuttle. Had Wilkinson known about the mission to Chronos Station beforehand? He couldn't have found out about it in the time they'd just happened to discover the combat shuttle the Ghosts had used. There was too much coincidence there for Connor's tastes. He didn't know whether to hate the old admiral or thank him. Wilkinson had seemed sincere in his message, and he'd served with Connor's father in the military. Connor still had no idea how Wilkinson had smuggled him aboard the Ark.

More than once he found himself looking for Kasey or Reisman. One of the reasons the Ghosts had been so successful was that Connor took the feedback from his team very seriously. In the end, the decision was always his and the team knew that, but he always tried to give his team the opportunity to share their expert opinions.

Connor approached a trio of young men who appeared to be in their late teens. Prolonging treatments could fool most people, but there was an unmistakable youthful vigor in the eyes of each.

"I'll be tagging along with you down to the colony," Connor said.

The tallest of the trio had straw-colored hair and blue eyes. He greeted Connor. "I'm Lars Mallory, Mr. Gates."

There weren't many people Connor had to look up to, but Lars was among the few. His broad shoulders and muscular body had the look of someone who was extremely active.

"You can call me Connor."

"Is it true you were a colonel in the special forces?" asked the shortest of the trio.

He had long brown hair tied back in a ponytail and his eyes were alight with excitement. Connor guessed he didn't get out much, considering his pale complexion.

"Sorry, I'm Noah. As you may have guessed, this is my ship," Noah said with a grin.

"The Genesis story," Connor said.

"Yup. Are you a religious type?"

"No, religion and I don't mix well," Connor said.

Noah's brows pulled together. "None of them?"

"Never mind him. He studies religions as a hobby. I'm Sean, by the way," said a sandy-haired youth with freckles on his face. His skin was bronzed by the sun.

"It's fine. I don't mind speaking about it," Connor said.

Noah's eyes lit up.

"How about we hold off on the theological discussion until we get on the cargo carrier shuttle," Lars said.

The trio was eager to get back to the planet, and Connor followed them into the hangar.

"So what do you guys do planet-side?" Connor asked.

Lars answered first. "Since we're eighteen, we get to rotate through different occupations in addition to our chosen professions. I'm back in Field Operations and Security, which is headed up by my father."

Connor nodded and looked at the other two.

Noah adjusted the straps of the pack he was carrying. "No field work for me. I work with the different scientists and help get their systems up and running. I also get to visit all the FORBs and set those systems up as well. Connect them back to the compound. That sort of thing."

"FORBs?" Connor asked.

"Forward Operating Research Bases. They're away from the main compound. Some of them are accessible via land transports and we need to fly to others. Someday, when we build the maglev train lines, they'll all be connected," Noah said.

Connor looked at Sean, who wouldn't make eye contact with him. "And you?"

Sean pressed his lips together in annoyance. "I rotate through like the others," he said and quickened his pace to march ahead of them.

"Did I say something wrong?" Connor asked.

"Nah, Sean always gets sensitive about that stuff. With his dad being the governor and all, that usually impacts what Sean gets to do," Noah said.

Lars led them to a cargo carrier that was fully loaded with equipment containers. They checked in with the deck officer and were allowed aboard. The deck officer scanned Connor's palm and then informed him that he'd get ID tags at the compound. Since Connor didn't have any belongings, he took his seat and strapped himself in.

Noah stored his gear and took the seat next to Connor.

"You never answered my question," Noah said.

Connor knew he hadn't answered the question about whether he was in the military and had hoped they'd let it go. Apparently not. "Yes, I was."

Noah's eyes widened. "Wow, are you able to talk about the missions you've been on? Have you been on a lot of them? Were they dangerous?"

"No, and I'm not at liberty to say," Connor said.

Noah's eyes drew downward in disappointment.

"So you set up systems, right?" Connor asked Noah, and he nodded in reply. "Are you any good with getting information off of the Ark's computer systems?"

"There are none better. The Ark systems are linked with the compound's. What is it you'd like to find out?"

"I have a list of things. I guess they'd be considered historical records now," Connor said.

"That wouldn't be a problem—" Noah began.

A woman in the row ahead cleared her throat and poked her auburn-haired head over the seat. "I didn't realize you had so much free time, Noah Barker," Lenora said. She glanced at Connor and gave him a wink.

"I don't, Dr. Bishop," Noah stammered.

"Are you sure?" Lenora asked and pursed her lips in thought. "Because it's been two weeks and our data link still isn't working right at FORB 97."

Noah nodded. "I know I've kept you waiting, but I've been working on it. There's something local that's interfering with the signal, and I'm working on a solution. We're trying additional sensors to bolster it."

"Uh huh," Lenora said, sounding unconvinced. "Then you won't mind accompanying me out to 97 to check out the systems yourself. I think you've done all you can from the compound."

Noah's face paled and then he sighed. "Oh, joy," he said.

Lenora smiled at Connor. "You could come too. You look like you'd make yourself useful."

Connor suspected Lenora would put anyone she could find to work for her. And with those eyelashes, he was sure many found it hard to say no to her.

"I'm sorry, Dr. Bishop, but Mr. Gates will be going through orientation for the next few days," Lars said.

Lenora shrugged, turned around, and sat in her seat.

Noah cleared his throat. "So you really don't believe in any religion?"

The carrier left the hangar, and Connor craned his neck to look out the window at the Ark. The Ark was the biggest ship he'd ever seen. They could have lined up all the battleship carriers in the NA Alliance fleet and they wouldn't have reached the end of the massive ship.

He turned back around. "Not one. Atheism isn't that uncommon anymore."

"The things I've read say that most people in the military do have faith in a religion. It's a pretty interesting statistic that pivots toward belief, especially for those with combat experience," Noah said.

"Religions are a destructive force responsible for thousands of years of war and bloodshed that stifled mankind's growth and prosperity. I don't need to believe there's a super being watching me in order to adhere to a moral code," Connor said.

"So you'd blame the institutions of religion because of the actions of certain members?"

"The scripture they follow is flawed and filled with contradictions. You can't preach tolerance and also have a clause in there that implies 'join us or die—if you don't believe what we believe, you'll go to a mythical hell.' That's all crap people use to control other people," Connor said.

"Religions have had to change a lot in the past few hundred years and acknowledge the flaws of their earlier practices," Noah said.

"Did God tell them to do that? Or was it common sense?" Connor asked.

"That's the real question, isn't it?"

"They had no choice. People were leaving them in droves. The old standards didn't make any sense. I don't have anything against anyone who chooses to have faith in something. Just don't try and push those viewpoints on me. I've spent a bulk of my career dealing with groups that thought they were divine in some way, be it with some crazy concept or luring people in with empty promises. The patterns are there, even if you strip away all the shiny things people like," Connor said.

Noah nodded. "Interesting viewpoint. People are so passionate about it regardless of what they believe."

"I think the framework of religion had a significant purpose in our history, but it's something we're meant to outgrow, that we *should* outgrow. Yet I still see those same tactics used to subvert people, whether it's religion or corporations," Connor said.

"So you don't like the institutions of religion, but God is okay?" Noah asked.

"One and the same for me. You're born, you live, and you die. That's it," Connor said.

"You must be the life of the party," Lenora called out.

Connor snorted. "So, did we bring two of each species from Earth on the ship?"

"We have the genetic materials for most species in the cryolabs, but we're years away from using any of that stuff," Noah said.

"And rightfully so. We can't go changing the ecosystem here to make this place seem more like Earth. We have to adjust to life here," Lenora said.

"If you tell me I can't have a dog, I'll never get to FORB 97," Noah said.

Lenora laughed. "If you fix the issue, I'll personally see to it that you get a puppy from the first litter."

"Hey, Lenora, how does religion fit into *your* line of work?" Connor asked.

Lenora twisted around and eyed him. "You're gonna burn," she said and laughed.

Connor chuckled.

"In all seriousness," Lenora said, "I'm a scientist. I believe there's an order to the universe that we don't fully understand. Just because we understand some mysteries doesn't mean we can do away with others. Call it whatever you want, but I don't think that you and I are here by accident."

Connor settled back in his seat and watched as they closed in on the planet. He hadn't seen distinct continents, only one large mass that stretched a long distance. There were vast mountain ranges that created a spider-work of peaks from one side of the vast continent to the other.

"We're heading toward the western reaches. It's heavily forested, with lots of freshwater springs. They still need to be purified, of course," Noah said.

"Have you explored much of the continent? It reminds me of the old references to the supercontinent Pangea," Connor said.

"The seed ship provided much of the survey data we have. There are strings of islands that go across the oceans, but we've only been exploring the western reaches of the continent. Don't forget there are only about twenty thousand of us awake at the moment," Noah said.

"How'd the site for the main compound get picked?" Connor asked.

"Oh, it was the Ark's artificial intelligence that took the data gathered from the seed ship and ran it through some pretty complex data models. We sent out probes of our own, along with survey crews, and Governor Quinn chose the first site," Noah said.

"Do you have family at the compound?" Connor asked.

Noah's features darkened. "No," he said.

The cargo carrier plunged through the upper atmosphere and leveled off its approach. Connor didn't press Noah for any more information. There was so much he didn't know about the planet. He kept thinking about different things he'd taken for granted on Earth and then wondered what it was going to truly be like on this planet. He recalled Lenora mentioning something about alien ruins, so there would have been an intelligent civilization that had evolved during the planet's history. If there were only ruins left, they must have died out for some reason.

Connor's stomach growled and he smacked his lips, thinking about real food and how he'd never have another beer and burger in Tub's Bar at the Wings Airfield in Colorado. His mind charged down the path of all the things he'd never have again, and at the same time, he looked around at the people in the cargo carrier and thought how they'd all volunteered to be part of the Ark program. They'd chosen to leave Earth and the other colonies in the solar system behind. How does one make that kind of decision? And yet, three hundred thousand colonists had been picked to be on the Ark.

Connor glanced out the window and saw that the landscape was much closer than it had been. They were flying over a vast lush forest that formed a treetop canopy. Their velocity was too fast for Connor to see the landscape in any detail, but a tree was a tree. As he took in the scenery, he kept thinking about what had happened to the Ark mission and how someone back on Earth had overridden the Ark's destination and added another hundred and twenty years to their trip so they could come here.

The compound was easy to spot, and the pilot circled around it once before making the final approach. Connor couldn't imagine that they did this for each flight down here and thought perhaps they'd done it for his benefit. He wasn't used to nice gestures like that. Until recently, his line of work frequently put him at odds with people who wanted to kill him.

The compound was a pretty large campus of buildings and farming areas. There was enough perimeter fencing to surround a small city.

The cargo carrier maneuvered to the landing strip, and the pilot set the large ship down. Connor pushed himself to his feet and felt a wave of dizziness creep over him.

"The planet's a bit bigger than Earth, but it won't take you long to adjust," Lars said.

"We can just breathe the air here?" Connor asked.

"Part of the revival cocktail you were given included an immune system booster to help it acclimate to the environment. You'll need to get treatments at least once every month since they're always discovering something new that hasn't been addressed, but it's a close match to Earth," Lars said.

Connor waited as the others gathered their belongings and he started to feel empty-handed. More than once he thought about his T49 assault rifle. Being armed was part of the life he'd led, and his lack of a weapon made him feel exposed.

The rear doors of the cargo carrier swung down, and a blast of humid air blew inside. The air smelled like a mix of sweet and musky, as if they were in a springtime bloom after a long winter. Were there any seasons? There must be. How long did they last?

Connor stepped outside and shielded his eyes from the bright sunlight. Lars handed him a pair of sunglasses and apologized for forgetting to do so earlier. Connor didn't really need the sunglasses because he had military-grade implants with a full nanite suite, but since they'd been offline for over two hundred years he didn't want to try turning them on again just yet.

To the south, the rings that surrounded the planet appeared gray but still clearly defined.

"What time is it?" Connor asked.

"The cycles are a bit different here, but a day takes a little over twenty-five hours and months are . . ." Noah's voice trailed off. "Don't worry about it. You'll cover all that stuff in orientation, and then you'll struggle to remember it like the rest of us. A year on this planet is three hundred and ninety days. I've been awake for almost four months and I still have trouble keeping it straight," Noah said.

"So when's Christmas?"

Noah glanced at him and chuckled.

"Everyone likes Christmas," Connor said.

He glanced around the airfield and saw a perimeter fence that looked quite robust and tall, considering the distance.

Lars followed his line of sight. "Thirty feet high and electrified to deter some of the local predators from coming around."

Connor frowned in thought. They'd surrounded the entire compound with a thirty-foot-tall electric fence, which made him wonder what they were trying to keep out. But it felt good to have his feet on solid ground again, and Connor recalled that they'd only started bringing people to the surface six months ago.

Noah and Sean hopped onto a ground transport vehicle that took them away while Connor followed Lars to the Field Operations and Security buildings located just off the airfield.

There was no shortage of buildings that looked to be constructed of previously fabricated parts. Connor wondered how long it would be before they built a real city at this location.

The area was flat and looked to be the same elevation beyond the perimeter walls, which would be easily defended. He expected the Forward Operating Research Bases to be comparably constructed but on a much smaller scale.

Connor noted that Field Ops personnel had comlinks attached to their ears. The comlinks hugged the ridgeline of the ear and rested against the head. Everywhere he looked he saw the same green jumpsuit and assumed this was the uniform of security personnel. The people they'd passed also noted Connor's clothing, which marked him as a newbie.

Inside the building, Connor followed Lars through a series of hallways leading to the interior. Cool, conditioned air blew through the air vents. They eventually stopped at an office outside what looked like a typical military command center. Connor glanced through the window. People were working at various workstations and there were large wallscreens that showed critical system statuses. He saw a reference to team deployment and some kind of schedule he didn't understand.

After gaining permission to do so, Lars took him into the office of Franklin Mallory. Connor noted that he was an older version of his son—nearly six foot five and broad-shouldered—but Franklin had a thick beard.

Franklin closed the video call he was on and came over to them. "Hello there. Franklin Mallory, head of security here."

Connor shook his hand and then took a seat.

"How was the trip down?" Franklin asked his son.

"Uneventful, as always," Lars said.

"Just what I like to hear. Charles has something for you in the pit, and I'll see you later for dinner. There are some things I need to talk to you about," Franklin said to his son.

Lars glanced at Connor.

"Thanks for getting me here. I appreciate it," Connor said.

Lars nodded and left the room. Franklin called for his son to close the door on his way out.

"So, I hear you're our unexpected colonist," Franklin said.

"So it seems. I think we can lay some things out on the table," Connor said. "I bet it's your job to evaluate whether I'm going to be any trouble. Does that sound about right?"

Franklin shrugged. "I told Tobias and Ashley I would evaluate you like I do anyone else, but I'm sure you understand that yours is a special case."

"How special?" Connor asked.

"You mean beyond the fact that someone snuck you onto the Ark? You're not the run-of-the-mill colonist, I'll tell you that. Everyone else chose to be here."

"Alright then, level with me," Connor said.

"You served in the military. There are few of us here," Franklin said.

"Where did you serve?"

"I was a colonel in the Military Police Division. They wanted someone who was good at organizing our security forces and investigations," Franklin said.

Connor didn't say anything, but he kept thinking that Franklin Mallory had zero combat experience.

"There aren't that many people from the military here. Tobias was adamant about having a police force equipped to keep the peace but not an actual military fighting force. I think they didn't want any tensions from the previous few hundred years before we left Earth to follow us here," Franklin said.

Now Connor understood. Despite the wishes of Tobias and the mission architects, *he* had shown up—an active member of elite special forces with more combat experience than anyone else here.

"So are they worried I'm going to get people to start fighting or something?" Connor asked.

"Colonists were vetted to determine whether they would thrive on a frontier-type colony. Candidates were tested to see if they could cope psychologically with a real break from home. Even our colonies in the solar system pretty much functioned as an extension of Earth, whereas things here would be different," Franklin said.

"Please don't tell me you came all this way and didn't bring a means to defend yourselves," Connor said.

Franklin chuckled. "Even though we don't have warships or grand carrier vessels, we can defend ourselves. Our tech and manufacturing platforms could enable us to build those things, but it's not the primary reason for being here."

"So where do I fit in?" Connor asked.

"The plan is still the same. You'll go through the basic orientation program, as well as go on a tour of the facilities. Tobias hopes you'll figure out your own place here."

"And you?"

Franklin regarded him for a moment. "I'm here in case you have trouble."

Connor didn't feel as if he were being threatened. Franklin had a job to do and was laying out the facts so they'd be on the same page.

"I'll assign personal escorts you are to take with you wherever you go," Franklin said.

Connor rolled his eyes. "You say I'm free to do what I want, but you're assigning me babysitters. How long will that last?"

"As long as I feel it's necessary," Franklin said.

Connor sighed.

"I looked at the records we have on file for you. You mentioned to Tobias that you led a platoon?" Franklin asked.

"We were part of the elite special forces battalion for the NA

Alliance. I commanded multiple squads and our call sign was Ghosts," Connor said.

"I've never heard of them, and I can't find any record of a group like that existing in the military."

Connor smirked. "That's because we did our jobs right. We had the high-risk missions that carried a high mortality rate for other groups. We hunted terrorist groups and rogue research outposts, but I focused primarily on a group that called themselves the Syndicate."

"That's something I'd like to hear more about," Franklin said.

Connor pressed his lips together. Officially, he wasn't supposed to divulge any information about the Ghosts to anyone outside their squad unless clearance was given by his commanding officer. It was one of the driving forces that had put a huge wedge between Connor and his ex-wife, Alyssa. She hadn't tolerated the confidentiality of his work.

"You do realize that you're not in the military anymore," Franklin said.

"I understand. Old habits die hard, I guess," Connor said.

Franklin shrugged. "Fair enough. So we'll need to get you sorted out. I'll have living quarters assigned to you that are befitting your former rank as an officer."

It was an olive branch, plain and simple. "I appreciate that," Connor said.

"I think someone with your experience could be extremely valuable in terms of what we're trying to do here. So as you go through the basic orientation, if you have ideas about things we can do better, I encourage you to share them," Franklin said.

"What about leaving the compound?" Connor asked.

"It's not safe to go off by yourself. We assign a small team of armed escorts to our field scientists," Franklin said.

"What's out there?"

"Some local predators are giving us some trouble. Pack hunters mainly, but there are others as well. We're still learning about the ecosystems here, and well . . . we're the aliens," Franklin said.

"I met an archaeologist on the Ark who said some ruins had been found," Connor said.

"Lenora Bishop. Yeah, she's keen to study the ruins. She believes that understanding the planet's history is the key to our future here." Franklin regarded him for a moment. "Lenora has turned more than a few heads here, so if she's caught your eye, you might have to stand in line."

Connor laughed. Lenora was a beautiful woman, but that wasn't what he had in mind, and said so.

Franklin held up his hands. "We're here to colonize, which includes making lots of babies."

Connor felt the blood drain from his face.

Franklin frowned for a moment. "Oh, dammit! I didn't think. I'm sorry. I read that you left a family behind. This must be difficult for you since there're so many families here and there'll be more. It's probably too soon to think about it, but there are also many people who aren't married. New life and new beginnings."

"I have a son . . . He'd be two hundred and eleven years old by now," Connor said.

"Wife?"

"Only for a while. Didn't cope too well with military life," Connor said.

"Takes a special kind of person to cope with it, and I bet it was even harder with the type of work you were doing," Franklin said.

"How does orientation work?" Connor asked.

"There are some basic classes and video instruction that I'm sure you'll breeze through. There are also qualifications for using land or air transport, but given your credentials, you'll know more about them than the local experts. There are field guides we can upload to your personal digital assistant," Franklin said.

"I do need to see a doctor. I have ZX-64 implants with a full suite of nanites. They're likely dormant, but I haven't switched them back on," Connor said.

Franklin's eyes widened. "Was your entire platoon outfitted with them?"

Connor nodded. "Allowed for swift communication and system interface capabilities regardless of how secure they were."

"I know who'd be interested in that. His name is Dr. Amir Marashi. He'd be the best one to help. You'll likely need to go into one of the med scanners. He'll want to reverse-engineer your implants if they can't find a reference to them in our data-libraries. Did Noah Barker come down with you?" Franklin asked.

"Yes."

"I know he's young, but he's one of the good ones. He's some kind of prodigy. Excels at pattern recognition and a bunch of other words that I have no idea what they mean. If you come across something you need help finding, he's your best asset. Navigating the archives can be a real bear sometimes. The AI helps but can be finicky at times," Franklin said and rose from his chair. "Also, your guides are there to assist you as well as keep an eye on you, so feel free to ask them questions. I'm assigning Corporal Diaz to you, and he'll rotate out with someone else."

"So am I free to go anywhere I want?" Connor asked.

"Inside the compound, yes, unless there are danger signs. There are some places we restrict access to, like the power station and weapons depot, that sort of thing, but think of yourself as a civilian," Franklin said.

Connor didn't know why, but thinking of himself as a civilian seemed harder than thinking of himself as a colonist. He'd been a colonel and now he was here.

"Diaz will show you where your quarters are, and you can get cleaned up. Your orientation begins tomorrow. Check in with me in a few days. Sooner, if you want to," Franklin said.

"How would I find you?"

"Your escorts will know, and once you get situated you'll find it's not that difficult to find the person you're looking for," Franklin said.

Connor left the office and found Corporal Diaz waiting for him outside. Diaz was short and built like a tank, with thick muscles.

"I'll take you to your quarters, sir," Diaz said.

Connor followed him, but he had every intention of exploring the compound. His quarters were in one of the temporary housing units located near the Field Operations and Security Headquarters. His accommodation was a one-room studio apartment that didn't have a kitchen, but he did have his own bathroom. Diaz explained that he'd only need to stay there for a few weeks before more permanent housing was built. Inside there was a bed and a dresser. On the bed was a pack that was full of clothing his size. Diaz left him alone, saying he'd be just outside.

Connor stifled a yawn and sat on the bed. Deciding to lie back just to see what the bed felt like, he was asleep in moments.

9

THE NEXT DAY a sharp knock on his door woke Connor from a deep sleep. He stumbled toward the door, but years of training quickly pushed back early morning disorientation. He opened the door to Corporal Diaz.

"Good morning, sir. Once I realized you were asleep, I left you alone. The revival cocktail can leave you groggy for a few days while your body acclimates to the planet. You have about an hour before your orientation begins," Diaz said.

Connor mumbled something about getting dressed.

"There's a shower in there. Don't be afraid to use it," Diaz said and chuckled.

Connor lifted up his arm and caught a whiff of foul odor. Laughing, he shut the door on Diaz and began to get ready for the day. In the shower, he blasted his body with hot water, feeling that there was nothing like a hot shower to make him feel like a new person. After his shower, Connor got dressed. His jumpsuits were all gray and had the golden sunburst on the sleeve. He put on thick black boots, and the smart mold inside contoured to the shape of his feet, providing superior support.

He checked his appearance in the mirror and took a deep breath.

"New beginnings."

Connor walked outside, and Corporal Diaz joined him. Connor arched an eyebrow. "How come you got stuck with babysitting duty?"

Diaz laughed. "Just lucky, I guess. I'll take you to the cafeteria to get some food. I know I'm hungry."

They started walking. The clothing they'd given Connor was quite comfortable, reminding him of his army fatigues—thick and durable.

"I don't understand the color codes of the uniforms. I assume green is for your division," Connor said.

"There isn't much to it, and it will most likely go away, except ours and any other government entity. Gray, like yours, is for generalist and people who are new," Diaz said.

Connor smelled food cooking before they reached the cafeteria, and his mouth started watering. They went inside and there were food stations set up along a buffet. Connor headed directly over to the omelet station and asked for a ginormous, four-egg omelet with bacon and onions and peppers.

"Make it good. My friend hasn't eaten in a while," Diaz said. "Hell, I'll take one too."

The cook reached for a large pan and heated up the oil. Connor watched as he sautéed the vegetables and then added bacon. After a minute, he poured on the eggs and shook the pan vigorously, then set it down and added cheese. Saliva gushed inside Connor's mouth.

Connor held out his plate as the precious omelet slid off the pan. He grabbed a cup of coffee and sat down at one of the empty tables, crushing the omelet in minutes. It hadn't stood a chance. Diaz joined him and Connor sipped his coffee.

Diaz whistled. "Did you even taste it?"

"You bet. Part of me wants another one, but I don't think I could fit it in," Connor said and took another sip of his coffee. "How long have you been here?"

Diaz finished chewing his food. "I was one of the early ones who came with the survey teams."

"So what made you decide to leave Earth behind?" Connor asked.

"That was easy. Traveling to another world. Come on, man, that's the stuff, right there," Diaz said.

"Which unit did you serve in?" Connor asked, playing a hunch.

"I was airborne division . . ." Diaz said, then frowned. "How'd you know?"

"If you're in the service long enough, you just know. It also makes sense for Mallory to have a former military person keeping an eye on me," Connor said.

They left the cafeteria and Diaz told him they were going to Central Processing for orientation. They took a two-seater all-terrain vehicle that had roll bars and thick knobby tires. The only sound the dark-green-colored ATV made was the thick tires on the ground.

"Do you like it here?" Connor asked.

"What's not to like about a new world to explore? Any chance I get to head to the FORBs, I take it. I have to say there are some strange-looking creatures here."

"Doesn't it bother you that this wasn't the original destination?"

Diaz shrugged. "Not really. I mean, when we first woke up a lot of people were freaking out, but we're here. We're not going to turn around and head back home. New Earth is here."

Connor shook his head. "I hope they come up with a better name than that."

"Oh, anyone can submit a suggestion for the name of this

place, but Governor Quinn said they wouldn't decide on a permanent name until everyone is out of stasis," Diaz said.

"I guess that's fair," Connor said and caught sight of the perimeter fences in the distance.

Diaz took him to a large tent and parked the ATV. Connor climbed out and they headed inside. There were chairs lined up and a big screen at the front. "Time to go to school," Diaz said.

There were fifty other people in gray jumpsuits, and Connor sat in the back. To his surprise, Diaz sat next to him.

A man in a blue uniform stood up in the front and smiled at them in greeting. "Welcome to your orientation. My name is Rich, and I'm going to tell you about our new home. By now, you've been told that this wasn't the original planet we were supposed to colonize. At a precise point during our journey, we received an update from Earth that changed the Ark's course. We're still piecing together why, but it may be years before we have a complete understanding. For now, I take comfort in believing that the reason was quite simple. They were looking out for us, and we're here.

"This planet is close to Earth in size and is quite conducive to supporting life. And the rings, of course," Rich said and looked around at all of them, "are really quite something. There's also a moon here. Planetary scientists have known for quite some time how important a moon is for stabilizing planetary tilt and how tidal shifts are required for life like ours to flourish on any planet. There are life forms on this planet that are similar to what we've seen on Earth, and there are some with striking differences. There are vast forests and jungles if you go to the southern reaches of the supercontinent. Deserts and prairies. The list goes on and on. Have a look at some of the birds we've observed."

An image came on the large wallscreen showing the leathery wings of a bat-like creature that had a hooked beak like a hawk and a large protrusion covering its head.

"We think the creature's large head is for extra cranial capacity, and we have scientists who are studying them now. They have an excellent sense of direction, and when a flock of them takes to the skies, it's truly a sight to behold. While their wings look leathery, they are in fact multilayers of translucent fibers. These things have double-jointed shoulder sockets that allow them to change how their wings work. They're able to lock their wings into position for lengthy glides that don't strain their muscles," Rich said.

One of the newcomers raised their hand. "How did you learn so much about them if we've only been here a short time?"

"Excellent question," Rich said and repeated it so everyone else could hear. "We've done field studies, but much of our research was gathered from drones. We've been careful not to disrupt their habitats and migration patterns. But if you want to see something truly strange, check this out."

The next image showed a creature that looked like evolution hadn't been able to decide what it was supposed to be. It stood on two clawed feet that bore a striking resemblance to a rooster's. There were two arms and four fingers with black claws, a tail that reached the ground, and small feathered wings. It had a small round head covered in dark hair, large dark eyes, and a mouth full of teeth.

"They're nocturnal. Some of our younger colonists insist on calling them nightcrawlers. Their wings enable them to fly short distances and they'll eat just about anything from small rodents to a variety of plants. They sing at night, which we think is part of their mating ritual. They average between one to two feet in height and, believe it or not, are most active during a full moon," Rich said.

The speaker paused to take a drink of water. "We could spend weeks learning about all the different animals here, but we're not going to do that. Your personal digital assistants—"

There were several chuckles from the crowd and Rich smiled.

"I know—a very old reference. Your PDA is equipped with a vast encyclopedia of knowledge that interfaces with most equipment, so if you're out and about and you see something you're not sure is dangerous, this can tell you."

Connor shook his head, thinking that if any of the colonists encountered something truly dangerous, they might not have the time to wait for the all-clear from their PDAs.

"As part of your orientation, we'll go out beyond the fence and acquaint you with the area. I'm not going to lie to you. Like Earth, there are some dangerous predators out there. It's important to remember not to let your preconceived notions about an animal fool you. It may look like a friendly cousin back on Earth but may be a dangerous predator here. The next images I'm going to show you are to make you aware of some of those predators," Rich said and took a breath. "Honestly, this one creeps me out a little bit."

The image showed four smaller pictures of a large tree limb. A long powerful tail coiled around it and was connected to a large armored body with four hairy legs that each ended in a claw. A beard made up of tentacles adorned a face with fearsome dark eyes and savage-looking canine teeth.

"If you spot this up in the trees, get the hell out of there because there are likely more of them. The creature uses ambush-predator tactics, so once it loses its surprise advantage, there's only a small chance of it chasing you. The armor is tough and, like everything else here, warrants closer study. We learn more every day, so check your PDAs frequently for any updates," Rich said.

Connor raised his hand, and Rich nodded for him to speak. "What predator is the perimeter fence meant to keep out?"

"There are some large herbivores that sometimes come near here, and they draw in some pack hunters. One of them looks like a giant centipede that has a pair of pinchers. They move pretty fast but are easily deterred with subsonic frequency transmissions. It drives them away. There's another one to be aware of, however,"

Rich said and put another picture on the wallscreen. "This resembles a prehistoric bear, but they roam together in packs and move more like wolves. There's usually an alpha, and they range in size from between six hundred to eight hundred pounds. They're capable of running long distances. We find them mostly on the open plains, but our drones have seen them in the forests as well. We call them berwolf," Rich said.

Connor glanced around the room and saw that many of the people looked scared.

"It's going to take some getting used to. The fauna here is sometimes bigger and more exotic than what we're familiar with, but in time this place will become familiar too," Rich said.

Connor had more questions but he didn't want to scare the group any more than they already were.

A woman raised her hand. "Has anyone been attacked?"

Rich nodded. "Yes, they have. There have even been some deaths. This is why we don't leave the compound without an armed escort."

The murmurings of several people swept across the room.

"I get it. You're new and some of this stuff is scary, but think about it. Anyone who lived out in the wilds back on Earth never went out without some kind of protection. The same principles apply here. That's why your next class will be in small arms training so you can protect yourselves and your loved ones," Rich said.

Diaz leaned over toward Connor. "I'm pretty sure you can skip that one."

"What do they arm them with?" Connor asked.

"Mostly deterrents like sonic-type weapons. Just enough to get the thing to pause and go off in another direction," Diaz said.

"What happens if it doesn't?"

"We do have gauss rifles and plasma pistols, some heavier

stuff, but we're not handing those out to the general colonist," Diaz said.

The other new colonists rose to their feet, and Connor did the same.

"Rich," Diaz called out. "My buddy, Connor, here, is already checked out of the next training sessions. We'll regroup with you later on."

Rich waved to them and then led the other colonists through the exit near the wallscreen.

"What do we do now?" Connor asked.

"You have an appointment with Dr. Marashi," Diaz said and smiled. "Then I get to clear you for weapons training myself. That will be fun."

They left the tent, and Diaz drove them to the neurological research facility. These buildings were also made up of prefab parts that had just needed to be put together. They went to the front desk and were told where Dr. Marashi's office was, which they found after a short walk.

Dr. Amir Marashi was an extremely thin man with a thick dark beard.

"Hello there, Connor. I was told to expect you," Dr. Marashi said. "Ashley warned me of your aversion to needles, so I'll assure you that we won't be needing any today."

Diaz glanced at Connor questioningly.

"I'll tell you about it later," Connor said.

"Let's get you loaded up onto the table and see what the med scanner can tell us about the state of your implants," Dr. Marashi said.

Connor climbed onto the table and lay down. "Do you have the restart protocols for the ZX-64?"

"Not exactly, but let's take a look first," Dr. Marashi said. "I assure you I won't do anything without your consent first."

Connor nearly grinned. He guessed his reputation had

preceded him. A large robotic arm extended from the ceiling, and Amir told him to lie still while a broad-spectrum laser pulsed from the end of the arm and proceeded to scan his body. A holoscreen appeared nearby that displayed an image of the results as they came up. The scan went on for a few minutes and then stopped. Connor sat up and watched as Dr. Marashi examined the information on the screen.

"The good news is that the nanites are intact. The scans show —and your biochip confirms—that their integrity hasn't been compromised due to the abnormally long stasis period," Dr. Marashi said.

"And the bad news?" Connor asked.

"I wouldn't call it bad news. I just can't be exactly sure what will happen if you re-enable your implants, but they'll more than likely function normally. Once active, the startup protocols should signal a diagnostic of your nanites with all the fail-safes designed to keep them from harming a person. The thing is, we can't be sure. Even if we fabricated another set of the ZX-64 series implants to the exact specifications, there's no way for me to reproduce what's already occurred," Dr. Marashi said.

Connor considered what the doctor had said for a moment. "Well, if anything were to go wrong, then I'd be in the right place."

"Brain implants are nothing new. We've been using them for over two hundred years. The fact that yours are designed for military application shouldn't affect that, but there is a degree of risk involved that I needed to make you aware of. An alternative I can offer you is to surgically remove them," Dr. Marashi said.

Connor frowned. He didn't like the idea of surgery. "I'm going to turn them on. If something goes wrong, you can always yank them out."

"I must warn you that the risk of turning them back on also extends to your brain," Dr. Marashi said.

"So what do you recommend?" Connor asked.

"I'd say you'll be fine."

"Turn 'em back on, doc," Connor said.

Dr. Marashi brought up a separate holo-interface on his console. "Okay, I'm going to send the startup protocols. You should experience the same sensations as when they were first installed."

Connor lay back down on the bed and told Amir to send the signal. There was a long pause, and Connor braced himself. Then he felt an extension of his consciousness come back online in the form of a disorienting buzz in the back of his mind. The throbbing in his head quickly gained in intensity. Connor squeezed his eyes shut and arched his back.

"What's wrong with him?" Diaz asked.

"His nanites are coming back online," Amir answered.

Connor cried out.

"He's in pain. Is this normal?" Diaz asked.

Connor's muscles went rigid as a strange pins-and-needles sensation spread throughout his body. His breath came in gasps and he focused on his breathing. Thankfully, the pain in his head slowly went away and he began to relax. He opened his eyes, and a familiar internal heads-up display overlaid his field of vision. He took several long blinks and felt his leg muscles twitch.

"I'd forgotten how painful that could be," Connor said.

"Are you alright?" Diaz asked.

"I think so," Connor said.

His implants were showing that they were online. Everything he was looking at was immediately classified, and his implants searched for the nearest network connection.

"I'm showing that your implants are online and the nanite activation sequence is progressing," Dr. Marashi said.

Diaz frowned. "How long does it take?"

"It can take a day to cycle through all of them," Connor said, and Dr. Marashi nodded.

"I'd offer you something for the pain, but your nanites should be taking care of that," Dr. Marashi said.

Connor nodded.

"You've got healing nanites that just stay in your system?" Diaz asked.

"Yeah, they've saved a lot of lives," Connor said.

Diaz looked at the doctor. "Can you reverse-engineer that? The healing nanites we use are temporary and just cycle out of a person's system."

"I'll look into it, but I'm not sure they're entirely safe," Dr. Marashi said and looked at Connor. "If you're willing to be scanned again, I think that—coupled with some test sequences for the implant-to-nanite interface—would reveal a lot about how they work," Dr. Marashi said.

"Go ahead, doctor," Connor said.

The deep-level scan took almost thirty minutes to complete. Dr. Marashi told Connor to use his implants, and Connor opened a connection to the compound's computer network. He spent the time trying to learn what had happened to the rest of the Ghosts, but there wasn't a trace of them. Wilkinson had covered his tracks well. He thought about looking up his son but changed his mind at the last second. He wasn't ready to face that just yet.

"Finished for now. If you wouldn't mind, please come back in a few days or at least forward me a diagnostic report of your implant's performance. I'd like to be sure there aren't any problems with the nanites. Meanwhile, I'll dig through the archives we have to see what the side effects were for prolonged nanite exposure," Dr. Marashi said.

Connor thanked him, and they left the neurological research building.

Diaz glanced at him. "You sure you're alright? You looked like you were in a lot of pain."

"I'm fine. The nanites do a good job managing the pain. What I'd really like to do is go for some target practice," Connor said.

Diaz let out a hungry laugh and they hopped back into the ATV.

Now that his internal heads-up display was active, he felt more like his old self and caught himself looking for Kasey and Reisman from Ghosts platoon. Thinking about them reminded him of the men who had died under his command on Chronos Station—Jefferson, who was calm and kept his shit together even in the stickiest of situations, and Malarkey, who was one of the medics serving with the Ghosts. Connor could always count on Malarkey to risk life and limb if there was a chance that one of them could be saved. He kept looking around for them, wanting those men near him—anything to create the illusion that he was home, even if it was just for a moment.

10

THE COMMUNICATOR on the ATV chimed, and Diaz hit the button. "Go ahead," Diaz said.

"Hey, Diaz, Vic here. Where you heading?"

"Sweet Victoria, your voice is enough to brighten anyone's day. I'm just taking my friend Connor to the firing range," Diaz said.

There was a pause and a chuckle. "Do you think you can swing by section seventy-three? I'm showing unauthorized access to the perimeter fences over there."

"You know I'd do anything for you, but aren't Mills and his group on patrol?" Diaz said.

"They're on their way, but they haven't checked in. Also, it's not far from the outer farms that have the new fruit you like," Victoria said.

Diaz looked over at Connor. "She gets me."

"If I get some, does that mean we can share that tasty fruit tonight?" Diaz asked.

"Stop being a pain and just do what I ask you to do," Victoria said.

"Roger that. I'll see you tonight," Diaz said and laughed.

The comms channel closed, and Diaz turned the ATV around.

"What's going on?" Connor asked.

"We started planting some local crops outside the fence and sometimes people take it upon themselves to go out there and harvest it. There should be guys out there working the field nearby, but I think Victoria just likes the sound of my voice," Diaz said.

"You guys together?" Connor asked.

"Every chance I get," Diaz said.

They headed toward the perimeter fence. There was an open area near the fence, and Connor could only glimpse what was on the other side.

"Do me a favor and reach behind us into the storage locker. There should be a CAR-74 semiautomatic hunting rifle in there," Diaz said.

Connor twisted around in his seat and opened the storage locker. Inside was a black rifle. He pulled it out and sat back in his seat. When he activated the gun's interface, it barked an alarm saying he wasn't authorized.

Diaz glanced over and nodded. "You're not cleared yet. Inside the glove compartment is an SD-15 you can use."

Connor opened the compartment and saw a bulky handheld weapon with a stubby barrel.

"That's the one. Activate it now so it's charged. The SD-15 is a sonic deterrent system capable of firing short-range frequency bursts. Have you used one before?" Diaz asked.

Connor held the SD in his hand and gave it a once-over. "I've used something like it. Are you expecting trouble?"

"Oh, you know, rather have it and not need it than need it and not have it," Diaz said.

They approached the perimeter gates and the guard immediately waved them through. Once through the gate, Connor held on while Diaz hooked the steering wheel to the left and put on the speed. There were at least a hundred yards between the perimeter fence and the edge of the forest. Everything from the plants to the trees was big and thick, and some of the plants were a variety of colors other than the dominant green. A short distance from them was a large ATV off to the side with four Field Operations security people working around it.

Diaz slowed down and stopped. "Hey there, boys. What seems to be the problem?"

The men were huddled around the ATV, which had a series of holes over the engine compartment. One of them turned around. The name Mills was written on his shirt.

"Vic got you here to check out activity on seventy-three?" Mills asked.

"That's right. She thought you were farther away," Diaz answered and introduced Connor.

"One of those berwolf shot out of the forest and sank his teeth into the engine compartment. He hit one of the power cables and got the shock of his life. Then he took off running back into the forest," Mills said.

"Are your comms down? Need me to radio in for a field mechanic?" Diaz offered.

"Nah, we got a spare cable here and we're changing it out. I think we've got a group of kids that decided to make a fruit run. Charlie's crew. Caught sight of some of them, but that's when that berwolf decided to try chewing on our ATV," Mills said.

"You're lucky it wasn't one of the big ones," Diaz said. "How many kids with Charlie?"

"Definitely saw four of them," Mills confirmed.

"Alright, we'll check it out," Diaz said.

They drove away, and Connor kept an eye on the forest. "Do your ATVs get attacked often?"

Diaz shook his head. "Nah, don't think that's happened before. A few months back I was in one of the more armored ones and was caught out there while a pack of those berwolfs was attacking a herd of herbivores. Other than a few glances at my vehicle, they didn't do anything to me."

Connor looked ahead of them and then back at the forest. "You should call in for backup," Connor said.

Diaz glanced over at him. "Why?"

"Pack hunters don't do anything without a reason. What if the animal Mills encountered was a scout and he just wanted to slow down the response for the real target?" Connor said.

Diaz's mouth formed a grim line and he activated the communicator. "Hey there, Vic. We found Mills. Their vehicle was having an issue with a power cable that's being replaced. Is there anyone else out here who can provide backup? Mills had a lone berwolf try to take a chunk out of his ATV," Diaz said.

"One moment," Victoria said.

They drove on, and Connor kept a sharp lookout. "How old are these kids?"

"Typical teenagers, like sixteen and seventeen. Mostly boys hang out with Charlie, but I've seen the occasional group of girls go with them as well," Diaz said.

The perimeter fence curved, and they went around the corner. Ahead of them was a plowed field that was lined with tall plants. Large yellow pods were bending the branches over.

"What's the status on that backup?" Diaz said.

"The section chief wants to know if you have visual confirmation of berwolfs in the area," Victoria said.

"Mills' report isn't good enough? We're at the crop fields now, and no, I don't see any of them, but that doesn't mean anything," Diaz said.

Connor set his implants on tracking mode and his vision became sharper. They were at a higher vantage point, and Connor saw workers with some machinery on the other side of the field several hundred meters from them. He peered at the area about halfway to the workers and his HUD showed an anomaly. Connor focused his attention on it and recognized the head-bobs of six distinct shapes.

"I've got 'em," Connor said. "About halfway to those workers, more toward the forest than the fence."

Diaz glanced at him in surprise. He gestured for the rifle and looked through the scope. After about a minute he'd found them too. "How the hell did you see that far?" Diaz asked.

"Implants," Connor said and scanned along the forest line. "Crap, looks like one of those berwolfs is following those kids. It's keeping its distance though."

Diaz slammed his palm on the communicator. "I have visual confirmation of a berwolf in the area. Now send us some damn backup," he said and closed the channel. "Switch it to broadband and try to get in touch with those guys. We've got to move," Diaz said.

Diaz gunned the ATV, and Connor held on while trying to operate the communicator. "They're not responding."

Diaz swore and started banging on the horn. They were closing in on the kids but the berwolf was still a lot closer. Connor unbuckled his seat belt and stood up while grabbing onto the roll bar. The ATV had large tires and he was able to see over the line of crops while standing. One of the kids turned around. The blaring horn startled the berwolf, who craned its thick neck around to peer in their direction. Connor pointed the SD-15 at it and fired. An invisible force flattened a swath toward the creature, but they were out of range. Connor glanced toward the teenagers, who were already running.

"Bring me in closer toward that thing," Connor said.

"Alright, I got you," Diaz said.

The ATV lurched toward the right and Connor aimed the SD-15 again. This time the creature turned around and started running.

"What's it doing?" Diaz asked.

"It's running along the tree line. Damn, those things are fast," Connor said.

Diaz took them out of the crops and was able to go much faster. Connor looked over to the left and saw that the bobbing heads of the teenagers were almost to the fence.

"Can they get through the fence over there?" Connor asked.

"The next gate is up ahead near those workers," Diaz said.

The berwolf cut to the right and dashed into the forest. Diaz eased up on the accelerator while Connor scanned the area. It was like the thing had disappeared, but everything in Connor's gut told him this wasn't over. Where was the main pack?

They were almost to the workforce and the security detail assigned to them. Hearing the commotion, the workers gathered by the security detail. Connor pressed his lips together at the way things were being run here. It was a miracle they'd survived this long.

Diaz brought the ATV to a stop, and he and Connor climbed out of the vehicle.

"Time to go. We've got berwolfs in the area," Diaz said.

One of the workers glanced fearfully toward the forest. "We're almost done."

"Well, get done," Diaz said.

The security detail closed in, and a woman with the name J. Scott on her shirt spoke first. "Did you say you saw a berwolf? We haven't seen anything all day."

Connor shook his head. He'd seen this before. Guard duty was tedious when it was uneventful, which led to the people on duty not paying attention. Two men from the detail turned around and approached the forest. Diaz kept speaking with Scott.

"Looks like Mills is finally going to join us," Diaz said.

Connor glanced behind and saw the large ATV almost upon them.

"Hey, we got nothing over here," one of the men said.

Connor turned back around. An alarm flashed on his internal heads-up display and then a large brown creature burst from the trees, snarling, and snatched one of the men backwards. The man screamed as he was dragged into the forest. The other man froze.

"We have to go get him!" Scott said.

"She's right," Mills said. "Everyone on Scott. Now!"

"No, wait," Connor said, but the Field Operations security people didn't hear him.

All eight of them ran into the forest, including Diaz. Connor followed behind. "Go slowly and stagger your approach."

Mills glanced over at him and noted Connor's gray apparel. "We know what we're doing," he said.

Diaz paused. "Maybe we should listen to him. He's—"

Diaz was cut off by the screams of the man who'd been dragged off. The way forward showed the forest closing in on them, and Connor kept looking for more of the berwolfs. He stomped over to Diaz.

"You have to listen to me. This is a trap. The berwolfs are laying a trap for us," Connor said.

Diaz's eyes widened.

"They're bringing this group to a choke point and then they're going to close in on all sides," Connor said.

"How could you know what they're going to do?" Diaz said.

"Where'd this guy come from?" Mills said. "Diaz, take the civilian back to the compound."

Diaz frowned and looked at Connor for a moment. "What if he's right?"

"You guys can trail behind if you want. Steve is one of my guys, and I'm going to get him," Scott said and quickened her pace.

Mills shook his head and followed along with the others.

Diaz looked at Connor. "What can we do? We can't let them go off alone," he said and started to follow.

Connor grabbed his arm. "Not that way. Let's circle around and flank them."

Diaz frowned and then nodded.

Connor set a quick pace. He checked the area as they angled their approach, circling around the others, who were calling out for Steve. Connor glanced back at Diaz and kept a sharp lookout, his face intense. They moved quickly in short bursts, stopping to check the area until eventually they were level with the other team, which was a short distance from them. Connor slowed down, and they moved quietly through the forest. He heard a deep grunt from a large creature, and Connor became still. He raised his fist and pointed to where he'd heard the noise. A berwolf was less than thirty meters from them, its muscular square head jutting out and its gaze fixed on the security detail. There was an answering grunt, followed by several more. He caught sight of the other team, which the berwolfs were about to attack.

Connor bellowed a loud roar and fired his weapon. Sonic bursts tore through the forest. Diaz fired his gun, aiming low so as not to hit the other team. The berwolfs reared in surprise and started running forward. Connor charged ahead and kept firing his weapon. He heard several screams and weapons fire from the other team. Connor ran past the others, pursuing the fleeing berwolfs, and then stopped. The terrain sloped upward, and two berwolfs had stopped on the ridgeline. They turned around. Connor stood up and had his weapon pointed at them but knew they were too far for him to reach, so he lowered it. The berwolfs regarded him in the cold, calculating way that a hunter used to measure the threat of another hunter. After a few moments the berwolfs turned around and ran down the other side of the ridge, away from them. There were several high-pitched yipping sounds and the answering calls by others. The sounds faded as the berwolfs headed off.

Diaz called out to him, and Connor ran back toward the

others. They were gathered around two men who had wounds on their legs. At the rate they were bleeding, Connor knew the main artery in the inner thigh had been missed. They'd live.

"He's dead!" J. Scott cried over Steve's body.

There were several large gashes on Steve's arms and shoulder, but the killing blow had come from the wound on his neck.

Mills stormed over to Connor. "I've got two wounded people because of you. You made them go right into us."

"They were about to attack. I took the element of surprise from them. Otherwise you'd all be dead," Connor said.

Mills swung his gaze to Diaz. "Who the hell is this guy? Never mind that," he said and glared at Connor. "You're coming with me. Bind him and toss him in the back of the ATV."

Connor's brows pushed forward and he clenched his teeth. Two of Mills' men came over and one had his weapon pointed at Connor. "Drop the weapon, sir," he said.

Connor blew out a breath and let the SD-15 fall to the ground. The other man started to come over with the bindings, but Diaz intercepted them. "Give me those things," Diaz said and tossed the bindings on the ground. "I'll take him back to headquarters and Mallory can decide what to do."

"Whatever, as long as he gets there. I'll be there shortly," Mills said.

The other men set up a perimeter while they called in med evac for the wounded men.

Diaz glanced at Connor. "Let's go," he said.

As Connor followed Diaz, he kept going over the berwolf encounter in his mind and tried to think of something he could have done differently. They'd been ready to attack. Connor knew his actions had been correct, but would Mallory see it that way?

"They were about to die. You saw it," Connor said.

Diaz looked shaken up and didn't answer him.

"How many of you have died like this?" Connor asked.

Diaz glared back at him. "You don't know what you're talking about. You could have just gotten lucky back there."

"You know it wasn't luck. It was a trap," Connor said.

"Yeah, how did you know?"

"Because it's how I've conducted operations before—pick off one of the weaker ones along the edge and pull the rest of your enemy away from their stronghold, then take them out. Pack hunters have been doing the same thing for millions of years," Connor said.

Diaz shook his head and cursed. "Dammit, this is going to be a real shit-storm."

Connor glanced up and saw a drone. The drone's serial number appeared on Connor's heads-up display, and he noted it for later. An emergency transport carrier flew overhead toward where the others were in the forest. Everything he'd seen so far spoke volumes as to how unprepared Field Operations and Security was at dealing with the challenges they faced.

They climbed back into the ATV, and Connor started making lists in his mind. Diaz didn't say anything to him as they went back through the gates.

"What about those kids?" Connor asked.

Diaz stopped the ATV and waved one of the guards over. "We saw a group of kids outside the fence. Did they make it back inside?"

The guard checked his tablet and nodded. "Yeah, they're at the next sector waiting to be taken back to the compound. They're pretty shaken up."

Diaz thanked the guard and drove away. Halfway to their destination, Diaz broke his silence. "Look, I gotta have a good think about what happened. It's been quiet along the fences for a while. I'm not saying I think you're wrong, but I have to go through the events in my mind to make sure we did the right thing."

An alert flashed on Diaz's PDA, and he thumbed through the interface.

"What is it?" Connor asked.

"You're overdue for your next scheduled orientation class," Diaz said.

Orientation was the furthest thing from Connor's mind. "I think they'll be able to carry on without me. Take me back to Frank Mallory and let's get this sorted out before Mills thinks I've gone rogue."

11

DIAZ KEPT DRIVING and every now and then shook his head as if he were having a conversation with himself. Connor remained quiet. Twenty minutes later they were back at the Field Operations and Security Headquarters. Diaz stowed the rifle in the ATV's storage compartment and led Connor inside.

"Hey," Connor said. "Thanks for sticking up for me back there."

Diaz nodded, and they headed to Franklin Mallory's office.

A short while later they stood outside the office and waited. Mallory's assistant wouldn't let them pass because he was on a call. Connor peeked inside the command center.

"Let's go inside," Diaz said and told the assistant they'd be next door.

The door slid open to the hustle of those working in the command center. Diaz walked over to the nearest workstation, where an older woman sat. She had on a headset, and Diaz tapped her on the shoulder.

"You causing trouble again, Juan?" she asked with a grin.

"Hey there, Alverez, this is Connor," Diaz said. "We had a

couple of our guys get hurt. Have you had any updates from the med evac team that was dispatched?"

"I'll check," Alverez said.

Her fingers zipped through the interface with practiced precision. "Here it is. I'm showing three—oh no! Looks like one person was killed. The other two made it to the medical center and are receiving treatment."

Diaz thanked her and they headed back to wait outside Franklin's office. They couldn't see inside, but Connor definitely heard raised voices.

"That sounds like Mills. Could he have gotten here ahead of us?" Connor asked.

"Probably hitched a ride with the med evac," Diaz said.

"Screw this," Connor said and stormed toward the door. He wasn't about to let Mills go on about how his people were attacked because of him.

Franklin's assistant tried to step into his way. Connor quickly weaved his way around the young man and opened the door. Franklin was sitting behind his desk and Mills was pacing around in front, his hands balled into fists. Mills stopped speaking and turned around, his face contorting in anger at the sight of Connor.

Connor ignored Mills and walked inside the office. Diaz followed.

Mallory's skinny assistant came in. "I tried to stop them, sir."

"It's alright, Gabe," Franklin said to his assistant and then looked at Connor. "I hear you're having a hell of a first day."

The door to Mallory's office shut.

Connor strode to Franklin's desk right in Mills' designated pacing stretch. "I hope you'll give me a chance to explain—"

"Explain what?" Mills snarled. "How you're responsible for two of my people getting critically injured? Or the fact that you caused a pack of berwolfs to charge at my team?"

Connor went rigid and swung his cold gaze toward Mills. Mills took a step back. "Cut me off again and you'll be eating out of a straw for the next few months."

Mills tucked his chin in and his nostrils flared.

Franklin stood up. "Alright, let's settle down."

Despite how satisfying it would have been to follow through with his threat to Mills, Connor looked at Mallory.

"Damon, why don't you go get a cup of coffee?" Franklin said.

"With all due respect, sir, he needs to hear what I have to say," Connor said.

"Fine, let's sit down then. Juan, you take the middle seat," Franklin said.

Diaz moved in front of the middle chair and adjusted his belt. The corporal only sat down after Mills and Connor did.

Franklin settled back down behind his desk. "Juan, why don't you give me your take on what happened outside the fence first."

Diaz laid out the facts of the day's events and left nothing out, recounting without a hint of conjecture. Diaz simply stated the facts as he saw them. More than once Franklin's gaze slid toward Connor, but he couldn't get a sense as to what the head of Field Operations was thinking.

"How did you know the berwolfs were laying out a trap?" Franklin asked.

"When you've been involved in as many missions as I have, you learn to see the signs. Otherwise you'll end up dead," Connor said.

"For Christ's sake. Do we really need to listen to this?" Mills asked.

"You don't know who you're talking to, Damon," Franklin said. "Connor Gates led an elite special forces team. I've had some time to look up some of his operations . . . well, the AI pointed me in the right direction by running an analysis of news headlines and found a pattern of events that were tied to Connor's reported whereabouts. So if the man says you were being ambushed, I'm inclined to believe him," Franklin said.

Mills pressed his lips together and glanced over at Connor.

"Don't take my word for it. Take a look at the drone feed we have," Franklin said.

An aerial video started playing on the wallscreen off to the side. It showed Diaz driving the ATV and Connor shooting the SD-15 to startle the berwolf that was stalking the kids. A secondary drone feed showed four other berwolfs just inside the tree line. Those berwolfs sprinted further into the forest, where the drone lost the visual. Franklin forwarded the video to where the first man was taken by the berwolf and dragged into the woods. Connor watched the security detail plunge into the forest despite his protests and he and Diaz circling around to flank the hunters. By the time they'd finish the video feed, Mills looked pale and at a loss for words.

"Paints a different picture, doesn't it? I think you owe Connor your thanks for saving your lives," Franklin said.

"Drone feeds are one thing, but being there is another," Mills said.

Connor cleared his throat. "Why don't the security details have access to the drone feeds? I know I didn't spot the drone until after the berwolfs had left."

"We rely on the tech on duty at Command Central to patch us the feed if they see something suspicious. The drones themselves don't have any type of combat-suite AI that can alert soldiers to an enemy nearby," Franklin said.

"The berwolfs have never done anything like this before," Diaz said.

"They're nothing but stupid animals that just got lucky," Mills said.

"You're wrong. They're quite intelligent, and you'll see more attacks like these in the future until we figure out why," Connor said.

"What makes you say that?" Franklin asked.

"They were probing defenses. Are there records of them showing up along the perimeter? Especially by the gates or where you have other crops outside the fence. Any place where people are likely to visit regularly," Connor asked.

Connor glanced around, and none of them knew the answer.

"I think this is something to look into, Damon," Franklin said to Mills.

"It looks like the kids were the original target, but we disrupted their approach, so they changed tactics. This was a coordinated attack. I'm no expert on animal behavior. Do you know someone on staff who can advise us on predatory behaviors? If you do, they should be brought in to give their opinion," Connor said.

Franklin nodded. "I'll bring someone in and have them evaluate the video. Another good suggestion. You look like you've got more to say."

"You might not like it," Connor warned.

"My pride probably won't, but if it saves lives, I can put that aside," Franklin said.

Both Mills and Diaz watched him, waiting for him to speak.

"Your protocols for dealing with field personnel are full of holes. They should be standardized to convey the importance of the communication at the outset. The operator who contacted Diaz either didn't know or didn't convey the level of suspicious activity, then acted as if Diaz could have refused the request," Connor said.

"I wouldn't have done that," Diaz said quickly.

"I know, but one thing that keeps getting drilled into my head is that this isn't Earth. We're the aliens. We need to remember one thing above all. Lives are at stake. Command Central didn't know where Mills or his crew were when they contacted us. We only learned that Mills' ATV had been attacked by a berwolf when we saw them pulled off the path repairing their own vehicle. That should have been reported," Connor said.

Mills frowned. "It was just a power cable, something we could easily replace."

Connor shook his head. "This is how lives are lost. Status updates, regardless of whether you think them trivial, need to be communicated back to Command Central so if you're overdue they can send a team out to investigate. What if the berwolfs had attacked you? I know you're armed, but what if one of you had gotten hurt or dragged off into the forest like what happened with the other team?" Connor asked.

"We'd radio to COMCENT for backup," Mills said.

"Really? Like you did when the other team had a team member get dragged into the forest? I'm not trying to insult you, but I don't believe it. But let's say for the sake of argument that you did just that. Then the people at Command Central, who didn't know where you were in the first place, would have to scramble to find someone to get out there to help you," Connor said and looked at Franklin. "There needs to be a clear chain of command and concrete protocols that your field teams and leaders follow to the letter. In addition, you need an emergency response team ready for deployment to deal with issues as they arise. Also, what about the kids who were out there? It was dumb luck that they even survived. While Diaz and I were trying to find that berwolf, we should have sent an update about those kids so when Mills came in behind us he could have checked on them before reaching the other team," Connor said.

Franklin pressed his lips together in thought. "You make a lot of good points."

Mills blew out a breath. "This is overkill, Franklin."

"Hold on a second, Damon," Franklin said. "Go on, Connor."

"I would need time to evaluate the teams you've got together.

I'm not sure if you have any advisories that are communicated to your field teams. If you have techs monitoring drones, why aren't they putting out a daily report on the activity they see? Based on what I saw today, it seems like you need an experienced direct-action force. Otherwise, you're going to lose more people until we properly evaluate the threat an animal like the berwolf poses," Connor said.

Mills laughed bitterly. "I can see you coming from a mile away. You come in here and dazzle them with your evaluation, all so you can lead a team of your own."

"Clearly you need the help," Connor said.

Mills rose to his feet and glared toward Franklin. "I don't have to sit here and listen to this. I want this taken up to Tobias for review. Until then, I have a compound to secure," he said and walked out of the office.

Franklin rubbed his fingertips on his desk and then looked at Connor. "I'm trying to remember that I asked for your opinion."

"You've got it. I'm not going to lie to you. The protocols being used here are entirely too lax," Connor said.

"And you don't pull any punches, it seems," Franklin said.

"What's Mills' role?" Connor asked.

"He's my second in command. So all that stuff you pointed out about how we've been doing things is basically like a slap in the face," Franklin said.

"I'm not trying to insult anybody," Connor said, and Franklin gave him a dubious look. "Fine, only a little bit, but lives are at stake."

"What would you propose I do? Just assign you a team and say have at it?"

"Well, for one, you can give some serious thought to the communications protocols and make your people use them. They need to be formalized. I think that'll have the greatest impact to start with. As for me, you need a highly skilled direct-action team," Connor said.

"Like your Ghosts?"

"No, I don't think so. We were mainly used for counterterrorism and intelligence gathering, as well as high-risk, high-reward missions. Some of the methodologies will carry over, but not all of it. Tobias told me to come down here and find a place in the colony. I think I found it," Connor said.

Franklin sucked in a deep breath and sighed. "You're awfully quiet there, Juan."

"Thinking about everything Connor just said, sir," Diaz said.

"And?" Franklin asked.

"I agree with him, sir. All of it, including my part."

Franklin nodded. "I'm not going to make any decisions right now. I'll talk to Tobias about this and your suggestions. In the meantime, I want you to finish orientation and have Diaz continue showing you around Field Operations."

"Sir, I have duty—"

"It's canceled. I'll have someone else take over," Franklin said. "As for you, Connor, continue your evaluation and come up with a real proposal for this new team and anything you think we could improve here."

Connor nodded. "I'll need access to personnel files."

"I can't just grant that kind of access, but I can work on it. For now, work with Juan. Oh, and I meant what I said before. You saved a lot of lives today. I know Mills doesn't see it yet, but he will. Eventually," Franklin said.

They left Mallory's office, and Connor was still trying to come to grips with what had happened. He hadn't gone in there with the goal of establishing a new security response team for the colony. He'd just pointed out all the flaws he'd seen with their current system and how he thought they should fix it. Is this what he even wanted? He didn't have a choice about being here, but everything beyond that was up to him. He glanced at the people who worked at the Field Operations Headquarters. They were just people trying to do the best job they could. Mallory had mentioned the lack of military personnel on staff. Who were these people? And were they even qualified to be doing the jobs they were being called upon to do? Connor glanced at Diaz. If Connor had to guess about Diaz's background, he would pin him as an infantryman for the Marines. He'd followed Connor's lead and his actions denoted some combat training. Ideally, he'd like to find more people like Juan Diaz, but the situation on this new world would definitely influence the makeup of the team he had in mind. Like it or not, he'd need the expertise of noncombatants.

Diaz took him back to orientation and Connor tried to pay attention, but in his mind he was already moving forward. Never one for sitting idly by, he had spent the bulk of his life throwing himself at his objectives, and this was no different. At least back home he'd had the chain of command to rely on, but here on New Earth *he* was all he had, and he'd need to convince Franklin and Tobias that they needed him more than they knew.

12

DURING THE NEXT FEW DAYS, Connor settled into a routine of attending the orientation required by all new colonists and working with Diaz in the off hours. Diaz had become a voice of reason, fulfilling a role once occupied by Kasey Douglass from the Ghosts. Diaz was adamant that Connor first needed to learn how they operated at the Field Operations Headquarters before making recommendations, and Connor conceded the point.

The colony's orientation program only lasted for a few days and was meant to give colonists a brief introduction to the planet, as well as a vision of what they could become. Basic system access was easily understood. Connor breezed through the qualification tests to demonstrate that he understood the materials presented to him. It was implied that the colonists would receive more of an introduction from their designated faction for work. The priorities of the colony were to learn as much as they could about their new home and build new habitats so more colonists could be brought down from the Ark.

He and Diaz had just finished eating dinner. The vatery was

able to produce any kind of meat they wanted and had been the solution for producing animal proteins for human consumption on Earth for hundreds of years. Noah had pointed out that there hadn't been an actual slaughterhouse on Earth for a hundred and fifty years.

"So in terms of equipment for the field teams, is this all you've got? Or is there stuff in storage that hasn't been brought down yet?" Connor asked.

Diaz groaned and took the last bite of his pork chop, savoring it. He surrendered his fork to his empty plate and wiped his mouth. "Connor, enough already. We've been at this for days. I need a break. Do you understand what I mean when I say I need a break?"

"I'm afraid I have no idea," Connor said mockingly.

Diaz sighed. "I have needs, Connor, needs that can't be fulfilled if you keep me trapped working late another night. Needs! Do you get me?"

Connor laughed. "Victoria off duty tonight?"

"Yes! So can we just take the night off? I know we have to meet with Tobias tomorrow and Damon will be there and all that. We can have an early start, but tonight, Connor, tonight I have to unleash the beast," Diaz said.

"Alright, go feed the beast. I'll see you tomorrow at oh six hundred," Connor said.

Diaz shot to his feet and grabbed both their trays. "How about oh six thirty?"

Connor chuckled. "Fine. Go have fun," he said.

It was his fourth day on the planet and he'd been working almost around the clock getting up to speed about how the colony worked. Diaz had been with him through most of it, and he could hardly fault the guy for wanting to take a day off.

"Hey there, rookie. Is this seat taken?"

Lenora sat down without waiting for an answer. She smiled at him while enjoying a vanilla ice cream cone.

"You didn't bring any for me?" Connor asked and then took a sip of his water.

Lenora stuck out her cone for a second and then snatched it back. "Why, Mr. Gates, I don't think I know you well enough to be giving you a sample from my ice cream cone."

Connor started coughing as the water went down the wrong pipe, and he felt a flush sweep across his face.

"I do believe I took your breath away," Lenora said and giggled.

Connor had to fight to keep from coughing, but there was still a tickle right on the cusp. "You do accents too?"

He let out one final cough and then glanced at his water, weighing whether he should risk taking another drink.

"My mother is from Atlanta and my father was from New York," Lenora said.

Connor nodded. "Want to take a walk?"

Lenora nodded.

They left the cafeteria. Nightfall had descended on New Earth and the sky was full of stars. Nearby there were a couple of people playing acoustic guitars and singing.

"How are things going at that research base?" Connor asked.

"Great, now that Noah got our systems up and running. Had to bring him back here earlier today, so I thought I'd stick around and head back out tomorrow morning," Lenora said.

"You flew him back here alone?" Connor asked.

"Yeah," she said and took another lick of her ice cream. "I decided early on that I wasn't going to wait for a pilot to take me where I needed to go, so I earned my flight clearance before going to sleep on the Ark," Lenora said.

"I thought all travel outside the compound required a security detail."

"Are you gonna turn me in?"

"It's for your protection."

Lenora's eyes widened. "You *do* care," she said.

Connor rolled his eyes.

"I appreciate your concern, but our security people were escorting some field ops near our base. Noah had to get back in time for some big meeting tomorrow," Lenora said.

"Oh, that's probably my fault then. I asked for him to be there. I'm meeting with Tobias tomorrow."

"So I have you to thank for dragging me away from my work," Lenora said.

"Who says you get to keep Noah all to yourself?"

Lenora smiled widely, and Connor found himself looking longer than he should have. She punched him in the arm. "I knew I liked you ever since you laid Barker out on his ass. So we're sixty light-years away from Earth instead of twenty-five. Big deal. Doesn't give him the right to be a jerk."

"You're not bothered by it?"

Lenora shook her head. "No, we were never going back to Earth. This place is incredible—a field scientist's dream."

"But still, the people back home didn't change the Ark mission on some whim. A lot of work had to have gone into it, and I wish I could understand why," Connor said.

"You and a lot of other people. For me, I'm going to concentrate on being here."

The band nearby began singing again and Lenora finished her ice cream cone.

"Since you're here, have you noticed any strange activity in your neck of the woods?" Connor asked.

"What do you mean?"

"A few days ago there was a berwolf attack," Connor said and told her what had happened.

Lenora frowned and shook her head. "There aren't any berwolfs out in our area, but I'll let my team know. We do see these . . . they're almost like a primate but different. They seem to show up now and then. They don't get close or attack or anything like that, but they do make their presence known."

"A primate? You mean like a monkey?"

"Something like it. This place certainly has a different mix of species than we had on Earth, and then at other times it seems quite similar," Lenora said.

Connor stifled a yawn.

"Jeez, am I putting you to sleep already?" Lenora asked.

"I'm so sorry. No, not at all. I've been putting in a lot of late nights," Connor said.

The light from the campfire cast a silhouette of Lenora's long hair. She yawned widely.

"Yawns are contagious," she said. "So, what's this meeting about?"

"I have some recommendations about how Field Operations and Security should run," Connor said.

Lenora laughed. "Now you're bumping heads with Damon Mills. You better watch your step."

"How come?"

"Damon has a lot of support from Field Operations."

"I don't have anything against him personally, but the way they run things is going to get people killed," Connor said.

Lenora sighed. "That's it right there. Direct. Straight to the point. Sometimes that can make people dig in their heels and resist all the good advice in the world."

"So you're saying I should be more tactful."

Lenora shrugged. "Couldn't hurt, and you might gain an ally instead of making another enemy."

Connor frowned in thought.

Lenora yawned again. "I'm gonna go. I intended to get my ship loaded with additional supplies before I set off tomorrow."

"Pursuing the alien ruins?"

"You bet. You know, if you get bored here you could always come out to our little research base and check things out. Tell us how secure we aren't," Lenora said with a grin.

"I'd like that. I might even be more tactful by then," Connor said.

Lenora left him, and Connor headed back to his quarters. It had been a long time since he'd just sat down and spoken with a woman—at least one not in the military. The last time he'd done something like this was with his ex-wife, and she'd given him an ultimatum. Alyssa had been domineering from the start, but he got the sense that Lenora was not like that at all. She seemed to state her opinion and then trust that you'd be smart enough to figure it out on your own.

Connor entered his quarters and sat down on the bed, closing his eyes and trying to build a picture of what his son looked like. The boy he remembered was three years old. He'd kept pictures of him in his office at their base near Earth, but he'd never interacted with him after he left. He'd just checked in on him from time to time. He'd often been tempted to reconnect with his son and be in Sean's life again, but the events on Chronos Station had changed all that, and now he was here on a planet sixty light-years from Earth, trying to picture what his son looked like. He recalled staying away because he'd felt that it was the right thing to do. So why did he feel like such a failure as a father? He couldn't even send him a message telling him how he felt and listen as Sean yelled at him for leaving. Connor deserved that, but now there would be no reconnection, no closure where his son was concerned. All Connor was left with was an ocean of regret and a new life to build. He didn't feel like he deserved it. His failure as a father and his inability to take down the

Syndicate made him feel hollow inside. Millions of people had died. He'd followed the breadcrumbs that led to Chronos Station and then recklessly stormed it. If he hadn't, would all those people still be alive? If he'd done things by the book, would his last encounter with the Syndicate have ended any differently? He lay back on his bed with his feet still on the floor and slept.

13

CONNOR WOKE up to a fist pounding on the door and Diaz's muffled voice shouting that it was after seven a.m. He shot up in bed and scrambled to open the door.

"Wow, you overslept," Diaz said with entirely too much delight.

"Yeah, I know," Connor muttered.

"And you're still in the same clothes you were in last night," Diaz said.

Connor glared at the corporal. "It's not like I have a closet full of clothes."

He only had four gray jumpsuits, which he was getting tired of. He just wanted some regular clothes or something other than gray.

"Don't worry, they're making clothes for you, unless you want all your stuff to have some other name on it," Diaz said.

Connor quickly washed his face and ran his fingers through his short hair, then put on his last clean gray jumpsuit. Would it be so hard to get a pair of pants? That shouldn't be hard.

"Come on, we should have just enough time to get some breakfast," Diaz said.

Connor glanced at his watch. He'd slept ten hours and felt completely refreshed. The doctor had told him it would take a few days to adjust to the reactivation of his implants, and he'd been right. Now he should only need a few hours' sleep a night.

They headed toward the cafeteria and met up with Noah.

"I heard you got the comms issues sorted out at that research base," Connor said.

"If by sorted out you mean I reconfigured the signal so the intensity is an order of magnitude above what should be required, then yeah, I guess I fixed it. You must have run into Dr. Bishop last night. Do *not* let her fly you anywhere," Noah said.

"Rough flight?" Connor asked and stuck a piece of bacon in his mouth.

Noah shivered. "You could say that. She scraped the bottom of the ship on the trees. Said she thought she saw the tip of an obelisk or something like that."

"Did you get a chance to look at the proposal I sent you?" Connor asked.

"Yeah, about the drones. It's possible, but we still need to define what the recognition software should recognize as dangerous versus what's benign," Noah said.

"How long will that take?"

"You know, you're starting to sound like the other department heads around here. I'll give you the same answer I give them. If you can get the request prioritized, you'll be moved to the top of my list. Otherwise, you'll have to wait," Noah said.

Diaz snorted. "Didn't you just get back from the research base?"

Noah nodded.

"How'd that become a priority?" Diaz asked.

"Oh, well, it's Dr. Bishop . . ."

Diaz frowned. "Oh, so a pretty doctor gets priority, but we don't?"

Noah's eyes widened. "No . . . Uh, no way. Have you met her? She's scary as hell. She basically kidnapped me."

Diaz glanced at Connor, unconvinced. "I don't know. Being kidnapped by a pretty doctor doesn't sound so bad to me."

Diaz was stoic for a moment and then burst out laughing. "But seriously . . ."

"Alright, leave him alone," Connor said and looked at Noah. "I get it. I'm pretty sure I can get to the top of that list."

Noah's eyebrows rose.

Connor didn't say anything else about it. They left the cafeteria and headed toward the Field Operations and Security Headquarters.

"So let me get this straight," Diaz said to Connor. "After I left you last night, you had dessert with the pretty doctor?"

"We talked for a bit," Connor said.

"Yeah, but did you have any dessert?" Diaz said.

"Shut the hell up." Connor chuckled, and Diaz started laughing.

"So, no dessert," Diaz said and slapped a beefy hand on Noah's shoulder. "I bet he'd like to though."

Noah was at a rare loss for words.

The playful banter all but ceased as they went inside the headquarters. Connor had spent a lot of time here when not attending orientation classes. He really needed to spend more time here, but Damon was pushing for Connor's request to form his own team for Field Operations to be rejected.

Ashley Quinn met them just inside and asked to speak to Connor alone for a minute. Diaz changed his whole demeanor when he saw her and treated her like his long-lost mother.

"I thought you said you'd stay out of trouble, and you found some on the first day. Thankfully, the past few days have been free of incidents," Ashley said.

"Hello, Dr. Quinn," Connor said.

"Don't give me that. It's Ashley now and forever. I got enough people calling me Dr. Quinn."

"Fine," Connor said. "Have you been able to . . . Is there anyone else . . ."

"Don't start stammering on me now. Spit it out."

"Did you find anyone else on the Ark like me? Who wasn't supposed to be there?" Connor asked.

Ashley's smile faltered. "No. We're still looking, but it's going to take a while."

Connor nodded and tried to hide his disappointment. He'd had a fool's hope that perhaps the rest of the Ghosts had been put into stasis along with him.

"So you think you've figured out what you want to do for the colony?" Ashley asked.

"I already made the suggestion. Now I'll find out whether or not they'll let me do it," Connor said.

Ashley nodded. "Tobias and the rest of the people who first conceived of the colony had a specific vision of what it was supposed to be. I don't think they anticipated some of the challenges we're facing."

"So you think they'll grant the request?"

"I think they'll let you make your case. Some of the things you suggested about communications and updates from those in the field made a lot of sense. Damon eventually came around to it. But what you're asking to create could be the beginning of something else that you probably don't even intend," Ashley said.

Connor frowned, trying to think of something but couldn't.

"You're asking to create a highly trained and highly capable group of people. Some might perceive it as a threat or that it might be misused in some way," Ashley said.

Connor shook his head in exasperation. "No, I don't want to take over the colony."

Ashley smiled. "I didn't think you did, but keep that in mind when you're speaking to the folks inside."

They headed to a small auditorium, and Connor stopped just inside the doorway. There were at least a hundred people in attendance. The walls and furnishings all had the uniform prefab look of something that was designed purely for function rather than aesthetics.

"Are all these people department heads?" Connor asked.

"No, this is an open forum. Tobias will want consensus before a decision is made," Ashley said and regarded him for a moment. "Does speaking in front of a crowd bother you?"

"No, not at all. It just wasn't what I was expecting." Connor frowned. "Does a public forum really get to decide matters of security?"

"No of course not, but their opinions matter. If they get to voice them here and feel that their concerns have been heard, it could stave off problems down the line," Ashley said.

Connor frowned in thought. He had only been expecting to speak to a few people and hadn't expected to be required to sway the public to his proposal.

The ground sloped downward toward a stage, and there were a couple of chairs set off to the side. Damon Mills and Franklin Mallory sat in two of the seats on stage.

Connor followed Ashley onto the stage, where she sat next to her husband. Connor took a moment to greet Tobias and acknowledge the other people sitting with him. There was a woman sitting next to Ashley who had red-rimmed eyes and a flushed face. Her gaze narrowed when she saw him looking at her.

Franklin waved him over from the other side of the stage and Connor sat down next to him.

"Are you ready?" Franklin asked.

"Always," Connor said with a confidence he didn't really feel.

He tended to do better speaking to other people like him, people who'd had similar training as him and he could speak to using a common frame of reference. He glanced over at Damon, who coolly returned his gaze. Connor took a deep breath and accepted that this was the arena in which he'd have to fight for what he believed. He hadn't given any thought to what he'd do if his request was denied.

Connor glanced at the first row of people and saw Lenora sitting there. Her long auburn hair hung down in front of her shoulders. She gave him a smile and slight nod of her head. Nearby, Diaz and Noah sat together. Diaz gave him a thumbs-up and a small fist pump.

Tobias stood up and went to the center podium. "Thank you all for coming," he said.

The ongoing discussions stopped and the room became quiet.

"I know we're all quite busy, so I'll be brief. There was an incident earlier this week involving a pack of berwolfs, and we lost Steven Bernstein of the Field Operations and Security group. Steven is survived by his wife, Grace, who is with us today. I'd like everyone to stand up and observe a moment of silence in remembrance of Steven, who made the ultimate sacrifice to keep others safe," Tobias said.

Connor came to his feet and bowed his head. He wasn't a religious man, but he believed wholeheartedly in honoring the sacrifice of those who wore the uniform. He looked over at the grieving widow sitting on the other side of the stage. Ashley had her arm around the widow's shoulders, consoling her.

"The events that transpired were something new, something we hadn't noticed before, and this was pointed out by one of our new colonists to whom I will introduce you in a minute. Franklin Mallory has had Field Operations and Security operating at a heightened state of readiness since the incident. In that time we've observed more berwolfs in the area. We consulted with Dr. Edwin Cummings and showed him the captured drone videos of the attack, as well as the eyewitness testimonies of the people who were there," Tobias said.

Connor frowned. No one had contacted him.

"I'll make Edwin's report available for everyone to review, but on the high level, the berwolfs executed a coordinated attack that demonstrated just how cunning a predator they can be. At this time, we don't know why they're targeting us, but we've made understanding the berwolfs one of our top priorities. Now, Franklin Mallory is going to come up here and speak about the changes that are happening at Field Operations," Tobias said.

Franklin stood up and went over to the podium. "I know many of you are quite concerned with this latest development. I won't sugarcoat it for any of you. This attack caught us almost entirely off guard. No, strike that, it *did* catch us off guard. One man, who is not part of Field Operations, made a huge difference that day and is responsible for saving the lives of the six teenagers who were the berwolfs' original targets. His name is Connor Gates, and he was not part of the Ark program. How he came to be aboard the Ark is a mystery even to Connor. I've met and spoken with Connor at length. So have Tobias and Ashley, and we know that Connor's presence here, while a mystery, was a stroke of luck for those six teenagers who are alive today. You see, Connor has a unique background. Back home he was part of an elite special forces group in the North American Alliance military. I'm telling you this because we all volunteered to be part of the Ark program. We're explorers and pioneers. Back on Earth, there was a shroud of secrecy that was prevalent in most facets of government, including the colonies of the solar system. That's not what we want to do here, which is why I'm disclosing the unique circumstances of how Connor came to be here in the first place. We can all agree that our journey to this planet has been nothing if not extraordinary. So when he comes up here to speak, please give his request careful consideration," Franklin said.

Connor stood up, and Franklin came over to him. "You could have warned me," Connor said.

Franklin shrugged. "You're here now."

Connor approached the podium and gazed out at the crowd. He took a deep breath, and remembering Lenora's advice about using tact, he glanced over at the grieving widow.

"Mrs. Bernstein, I didn't know your husband. I have no idea what kind of man he was, but I know what it takes to put on a uniform and put your life at risk every day for the safety of others, and I know the terrible toll it takes on the loved ones who are left behind. I offer you my sincerest condolences for your loss and my solemn vow to work my hardest to help prevent something like this from happening again," Connor said.

Tears streamed down Grace's face, but she held her head high and refused to let her grief steal her resolve. Connor turned to address the crowd. "I'm an outsider. I figured I'd get that out of the way right off the bat. I wasn't supposed to be here. Until a week ago, the only thing I knew about the Ark program was an infomercial I saw in a transit tube on a space station. Next thing I knew, I was here. I'm not going into the details of my past, and if you must know the details, you can come to me directly or see Tobias," Connor said and gestured toward the governor. "Some of the things I'm going to say will appear harsh and have been met with heavy resistance from those who've been here longer than I have.

"I've spent the bulk of my career evaluating enemy forces and overcoming obstacles. What I saw in the berwolf attack was a strategic execution used by predators but also by people with training similar to mine. We need to adapt if we're to survive here." Connor stepped away from the podium and took a few steps closer to the audience. "If I were you, I'd be thinking: why should I listen to this guy? He can't possibly know what he's talking about. I get it. I'm new and I haven't proven myself to you yet. I wasn't alone the other day when the attack happened. Corporal Diaz was escorting me around that day. He was there and was just as pivotal to the survival of those kids. Since then, I've been learning about how Field Operations and Security conducts its work and achieves its primary objective, which is to keep all of you safe. I'm not going to stand up here and list a bunch of flaws and start pointing fingers at anyone. I've made my suggestions to Franklin, who's considering them. I'm hoping my suggestions will help save lives because that's what this is all about—keeping you alive and keeping the people at Field Operations alive. What I've come prepared to speak about is a new team that is to be part of Field Operations, although I thought my audience was just going to be Tobias," Connor said.

There were a few chuckles from the audience.

"See, I'm still learning too. My proposal is to form a new division within Field Operations with the purpose of providing support to Field Ops teams both here in the compound and out at the research bases. I would like a team of volunteers to train and make into a highly specialized direct-action force, the purpose of which is providing rescue operations and field reconnaissance so that at some point in the future we don't need to live behind a wall," Connor said.

Damon Mills stood up. "How is what you're proposing different than what we already have? I have teams already designated for those jobs."

"I don't think this is the right place for that discussion," Connor replied.

"Why is that? Is it because you don't have an answer to the question?" Damon said coldly.

"Because that discussion is best served between professionals," Connor said.

"Okay, so you don't have an answer then," Damon said and sat down.

Connor gritted his teeth. He'd wanted to keep this civil. "I'll answer the question. Your methods and protocols are putting people's lives at risk. More tragedies like what happened to Steve Bernstein will happen. It's not a matter of *if*, it's a matter of *when*, unless we adapt. How many will have to die before you admit you're not equal to the task that's been given to you? With the right training, you could be."

Damon shot to his feet, his face purple with rage. "This is outrageous! How dare you imply that Steve's death is because of me?"

"I didn't say it was because of you. But the fact that you and the other team plunged headlong into the berwolf trap didn't help. Instead of one tragedy, we might have had eight. I told you to wait, and instead you did just as the berwolfs wanted you to do," Connor said.

Damon took a step closer and stopped himself. "One of those things took a member of my team. I wasn't just going to let that happen. No one in Field Ops would do such a thing."

"That's good. There *should* be that kind of camaraderie in our line of work. I'm not questioning the courage of your team. I'm questioning how you handled the situation. A real team that's been properly trained stands a better chance of changing the outcome the next time the berwolfs, or some other creature, attacks," Connor said.

"Right. So how would you have done it?"

"The team I have in mind would be comprised of specialists equipped to deal with the situation. I would have used the drones, set my sharpshooters up high. They don't need to go running through the forest to get a clear shot. I'd have had the rest of my team stagger their approach so we'd cover each other while we went in and got our man," Connor said.

Damon shook his head. "Sounds good while we're here, but out there it's different. If another of my men got taken tomorrow, I'd go in there and get him as quick as I could."

"You'd prefer to go on with business as usual. If you do that, more people will die," Connor said and turned toward the audience. "Is Dr. Cummings here?"

A short balding man stood up in the crowd and raised his hand.

"Just a quick question for you. In nature, once predators begin probing defenses, do they simply go away?" Connor asked.

Dr. Cummings glanced over at Tobias, who nodded for him to answer. "Predators have been known to stalk their prey for extended periods of time. However, when a predator believes there is a competing predator encroaching on their territory, some will never leave and will fight to preserve what's theirs. They'll keep coming until the threat is annihilated or they cannot perceive a way to overcome the stronger predator."

"You see, Damon, it's not me. These are facts based on what we learned back home, except that the predators here seem more intelligent than what we had back home. Why else would they incapacitate your ATV before moving in on their intended target?" Connor said.

Mills shook his head and looked away.

"I'm not asking to take over Field Operations. I'm asking to train a new team as a proof of concept that will help secure the colony."

Tobias stood up and came over to Connor. "I think we understand what you're asking for, and I have a suggestion of my own for how best to handle this. Damon, you supervise field operations and will continue to do so, executing your duties as you see fit. I need you, but I also want you to consider what Connor has said."

Damon glared at Connor, then gave a jerk of his head.

"I'm going to give Connor's proposal of forming a new team a chance. I believe that in the original request Connor called them a platoon. This is on a provisional basis to get a better idea of how such a team would perform," Tobias said. "Now, who has questions?"

"I have a question," Damon said. "Where do you intend to get your volunteers? I won't order any of my people to do this because it's not something I'd do myself."

"I only want volunteers. I'll speak to various Field Operations personnel in groups," Connor said and then turned toward the audience. "I will also be coming to your respective divisions because we'll need the expertise of people like you and your departments to provide consultancies. Not all consultancies can be done from the safety of the compound."

Multiple people began shouting their displeasure at this request.

Lenora stood up. "This is a perfectly reasonable request. Don't you see that this is for our own protection? He's not asking you to join the army. He's asking for at least one member of your staff to be field qualified in the event they need your help. The better those guys can do their jobs, the safer we all are. I know when I go out in the field the security details that are assigned to my group do an excellent job at trying to keep us safe. But if someone like Mr. Gates can offer something better and lower the risk to our lives, we should give him our support. If you don't, you forfeit your right to complain when it's you out in the field and it's your life on the line."

Connor's mouth hung open and he took a moment to recover. "Thank you."

Lenora sat back down.

"Just remember, the motivation for all of this is to save lives. I'm not going to force anyone out into the field. This is our new home. We have to adapt to it, and that means sharing some of the burdens, which includes risk."

"Thank you, Connor. You've certainly given us some things to think about. That's it for today's session. I hope you all have a wonderful day," Tobias said.

Connor leaned in so Tobias could hear him. "I still need to speak with you."

Tobias nodded. "I expected as much. Once the audience leaves we can talk."

It didn't take long for the audience to start emptying out. Lenora waved to him and left. Connor felt a soft tap on his shoulder and turned around.

Grace Bernstein stared up at him. "Is what you said true? If Steven had been part of your group, would he have survived?" she asked.

Connor saw the anguish in her eyes and the longing for some fleeting hope that could give her husband back to her.

"No, ma'am, I can't make that guarantee. No one can," Connor said softly.

Grace nodded and then allowed herself to be guided away.

"Nice performance," Damon said. "Just now, I mean."

Connor glared at the man, and his knuckles ached to strike the man's jaw. "You're a piece of work."

"You're the one selling these people on something you can't deliver. A life without fences here on this planet isn't possible," Damon said.

"We'll see," Connor replied.

"You've only been here a few days. Talk to me after you've been here as long as I have. You don't know the half of it. You act as if the berwolfs are the worst things waiting for us out there," Damon said.

Before Connor could reply, Franklin called them over. Juan

Diaz and Noah Barker were standing with him, along with Tobias and Ashley Quinn.

They all went into a nearby conference room located behind the stage. A fresh pot of coffee waited for them, and they all sat down.

"Governor, I don't see why we need to indulge this request. There's a lot more to worry about—bigger things than the local wildlife," Damon said.

Connor frowned in confusion. What was Damon talking about?

Tobias held up his hand. "Not now, Damon. The decision's been made," the governor said and turned to Connor. "Alright, Connor, we're all ears. What is it you want to do?"

"I'll need a designated space to train my team," Connor said.

"We can provide space here at the compound—" Tobias began, but stopped when he noticed Connor shaking his head.

"Not here. I need to train them away from here. There are too many distractions, too much comfort. Are all the forward operating research bases in use?" Connor asked.

Tobias pinched his lips together and looked over at Franklin.

"How far away did you want to go?" Franklin asked.

"Doesn't have to be on the frontier or anything like that. Just more than a few days' walk from here," Connor said.

"Are you serious? What are you going to do with this team?" Damon asked.

"I'm going to train them, make them into a cohesive unit that's highly disciplined and able to adapt to new situations," Connor replied.

"You mean you're turning them into soldiers," Damon said.

"If that's what it takes, but you can't argue with the thousands of years of history backing me up. Were you a soldier?" Connor asked.

Damon shook his head. "No, I was in law enforcement."

Connor held in his surprise. Tobias had people with only a law enforcement background running security for the whole damn compound? Mallory was a good man, but he had to know he was getting in over his head.

Franklin cleared his throat. "How many people do you intend to bring?"

"Ideally between thirty and fifty, but I'll start with as few as ten. There'll be some who will quit and there'll be some who won't make the cut. We'll need some equipment and supplies, but we'll be somewhat self-sufficient," Connor said.

"We have a research base just twelve kilometers away that's underutilized. You'd need to share it with the field team that's there, but I think it could work if we had a barracks there. What else?" Franklin said.

"Weapons. Diaz informed me that you restrict their use and prefer to use deterrent-type force like the SD-15s. Nonlethal weapons have their uses, but there comes a time when a deterrent isn't enough and more than one predator will need to be put down to make them leave us alone," Connor said.

"That is out of the question," Tobias said.

"You need to reconsider because no matter how we frame it, we're the invaders here. I prefer a peaceful resolution, but sometimes it comes down to them or us, and we need to be prepared. Locking up the military-grade weaponry isn't going to prevent that. Please, Tobias, trust me to do my job. My team needs not only to learn how to use the weapons we have, but they must be comfortable with them. But I'm not going to have them annihilate a species so we can be comfortable," Connor said.

Tobias drew in a breath and glanced at his wife. "I don't like this, but I'll give you clearance for them."

"The other thing I'll need is priority access to engineering teams and Noah," Connor said.

Noah had been nodding and listening, then gave a start when his name was mentioned. "Me? What do you need me for?"

"To help us with some of our technological hurdles," Connor said.

"I'm happy to help you, Connor, you know that, but there are so many people waiting for me already with projects of their own," Noah said.

"Do those projects directly impact the survivability of the people involved?" Connor asked.

Noah swallowed hard and looked at Tobias helplessly.

Franklin cleared his throat. "We have some engineers on staff who can help."

"I'm sure they're very good, but I need the best, and by most accounts I've heard, that's Noah," Connor said.

Franklin looked at Tobias. "How about we designate a chunk of Noah's allocation to what Connor needs each week and take it from there?"

"Don't I get a say in this?" Noah asked.

Tobias smiled. "Of course, go right ahead."

"What do you need that you think only I can do?" Noah asked.

"For starters, we'll need changes to the standard Field Operations equipment that will require upgrades to things like suit computers. I want to be able to deploy my own drones and have them fly reconnaissance that's patched directly to us and not Command Central. And about three or four more things," Connor said.

Noah looked intrigued. "I'm sure I can do some of that an—"

"We'll work something out," Tobias said, cutting Noah off.

"I need command authority within Field Operations and Security," Connor said.

"Why?" Tobias asked.

"We're going to be working together, and I don't need anyone having to run to someone like Mills to see whether they should follow an order from me when we're out in the field," Connor said.

Tobias glanced at Franklin, eyebrows raised.

"It's done," Franklin said.

"That's it? You're just giving him command authority?" Damon snarled.

Franklin's brows pushed forward. "The man was a colonel in the NA Alliance military with decades of experience commanding platoons like the one he's proposing. What more do you need?"

Damon clamped his mouth shut and just shook his head.

"How's this going to work?" Tobias asked. "Officially, Field Operations and Security isn't a military by itself. It's more of a law enforcement agency mixed with the old-style park rangers."

"Well, we'll need a new division then, one that'll provide the framework Connor needs to put his team together so we can all work in concert," Franklin said.

"I'll consider it. For now, you're Search and Rescue," Tobias said.

"I'd like you to transfer Corporal Diaz under my command," Connor said.

"Now wait just a damn minute," Damon snarled.

"Hold on a minute," Diaz said. "I volunteer. I've been working with Connor all week. I want to join his team, and to be honest, Connor is going to need all the help he can get." Diaz turned to Damon. "Meaning no disrespect to you, sir, but I think it would be the best fit for me."

Damon's nostrils flared. "Fine," he said and looked at Franklin. "Are we done?"

"Not yet," Connor said. "I'll want to speak to your direct reports tomorrow morning."

Damon looked like he was about to spew fire. "Tobias, I want to confirm that I have the authority to block transfers of individuals whose roles are critical to Field Operations."

"I'll leave that to Franklin," Tobias said.

"I'll give final approval for any transfers, but you can certainly bring me your concerns," Franklin said.

Connor tried not to smile, and that seemed to infuriate Damon more. The Field Operations commander left them, and Tobias blew out a low whistle.

"He'll come around," Franklin said. "Mills is a good man."

Connor didn't say anything, but he wasn't convinced that he and Damon could work together. The man was territorial and took everything personally—not the best traits in a commander.

"Well then, I wish you luck with this," Tobias said to Connor.

"I appreciate the show of support. I know this can't be easy," Connor said.

"Why? Because you're not supposed to be here?" Tobias asked.

"That's part of it."

"We'll see what happens," Tobias said.

"Come on, Connor," Franklin said. "Let's get you set up. I'll find a place at headquarters for you and Diaz to work while you get this up and running."

"Thank you. Oh, one more thing for Tobias," Connor said. "Mills is right. There are only so many people I can pilfer from Field Ops before it becomes a problem. I know you have a schedule for waking up the colonists on the Ark, but can you prioritize certain types of individuals? Former military experience would be good, people like Diaz who have infantry experience, anyone with hunting and survival experience. People like that."

Tobias glanced at his wife. "You said he wouldn't be trouble, and now he's treating the people on the Ark like a mail order catalog."

Ashley gave him a playful slap on the shoulder. "No one said starting a colony would be easy, love."

"I'll see what I can do," Tobias said.

"Really? I've been asking for additional personnel and you've been putting me off, but Connor gets special treatment." Franklin laughed and looked at Connor. "Tomorrow you get to try to convince a bunch of people who are settled to leave all that behind for a while to be trained in a job they might not want," Franklin said.

"Sometimes people will surprise you," Connor said.

They left the auditorium conference room, and Connor was already making lists in his head. He pulled Diaz and Noah aside.

"Thanks, guys. If you know someone who would be a good fit for the team, I want to know about it. Don't be shy about it either, Noah," Connor said.

"Wait. I'm just on loan," Noah said.

Connor grinned. "For now."

"But I'm not a soldier," Noah protested.

"Neither was I," Connor said. "Don't look so scared. I want your input on the technical stuff, and I'll show you things like how to shoot a rifle. It'll be fun. Plus you'll gain a valuable perspective by doing some fieldwork."

Noah considered it for a moment and then nodded.

"Let's get to it," Connor said.

Now the real work would begin. Building the team he had in mind wasn't going to be easy. He and Diaz had their work cut out for them, but it was a start—at least for now.

14

IN THE WEEKS THAT FOLLOWED, Connor worked nearly around the clock. He only needed a few hours' sleep in order to function, which was one of the benefits of the nanite suite he had. Dr. Marashi had taken a sample of the nanites from Connor's blood to see if he could duplicate them. Long-term exposure carried a risk of the body rejecting the nanites, rendering them ineffectual. The nanites Connor had in his system were experimental and cutting edge, which was why only his old platoon had access to them. They'd needed to cycle them at least once a year to avoid complications. Since Dr. Marashi hadn't been able to reproduce the nanites, Connor was reluctant to let them go. They simply offered him too many advantages, including quick healing abilities, for him to go back to living without them.

"Are you sure about this?" Diaz asked, glancing down at the three chevrons that adorned the arms of his uniform.

"If I wasn't sure, you wouldn't be here," Connor said.

Field Operations had a similar command structure as the NA Alliance military, which Connor attributed more to Franklin Mallory than Tobias Quinn. Quinn was adamant about not having anything that functioned as a military, believing that having standing militaries created as many problems as it solved.

"I have to say I really didn't think Mallory would go for the change in plans," Diaz said.

"You saw that research base. It wasn't going to work," Connor replied.

They were standing in Connor's temporary office at the Field Operations Headquarters. The interactive wallscreen had lists of supplies and personnel records of the squad they'd put together.

"That's another thing. We easily had more volunteers. Why aren't we taking everyone we can get?" Diaz asked.

"This is only the first bunch. Search and Rescue is just the two of us right now. A dozen recruits is a good start," Connor said.

"Mallory was surprised by the short list," Diaz said.

"I'd thought of bringing more recruits and then whittling them down, but there simply aren't enough people to go around for that. We can replace anyone on the team if it comes to that," Connor said.

Diaz glanced at the list of recruits. "You better keep that backup list handy, Colonel."

Mallory had reinstated Connor's previous rank, which made him equal to Chief Mills and second in rank to Mallory himself. Whereas Mills had multiple squads totaling nearly three hundred people in Field Operations and Security, Connor just had himself, Diaz, and twelve recruits.

There was a knock on the office door, and Diaz went to open it.

"We have a visitor, sir," Diaz said.

Sean Quinn was standing outside. The sandy-haired youth waved from the doorway, and Connor gestured for him to come inside.

"What can I do for you?" Connor asked.

Sean walked in and did a pretty good impression of standing at attention. "I'd like to join Search and Rescue, sir."

Diaz's mouth rounded in surprise, but since he stood behind the governor's son, only Connor could see.

"Why?" Connor asked.

"There have been more incidents with the berwolfs stalking the teams—not only here, but at some of the research bases. You were right, sir, and I want to join you so I can help do something about it," Sean said.

Connor regarded the youth for a moment. He had a few freckles on his face and his tanned skin indicated that he spent much of his time outside, but there was still that uncertainty in his gaze that suggested Sean was running from something.

"How old are you?" Connor asked.

Sean's shoulders slumped. "Seventeen, sir."

"You're too young for this. Come back to me next year," Connor said and walked behind his desk, giving the young man a moment to school his features.

"Sir, I'll be eighteen in just a few weeks. What difference will the time make?"

"Not much from your perspective. What matters is where we draw the line. Do your parents know you're here, asking for this?" Connor asked.

Sean's eyes flashed angrily. "No, sir."

"Do you think they'd give their consent for you to do something like this?"

"I'm not sure, sir."

"What do you think we're going to be doing?" Connor asked.

"Helping people out, being the strongest of the strong, the best trained, sir."

"You can be all those things without joining Search and Rescue," Connor said.

Diaz opened the door and the busy sounds from the corridor beyond echoed inside.

Sean stood in the same spot, his gaze on the floor. "Please, sir."

Connor shook his head. "Look at me. What we're doing is dangerous. I'm not running a day camp where you get to 'find' yourself to determine whether you're worth something. You can 'find' yourself without me. Go out there and make a difference and then, maybe, I'll consider letting you join. Now get out of here."

Sean sucked in a breath and fled.

Diaz closed the door and made a low whistling sound. "Is this what you're gonna be like once we get to our camp?"

Connor shook his head. "Worse. Besides, I don't have time for that right now."

Another knock came as the door opened and Noah stuck his head inside. "Am I interrupting?"

"Not at all. Come inside," Connor said.

"I have good news. The drones you asked for are ready," Noah said.

"Excellent! Are they in the supply crates?" Connor asked.

"All twenty-five of them are being loaded as we speak," Noah said.

"Great, so you're coming with us then," Connor said.

"I'll be out there in a few days. Mills has me doing some things for Field Ops now," Noah said.

With the onset of Search and Rescue, Damon Mills had suddenly begun making changes to Field Ops, improving their response times and security.

"Mills has plenty of engineers working for him," Connor said.

Noah glanced over at the wallscreen. "And I see you have one, too."

Connor caught Noah's gaze lingering on the list. "Is there something I should know?"

Noah shook his head. "It's nothing. I'll be working on the suit upgrades for your squad and will come out to the camp when they get delivered."

Connor eyed the young tech specialist. "It's your squad too."

"You're relentless," Noah said and left the room.

"The funny thing is he thinks he has a choice." Diaz snorted.

"Don't be crazy. They all have a choice. They might not like the choices they have, but they'll always have a choice," Connor said.

He killed his open session on the wallscreen and looked around his office. Everything was in its place and there was nothing he'd forgotten. Connor stepped outside the office and heard his name being called.

Franklin Mallory caught up to him. "I thought I'd walk you out."

"I was just coming to your office to let you know we were leaving," Connor said.

Diaz said he'd meet them on the tarmac and quickened his pace.

"So, you're all ready?" Franklin asked.

"As we'll ever be," Connor said.

"I have to be honest. I'd feel a whole lot better if you were going to the research base as we originally planned."

"Isolation is key, for the first few weeks anyway. Most of them have been too comfortable living at the compound," Connor said.

"Yeah, but that camp is rustic, to say the least. I saw on the manifest that you're only bringing one small power generator and a light backup."

"They already know how to operate here. We strip everything away and gradually reintroduce things. Also, it measures their commitment," Connor said.

Franklin nodded. "I know. I know. We've been through this a half dozen times. You'll be off the grid."

"With regular check-ins. Diaz and I have been out to the site and have a pretty good knowledge of the area. We have all the data collected so far, and we've had a Field Ops drone in the area doing reconnaissance," Connor said.

Franklin glanced at him. "You're excited about this, aren't you?"

"Absolutely. And remember our agreement. No inspections for at least a month," Connor said.

They exited the headquarters and climbed into the waiting ground transport that would take him to the airfield.

"I hear the berwolfs have been coming back around," Connor said.

Franklin nodded grimly. "Yes, they have. Some of the new protocols have helped."

Connor was glad to hear it. He hadn't been convinced that Damon Mills would make any changes. "How's Mills handling it?"

"He cares about his people. It's just you he doesn't like," Franklin said.

They arrived at one of the smaller landing areas of the airfield, but there was still quite a bit of traffic going to and from the Ark. Outside a cargo carrier, Sergeant Diaz was shouting at a ragtag group.

"Form a line. Now!" Diaz bellowed. "It's not that hard."

Connor and Franklin walked over. Diaz turned around and snapped a salute. "Search and Rescue trainee squad awaits inspection, sir."

"Thank you, Sergeant," Connor said, returning his salute.

Twelve men and women formed two lines of six, varying in age and experience. Off to the side was a pile of personal items that had no business going to their camp. More than a few of the recruits glanced over at the pile.

"Your stuff will be returned to you once your training is complete. We'll do formal introductions later," Connor said.

"Sir, yes, sir," the squad shouted.

Connor suppressed a smile. Diaz must have given them some preliminary instruction before he arrived. Connor stood next to Diaz and snapped a salute to Mallory.

Franklin regarded them with a nod to a time long gone. "The clock is ticking. I'll let you get to it."

Connor turned toward Diaz. "Get them on board, Sergeant."

"Yes, sir," Diaz said and turned to face the new recruits. "Alright, you heard him. Grab your gear and get on board the ship. Debriefing will occur once we're on site."

"Good luck," Franklin said.

Connor shook his hand. "I'll see you in a few weeks."

Franklin returned to the ground transport, and Connor caught a glimpse of a man standing off to the side. A tele-view of the man appeared on his internal heads-up display. Damon Mills watched him, stone-faced and impossible to read. Connor regarded Mills for a moment, and though there were a hundred meters between them, it wasn't far enough in Connor's mind.

Connor turned around and walked up the ramp to enter the cargo carrier, the last one to board. He walked past the supply crates, and as he came to his new recruits, their conversations hushed. Connor headed to the cockpit where the pilots sat.

A pilot named Mitchell greeted him. "We're clear for takeoff."

Connor nodded. "Good. Once we're in the air I have a new set of coordinates for you."

"I'm afraid I don't understand," Mitchell said.

"It's fine. You will," Connor said.

The cargo carrier thrusters were engaged and the ship lifted off the ground. Once they were high enough, the carrier sped off.

Connor used his implants to interface with the ship's systems and uploaded the coordinates and his authorization.

The new coordinates appeared on Mitchell's terminal, and the pilot frowned. "I have the new destination, but sir, there isn't any research base at this location."

"I know," Connor said. "We'll also be doing a low-altitude deployment."

"I wasn't aware of that," Mitchell stammered.

"I'm making you aware of it now. Will there be a problem?" Connor asked.

"The passengers aren't equipped for a low-altitude drop, sir."

Connor glanced behind him, making a show of considering what the pilot was saying. "Oh, that. Don't worry about it. They'll be fine. Just get us over those coordinates, dump us out, and go back home."

The pilot nodded. "Yes, sir."

Connor went over to see that Diaz was already wearing a vest with repulsor jets on the back. They were designed for low-altitude jumps. The jets would fire to slow the wearer's descent enough for them to make a soft landing. Connor put his own repulsor vest on and waited.

"Sir, we're approaching the drop zone. I'll just warn the passengers in the cabin of the flight status," Mitchell said.

"That won't be necessary," Connor said.

"But, sir—"

Connor gave him a hard look. "Are they all strapped into their seats?"

The pilot did a quick check of the status of the passengers. "Yes, sir."

"Then when we're over the drop zone, dump them out," Connor said.

He glanced at Diaz and headed to the cargo area.

"You believe that guy?" Connor heard Mitchell ask his copilot when he thought they were away. Connor closed the door. He was facing his new recruits, and the nearest one raised her hand.

"Yes," Connor said.

"How long till we get there, sir?" she asked.

She had thick blond hair and pale skin. The name A. Blake was stenciled into her jacket.

"What did you say?" Connor asked.

He'd heard her, he was just delaying his answer. The recruits nearby were actively listening when suddenly a klaxon alarm sounded and the interior lights changed to red. A few seconds later the cargo bay doors opened and wind roared through the airship. The recruits looked behind them in horror as the locking mechanism holding large storage crates in place shifted and the crates were pulled from the cargo area.

"I can't get my straps undone!" one of the recruits cried.

Connor kicked the emergency lever. The recruits all angled backward and screamed as their seats raced on tracks toward the exit. At the last second, small rockets fired as their seats detached from the ship and they were tossed out of the cargo ship.

The cargo area was clear. Connor glanced across at Diaz, who gave him a thumbs-up. Together they ran down the ramp and jumped into the air. Diaz let out a loud woot and bellowed a laugh almost the whole way to the ground.

15

THE WIND SLAPPED against Connor's face as he jumped out of the cargo ship and noted multiple chute deployments from his new recruits. Their chairs were bolted together and designed for this type of emergency. He scanned ahead for the hardened cargo crates and made a quick count. Connor looked at Diaz and gave him a thumbs-up. Without parachutes of their own, they quickly overtook his new recruits. The pilots had done their jobs well, because they were right on target, and they approached the wide-open glade he'd designated as the spot for their new camp over a week ago.

He and Diaz used their arms to angle away from each other. Landing with a repulsor jet pack wasn't for the faint of heart. They were required to change the angle of their approach; otherwise, the small repulsor engines would speed them to their deaths. Connor brought his arms in and dove forward. The momentum of his body aligned his feet with the ground below, and he fired his engines for a few moments. He slowed down, but not enough, so he fired his engines again in a controlled burst and his velocity quickly decreased. His feet scraped the ground and he pumped his legs, then killed the jets and ran a short distance before stopping. Diaz landed nearby, and the sergeant immediately started scanning the area. He had his SD-15 in his hand.

Connor kept his SD holstered and patched into the recon drone they had in the area. There were no berwolfs nearby. The cargo crates landed close by, followed by his harried-looking recruits. Some of them had vomit on their shirts.

He did a quick visual. "Alright. Fall in line. Let's go. I haven't got all day. What are you waiting for? Get up!" Connor shouted.

Diaz was on them, coming from the other side, shouting for them to get up. The recruits unstrapped themselves and tried to stand up, but most of them immediately fell because their wobbly legs refused to hold them up.

"On your feet. Line up, people," Connor said.

All twelve recruits lined up, most of them looking completely out of sorts as if they couldn't believe what had just happened.

"Welcome, Lightning Platoon, to Search and Rescue training. Over the next few weeks you will be challenged and tested to see if you have what it takes to be on my team," Connor said. He walked down the line as he spoke. "I know many of you have questions," Connor said.

Five recruits' hands shot into the air.

"Put your hands down," Diaz snapped. "The commander didn't ask you if you had questions. He made a statement."

The recruits reluctantly put their hands down.

"Thank you, Sergeant Diaz," Connor said. "You're wondering where the research base is that you were told about, the one that was just twenty klicks from the compound. I lied."

A recruit glanced over at her fellow recruit, and Connor immediately stepped in front of her. "Is there a problem, Owens?"

Amy Owens had thick dark hair and a plump body. She wasn't overweight, but she'd never be what you'd call slender either. "Uh, no, sir."

"Then why were you looking at Deacon when I was speaking to you?" Connor asked.

Owens glanced over at Deacon.

"Again!" Connor shouted. "Henry Deacon, maybe you can tell me why Owens keeps looking at you during my debrief."

"Sir, I think she's just scared from the drop, sir," Deacon said.

Connor nodded. "Perhaps she likes you. What do you think, Sergeant Diaz?"

Diaz stalked over to them. "I definitely sense some animal magnetism going on here, Commander."

Owens' face flushed.

"Indeed, we got ourselves a real Hot Rod here," Connor said. "In fact, from here on out your name is Hot Rod. How's that sound?"

"Sounds great," Deacon said.

Diaz got up in Deacon's face. "Hot Rod, you're addressing a superior officer. Fifty pushups. Count them off."

Hot Rod dropped and immediately began doing pushups.

Connor went back to Owens. "You're my tech specialist. Is that right, Owens?"

"Yes," Owens said. "Sir, I meant yes, sir, sir."

Diaz was about to start in on her, but Connor held up his hand. "That's alright, Sergeant. We got ourselves a regular Einstein here. Do you know who Einstein is, Owens?" Connor asked.

"Yes, sir. He came up with the theory of relativity, sir," Owens said.

Connor grinned. "Outstanding, Owens, except you forgot one thing. Anyone can spout out the accomplishments of a historical figure. They overlook the fact that he was a man of innovation. You'll be called upon to do complex things with limited resources. Each time you think you don't have what you need, I want you to remember our good friend Albert. What did he have? The man conceived theories that couldn't be proven for over a hundred years after he died. From now on I'm going to call you Einstein."

"Yes, sir," she said.

Connor moved down the line and peered at a lanky young man. Even the man's fingers were long and spindly. His short black hair and tan skin announced his Spanish heritage. "Ramirez, Joseph," Connor said.

"Yes, sir," Ramirez said.

"You are the thinnest man I've ever seen," Connor said and glanced over at Diaz, who repeated the same. "You can almost see his bones. In fact, that's what I'm going to call you. Bones. How's that name sound?"

"It sounds good to me, sir," Bones said.

Connor nodded and moved on to the next recruit. "Elyse Winters, is that your name?" Connor asked.

"Sir, yes, sir," Winters said.

She had blond hair that was tied into a bun and her blue eyes were fixed decidedly ahead.

Connor smiled and pretended to get the chills. "You're one cool customer, Winters. I bet not much shakes that resolve of yours."

"Sir, yes, sir," Winters said.

"Yes, what? You're one cool customer? Or nothing shakes your resolve?"

"Both, sir," Winters said.

Connor grinned and gave Diaz an approving nod. "Very frosty. In fact, that's your new name. In fact, Frost, I want you to drop and give me fifty pushups."

Frost dropped down and immediately started counting off her pushups. Connor couldn't help but be impressed. He'd just thrown them out of a perfectly good cargo ship and they were out in the middle of nowhere, yet Winters, now Frost, followed instructions to the letter. She was a keeper for sure.

Connor glanced at Diaz. "I guess engineers are predisposed to work well under pressure."

"Sir, yes, sir," Winters said while doing her pushups.

"Where are my hunters?" Connor said.

He glanced down the line.

"Over here, sir," a woman said.

Connor walked over to her and glanced at the man next to her. "Donna Marten?"

"Yes, sir," Marten said.

Donna Marten was lean and in great shape. Connor was sure he could give her two hundred pushups and she'd hardly break a sweat.

Connor glanced at the man. "And you're Nate Poe?"

The man had long straight black hair tied back from his face and brown skin. "Yes, sir."

Both hunters were tall—easily six feet.

"First, it's convenient that you guys chose to stand together. Otherwise, I'd have to do this whole song and dance again. Don't you agree?" Connor asked.

Poe frowned. "I guess so, sir."

Connor looked at Marten. "What about you?"

"No, sir," Marten said.

Connor stepped back. "Did the rest of you hear that? Recruit Donna Marten doesn't agree that it was a good idea for her and her fellow hunter to stand together in the line."

"She's got some nerve, sir," Diaz said.

"Nerve indeed. Got ourselves a regular Boone right here. In fact, Marten, that's going to be your new name. Boone," Connor said. "It just so happens that Recruit Boone is absolutely right. It's a terrible idea for my specialists to be so close to one another. Does anyone besides Boone know why?"

"Sir," said a huge man from further down the line.

"Randle, Wayne, go ahead and tell us why," Connor said.

"Because if we're attacked, we run the risk of two people with the same skill sets being lost," Randle said.

Connor nodded. "That's exactly right, Randle. Outstanding. From now on, when we're outside of the camp, you are to stagger yourselves from anyone who has the same specialty as you. We have comlinks, and you can always speak that way. Is that understood?"

"Sir, yes, sir," the recruits replied in unison.

Connor looked back at Randle. "I recognize you from Field Operations."

Randle nodded. "Sir, I was on patrol the day of the berwolf attack, sir."

"That's right. You're one of my weapons specialists. Where is my other weapons specialist?" Connor asked.

"Over here, sir," a man said from further down the line.

"Compton, Neal. Good job, the both of you," Connor said.

"Thank you, sir," they both said.

"It could have been luck, but I'm sure the fact that you both were infantrymen back home had something to do with it," Connor said and walked to the middle of the line. "We'll have to continue the introductions a little bit later. As you can see, we're not at a research base. We're out in the middle of nowhere, roughly fifty kilometers from the compound," he said and looked down the line for his next victim.

"Blake, Allison," Connor said. "What's our situation?"

Blake's brows drew upward and her hazel eyes widened. "I'm not sure, sir," she said softly.

Diaz shook his head. "Recruit! Your commanding officer asked you a question. You will speak loudly and clearly. Now!"

"I'm not sure, sir," Allison said much louder this time.

"Why not?" Connor asked.

Blake started to look at the recruits on either side of her but caught herself. "I'm not sure what you're asking me, sir."

"It's a simple question. What's our situation?" Connor asked.

Blake's chin crumpled and she took shallow breaths.

"Calm down," Connor said. "You're one of my medics, right? Take the same skills you'd use to assess a patient and apply them to us right now."

Blake swallowed hard and she glanced around. "We're exposed out here and it will be dark soon."

Connor smiled. "Excellent. So what do you think we should do?"

"Set up camp, sir?"

"Outstanding," Connor said. "You heard Babyface. We need to set up camp. In that first storage crate, you'll find fencing to set up a perimeter. Split up into two teams and get it set up first."

"Sir, where are we going to sleep tonight?" Compton asked.

Connor's gaze narrowed. "Who said anything about sleeping?" he asked.

"Yes, sir," Compton said.

"Bones and Frost, there's a power generator in one of these crates. Find it and check with Diaz about where to set it up. Then help with the fence," Connor said.

"Dismissed," Diaz shouted. "Time to get to work, people."

Randle walked over to Connor. "Sir, shouldn't some of us be armed in case there are predators around? Some of them start coming out during this time, sir."

"Listen up," Connor said, and the recruits stopped what they were doing. "Sergeant Diaz and I are the only ones cleared for weapons, so the more time we have to spend answering your pitiful questions, the less time we have to keep watch for any predators in the area, which means one of you might become dinner. Now get that fence up."

Randle snapped a salute and ran over to the large container. Connor watched as the recruits started offloading the crate.

"Recruits, if that fence isn't set up within three hours, I'll make sure you'll be sleeping in a tent on the other side," Connor said.

The recruits quickened their pace. Connor knew there weren't any predators in the area, but he wanted to deploy the new drones Noah had given them. He retrieved his tablet computer from his pack and brought up the manifest, found the crate that contained specialized equipment, and entered the security code. There was a snap-hiss sound as the crate opened. Squished inside, looking uncomfortable as hell, was Sean Quinn.

16

CONNOR'S MOUTH HUNG OPEN. Of all the things he'd expected to encounter, a stowaway in a cargo crate wasn't among them.

"Get out of there," Connor said.

Sean climbed out of the crate and winced. His hand went to his side.

"How did you get inside the crate? When did you even have time? I just saw you a little while ago on base," Connor said.

Sean tried to stand up straight and winced again. "After I left your office, I bumped into Noah. He told me he was just coming from the airfield and that you were leaving to begin training the new recruits. So . . . I went to the airfield and snuck aboard."

Connor regarded him for a moment and pushed away his irritation at the utter lack of security at the airfield. "Hard landing in that crate, wasn't it?" he said.

"I didn't know they were going to be dropped out of the ship —" Sean began to say.

"You could have been killed. Those crates are designed to land without a chute. We put chutes on those with delicate equipment. It was dumb luck that you weren't seriously hurt," Connor said.

Sean pressed his side and winced. "I think I might be hurt a little bit."

"And now this is my problem to deal with. I don't want to explain to your parents how their idiot son decided he'd stowed away in a crate because he's having rebellion issues, but you've given me no choice," Connor said.

"Please don't!" Sean pleaded. "Don't do it. I'll do anything you tell me to. Just don't send me back there."

"What's your problem? Why don't you want to go back to the compound? You can do whatever the hell you want there and be someone else's problem," Connor said.

Sean looked away. "No, I can't. I can't do anything."

Connor watched as Sean winced again, and this time his hand rubbed the side of his head.

"Sit down," Connor ordered.

He stepped back and looked over to where the recruits were emptying a storage crate about forty meters from them. "Sergeant Diaz!" Connor shouted.

One of the recruits heard him and told Diaz. Diaz came around the storage crate.

"Send over Babyface. I need a medic," Connor said.

He heard Diaz shout for the recruit to go to Connor, and Recruit Blake ran over. Her pretty face was a grim line of determination, but Connor could tell she was barely coping. She reached them and came to a halt, glanced at Sean sitting on the ground, and then remembered to stand at attention and salute Connor.

"Recruit Babyface, please put your skills as medic to good use and examine Recruit Bling here," Connor said.

"Yes, sir," Babyface replied.

She immediately squatted down and set about assessing Sean Quinn for injuries. Connor stepped around them and searched for the container of drones Noah had packed for them. There were three silver cases marked with the golden sunburst, and Connor pulled them out one at a time, setting them down a short distance from the others. He listened to Blake question Sean and check his injuries. Connor had his back to them, but he could hear everything that they were saying. Despite the shakeup of the circumstances and the fact that they were utterly exposed to New Earth's vibrant ecosystem, the young medic went about her assessment with the practicality that only came from experience.

Connor heard footsteps approaching and turned around.

"Sir, Recruit Bling has some minor bruising of the ribs and a headache that was caused by the jolting he experienced while inside the storage crate, sir," she said.

"Excellent. Return to the others and get the fence set up," Connor ordered.

He looked at Sean, who was sitting on the ground but hastily got to his feet.

"I don't know what I'm going to do with you. We'll have communications up in a little while. In the meantime, there's no way I'm going to let an extra pair of hands go to waste, even ones as dainty as yours. From here on out, you'll be called Bling. While you're here, you will follow my orders without question. Is that understood?"

"Yes, sir," Sean said and tried to keep the smile from his face.

"Now, go report to Sergeant Diaz. He'll put you to work. Tell him I said to give you the dirtiest task he has. Now repeat my order," Connor said.

"Report to Sergeant Diaz and tell him to give me the dirtiest task he has, sir."

"Good. Now leave," Connor said.

The kid ran off to join the others, and Connor put thoughts of him out of his mind. He had other things to worry about. Grabbing the first case, he used his implants to authenticate the lock, and it sprang open. The oval-shaped drones had the look of a decapitated head from a robot. Two optics in the front glowed when he activated the drone. There were also different sensors along the tubes on the side that gave it a more streamlined look, and the metallic compound the hull was made of was light and strong.

Connor checked the drone's status and video-feed output using his implants. A sub window appeared on his internal heads-up display that showed anything he pointed the drone at while the drone's target-awareness computer identified and classified anything that came into view. He set the dark gray drone on the ground and put it in patrol mode. The drone rose up into the air and sped off, hardly making any noise. He uploaded the transponder identification for Diaz's PDA. Connor activated the rest of the drones from all the cases and broke them up into groups. Their patrols would send them into different vicinities outward from the camp. Connor connected to drone seven and set it to locate Diaz. He watched the video feed as the drone made a quick sweep of the camp and quickly identified Sergeant Juan Diaz. Connor acknowledged the recorded success and put the drone in patrol mode. Noah had assured him that the drones could identify the known predators and would alert Connor if anything should happen to be heading toward their camp. Once they set up their small operations center, the recruits would rotate through monitoring duty. He and Diaz would need to review the unknown detections to help the drones' artificial intelligence learn what the misidentified creatures were. It was a pain but definitely worth the effort.

Connor set the empty cases to the side. The drones still had to prove themselves, so he set about doing a patrol of his own just to be sure no berwolfs or anything else were coming to investigate the camp while it was being built. A short while later Diaz caught up to him.

"Excuse me, sir," Diaz said.

They'd agreed that they would maintain formal communications while the recruits were around them.

"Are you aware that we have an extra recruit in our midst, sir?" Diaz asked.

"I am," Connor replied.

"You do realize he's the governor's son, sir?"

"I do," Connor said and waved Diaz closer. "He stored himself in one of the crates. I had to do something with him."

Diaz grinned. "I've got him digging a latrine—that is, of course, until we get the rest of the camp set up."

Connor glanced over at the recruits who were working on building the perimeter fences. He and Diaz had given them the orders and were evaluating how well they could work together. Connor had trained soldiers before, and every task, large and small, was a test. The sooner these recruits learned that, the better.

"How do you think it's going so far?" Connor asked.

"No one has died, sir," Diaz said.

Connor made a face at the sergeant. Diaz grinned and went back over to the recruits, shouting that they'd better get a move on. Connor walked over to his two engineers, who were making excellent progress setting up the power generators.

"Bones, I need you to help out the others with the fence," Connor said.

"Yes, sir," Bones said. He returned his tools to the kit and ran off to help the others.

Elyse Winters, now known as Frost, continued working on the main generator. Frost hardly paid Connor any notice at all and just focused on what she was doing.

There was a loud slam as one of the fence sections hit the ground, and Diaz's shouts could be heard echoing around them. Connor glanced over and saw that several recruits were now doing pushups.

"Sir, may I ask you a question?"

"Go ahead, Frost," Connor said.

"Why did you pick such a remote location to train us, sir?" Frost asked.

"You were in the military before?" Connor asked.

"Yes, sir, same kind of job. Different location, sir."

"Then you already know the answer to that question," Connor said.

"Joe and I . . . uh, Bones and I have served before. We understand the discipline you're trying to instill, but some of the others have no idea, sir," Frost said.

"They'll learn or they'll go back to the compound," Connor said.

"This is done, sir," Frost said and gestured toward the power generator.

Connor thought it would have taken another half hour to put it together, but he looked it over and everything seemed to be in order. Frost engaged the generator's startup sequence and it went through several self-diagnostics before returning the ready status.

"Good work," Connor said.

"Thank you, sir. You wanted the best, sir," Frost said.

She wasn't lacking in confidence. "That remains to be seen. Lay out the wiring for the fence and then rejoin the others," Connor said.

Connor left his engineer and headed toward the others. The fully constructed fence sections were over twelve feet tall, but inside the crate they were folded over and only half that height. Most of the recruits carried the sections together except for Randle and Compton, who each took a section of their own. The progress they were making was painstakingly slow. At the rate they were going, the fence wouldn't be complete until well after nightfall, which was unacceptable.

"I think we have ourselves a competition going on here,"

Connor said. "Randle, you're strong as a bull. In fact, that's your name now. And Compton is like a bear."

"A grizzly bear, sir," Diaz said.

"Grizzly, I like that. Do you like it, Compton?" Connor asked.

"Yes, sir," he answered.

"Well, see how many sections Bull and Grizzly can handle on their own. Let's see how many they can lift up together. Any bets?" Connor asked.

"I say six sections, sir," said Henry "Hot Rod" Deacon.

"Whatever it is, I know I can equal it, sir," Bones said.

Connor laughed with the rest of them. "The gauntlet has been thrown. Show us what you can do."

Bull went inside the large crate and came out with two sections of fencing. Each section was ten feet in length. He laid the sections on the ground, one atop the other. Grizzly continued stacking until they had eight sections in a neat pile. Each section weighed about fifty pounds. Neal "Grizzly" Compton and Wayne "Bull" Randle squatted down and easily lifted them up. They carried the fencing a hundred meters from the storage container toward the end of the fence that was already up. By the time they reached the end, both men were gasping and drenched in sweat. They set the sections down and hunched over with their hands on their knees, trying to catch their breath.

"Alright, Bones, you're up. Eight sections," Connor said.

"No problem, sir," Bones said.

"This should be interesting," Connor said and glanced over to see Boone and Nate beginning to offload a section of fencing. "Hold off on that a second. I want everyone to watch how Bones is going to pull this off."

Bones smiled widely. "I'll need one volunteer to help me."

"Now wait a minute," Bull said. "You said you could beat us alone."

"That's not what I said. I said I could equal it," Bones replied.

Bull looked at Connor. "Sir?"

"Let's see what he does," Connor said.

They went back to the storage crate, and Bones stood in the entrance. "Sir, I need one volunteer."

"Me, sir, I'll do it," Blake "Babyface" Allison said and ran forward before anyone could stop her.

Bones frowned for a moment, then shrugged and gestured for her to follow him inside.

The two of them carried out eight more sections of fencing one section at a time and stacked them together. The rest of the recruits looked on with slightly bemused expressions. If Bull and Grizzly—who were both six feet, six inches tall and close to three hundred pounds of solid muscle—had trouble, they assumed that the team of Bones and Babyface certainly couldn't do it.

Bones went back into the storage container and pulled out the straps from inside. The engineer got down on his hands and knees and weaved the cord through the slats at the bottom section of fencing. Babyface helped him and after a few minutes they had multiple crisscross sections weaved throughout. Bones cut the remaining cords into smaller sections and weaved those in, leaving enough slack at the end to make a harness.

Bones called Babyface over and gave her some instructions. She nodded and knelt on the ground. Bones looped the cords around her middle and then crossed them behind her neck, then ran to the other side and got himself set up with a makeshift harness.

"Okay, Blake . . . I mean Babyface, on three we lift together," Bones said.

Bones counted down and then pushed up from a squat to a standing position. Babyface did the same and, much to the recruits' surprise, the stack of fencing rose off the ground, entirely stable.

"Good job!" Boone shouted and clapped.

Bull and Grizzly just stood with their mouths hanging open.

"Okay, one step at a time. Just a walk in the park," Bones said.

Connor watched as the two recruits carried eight fence sections over a hundred meters and set their stack down near the other stack. Both of them were sweating and slightly winded from the effort.

Connor grinned. "You see, brains and brawn can work just fine apart, but together you can accomplish so much more."

Bull went over to Bones. "You've got to show us how you did that."

"It's easy. I can show you," Bones said and led some of the others back toward the storage crate.

Connor saw Babyface watching him, so he gave an approving nod. She beamed at the acknowledgment.

The recruits broke themselves up into two teams. One team carried the fencing sections out from the storage crate while the others set them up and connected the sections together. They progressed much quicker because of it, but Connor knew there was no way they were going to finish in the time he'd given them. They did manage to get well past the midpoint using Bones' new method of carrying. Connor looked around and saw that they were now leaving stacks of fence sections along the perimeter of their new camp. Neither he nor Diaz yelled at them to move faster. They'd achieved each objective he'd set for them, which was to set up the perimeter fence and work quickly and efficiently as a team. To the casual onlooker, what Connor was about to do would seem cruel, but anyone who'd trained soldiers would know it was necessary.

The sun was getting lower in the sky, and his team of recruits lined up. They were grimy and sweaty and starting to smell pretty ripe.

"Recruits, we have a temporary addition to our team. Recruit Bling, get up here and face the squad," Connor said.

Sean Quinn was covered in dirt from the trench he'd dug to serve as their latrine. He stood at attention.

"I see that some of you recognize Recruit Bling, but for those of you who don't know him, his name is Sean Quinn. His father, Tobias, is the governor of our colony and his mother, Ashley, is chief of medicine on the Ark. Bling decided it would be a good idea to store himself in one of the crates, and I didn't find him until after we'd gotten here," Connor said and circled around Sean while addressing the other recruits. "He complained that the other people at the compound give him too much preferential treatment. He wants to join Search and Rescue to be part of something important. He says he's committed to us and to you. Over the next few days, before our next shipment of supplies comes in, I'll need to decide what his level of commitment is. The reason I'm telling you this is because I didn't want anyone to give this young man any preferential treatment, but now I'm not sure I agree with that. He's used to getting special treatment, so I'm going to hold with that tradition. For every mistake Recruit Bling makes, you all will join him in his punishment. For every mistake, lapse in judgment, trip, fall, complaint, or anything else the rest of you do that Sergeant Diaz and myself don't like, Recruit Bling here will do *double* your punishment," Connor said and turned toward Sean Quinn. "How's that sound to you, Bling?"

"Sir, it sounds outstanding, sir," Sean replied.

"Get back in line," Connor said.

Sean scurried back to his place and stumbled into Bull. He whispered a hasty apology and took his place.

"Recruit Bling, come back here," Connor snapped.

Sean ran back to the front.

"Did you understand my order, recruit?" Connor asked.

Sean frowned. "Yes, sir."

"Repeat the order for me," Connor said.

"Sir, you said to get back in line, sir," Sean said.

"That's right. Then why did you assault Recruit Bull?"

Sean's eyes widened. "I'm sorry, sir. It just sort of happened."

"Just sort of happened?" Connor asked and looked at Diaz. "Sergeant Diaz, do you believe in magic?"

"No, sir."

Connor glared at Sean. "I assume you know how to walk straight, is that right?"

"Yes, sir, it won't—"

"Recruit!" Diaz bellowed. "The commander didn't ask for an excuse."

"Sergeant Diaz, what's our standard punishment for this kind of infraction?"

"Fifty pushups, sir," Diaz said.

Connor stood in front of Sean. "That means you get to do a hundred pushups and the rest of you get to do fifty. Count them off right now."

"But, sir—"

"I'm not interested in your opinion!" Connor bellowed. "If I want your opinion, I'll give it to you."

Sean immediately dropped to the ground and started counting off pushups. The rest of the team dropped and began their pushups.

Connor paced in front of them. "I know you've become accustomed to voicing your opinions the moment they become a thought in your brain, but during training we're not interested in your opinions. When you make a mistake, don't offer up excuses and try to tell Sergeant Diaz or myself that it won't happen again. Words are cheap." Connor paused and watched as Recruit Allison struggled with her pushups. She glanced at Connor's feet as he stood by her and doubled her efforts.

"Sergeant Diaz, do you know what an excuse is?" Connor asked.

"I'm sure I do, sir, but I never get tired of hearing you say it," Diaz replied.

"An excuse is another word for failure. No amount of words will erase the failure. Now, you say it," Connor ordered the recruits.

The recruits repeated it, and Connor had them do it again. They finished their pushups, with the exception of Bling.

"The rest of you have a hundred and twenty seconds to use the latrine and return here or you'll join Recruit Bling for more pushups," Connor said.

Half the recruits immediately ran toward the trench at the far side of the camp.

"Excuse me, sir," Owens said.

"Einstein, I don't recall giving you permission to ask me anything. You have your orders," Connor said.

"But, sir, I don't think I can in front of everybody, sir," Owens said.

"Hold on. Recruits, get back here," Connor shouted.

Diaz yelled at the other recruits to get back. Several stumbled back, pulling up their pants and looking annoyed.

"Line up!" Diaz said.

Several glared ahead and refused to look at him.

"The reason you were called back was because Recruit Einstein didn't think she could handle the pressure of relieving herself in front of all of you. Apparently she's pee-pee shy. So now we get to do a little bit of running. Thirty laps, following the fence. You will stay in formation. Recruit Bling, that will be sixty laps for you," Connor said.

Sean turned around and started running.

"Recruits, you heard the man. Fall out!" Diaz said.

Connor led them along the perimeter of the fence and heard the footfalls of the recruits behind him.

"Hey, Bones, how far is thirty laps?" Compton asked.

"Six miles," Bones answered, and several recruits started groaning.

Connor turned around and jogged backwards. "There is no talking on this run, recruits."

The first two miles passed without anyone complaining. The third mile brought on a few groans and the fourth mile added to that.

Diaz pulled out a shock stick from his belt. "If any of you lag behind, you'll get to feel the love from my stunner."

The recruits immediately shut their mouths. At six miles, Connor brought them to a halt. He told Diaz to get them lined up and ran with Sean Quinn.

"Ready to call it quits?" Connor asked.

"No, sir."

"Why not? All you have to do is get to a comlink and make that call. Mommy and Daddy will come and take you home. Acknowledge this was all a big mistake and promise never to do it again," Connor said.

"I won't quit, sir," Sean said.

"Are you sure? I can get communications up in no time," Connor said.

"I'm not gonna quit, sir."

"We'll see, Bling. We'll see," Connor said and stopped running. "If you finish the rest of the run in forty-five minutes, you get to stay for another hour. Otherwise, I'm going to make the call."

Connor watched as Sean quickened his pace.

Connor returned to the others and regarded his recruits for a moment. There were already a few soldiers in the bunch, but by the time he was done, they'd all be much closer to being soldiers than they were right now.

"Let's try this again. You have one hundred and twenty seconds to use the latrine and return here," Connor said.

Diaz repeated the order, and this time the recruits hastened toward the latrine without comment. Diaz walked over to his side.

"Going to be a long night," Diaz said.

"I thought you liked to stay up all night," Connor chided.

"I do, but we don't all have those fancy implants and nanites that let us get by on two hours of sleep," Diaz said.

"I think it's time for a water ration. Would you get the canteens and bring them back here? Take Boone and Einstein to do the heavy lifting," Connor said.

Diaz grinned. "At once, sir. Right away, sir."

Diaz jogged away and called the recruits over to him while Connor made a show of checking his PDA for the time. He had a timer showing on his internal heads-up display, but the recruits couldn't see that. Connor watched as Deacon shouted that their time was running out. The warning was repeated by several of the others. The recruits finished their business and sprinted back toward Connor, lining up in two rows.

"Congratulations, you *just* made it and have proficiently demonstrated your ability to follow simple commands," Connor said.

Relief shone on most of their faces. Elyse Winters had no reaction and neither had Joe Ramirez nor Nate Poe. The three were in the best physical shape of the bunch. Wayne Randle and Neal Compton didn't look that much worse for wear, but during the run Connor had heard them huffing and puffing quite a bit. Connor glanced at Allison Blake, who wore a determined expression.

Diaz returned with Boone and Einstein.

"Go get your water ration and get back in line," Connor said.

The recruits quickly retrieved their canteens, and Wayne Randle drank from it greedily. Joe Ramirez did the same, but none of the other recruits did.

"Bull, do you have trouble hearing? I didn't read in your file that you had issues with hearing," Connor said.

Randle looked guiltily at the canteen in his hands and closed his eyes for a moment. "No, sir," he said.

"What about you, Bones? Is there something wrong with your hearing that I'm not aware of?" Connor asked.

"No, sir," Ramirez said.

"Come out here and stand in the front. Both of you," Connor said. "The rest of you may drink since you know how to follow orders.

"It seems that both of you need a lesson in following orders again, so we're going to do a little exercise to drive that point home," Connor said.

"Yes, sir," both recruits said in unison.

"Do either of you know what burpees are?" Connor asked.

"No, sir," Ramirez said.

"Yes, sir. It's hands to the ground by your feet, jump your feet back, then do a pushup, bring your feet back in, then jump into the air, sir," Randle said.

Connor smiled and gave an approving nod to Diaz. "Outstanding. Do forty now."

Both men immediately started doing the burpees. Ramirez followed along, awkwardly at first, but then easily got the hang of it. By the time they both reached twenty-five, each man was breathing heavily and had spit up the water they'd drunk.

"As entertaining as this is, we have more work to do," Connor said.

There were several soft groans.

"But if you would like to join Bull and Bones, that can easily be arranged," Connor said.

All groans ceased immediately and there was silence but for the footfalls of Sean Quinn running along the perimeter fence nearby.

"We have four tents to set up. There'll be two cots in one tent. The remaining tents will be divided among you. One tent will have five cots since we're now a team of lucky thirteen. You have one hour to complete this task," Connor said.

There were no comments or questions. The recruits simply followed Diaz to the supply crate that held the tents. Exactly thirty minutes later, Sean Quinn finished his run early. He panted, and Connor regarded him for a minute. To Sean it seemed that Connor was staring at him as a form of intimidation, but what Connor was really doing was giving the young recruit some recovery time.

"That canteen of water contains your water ration," Connor said.

"Yes, sir," Sean said but didn't move. He immediately began doing burpees and counting them off.

Connor watched as Sean used every ounce of his remaining strength toward completing the exercise.

"You got this!" Deacon shouted from where they were assembling the tents.

Sean collapsed at forty up/downs, gasping for breath.

"Get up, Bling. You can do it!" Randle's deep voice bellowed.

The other recruits shouted for Sean to get up.

Connor squatted down. "They believe in you. Do you really want to let them down?"

Sean growled as he came to his feet. "Search and Rescue!" he shouted.

The rest of the recruits cheered, and Connor shared a look with Diaz. Neither one of them cracked a smile, but their chests filled with pride for the young man. When Sean reached eighty he could hardly catch his breath. He was on his hands and knees.

"Go on over and help them get the tents set up," Connor said and walked away.

Randle and Compton ran over to Sean and helped him to his feet. One retrieved a canteen of water and urged him to drink.

Sean Quinn glanced over at Connor with a burning intensity in his eyes. It wasn't until that moment that Connor believed the young man really wanted to be part of the team.

Over the next few hours the recruits had one break to feast on a pack of field rations. There weren't any complaints since they only had five minutes to eat before the next task was given to them. The recruits set up other mobile structures, which were basically tents designed for a purpose. With the power generator up, the perimeter fence had electrical current running through it. It wasn't a constant high-voltage charge since that would have been inefficient, even with the advanced battery capabilities they had. They set up motion sensors that would cause the fence to go full charge if an animal large enough to be a threat was detected.

It was well past midnight, and the recruits were almost asleep on their feet.

"Time for some rack time. Two of you will patrol the perimeter of the fence for the next hour and then the next set will rotate in. You will alert either me or Sergeant Diaz if you see anything suspicious outside our perimeter," Connor said.

"Sir, may I ask a question?" Donna Marten asked.

"Go ahead, Boone," Connor replied.

"Will we be armed for patrol?"

"Negative. Weapons training will be tomorrow. Until I've assessed your abilities, you will not be armed," Connor said.

"Dismissed," Diaz said.

As the recruits walked toward their tents—some of them limping—Connor and Diaz watched. At the last second, Boone and Grizzly headed away from the tent to take the first patrol.

"Go on and get some rack time," Connor said.

"I'll see you in few hours, sir," Diaz said and went to the tent they were sharing.

Connor went to the command tent, where there were several crates of computer equipment waiting to be set up. Noah wouldn't be there for a few days, and Connor was sure that either Ramirez or Winters could set it up, but he wanted at least one monitoring station up and knew he could handle it. It had been a long day for them all, but Connor wasn't the least bit tired. If anything, he was excited to finally be doing something. He believed building his own team was the best way he could contribute to the colony.

Throughout the day he and Diaz had recorded the recruits' strengths and weaknesses, both of which would be tested over the coming days and weeks.

He heard the sound of hushed conversation as Boone and Grizzly walked the perimeter. He hadn't given them specific orders on how to stand watch and was curious to see what each pair of recruits would do. He had one of the drones following them, but doubted the recruits knew the drone was there.

Connor finished setting up the monitoring station and brought it up. Drone feeds began to upload their data, and Connor noticed that they had limited communications capability with the main compound. A chat window opened up.

::Couldn't wait for me to get there to set up a monitoring station I see,:: N. Bates said.

"Noah," Connor muttered.

::SR-Camp is up. Drones are on patrol and checking in,:: C. Gates said.

::Sweet! I'll run diagnostics on them when I'm out there in a few days. How's the training going?:: N. Bates asked.

::We're missing our second tech specialist,:: C. Gates replied.

::Owens is good. I hope you're being nice to her,:: N. Bates said.

The amber text window became outlined in green.

::I've encrypted this session,:: N. Bates said.

Connor frowned. ::Okay, why?::

::We've received a data burst from the space buoy network. If you *recall, the data we received from Earth was sent sometime in the past two hundred years,*:: N. Bates said.

::*What did you receive?*::

::*Only the header of the data burst, which had a reference called EOD-Extinction Critical Alpha. What follows is a set of programming instructions for the Ark,*:: N. Bates said.

::*Are you trying to play a joke on me?*::

::*It's tempting, but no. There's also a mention of M. Wilkinson.*::

Connor felt something sink into the pit of his stomach. ::*Can you send me what you have?*::

::*No, it's too much for this connection. I only have a partial dump because access to buoy transmissions is restricted until they're reviewed by the Governor's office,*:: N. Bates said.

Connor leaned back in his chair and rubbed his chin. ::*Okay, show me what you've got when you get here in a few days. I would suggest not showing this around to anyone else.*::

::*You don't have to tell me twice.*::

::*I need you to do something for me. Sean Quinn stored himself in one of our crates. He requested to join the Search and Rescue squad, which I initially refused. Since he's here, I have him training with the rest. Can you send a message to Ashley?*:: C. Gates asked.

::*Oh boy, that's not good. I'll let her know.*::

The chat session ended, and Connor thought about the partial data dump from the space buoy network. Tobias normally had a policy for transparency, so why would any information received from Earth be restricted? He recalled some of the conversations on the Ark and that Ashley and Tobias had explained how their mission had been overwritten to bring them here instead of their original destination. That override added over a hundred years to the mission.

Connor got up from his seat and stepped outside the tent, looking over at the tents nearby and thinking about Sean Quinn. Could Sean know something about why the mission had been changed? Did he know why Tobias was keeping information from the colony? Was that the reason Sean was determined to join Connor's new team? Or was he just doing what normal teenage kids who are on the cusp of adulthood and carving out their own niche in the world do?

Connor looked up at the night sky. A blanket of stars shined along with the moon. His gaze was then drawn to the south, where the ring that surrounded the planet brightened the night sky. Connor doubted there was ever a pitch-black night on this planet. The surrounding area was alive with chirping insects, and when Connor closed his eyes, he could almost imagine he was back on Earth, but the rhythm of sounds from the nightly critters was of a different cadence, and his brain kept registering that fact.

Connor walked over to one of the armored storage crates and placed his hand on the palm reader. At the same time, he used his implants to engage the locking interface with his biometric information and the lock disengaged. Connor pulled the large doors open. Inside was a mobile armory that held a variety of weapons they'd be training with in the coming weeks. It had taken a fair amount of negotiating with Tobias, but Connor had been able to access the weapons manifest from the Ark. Tobias may have no intention of starting a formal military, but that didn't mean he couldn't arm one if it came down to it. Someone had the foresight to include military-grade assault rifles and other types of weapons.

Connor unloaded the weapons crates he wanted to use with the recruits and stacked them just outside the container. There was only so much time he'd allocated for training these recruits who'd ostensibly come with at least some experience in a field he needed for Search and Rescue.

Connor heard two recruits walking along the perimeter fence. When they noticed him, they jogged over.

"Do you need some help, sir?" Deacon asked.

It appeared that Connor had been working long enough for a shift change. "Grab a crate and follow me," Connor said.

Deacon and Poe each took a crate, and Connor grabbed the last one. He led them over to the command tent, where he'd set up the monitoring station, and put his case down. The others put theirs down next to his.

Connor thanked them, and they returned to their patrol. Connor went to his tent just as Diaz was leaving.

"I was just coming to find you," Diaz said.

"I set up a monitoring station and there are three crates of CAR-74s in the tent," Connor said.

Diaz nodded. "Couldn't you get the mess tent set up and get some eggs going?"

"We'll see how they perform today. If they earn it, they'll get a hot meal at the end. If not, then more rations," Connor said and went inside the tent.

He sat down on his cot, removed his boots, lay down, and shut his eyes. The last time he'd trained recruits like this he'd had a staff of twelve instructors with rotations. Here, he and Diaz just had each other. He thought about the Ghosts. More than once, images of Kasey and Reisman came to mind, along with Samson and Oslo. Randle and Compton reminded him a lot of Samson and Oslo, who'd carried heavy weapons in his unit. Connor went to sleep dreaming about lost friends and family. The Ghosts had been both to him. Today he'd kept comparing the recruits to the professional level of the elite special forces that made up the Ghosts. Perhaps he was being too hard on them, but the more ruthless side of Connor dismissed such thoughts. They trained because they'd be called upon to deal with the most dangerous of situations. They'd be facing the unknown, and in order to do that, they'd all need to perform at their best. This meant Connor had to push the recruits past their limits to see what they were truly capable of.

17

CONNOR SLEPT for two hours and woke up completely refreshed. He glanced outside the tent and saw that the sun was starting to rise, and he heard Diaz let out a hearty laugh. Connor put on his boots and didn't have to smell his underarms to know he smelled just as bad as the recruits. It had never bothered him before and certainly wasn't going to today. He put on a fresh shirt and went outside.

Diaz had the recruits lined up, and he turned around to face Connor.

"Good morning, Commander," the entire team said.

"Good morning," Connor replied.

Diaz's eyes were gleaming.

"Report, Sergeant."

"Quiet night. All is secure, Commander," Diaz replied.

"Excellent. Let's start our morning with some PT," Connor said.

Blake went pale, and Owens swayed on her feet. For the next hour Connor led them through various exercises, and he and Diaz performed them right along with the recruits. Sean Quinn stood with the others. Despite all the extra physical activity, he kept up with them. Connor led them on a six-mile run inside the perimeter fence, which he was already getting tired of. Running around in circles had never been his thing. Soon it would be time for their morning exercises to be performed outside the protective confines of the fence.

They ate breakfast in the form of field rations. He and Diaz divided the recruits into groups and assigned them tasks for setting up the rest of their camp. The first and foremost was setting up useable porta-toilets. While the latrine Sean had dug yesterday held a certain amusement factor, Connor didn't relish the thought of dropping anchor over a trench again today. He assigned Elyse Winters the task of digging a well, which wasn't as labor intensive as it once was. Connecting their water supply to their mess hall and showers with a flex-pipe wouldn't take much time at all.

By midafternoon, sore muscles were beginning to stiffen up. Now that they had a fresh supply of water, Connor ended water rationing. They had more field rations as their midday meal, and he promised them that if they continued to perform there would be a hot meal for dinner.

They assembled in the yard away from the tents, and Diaz had them line up.

"We're going to start weapons testing. Inside the crates behind me is the CAR-74 semiautomatic hunting rifle. It's standard issue for Field Operations and is a good, basic firearm," Connor said.

Nate Poe raised his hand, and Connor nodded for him to speak. "Sir, I thought we'd be using weapons with a bit more stopping power. Presumably, Search and Rescue will be going into some of the worst situations. Wouldn't that mean we get to use more powerful firearms, sir?"

"Some of you haven't fired anything but the SD-15 Sonic Hand Blaster, and others have used the CAR-74 and on up to the AR-71 assault rifle. We'll get to the more powerful weapons. The purpose of using the CAR-74 is to teach basic marksmanship and to see if you can even fire a weapon accurately. And weapons testing will require that we leave the safety of the camp. We'll only be going just outside the fence. Either myself or Sergeant Diaz will be keeping watch at all times while we're outside. If you see something, do not fire your weapon at it unless your life is in danger. Instead, let us know," Connor said.

"Yes, sir," the recruits said.

Connor bent over and opened the crate full of the CAR-74 semiautomatic hunting rifles and picked one up. "The compact design should fit comfortably in your hands and uses smart rounds for ammunition. There's a full automatic setting, but you will never go full automatic out in the field. The reason for this is that you would use up all your ammo inside a minute," Connor said.

He proceeded to show them the different features of the rifle, along with safety instructions. Each of the recruits picked up a weapon.

"Sir, I'm not able to turn off the safety setting," Deacon said.

"That's because I don't want you to shoot anyone yet. The only weapons cleared for use are the ones Sergeant Diaz and I are holding. When I authorize you to shoot, you'll be able to disengage the safety on your weapon," Connor said.

They marched to the gate and left the safety of the camp. Connor led them away from the gate and had six of them line up while Diaz kept an eye on the forest nearby. So far, the berwolfs hadn't seen fit to pay them a visit. Connor took a small case from his pack and opened it. Inside were six target drones, which he set to fifty yards away. The drones raced to the configured distance and hovered a foot off the ground. Above the drones, six holographic targets appeared.

"Cute," Poe said.

"Successfully hit the target and the drone will move farther away to a limit of five hundred yards. I will demonstrate," Connor said.

Connor knelt down on one knee and aimed his rifle. He fired one round and hit his target dead center. The drone moved back to seventy-five yards and Connor repeated the feat. Based on the ease with which Connor hit the target, the drone doubled the distance to a hundred and fifty yards. Connor lay down on the ground and used the legs at the end of the barrel to rest the weapon on. He quickly aimed the rifle and hit the center again. The target was hit two more times—once at three hundred yards and then again at five hundred.

Connor stood up. "Now it's your turn. First group, line up and fire from either a kneeling or ground position."

Nate Poe went to the first position, followed by Donna Marten. Randle and Compton came next, with Elyse Winters and Jo Ramirez next.

Poe and Marten quickly completed the exercise without missing a single shot. Connor expected nothing less from his two hunters. Deacon and Owens took the two open positions. Randle got stuck at three hundred yards but eventually made it to five hundred. Compton also performed the exercise without missing the target.

Deacon got stuck at a hundred and fifty yards and slammed his fist into the ground. "Sir, I believe there's something wrong with my rifle, sir," Deacon said.

Diaz went over and checked the weapon. He took one shot and hit the target. "The only problem here is that you can't shoot straight. Keep at it, Hot Rod."

Allison Blake dropped her rifle, and Connor was on her in seconds. "I won't have another member of this team get shot because you can't hold on to a damn hunting rifle. Fifty burpees now, recruit," Connor ordered.

Sean Quinn went over to her and began performing the burpees alongside her. Connor heard her whisper that she was sorry.

Connor turned his attention back to the others, and Amy Owens was trying to hit her target set at a hundred yards. She was joined by Jackson and Cooper. A few minutes later, Allison Blake returned to the line, and this time she held onto her weapon. She fired a shot at the target and completely missed. Connor lay down next to her and began giving her some guidance. After a few more tries she hit the target at fifty yards and let out a squeal of delight. The drone moved the target to seventy-five yards and Connor left her to it.

Connor had set a hundred-round limit, and Blake didn't make it past a hundred yards, but she was happy to make it that far. Connor knew she hadn't fired any type of firearm before. Sean Quinn was last to go. He lay down on the ground and aimed the CAR-74 hunting rifle as if he'd used one many times before. In five shots he also achieved the five-hundred-yard mark.

Connor stood behind him. "Excellent job, Recruit Bling. Are there any other hidden talents I should know about?"

"No, sir," Sean replied.

Connor had them line up again. "Not bad. For some of you, this was easy. Probably too easy. We'll be practicing each day and all of you will improve. The CAR-74 is a good introductory weapon. We'll only practice with it part of the time and only because it's standard issue for Field Operations. The likelihood of you encountering this weapon again is high, so you will know all its capabilities. Several of you will start on the M-Viper Sniper Rifle," Connor said.

This announcement brought several excited grins.

"When I call your name, I want you to line up next to me," Connor said.

"Yes, sir," the recruits said.

"Boone and Poe, obviously, and Grizzly," Connor said and made a show of surveying the rest. "Bling," he said.

Boone and Grizzly started clapping as the very surprised Sean Quinn joined the others.

"You're now my sharpshooters. You will train with me using the M-Viper and we'll focus on vantage points and other tactics unique to that kind of weapon. Rejoin the others," Connor said. After his sharpshooters got back in line, Connor continued. "Now that you're well rested, we're going to go for a nice run. From here on out you'll be armed everywhere you go. For today, it's going to be the CAR-74, and tomorrow it will be something different. Before we start our run, I'll open up the floor for a couple of questions," Connor said.

"Sir," Owens said. "What does CAR stand for in the CAR-74?"

"Good question. CAR stands for civilian assault rifle and the number is the series number," Connor said.

Deacon smiled and raised his hand. "Sir, is dinner soon? I'm starting to get hungry."

This brought more than a few laughs from the other recruits.

"Thanks for volunteering, Hot Rod," Connor said.

Deacon's face became pale. "Sir?"

"You've just volunteered for cleanup duty in our mess hall for the next two days. It comes with the added benefit of eating last," Connor said.

"Yes, sir," Deacon said.

"Recruits, be sure the safety on your rifles is on. Our run is going to be a little more scenic this time," Connor said.

He nodded to Diaz.

"Recruits, form two lines," Diaz ordered.

Connor took point. He had the surveillance drones in patrol mode, but there hadn't been enough time to allow the system to mature. Regardless, they were armed, and he and Diaz had already been to the area they were going to run to before they brought the recruits here. Connor set off at a slow pace down a rough trail that took them into the forest. As the forest thickened, shafts of sunlight poked through the canopy high above them. Connor glanced up and saw several creatures moving near the treetops. Their long arms were used to grasp thick vines and swing among the dizzying heights. Connor pulled up a drone feed on his internal heads-up display to get a closer look at them. The tree creatures looked to have thick skin that was a mix of grays to pale yellow stripes going to their elongated, three-fingered hands. Each finger looked as thick as his forearm. The lower half of the creatures' bodies split into two thick tails. Their ears ended in a point on either side of their reptilian faces. One of the creatures carried a smaller version of itself. The creature swung its young onto its back, where it held on, and then the group followed Connor and the recruits from the lofty heights of the treetops.

"We've got company," Randle said.

"Bull, put your gun down," Marten hissed at him.

"Won't they attack us?" Randle asked, clutching the weapon to his chest.

"No, they're just watching us," Marten said.

"Boone is right, you should listen to her," Connor said.

Randle lowered his gun and kept running. "Yes, sir."

"What are they called?" Deacon asked.

"They don't have a name, just a designation. TCL, for tree climber, large, and I can't remember the number associated with it. I do know they pretty much stay in the trees but can come onto the ground and use their split tails to move them around," Sean Quinn answered.

The tree climbers kept up with them.

"This is our new home. We need to learn to survive here. As part of our training, we'll be going outside the camp a lot, and eventually we'll be spending multiple nights away from camp," Connor said.

"Oh boy, I can't wait," Deacon said with mock enthusiasm.

"You'll be fine, Hot Rod. I'll protect you," Marten said.

"I always like a strong woman to keep me safe and warm," Deacon replied.

Several of the other recruits laughed. Connor used his implants to connect to a drone ahead of them that was located in an open plain similar to where they'd made their camp. After thirty minutes of navigating the rocky terrain of the forest path, they emerged onto a grassy field. The field led to a shallow valley, and Connor stopped running.

Ramirez gasped and pointed down into the valley. Two hundred yards away moved a herd of long-legged creatures that had thick, muscular bodies on top and were covered in shaggy brown hair.

"They've got to be twenty feet tall, maybe even taller," Ramirez said.

"Look how many of them there are," Blake said.

One of the creatures swung its head toward them. The short tentacles along its mouth gave it a bearded look. The creature blew out a blast of air and the call was taken on by the others.

"We don't want to get any closer," Sean warned. "They'll leave us alone if we don't bother them, but the alphas will defend the herd."

Another creature made a sound that reminded Connor of a deep horn blast. The herd perked up at this and started running away from them.

"Looks like we spooked them," Owens said.

Connor frowned and tried to see if there were any drones on the far side of the valley.

"They're not frightened of us," Marten said. She raised the scope of her rifle and peered across the valley.

Connor couldn't hear anything but the pounding legs of the giant creatures as they sped away.

"How fast can they run?" Randle asked.

"They can get up to a hundred and thirty kilometers an hour on an open field like this," Sean said.

"You know an awful lot about the creatures that live here," Randle said.

"Sergeant Diaz, we might have a planetary expert in our midst," Connor said.

A piercing scream echoed throughout the valley. Across from them, one of the long-legged creatures was pulled down by a group of spotted predators. They'd darted from the forest on the other side and sunk their claws into it. The predators looked as if they wore the pelt of a leopard that gave way to black skin and two sets of arms.

The long-legged beast had bleated a final cry before the spotted predators silenced it with harsh growls.

Connor looked at Sean. "Know what they are?"

Sean Quinn squinted his eyes and then shook his head.

"Boone?" Connor asked.

"No, sir, we haven't encountered those before," Donna Marten said.

"That's our cue to leave. Sergeant Diaz, take point," Connor said.

They quietly withdrew back into the forest. Connor was about to turn around and follow the others when he caught sight of a spotted predator that wasn't feasting on the fresh kill. It was facing him.

"Shit," Connor said.

He raised his rifle and looked at the creature through his scope, taking off the safety and silently pleading with it not to attack him. It had no element of surprise, and no ambush predator would run across a field to attack its prey when there was a fresh kill waiting to be eaten.

The predator's muscular chest heaved as it drew breath. It had a set of smaller arms, followed by a set of longer arms behind it. The shoulder joint for the second pair of arms angled forward, and Connor was willing to bet that it could use those arms to help it run faster—a lot faster than Connor could ever run, that was for sure. There was no doubt in Connor's mind that the predator was looking at him. There were thick protrusions from the creature's cheekbones, which ended in red, giving it the look of fresh blood from its latest kill. Connor shivered and slowly eased his way backward. He'd thought the berwolfs were the apex predator in this area, but he might have been wrong.

As soon as Connor was within the cover of the trees, he turned around and ran, eager to catch up with the others. He tasked a drone to follow that creature and kept the video feed on his internal heads-up display. It hadn't followed him, but it definitely noticed him. He didn't know if he was seeing the curiosity of encountering a new life form or whether that creature was judging how much of a threat Connor was. Either way, he didn't want to find out, especially since he was armed with only a civilian hunting rifle.

18

THAT EVENING they had their first hot meal and the recruits also got their first taste of free time to eat and shower, which they all took advantage of. The only one pressed for time was Henry Deacon, whose comments had landed him on cleanup duty.

They met again for further instruction, as well as information regarding the expectations Connor had for his Search and Rescue platoon. The class environment was more interactive since each recruit had professional experience in their chosen field that applied to what Connor was trying to accomplish with them. Nate Poe and Donna Marten had both been on security details, rotating through the research bases. They had an excellent working knowledge of the creatures and plants they should be careful of and things that weren't a threat. Much to Connor's surprise, Sean Quinn possessed a breadth of knowledge about the planet and its creatures. Admittedly, Connor had mistaken the sandy-haired youth for just another kid, but he'd proven to be intelligent. Given Sean's parents, Connor supposed he shouldn't have been too surprised.

Over the next few days their time was broken down to physical training followed immediately by weapons instruction that included hand-to-hand combat. They also hiked into the forest beyond the camp. There were no reports from the drones about the spotted predator they'd encountered in the valley, but Connor still stayed away from the valley just to be on the safe side until the recruits were more experienced with their weapons.

They'd built elevated platforms inside the camp, where they'd practiced rescue scenarios of extracting trapped victims. As they were completing their second round of PT one day, a small cargo ship flew over the horizon. The wings folded upward and the pilot landed the ship in the marked area of the camp.

The cargo doors opened, and Diaz had the recruits start offloading the containers. Connor approached the side hatch, where Noah Barker exited the ship, followed by Ashley Quinn. Her gaze narrowed when she saw him. Ashley glanced to the side and saw her son offloading the plane. Her gaze softened for a moment and then she turned to Connor.

"Noah explained what happened," Ashley said.

Connor nodded and glanced at Noah. He was carrying a backpack and glanced around the camp as if he were deciding whether he could get back on the ship.

"Welcome to Search and Rescue. You can stow your gear in the tent and then meet up with the rest of the recruits when we assemble," Connor said to him.

Noah, recognizing a dismissal when he heard one, left Connor alone with Ashley.

"Sergeant Diaz," Connor said, "can you send Recruit Bling here?"

Ashley frowned in confusion until she saw her son running toward them. Sean came to a stop and snapped a salute at Connor before standing at attention.

"At ease. Give your mother a hug," Connor said.

Ashley pulled her son into her arms, and Connor took a few

steps away to give them some privacy. He glanced over and Ashley was speaking in a stern tone to her son.

Connor caught snippets of the conversation. There were a few "crazies" and "your fathers" worked in.

"Connor, would you come here?" Ashley called.

Connor walked over and she had Sean give them a moment.

"How could you let this happen? This isn't what I want for my son," Ashley said.

"By the time I noticed he was here the ship had already gone back to headquarters. Training my recruits was more important at the time," Connor said and stepped closer. "Look, if he'd been hurt I would have called in a transport for him. He wants to be here. Believe me, I tried to dissuade him from training with us."

Ashley shook her head. "Yes, I'm quite aware of the level of training you're subjecting your recruits to."

Connor frowned. "What's that supposed to mean?"

"Come on, Connor, we've been keeping an eye on you. I'm not disputing your training methods. You have specific goals you're trying to achieve, and as an expert, I recognize that. But as a mother, it's tough to see. Why is Sean given double the punishment? Couldn't you take it easier on him?" Ashley asked.

"No. He locked himself in a storage crate to get away from special treatment. He did that to get away from the fact that you and Tobias are the head of the colony and Sean gets special treatment because of it. The fact that he handles everything I put him through is a clear indication of the man he wishes to become," Connor said.

"I think you underestimate how influential you can be. He's still a boy," Ashley said.

"He's almost eighteen. Old enough to be counted as an adult," Connor said.

Ashley scowled. "What do you know about—" she began to say but stopped herself from speaking.

"You were going to say: What do I know about being a parent? Not nearly as much as you. You know that," Connor said and squelched the pang of regret that threatened to rise up inside him. "But I know about training soldiers. Your son has what it takes."

"We didn't bring him here to become a soldier," Ashley said.

Connor sucked in a deep breath. Ashley's maternal instincts were in high gear, and this was an argument he couldn't win. He turned toward Sean and waved him over.

"Wait. I'm not finished speaking to you," Ashley said.

After nearly a week of being conditioned to follow orders, Sean Quinn was already coming toward them.

"Sean, your mother has made it quite clear that she doesn't want you here. Before you decide what you want to do, there's something I want to say to you," Connor said.

Sean glanced at his mother and then back at Connor. "Yes, sir?"

"You've recognized that you're at a crossroads in your life and that it's time to start forging your own path and have a say in what your life is to become, whether it's here or some other part of the colony. I have one question for you, and whatever you decide will not influence my opinion of you. Understand?" Connor asked.

"Yes, sir," Sean answered.

"Do you want to be known as the governor's son or Sean Quinn? Because the governor's son has no place on the Search and Rescue team, but Sean Quinn can earn a spot. Your actions over the past week have given you the right to try to be here in a more official capacity. That's all I wanted to say. I'll leave you to your mother and wait to hear your decision," Connor said.

Connor started to walk away, but before he could get too far, Sean called out to him.

"Commander, I'd like to stay, sir."

Connor glanced at Ashley. The chief of medicine was seething, but when her son looked at her, she smiled at him.

"I'll tell your father your decision. I don't have to tell you that he won't like it, but I'll share your reasons with him," Ashley said.

Sean's eyes lit up and he gave his mother a peck on the cheek.

"Be . . . careful," Ashley said quietly.

"I promise I'll look after him," Connor said.

"I'm sure you will. Would you mind walking me back to the ship? There's something I'd like to talk to you about," Ashley said.

"Of course," Connor said.

He followed Ashley back to the ship and she led him up the loading ramp beyond where the recruits were finishing offloading the ship. Once they were alone, Ashley spun around and punched Connor right in the stomach.

Connor doubled over, gasping for air. Ashley loomed over him with a satisfied smirk on her face as he straightened up.

"As a mother, you owed me that and you know it," Ashley said.

Connor sighed and nodded. "Alright, I'll give you that, but I meant what I said about your son."

"Oh, I know you believe it. Somehow Sean has come to idolize you. While I do think you're one of the good ones, you have a more dangerous side that I'd rather my son not emulate," Ashley said.

"This is supposed to be a place for fresh starts. I have a past that I won't apologize for. I'm here, and I'm doing the best I can to contribute to the colony."

"I know you are. That's the only reason I'm letting Sean stay here."

"Oh really? I don't think you'd be able to stop him. Not anymore."

The pilot stuck his head out of the cockpit. "Ma'am, we're ready to go."

"That's my cue to leave," Connor said.

"Oh, I do have an update for you. Noah will be here for the duration of the training. And I'm showing that you requested one of the Hellcats for training purposes?" Ashley asked.

"It's a troop carrier vessel that I know is on the Ark. We're Search and Rescue, and I want that to be one of our primary vehicles. We can rotate the ATVs as needed. Most of them know how to operate those anyway, but the Hellcat is different," Connor said.

"Who's cleared to fly it?" Ashley asked.

"Well I am, for one, and Juan Diaz for another. Unless you want to officially transfer a pilot to my group?" Connor asked.

"Nope, not yet. I'll see to it that you get your Hellcat, but it will take a few weeks," Ashley said.

"I appreciate the effort," Connor said.

Ashley narrowed her gaze in mock vehemence. "Don't try using that charm of yours on me. Now get out of here."

Connor laughed and wished her well. He exited the ship and cleared the area, waving to the pilot as he went. The pitch of the repulsor engines increased as more power was pumped into them and the ship rose into the air and sped away.

The recruits were moving the cargo crates over to their supply area.

"Commander," Diaz said.

"What is it, Sergeant?"

"Does this mean Recruit Bling is officially part of the Search and Rescue platoon, sir?"

The nearby recruits, including Sean Quinn, stopped so they could listen.

"Affirmative, Recruit Bling is part of Search and Rescue now," Connor confirmed.

Compton hooted loudly and gave Sean a healthy slap on the back. The sentiment was shared by the other recruits. Diaz walked over to Connor and barked for the recruits to get moving.

"So you're keeping the governor's son here," Diaz said. He spoke quietly so the others couldn't hear.

"He earned it. You know that," Connor said.

"I do, but some might read it as a political move," Diaz said.

"You mean my good friend, Damon Mills?"

"Among some others," Diaz said.

Connor pressed his lips together. "What are you saying? I shouldn't have let Sean stay?"

"No, I agree with you, and it wouldn't matter if I didn't. You'd just do as you please anyway. If something happens to that kid—he gets hurt or killed—then that will be on you," Diaz said.

"If something like that happens to any of them, it will be on me," Connor replied.

"True, but Tobias Quinn can be a dangerous enemy to have. I'm not speaking to you as a sergeant. I'm speaking to you as a friend. Just keep that in mind," Diaz said.

"Well, as your friend I appreciate it," Connor said. "I also doubt we'll get many delays in our equipment requests from here on out."

Diaz's eyes widened and he grinned. "You're a piece of work. And you say you don't play politics."

"I don't. I'm just using the cards I've been dealt," Connor said.

Later that day Connor went into the tent that served as his command center. Noah Barker was hard at work setting up additional systems and checking the ones that they'd put in place.

Noah turned around as Connor came inside. "Who set up this monitoring station? It's like they just jammed all the connections in. Whoever did it didn't know what the hell they were doing. I swear I spend more time going behind people, fixing their mistakes, whereas if they'd just let me do the install in the first place it would work perfectly. I bet it cuts out on you a bunch, doesn't it?" Noah said.

Connor glanced at Diaz, who had followed him inside the tent. The sergeant's stone-faced expression didn't reveal a thing. Only his eyes hinted at the barely contained mirth threatening to break free.

"Is anything broken?" Connor asked.

The monitoring station *had* been cutting out on them, but he hadn't been able to figure out why.

Noah stood up and rubbed his hands together. "Nothing I can't fix. So are you going to tell me?"

"What?" Connor asked.

Noah frowned. "Which of your recruits do I have to thank for botching up this install? They'll need to be trained to do it right."

Connor walked to the other side of the tent and looked away, feeling a flush creep across his face. "That won't be necessary."

"Why not? Look, I won't be that hard on them," Noah said.

Diaz started laughing, unable to contain himself any longer. "*He* put it together," Diaz said when he caught his breath.

Noah's eyes widened. "Oh, my God! I'm sorry—uh, I didn't mean all that. You know I was just being dramatic. It wasn't so bad."

"Just stop," Connor said. "It's not going to crush me that I can't install a monitoring station with the same skill as you. Just fix it so it stops cutting out on us."

"I'm almost done," Noah said.

He ducked behind the workstation and fiddled with the control panel, then came around and powered it on. This time there was no interference registering on the screen.

"Oh good, you've had the drones patrolling," Noah said.

"Yeah, and we stumbled onto a new type of predator. The drones have some footage to upload that I want sent back to the compound," Connor said.

Noah nodded. "They'll be able to upload their stored data now."

"That's good because we were only able to get live feeds from them and nothing prerecorded," Connor said.

"That's because you didn't connect the monitoring station to the storage array," Noah said.

Diaz started laughing again and spread his arms wide when Connor looked over at him.

"You've got to admit, it's pretty funny," Diaz said.

Connor chuckled. "I get it. Oh, and Noah, did you bring the other thing with you?"

Noah feigned ignorance. "I'm not sure what you mean."

"I told Diaz what you showed me—the data burst from the space buoy network," Connor said.

Noah glanced at Diaz and then back at Connor. "I did. You should know that after our little chat, Damon Mills paid me a visit asking about why our chat session was encrypted."

"What did you tell him?"

"I told him you wanted to test the secure communications features of the monitoring station," Noah said.

"Did he believe you?" Connor asked.

Noah shrugged. "I think so. He stopped asking me about it, but he started hanging around wherever I was working. It was enough for me to notice."

"Maybe Mills knows about the data burst somehow," Connor said.

Diaz nodded. "Probably. He and Franklin Mallory were among the first to be awakened on the Ark. They'd definitely be in the know."

"So do you have a full dump of the data burst?" Connor asked.

Noah shook his head. "Just the partial. With Mills hanging around, I didn't want to take a chance and go poking around at the Field Operations Headquarters. So I was thinking . . ."

"You want to work on this here," Connor said.

"It's remote and isolated," Noah replied.

"Show me what you have and then I'll decide," Connor said.

Noah reached into his pack and pulled out his tablet computer. He navigated through the interface and then flicked his hand toward the large holoscreen above the monitoring station.

"Here's the header that has the totally uplifting and non-scary reference to EOD-Extinction Critical Alpha," Noah said.

"EOD," Diaz repeated. "What the hell does that mean?"

Connor stared at the information on the screen. His brows pushed forward in concentration and he glanced at the others. "End of Days," he said.

Noah's face paled. "I've got a bad feeling about this."

"Are you sure the translation is right?" Diaz asked.

"Yes, this first part of the message was in the clear before the main data burst, which is why we're able to read it," Noah said.

"We shouldn't jump to conclusions," Connor said.

"Are you serious? A data burst from Earth that has the words 'extinction' and 'end of days,' and you don't want to jump to conclusions?" Noah asked.

"That's exactly what I'm saying. Something like this could spread like wildfire across the colony. We need to fully understand what's in that data before we decide what to do next," Connor said.

"So if it's bad, can I freak out then?" Noah asked only half-jokingly.

"We'll see. Where's the rest of it?"

"The main data burst has to be decoded. I thought of writing up my own decoder to do the job, but that could take a really long time. So I think I can access it from the Ark's computer system," Noah said.

"They'll detect it," Connor said.

"How do you know?" Noah asked.

"How do you *not* know? You think there won't be a digital trail if you try to access secure information?"

Noah thought about it for a moment. "Okay, I bet if I can just see the framework of the algorithm used to decode communications from the space buoy network, we should be able to see what the rest of the message says."

"Okay, but this is a part-time effort for you. You've missed a week's worth of training and you need to get caught up," Connor said.

Noah looked at both Connor and Diaz in alarm. "I thought I was just consulting with Search and Rescue," he said.

Connor smiled. "Keep telling yourself that. Welcome to the team. Now go put on a uniform like the rest of the recruits."

Noah's laugh became silent as he realized Connor was serious.

"Don't worry, we'll take good care of you," Diaz said.

Noah left the tent.

"This is some next-level stuff," Diaz said.

"Too soon to really know what it means," Connor said. The references did worry him, but it wasn't enough for him to drop everything he was doing and confront Tobias about it. "Whatever it means, it won't change what we're doing here. So let's get back to work."

19

OVER THE NEXT SIX WEEKS, Connor and Diaz trained the first class of Search and Rescue. Franklin Mallory, the Director of Field Operations and Security, visited the camp twice. Both visits had left the director impressed and eager to put them in the field. After Mallory's first visit, the recruits had become preoccupied with giving their camp an official name rather than some alpha-numeric designation. The name Camp Gates had been tossed around, but Connor put a stop to that quickly. The next name suggestion came from Blake, who called it Camp Mutt. Blake confessed that she was a dog lover, and as a field biologist as well as a medic, she championed to the idea that genetic diversity led to a superior species. Randle offered his services for providing genetic diversity when it came time to procreate for the sake of the colony. As far as Connor knew, no one had taken him up on his offer.

Connor checked the time and brought up the schedule for the day. He was in the command center working at his terminal. They had an active connection back to the compound, which he authorized the recruits to use at the end of the week so they could contact friends and family. After being completely isolated for six weeks, most recruits welcomed the opportunity. They'd earned it. Their initial training would be completed soon, and Connor already had his eye on at least two of them to lead squads of their own someday.

Noah walked into the tent. He had his travel bag all packed up and ready to go.

"I'm really sorry, sir," Noah said.

Connor glanced at him. "You'll be back."

"I'll just be gone for a few weeks. Dr. Bishop made a huge discovery at the forward operating research base and needs a technical consultant," Noah said.

"She found alien tech," Connor said.

"That's what the report said. She found more ruins built by the civilization that used to be here," Noah said.

"They died out. There are living people here who need us right now. Berwolf ambush attempts have been steadily escalating."

"I know. I see the same reports. They're at the compound and at some of the research bases," Noah said.

"Yeah, so why haven't you requested to take your weapon with you?" Connor asked.

Noah blinked for a while. "I didn't think it was allowed."

"You're field-weapons qualified now, and as long as you're officially a member of my team, you're part of Field Operations. You're authorized to carry your weapon with you. As far as I'm concerned, this is an extended field assignment," Connor said.

Noah smiled. "I didn't . . . Uh, thank you, sir."

Connor feigned sternness. "You'll have to complete survival week with the next class that comes through here."

The smile on Noah's face faltered. "You're joking, right?"

"Do I look like I'm joking?"

Noah swallowed hard and then recovered. "Looking forward to it, sir."

"It won't be as bad as you think it's going to be. By now, going out into the forest isn't the mystery it once was," Connor said.

"That first time you came through the gate while I was on patrol scared the crap out of me. I thought that new predator you found, the ryklars, had learned to open gates," Noah said.

"Haven't seen them in a while. According to the field biologist at the compound, they're predators that follow the herds, so it's likely they just migrate from place to place with the herds," Connor said.

"I've meant to ask why you've been going into the forest at night," Noah said. "I mean, beyond the training you make us do."

"One of the most useful things we can do to adjust to living here is to get to know the planet," Connor said.

Noah snorted. "As long as you're armed with an assault rifle and night vision, along with an additional reconnaissance drone, you're good to go."

"Those things certainly do help."

"So, this survival week you've got planned . . . What equipment are you allowing us to bring?" Noah asked.

Connor raised a brow. "You didn't really think I was going to give anything away. That's a need-to-know, which you don't."

Outside the tent, they heard the approach of a transport ship. The sound from the engines came closer, and Connor frowned.

"Sounds like they're coming in too fast," Connor said.

Noah's eyes widened.

"Lenora!" they both said at the same time.

Connor and Noah raced outside. The camp was larger than it had been when they'd first gotten there to accommodate their Hellcat troop carrier ship, and they'd had to extend the perimeter fence to allow for other drop ships to visit the camp. It was a tight fit for experienced pilots, which Dr. Lenora Bishop, Head of Archaeological Studies, definitely was not.

Connor opened a comlink to the approaching ship.

"Hello, Connor," Lenora said.

"Don't destroy my camp with a bad landing. If you're not comfortable landing here, put the ship down outside the fence and we'll escort you in," Connor said.

"Where's the fun in that?" Lenora said.

The transport ship circled the camp and then approached the landing zone.

Connor glanced at Noah. "Why doesn't she use a pilot?"

"They kept telling her they couldn't fly the ship where she wanted it to go, so she fired them," Noah said.

The transport ship started its descent over the painted white circle and started to drift toward the fence. Connor brought his hands up to his head and winced. That ship could tear a hole in the perimeter fence. At the last second, Lenora course corrected and set it down. Half the landing gear was outside the designated landing area.

Connor ran his palm over his face and blew out a breath. "Are you sure you want to go with her? It might be safer out in the forest. You could take your chances with the local predators."

Noah's face was already pale from watching Lenora's nearly catastrophic landing attempt. "I'll be right back," he said and hastened away.

Lenora stepped out the side door of the ship and her auburn hair surrounded her head like a mane of pure femininity. She saw him and waved. Connor walked over and nearly forgot how she almost just destroyed his camp. Her cupid's-bow lips lifted into a playful smirk as he got closer.

"You stuck the landing," Connor said.

"You should have seen the last one I did," Lenora said.

She glanced around the camp and saw that the recruits were doing various exercises. One group was rappelling down an elevated platform while the others were using the repulsor vests. Connor noted that Neal Compton was the victim being lowered in a harness from the fifty-foot-tall platform. Owens, Jackson, and Cooper were slowly lowering Compton's three-hundred-pound body.

"Things have really come along here," Lenora said.

"Yes they have, but this is the first time you've ever been here," Connor said.

"You caught me. I met with Ashley on one of the supply runs at the compound two weeks ago," Lenora said.

Connor arched an eyebrow. "You were looking for Noah," he said.

"You bet I was. I swear the little squirrel can hide with the best of them."

"I see," Connor said.

Lenora gave him a challenging look. "It's easy to say no on a vid, but get him in person . . ."

"And he melts. I get it," Connor said.

"You got it. This is really quite a setup you got here. You still haven't taken me up on that offer to come out and see the ruins we found," Lenora said.

She looked at him with those beautiful eyes of hers, and Connor almost found himself agreeing to go.

"I'd like to, but we've got something big planned for them this week," Connor said.

"I bet they wouldn't mind if you gave them the week off," Lenora said. Cupping her hands around her mouth, she shouted, "Do you guys want a week's vacation?"

Connor's mouth hung open as he heard Ramirez shout to the others about getting time off.

Lenora laughed.

"You're unbelievable! I can't believe you just did that," Connor said and snorted.

Lenora patted him on the arm. "Live a little, will you?"

Connor chuckled. "I will. When things calm down here, I'll come out to your base and see what all the fuss is about."

Lenora held him in her gaze. "I'll hold you to that."

Connor had little doubt that she would. "Since you're here, have there been any increased sightings of the local predators? We've seen reports of heightened berwolf activity around the compound and some of the research bases."

"I saw that, but there's been no berwolf activity out by us. We've seen the new species that you spotted—the ryklars, four arms and two legs. Looks mean as hell. Leopard spots on its back," Lenora said.

"Have they attacked anyone?"

Lenora shook her head. "No, they just make their presence known. I've only seen them at a distance. Rogers has seen them much closer, like across-this-camp kind of close. He kept saying that the creature seemed more intelligent than he thought it should be."

Connor nodded. "I know what he means. Be careful. I know they're smaller than the berwolfs, but I think they're more dangerous."

Lenora smiled and leaned in as if she wanted to whisper something, so Connor met her halfway and she gave him a kiss on the cheek.

"That's for being sweet," Lenora said.

Connor felt his cheeks redden. He couldn't get a bead on this woman. One moment she acted like one of the guys and the next . . . He didn't know what to think.

"It's about time. I haven't got all day," Lenora said, looking past Connor.

"I had to get my stuff," Noah replied. "I can't do an analysis of the alien tech you found without my equipment."

"Great, and now you're armed too," Lenora said.

Noah carried his AR-71 rifle along with his utility bag in his other hand.

"I see all this physical training suits you. Got some muscles now," Lenora said.

Noah smiled, made a show of flexing his biceps, and climbed into the ship.

Lenora turned back to Connor. "It seems like the moment I get to talk to you I have to leave a few minutes later. I'll take care of Noah for you. He's one of the good ones, and I like to make sure he's doing okay."

"He's lucky to have you looking out for him," Connor said.

Noah was alone in the colony—one of the colonists from the Ark program who didn't come with any family or significant others. Noah had explained that his family sacrificed a lot to get him qualified to even come on the Ark. Connor was positive that Noah's aptitude and high intelligence had determined his candidacy for the Ark program rather than the lottery randomly awarding him a spot.

"I'll see you around, and don't forget about that invitation," Lenora said.

She headed back to the ship and waved over at Diaz, who was on his way over to Connor.

Connor glanced at Diaz. "We should probably back up. I don't know if her takeoffs are any better than her landings."

They backed up, and the transport ship's engines burst to life. The ship rose steadily into the air and Connor could see Lenora and Noah sitting in the cockpit. He waved, and the ship sped away.

Diaz snapped his fingers in front of Connor's face. "Snap out of it. We've got work to do. I mean, I know she's a rare beauty, that one, but come on. Focus, sir."

"Stop," Connor said. "It's really not like that."

Diaz gave him a pointed look. "You mean to tell me you couldn't tell she was flirting with you?"

Connor frowned. "Give me a break. She's just being friendly."

"Well, she can be friendly like that with me anytime then, or with half the guys here or anywhere else," Diaz said.

Connor glanced at Diaz with a disapproving frown.

"Yes, sir, I'm Connor Gates. I can't afford any personal attachments," Diaz said.

Connor shook his head. "Let's get back to work."

"We got a minute. Let's explore this a bit," Diaz pressed.

"There's nothing to explore, and there's nothing going on with Lenora," Connor insisted.

Diaz nodded. "Lenora, you say. You mean Dr. Bishop? The world-class archaeologist? What's the problem? I'm not telling you to get married, but you know . . ." he said and shrugged.

"It's not appropriate," Connor said.

"What's not appropriate? You're a man. She's a woman. You're natures' designated mating pair."

"It's not that simple. I've left—"

"People behind. We all did, and you told me you hadn't spoken to your wife in over five years. You said there was always another mission," Diaz said.

Connor glared at him, losing his patience. "Are you done?"

Diaz smoothed his features, feigning disinterest. "I'm done. Let's get back to work."

Connor glanced in the direction the ship had gone and spied a creature beyond the fence near the forest line. He stopped moving and peered in that direction, trying to decide whether it was just a trick of the light or something else. The forest line was a mass of overgrowth, with thorny vines and large leaves, but mixed in with all the foliage were the thick, bloody red protrusions on the elongated head of a ryklar. Within the thick, muscular folds were dark slits for the creature's eyes.

"Diaz, follow my line of sight toward those trees over there beyond the fence. About seven feet off the ground mixed in with that thorny mess. Do you see anything?" Connor asked.

Diaz peered in the direction. "I don't see anything, but I haven't got eyes like yours."

Connor used his implants to recall the nearest drone and sent it toward the target location. "I think it's a ryklar, but I only see one of them."

He headed toward the fencing and Diaz walked beside him. Connor heard the drone zooming over the camp and looked back to the creature, but it was gone, so he brought up the drone's feeds on his internal heads-up display and set it to pursue. The drone plunged into the forest, and Connor had a bird's-eye view of the ground. He saw the swaying of plants that marked the creature's passing and he had the drone move forward around the corner of a large tree, but there was nothing there. He engaged the drone's other cameras, giving him a three-hundred-sixty-degree visual of the area, but there was nothing there. Switching the view to infrared, he looked for a heat signature.

"Did you find it?" Diaz said.

Connor shook his head and released his control of the drone, setting it on patrol mode. "No. Let's grab some gear and go check it out."

"Are you sure? We have to debrief the recruits in fifteen minutes," Diaz said.

"I just want to go out into that area and see if there are any tracks," Connor said.

Connor went over to their armor depot and retrieved his AR-71. Donna Marten caught sight of them and jogged over. She was already carrying her weapon.

"Need some help, sir?" Marten asked.

Connor waved her over and they headed toward the gate. "Yeah, I thought I saw a ryklar across the way over there. I just want to see if there are any tracks."

Nate Poe and the other recruits saw them leaving and raced over to them, wondering what was happening.

"We're just going to check something out. Poe, why don't you and Bling get up on the observation platform with your Vipers. The rest of you man the gates," Connor said.

The recruits deployed, following his orders without question. Sean Quinn and Nate Poe retrieved their M-Viper sniper rifles and were climbing the observation platform soon after Connor and the others left the gate.

Connor focused on the way ahead of them while Diaz and Marten divided their attention between the sides and the front. As Connor closed in on the area, he wondered how the creature would have been able to climb up the dense thorny mess just to take a look at them.

Connor made a circling gesture, and they moved around the thicket. The drones hadn't detected anything and there didn't seem to be anything around. They went a short distance beyond the tree line, and Connor looked on the ground for some evidence of clawed footprints.

"Sir, I think I found something," Marten said.

Connor turned around and headed toward Marten, who was looking at the area behind the thicket. She squatted down and gestured toward a shallow slash in the soft ground. It was just a single slash, with only the shallow impressions of two prongs from the creature's other foot.

"I don't get it. Why is there only one track?" Diaz asked.

"Because this is where it could have leaped down from up there," Marten said and gestured toward the overgrowth that Connor could now see covered the remnant of a log. "It wouldn't be all that comfortable, but it would give a nice view into our camp while providing excellent coverage."

Connor glanced at the area where the creature had been and then down at the shallow track, trying to determine where it had gone and why there were no other tracks. The recent rainfall had the plants swelling with water, so there would be nothing broken to mark the creature's passing.

"Could you track it?" Connor asked.

Marten stood up and took an appraising look around. "I could search the area for more tracks and maybe I could track it then."

Connor nodded, considering.

"What do you want to do, sir?" Diaz asked.

"Let's go back. If the drones pick it up, we'll investigate," Connor said.

They headed back to camp, Connor deep in contemplation. Since ryklars were ambush hunters, why would a single one come near the camp? A scout perhaps, but even scouts didn't venture far from the pack. Maybe he hadn't seen what he thought he had after all.

They reentered the camp, and Diaz announced it had been a false alarm. Poe and Sean hadn't seen anything from the observation platform. As the recruits gathered in the assembly area for debriefing and classroom instruction, Connor and Diaz moved to the front.

Connor took a moment to look at all of them, and his eyes lingered on Blake, a.k.a. Babyface. She now carried herself with a sense of confidence that he'd only seen her exhibit when doing medical examinations before, and he saw the same confidence gleaming from the other recruits. At this point in their training, they had a better idea of their capabilities and knew where their weaknesses were.

"Welcome to the final week of training. You've all worked very hard and have come a long way from where you were just six short weeks ago," Connor said.

There were several chuckles from them and Connor knew that none of them had thought any part of their training had been short or easy. They'd taken the brunt of breaking in a new training program, and they were the first class of what he hoped would be many. And as with many of life's circumstances, the first was always most memorable.

"This final week is a make-or-break moment for you, a culmination of all you've learned. To prove that you've mastered what's required of you and that you can function as effective teams, you'll be divided into two groups and flown out to two remote locations. You'll need to work your way to a different location for extraction, and you'll have four days to complete this exercise," Connor said.

Amy Owens raised her hand. "Why four days, sir?"

"If you can survive out there for four days, there's no reason to believe you couldn't survive together for longer periods of time. Other climates may require different skill sets, but the basics are the same—water, shelter, food. Those are priorities. You'll be required to function as a team and use the skills you've learned here, putting them to practical application. Let me be clear on one thing. You either pass this exercise as a group or you fail it as a group. This survival training exercise is not a graded exercise. It's strictly pass or fail and is required to earn your badges," Connor said.

Ramirez raised his hand.

"Go ahead, Bones."

"What happens if we fail, sir?" Ramirez asked.

Connor fixed them all with a hard stare. "Then you would have failed basic Search and Rescue training."

Ramirez swallowed hard. "Sir—"

"One second, Bones—and this is for the rest of you as well—Sergeant Diaz and I will be monitoring your progress, and if you fail to reach your objective, your performance will be evaluated as a group," Connor said.

There were no other questions, so Connor continued. "You'll also be required to locate several victims in your area. Somewhere between your drop-off point and the extraction point, you'll receive a distress call and you'll investigate. Could be more than one. You'll need to determine how best to proceed," Connor said and gave them a knowing smile, something the recruits had come to dread. "The purpose of this is to give you a taste of what we'll be called upon to do. Sergeant Diaz and I have reviewed the records for rescues that Field Operations has on file. They range from minor injuries to vehicle breakdowns, people getting lost, and serious injury. It will be up to you and your team leader as to how best to deal with it. I've selected two team leaders for this exercise, but before I tell you who they are, I want to make a few more points. One, any one of you may be called upon to step into the role of team leader. Two, this isn't a popularity contest. And three, you will respect the chain of command. For the purposes of this exercise, the team leaders have operational authority. Is that understood?"

"Yes, sir," the recruits replied in unison.

"Okay, since Noah had to leave, the teams will be split evenly. Team Alpha will be the following: Owens, Winters, Deacon, Poe, Jackson, and Compton. Your team leader will be Winters," Connor said.

Those recruits glanced at each other and gave an acknowledging nod.

"Team Bravo will be the following: Ramirez, Allison, Marten, Cooper, Randle, and Quinn. Your team leader will be Randle," Connor said and gave them a moment. "You're all aware of the dangers waiting for you out on the frontier, and this entire planet is the frontier. I expect daily reports to be sent back to camp from the team leaders."

Randle raised his hand. The big man appeared extremely uncomfortable. "Sir, what do we do with the victims we find?"

"What do you think, recruit?" Diaz said. "We're Search and Rescue. Treat this exercise as a live simulation."

Randle shook his head and quickly apologized.

"As I said before, Sergeant Diaz and I will be observing your progress and will not be far. We'll also function as COMCENT for this exercise. The team that finishes first gets the honor of setting the camp record," Connor said.

Winters narrowed her gaze. "Will you be out in the field with us, sir?"

"Perhaps, recruit," Connor said. "The official kickoff for this exercise is at oh six hundred. Dismissed."

The recruits stood up and snapped a salute. The remainder of the day was spent with the recruits gathering the equipment they'd need for deployment. Connor shared a knowing look with Diaz. They'd spent much of the last six weeks doing everything in their power to keep the recruits on their toes, and this would be no different.

When Connor noticed Sean Quinn watching him, the recruit went inside his tent to get some rack time.

20

Connor met Diaz outside the command center at oh one hundred hours. They wore full combat gear and green camouflage uniforms.

"Almost go time," Connor said.

"If they thought we were going to let them have a full night's sleep, we may not have done our jobs," Diaz said.

"I think some of them suspect something," Connor said and glanced toward the observation tower where Randle and Jackson were on watch.

Connor and Diaz received an updated ETA for the two transport ships coming from the compound.

"They're twenty minutes out," Diaz said and gave Connor a sidelong look. "You're looking forward to this, aren't you?"

Connor nodded enthusiastically. "This is the fun part—deployment out in the field, where we can observe them and put a few obstacles in their way. I ran a check on the distress beacons and they're all ready."

"Then it's time to sound the alarm," Diaz said with a hearty laugh.

Klaxon alarms blared and the exterior lights for the camp came on simultaneously. Connor and Diaz went into the recruits' tents, yelling for them to wake up.

A few minutes later the recruits were lined up in full combat gear with their weapons ready for inspection. Connor and Diaz walked among them, checking that their equipment was ready. None of them failed the inspection, and they shouldn't because Connor had drilled them for this.

"In the next few minutes, troop carrier ships will be here to take you away and this exercise will officially have begun. The mission for Team Alpha: An expedition exploring mineral deposits has become overdue, and their last known position will be transmitted to your PDA. Your job is to sweep the area and look for any survivors. Time is of the essence since we've already received two distress beacons," Connor said, transferring the mission brief to Elyse Winters.

"Sir, I've received mission details," Winters acknowledged.

"Fall out, Team Alpha. Your ride is here. Make us proud," Connor said.

Winters led her team over to the landing area, where a troop transport was coming in for a landing. Diaz followed at a short distance behind to observe.

"Team Bravo: A downed survey ship is reported in zeta quadrant. There were four members of the survey team on that ship. Your job is to find out what happened to them," Connor said and transferred the mission brief to Wayne Randle.

"Sir, I've received mission details," Randle said and read the information on his PDA.

The second troop carrier ship was approaching the landing area, and Randle called for his team to head over to the landing zone.

Sean Quinn lagged behind for a moment. "Sir, are you coming with us?" he asked.

"You're focusing on the wrong thing, recruit. You have a job to do. Now go do it," Connor replied.

Sean Quinn sprinted over to the rest of Team Bravo and Connor walked over. He watched as Randle ordered his group to double-check their equipment, particularly their ammunition, food and water rations, and their medical supplies. He assigned individuals specific jobs. Randle looked at Sean Quinn's equipment and noted that he had the M-Viper with him.

"There's no need for two people on the team to have that rifle for this mission. Go get the AR-71 and put a scope on it. You can multipurpose with that setup, alright, Bling?" Randle said.

Sean Quinn saluted the Team Bravo leader and ran off to exchange his weapon. Connor made a note on his tablet computer regarding Randle's forethought into how his team was equipped before embarking on the four-day mission. It played to the recruits' strengths.

Connor headed over to Diaz. Team Alpha was climbing aboard the troop carrier. Winters stood at attention and saluted Connor, then followed her team into the ship.

"Everything checks out for Team Alpha, sir," Diaz said.

Connor nodded. "Good. I expect Winters will do a good job leading them."

"That she will," Diaz said and frowned.

"You have doubts?" Connor asked.

Diaz shook his head quickly. "No, I have no doubts about what any of the recruits can do. It's just that . . ."

Connor smiled. Diaz had never trained a platoon before. "I see. We train them and teach them as best we can. Now it's up to them to put it to use."

"I'd be lying if I said I didn't want to be out there with them."

"Me too. Soon. This is for them to prove themselves, and there will come a time when neither you nor I will be there for them to lean on," Connor said.

The first troop carrier ship rose into the air and headed off into the northeast. The second ship took off soon after that, heading in a different direction. The sounds of the engines faded and all was quiet but for the nightly hum of New Earth. Connor glanced over at the Hellcat. Their gear was already on board, but they wouldn't be flying out just yet. He and Diaz would be monitoring the two teams from the command center for a time and then head out after that. None of the recruits knew for sure whether Connor or Diaz would be out in the field with them, but Connor suspected they knew there'd be a good chance they would be.

They walked back to the command center and Connor brought up a map on the main holoscreen, then launched a secondary window to run a check through the automated protocols Noah had set up for him. He'd dispatched a trio of drones to monitor the two quadrants where his recruits would be. As part of the standard deployment, Connor had equipped both teams with a drone of their own to use as they saw fit, but the tactical drones the teams were using were smaller and didn't have the range that Connor's patrol drones had.

Diaz poured them both a cup of coffee that they drank while watching the progress the two troop carriers made as they approached their destinations. Connor uploaded a report back to Field Operations so the monitoring division was aware that the scheduled training mission had begun. They monitored each of the troop carrier's comlinks, and Team Alpha had just reached their drop-off location. The drop feed showed each of the recruits' heat signatures on the ground. Their names appeared on screen as their locators transmitted their position to the GPS satellites in orbit. Winters had Compton and Jackson on point, and Connor brought up the output from Winter's PDA. She already had the location of the expedition marked on their map, and a few minutes later they started heading toward it. The second distress beacon call was also designated in the vicinity of the last known location of the expedition.

"There they go," Diaz said.

"We've run enough nighttime exercises for them to function in those conditions," Connor said.

Team Bravo reached their location at the edge of a canyon. They would need to find a way into the canyon to reach the survey ship.

"I wonder how long it will take Randle to find a path down into the canyon at night," Diaz said.

"If it were me, I'd check in with Command Central for a survey map of the area, and if I didn't have that, I'd split into two groups to scout for a way down into the canyon," Connor said.

A few minutes later Randle called in, asking for a topographical map of the quadrant he was in, and Connor transferred the information back to them. There was more than one way to achieve the objective, but time was always of the essence.

The hours went by quickly as they monitored each team's steady progress. They moved quicker once it was daytime. Team Bravo would reach their first victim soon. As part of the exercise, Connor and Diaz had built in tripwires that would create different situations, depending on when the teams reached them. The distress beacon that Team Alpha was moving toward went offline. They quickened their pace, and Winters sent an update back to them.

"Almost time for us to take this show on the road," Diaz said. Working from his own holoscreen, he frowned. "What the hell is that?"

Connor glanced over but didn't see anything on the screen. "Play back the drone feed from thirty seconds ago."

Several hundred meters away, the infrared spectrum of the feed revealed several creatures following the recruits on Team

Bravo. Then they disappeared, as if the creatures were suddenly cloaked in a shroud of cold that prevented them from being detected.

They had the drone focus in on the area but couldn't find anything.

"I'm not sure what they were. Could be they've got something following them," Diaz said.

"We can do a flyover with the Hellcat once they call in a pickup for the first victim," Connor said.

"Is that the broken leg?"

"That's the one," Connor said.

A few minutes later, Randle called in to Command Central for a pickup. They'd found the first person from the survey ship.

"Where are the other survivors?" Connor asked.

"The victim has lost consciousness due to the pain of his injuries and is not responsive, sir," Randle replied.

"Understood. Hellcat is being deployed and will be at your position within the next thirty minutes," Connor said.

They set the camp systems to follow passive protocols, including the fence remaining electrified to deter any curious creatures, and left the command center. Connor and Diaz walked over to the Hellcat troop carrier that had been assigned to Search and Rescue. Connor used his implants to send his authorization, and the side entrance door opened. He climbed aboard and headed to the cockpit. The Hellcat's systems came online, and he established a connection to the camp's computer system. All data feeds would funnel through there. Diaz joined him in the cockpit and sat down in the copilot's seat.

Diaz checked the ship's systems. "All systems ready."

Connor engaged the engines and the Hellcat rose into the air. His heads-up display showed Team Bravo's location through the retrieval beacon they'd set up. Connor punched the coordinates into the navigation system and pushed the throttle. Their velocity took Diaz by surprise.

"A little warning would have been nice," Diaz said.

Connor had spiked the velocity, which caused a delay in compensation by the inertia dampeners. He'd been expecting it, so he was ready when the brief gravitational forces pressed him into the seat. Diaz wasn't.

"This is payback for all those comments about Lenora, isn't it?" Diaz said.

"I don't know what you're talking about. We have an unconscious victim who requires medical attention, so I maximized the speed," Connor replied innocently.

Diaz snorted. "Right," he said, sounding unconvinced.

The Hellcat sped across the skies, and fifteen minutes later they were closing in on Team Bravo's position. Randle waved at them. The Hellcat was a highly maneuverable carrier ship that could navigate the small spaces inside the canyon if required, but Team Bravo had harnessed the victim and brought him up to the top of the canyon to expedite the rescue operation. Connor set the Hellcat down and opened the rear doors. He and Diaz raced to the back of the ship. Recruit Blake was there, along with Ramirez and Quinn. They carried the ballistics-gel form of a one-hundred-and-eighty-pound man.

"Sir, the victim's injuries were sustained from a fall while climbing down the canyon wall. Bruising and basic med scans indicate several bone fractures on the victim's right leg, including the femur. There is no evidence of internal bleeding, but the victim should be put into a medical capsule immediately and treated by the doctors at the main compound," Blake said.

Diaz had a stretcher ready to go, and Ramirez and Quinn helped transfer the victim onto it.

"Confirmed transfer of the victim. We'll get him the help he needs. Was he alone?" Connor asked.

"Sir, we believe the victim was going for help when the accident occurred. No distress beacons have been detected, but we've found evidence of the trail the victim was following. We intend to follow it and hopefully find the other members of the survey team," Randle said.

"Understood. We'll update Command Central with the status and alert the hospital at the main compound," Connor replied.

He and Diaz were playing the part of the emergency response team. Randle left the Hellcat and joined the rest of his team that was following Marten, who'd found the victim's trail.

He and Diaz secured the victim and updated Team Bravo's performance ratings for the exercise.

"They did a good job," Diaz said when they were back in the cockpit.

Connor lifted off. "They did everything by the book. The next one won't be so easy."

Some of the victims had timers counting down, and the more time it took the rescue team to find them, the worse their injuries would become until the victim eventually died. As with any search and rescue operation, they were always running against the clock. Team Bravo had handled themselves professionally and stuck to established protocols. Connor couldn't be prouder of them.

"Let's do a sweep of the area," Connor said.

Diaz cleared the view on the heads-up display, and the onboard cameras piped in a live video feed. In a few moments, they were over where Diaz had spotted the creatures that might have been stalking Team Bravo.

"I got nothing," Diaz said. He cycled the feeds through several visual spectrums, and while there were some forms of wildlife, they weren't what they'd seen before.

"Maybe whatever it was has moved on," Connor said.

He glanced at one of the feeds and saw a herd of landrunners moving south. Their long legs propelled them at great speeds that people could only match using machines.

"Sean says they can maintain that speed all day," Diaz said.

Connor nodded. The landrunner herds hadn't gone anywhere near the main compound, which was why it was such a shock for Connor when he'd first encountered them while scouting for an area to establish the training camp.

"Let's see what Team Alpha's doing," Connor said and brought up the map.

"She split the team. I was wondering how she'd handle the second beacon," Diaz said.

Elyse Winters had split her six-person team into two groups of three. Preferring not to waste fuel, Connor set the Hellcat down while they watched Team Alpha's progress. The first group closed in on the distress beacon and later reported that they'd found a colonist who'd gotten separated from the expedition and was now traveling with the team.

"They found the hologram of the lost colonist," Connor said.

The small team was now working their way toward Winters and the others. Winters opened a comlink to Command Central.

"This is COMCENT. Go ahead, Team Alpha," Connor said.

"Winters reporting in. We've located the second distress beacon, but there are no colonists nearby. We'll continue to do a sweep of the area and look for signs of where they may have gone. We've found berwolf tracks near the beacon and suspect the colonist left the area to take refuge on higher ground."

"Acknowledged, Team Alpha. Proceed with caution," Connor replied.

He closed the connection.

"I thought the tracks were a nice touch," Diaz said.

A warning of inclement weather broadcasted from the main compound.

"Looks like we're gonna get some storms moving through the

area," Connor said. He brought up the weather feed, which showed projections for high winds and thunderstorms.

Diaz peered at the feed. "They might have to hunker down until it passes."

Connor forwarded the weather alert to the two teams, along with the standard recommendation for taking shelter. Over the next hour, the skies became dark with storm clouds and distant thunder boomed across the sky. If the wind got bad enough, he'd have to send the patrol drones to a safe area until the storm passed. The storm system moving in looked like it was going to be around for a few hours, and with the onset of nightfall, both teams would be searching in the dark. Team Bravo had found an overhang under which to weather the storm, but Team Alpha was still moving.

"She should have found shelter by now," Diaz said.

"She's determined to find the rest of the expedition," Connor said.

"Yeah, but they're in a flood plain, and if there are flash floods, this could become a real rescue mission," Diaz said.

The drone feed showed Team Alpha navigating across a rocky terrain, angling upward. Connor had the drone pan the camera up and saw a cave.

"Shit," Connor said in surprise. He'd been so distracted by the storm that he hadn't paid attention to where Team Alpha was.

"Is that the entrance to the cave where you put the rest of the expedition?" Diaz asked.

"Yeah, but Winters found a faster way to it. We assumed she'd follow the path over it and have to rappel down to the entrance once they'd found it," Connor said.

That was the original plan. Winters must have done her own area surveys and narrowed down the potential locations the expedition would have used for shelter.

The storm blew in and lasted for most of the night. Both

teams had checked in, and Winters reported the successful rescue of the expedition that had become lost while scouting for potential mineral deposits. The members of the expedition suffered from dehydration and exposure because they didn't have their survival packs with them. Winters completed the rescue simulation and, in actuality, retrieved the holograms Connor had placed in the cave.

"Winters is doing a great job. She could lead her own team," Diaz said.

They were standing outside the cockpit, stretching their legs and taking advantage of the downtime to rest while the storm blew through the area. Diaz's snoring had echoed from the cargo area most of the night. Connor only needed a few hours' sleep, so he'd spent the time monitoring the teams and writing up his own evaluation of their simulated survival mission mixed with a search and rescue exercise.

"She's doing well. I reviewed the drones I had assigned to Team Alpha and saw that she took a gamble by leading the team through a ravine to reach that cave. In this case, it paid off, but that may not work the next time," Connor said.

"Maybe. She made a decision and took a risk based on the information she had. What would you have done differently?" Diaz asked.

"I would have stayed with the high ground as long as I could before committing to going to the cave. We'll need to account for that when we train the next group," Connor said.

Diaz rolled his shoulders and cracked his neck. The sound of it sent a shudder through Connor. He couldn't even stand the sound of someone cracking their knuckles.

"Think there'll be another group?" Diaz asked.

"You bet. This class is good. Most of them came to us with *some* training, with the obvious exception, but even Sean Quinn has shown a level of commitment I hadn't expected," Connor said.

"That kid looks up to you. I think you're the first person to really challenge him," Diaz said.

They had a quick breakfast of some tasty field rations, and Diaz grumbled about the lack of coffee. They'd returned to the Hellcat's cockpit when a comlink from Team Bravo reached them.

"This is COMCENT. Go ahead," Connor said.

"This is Team Bravo. We've found the survey ship and three remaining members of the survey team—one survivor and two casualties," Randle said.

"Confirm one survivor and two casualties. What was the cause of death for the two casualties?" Connor asked.

"One person died from injuries sustained during an emergency landing. The second person survived the emergency landing but bled out from her injuries after eighteen hours," Randle said.

Connor heard the bitter tone of failure in Randle's voice. This was a hard lesson for them to learn. Had the storm not come in, they might have saved the second person. This was one of the reasons Connor used adaptive simulations so the outcomes would change as the exercise progressed.

"Understood, Team Bravo. Rescue simulation complete. Updated mission parameters being transmitted to you now. You have forty-eight hours to reach the extraction point," Connor said.

There was a long pause and Connor knew Randle was blaming himself, but Connor knew better than to break protocol. Team Bravo hadn't failed this exercise. How Randle handled himself would be a clear indication of what kind of soldier he'd be. The same went for the rest of the team.

"Acknowledged. Received updated coordinates. Team Bravo, out," Randle said.

The comlink closed. Connor had decided last night to change the extraction point for each team and had more updates for them as they closed in on their destinations.

"Sir, are we asking too much from the recruits with all these changes?" Diaz asked.

"They need to be challenged and be able to deal with unanticipated events. If we just gave them a set of coordinates and said get there at a predetermined time, that might challenge them, but I'm aiming to keep them off balance. They need to be able to adapt," Connor said.

He glanced at one of the video feeds that showed the area ahead of the ship. A shadow passed beyond the view of the camera, and Connor adjusted it. They were in a small clearing surrounded by forest. Grassy plains stretched out before them until the forest started back up again. Connor brought the video feed to the main holoscreen.

"What is it?" Diaz asked.

"I thought I saw something—" Connor began and stopped.

Ahead of them Connor saw the spotted back of a ryklar standing up and glancing toward their ship. If it hadn't moved, he might have missed it. The red-colored protrusions around the creature's mouth made it look as if it had recently killed something.

"Crap! Where'd that thing come from?" Diaz said.

"There've got to be more of them," Connor said.

"What's it doing just standing there?" Diaz said and blew out a breath. "That thing is creepy."

The ryklar's muscular chest heaved and it backed up toward the forest.

"I think it wanted to be seen," Connor said.

"Seriously? What the hell for?"

"I bet it wants us to follow it," Connor said.

Diaz's eyes widened. He accessed the video feed interface, and a row of feeds appeared, showing the area surrounding the ship.

"I wonder . . ." Connor said.

"Please tell me you're not going out there," Diaz said.

Connor shook his head. "No, but let's see if it responds."

Connor activated the searchlight on the nose of the ship. He powered it off and on three times before leaving it off. The ryklar jumped back, startled by the light. Then the creature let out a shrill scream and charged forward a few steps before pounding its clawed fists on the ground.

"I think you just made it angry," Diaz said.

"Nah, I think it's just trying to prove it's not afraid of us," Connor said.

Diaz looked at the sub-screens below the main holoscreen and gasped. "They're all around us."

Ryklars stood up, revealing themselves. There were at least ten of them. Connor frowned and brought up the different sensor spectrums. He stopped on infrared and detected the body heat from the creatures. Their dark red figures stood in sharp contrast to the surrounding area. Then, one by one, they disappeared. The ryklars hadn't moved. It was as if they'd stopped producing body heat.

"Where the hell did they go?" Diaz asked.

Connor's hand brought up a secondary interface. "I think they're still there," he said and brought up the sonic wave detector. The ship's computers quickly analyzed the ambient sounds and Connor applied the filter to detect the rhythmic sounds of breathing. The holodisplay background changed to a pale blue screen and showed faint outlines of anything that made noise. Dark outlines of the ryklars showed up again.

"How'd you do that?" Diaz asked.

"Sonic detectors show the sources of any noises in the area, and I applied a filter to focus in on a creature's breathing," Connor said.

Diaz's mouth hung open. "I didn't know it could be fine-tuned like that."

"Most combat suits trap body heat to reduce the risk of being detected, so we had to rely on sound to find out where our enemies were hiding," Connor said.

Diaz nodded. "One day you're going to have to tell me more about your old unit."

Connor snorted and then his stomach clenched. If the ryklars were here, there could be more of them in the area. Diaz must have had the same thought.

"We have to warn them," Diaz said.

Connor made a swiping motion with his hand, and the video feeds all minimized to the lower right corner of the main holoscreen. He brought up the drone feeds, and two of his six drones were offline. Connor maximized the limited sonic abilities of the drones.

There was a loud bang on the side of the ship, followed by more on top. The local video feeds show the ryklars trying to get inside. One of the creatures slammed its claws repeatedly into the same spot. The harsh clang echoed throughout the ship, accompanied by loud stomping on the roof. Connor started the engines, and the sound of it startled the creatures. All banging on the hull ceased. He did a quick preflight check and engaged the engines. The Hellcat rose into the air and Connor set it to auto-hover a hundred feet off the ground. The video feeds showed the ryklars scurrying away.

Connor brought the drone interface back up, and he still only had four drones to work with. They were flying low, marking the progress of the two teams of recruits. He had the drones make a sweep of the area using the creature-recognition software to alert on ryklars.

He opened a comlink to Team Alpha. "Winters, have your team find a defensible position and await further instruction—"

The comlink was severed, and they heard the sound of metal being torn from the hull. Connor engaged the thrusters and banked hard to the right. He circled around and saw a ryklar falling to its death.

"Communications offline. That thing must have torn off the array," Diaz said.

Connor swore. With their communications offline, they didn't have access to the drone feeds. "I'm calling it. This exercise is canceled."

"Are you sure? We can head back to camp and get the drone feeds there," Diaz said.

Connor shook his head. "It'll take too much time. If we go back there only to find out there are more ryklar hunting both teams, we might lose them. They're armed, so they should be able to hold out, but they don't know that those things can camouflage themselves from detection."

Connor brought up the map, and the last known locations of each team appeared. Their ship was right in the middle between the two. He couldn't recall which two drones were offline. Could the ryklars have taken them out?

"Okay, this is what we're going to do. You're going to drop me off at this point here, north of Team Alpha's position. I'll cut across and flank them. I want you to take the Hellcat and extract Team Bravo. They're on a more open plain, so even if the ryklars decided to ambush Randle and the others, they should see them coming," Connor said.

"I don't like just leaving you in the middle of nowhere. You're breaking your own rule about solo missions," Diaz said.

"I know. We need to adapt, and I can move faster alone than we can together," Connor said.

Connor left the cockpit and slipped into his Nexar combat suit armor. The combat suit was designed to be donned quickly, and he used his implants to send the command for the power armor to open. Connor stepped inside and the armored sections closed in rapid succession. The suit was military grade and part of their arsenal of equipment, most of which remained on the Ark. Connor pulled the helmet on, and the power armor computer systems came online. His implants immediately connected to the internal systems. Connor grabbed his AR-71 assault rifle with grenade launcher and loaded the high-density nano-robotic ammunition. His helmet's internal heads-up display showed the ammunition count in the upper right corner.

Connor walked to the back of the ship and opened a comms channel to the cockpit.

"Maintain speed and heading," Connor said.

"I can slow down and give you a softer landing."

"No. Do not slow down. The suit jets are enough for me to make a hard landing and move on. Speed is our most important asset. Since comms is down, we have no way to warn them. Retrieve Team Bravo and then come pick us up. You're cleared to use the Hellcat's weapons at your discretion," Connor said.

Connor was still patched into the Hellcat's flight systems and saw that they were rapidly approaching the drop zone. He grabbed onto the handle and engaged his mag boots so he wouldn't be sucked out of the ship when he hit the button to open the rear doors. The treetop canopy zipped past below him in one green blur. After the initial blast of air that threatened to pull him off the ship, Connor disengaged the mag boots and released his hold on the handle. With two hands on the AR-71, he made a running leap from the ship.

The combat suit's systems sensed the drop in altitude and deployed flaps to help slow his descent, and Connor pulsed the suit's jets to further slow himself down. He clutched his legs together, his armored body becoming a missile, and sank below the treetop canopy. He used his suit jets to maneuver past thick tree branches as best he could, but it wasn't enough to avoid them all. He bounced between two thick trees and gritted his teeth as he crashed to the ground. The combat suit kept his body protected, but the bone-jarring landing left his brain addled for a few moments.

Connor regained his feet and swung around to face in the direction of Team Alpha's last known position. He set the combat suit's systems to scan everywhere he looked. The software would run real-time analyses of the different spectrums, noting any anomalies and immediately alerting Connor. He was ten kilometers from where Team Alpha had last been, and he darted off in a southerly direction.

As he ran through the forest, he tried to keep watch for any ryklars in the area. Their sudden appearance now—and even at the camp two days ago—made him wonder just how intelligent these creatures actually were. The compound didn't have a population count because the ryklars were so hard to find. After his first encounter with the creatures, Connor had searched the Ark database on the known predators and their hunting habits. Most hunted for food, but the ryklars' behavior toward the Hellcat denoted a higher intelligence akin to that of humans.

He set the ammo configuration of the AR-71 for incendiary rounds. He'd have fewer shots than a standard round, but he aimed to intimidate the ryklars by the sheer force of the weapon's capability and hoped the creatures would react like any other animal and run from a stronger foe.

The recruits had their weapons, but they didn't have the military-grade combat suit Connor wore. They hadn't been trained in its use and didn't have the upgraded implants to interface with the advanced computer systems of the suit. The combat suit also assisted Connor with moving much faster than he would be able to without it, but the recruits wore the standard body armor issued by Field Operations and Security.

Connor slowed his pace when he crossed the two-kilometer threshold from Team Alpha's last known position, then stopped and listened. He used the limited communications systems of the suit to try to connect with any drones nearby, but he couldn't find any. Connor started moving again at a slower pace and a few minutes later heard the sharp sound of an M-Viper sniper rifle being fired. He quickened his pace toward the sound and found a large tree he could climb. He slung his rifle on his back and quickly gained a panoramic view.

The forest floor sloped downward toward a nearby stream. Connor peered across to the other side of the small valley, and the way was clear, so he dropped down from the tree and raced across the depression. The sounds of a semiautomatic AR-71 set for three-round bursts echoed above him. Connor crossed the shallow stream and ran up to the top of the hill, where he came to a halt and squatted down to stay under cover. A short distance to his left he caught his first sight of Team Alpha being set upon by twelve ryklars. His combat suit's targeting computer showed six more trying to circle around and flank the recruits. The ryklars used the trees for cover but steadily moved forward. The bodies of several creatures lay unmoving nearby. Connor saw Winters bring her M-Viper up and take a shot. The ryklars dove for cover.

Connor opened a comlink to Winters. "I'm northwest of your position. There are six bogies trying to circle around you to your left."

Connor saw her turn to the left and signal Compton to lay down suppressing fire.

"I can hardly see them, sir," Winters said.

"They've taken cover," Connor replied.

"Sir, they came out of nowhere. Our drone didn't pick them up and our equipment doesn't register them. We tried to reach COMCENT, but we've been cut off."

"Understood. You're doing fine. Keep them pinned down. I want you to start falling back to a more defensible position," Connor said.

He saw Winters glance over toward him, and Connor flashed his IR tag.

"There's a rock wall about half a klick from your position. You should be able to climb it and hold that position," Connor said.

"Sir, these things are smart and they're hard to kill. They'll figure out what we're doing," Winters said.

"They don't know I'm here. They'll follow you, which is what I want, and when they bunch together, I have something special in mind for them," Connor said.

He heard Winters relay his orders.

"Sir, we're ready, but once you reveal yourself they'll pounce on you. If you coordinate with me, I can have the team provide covering fire for you," Winters said.

Connor smiled. "Good job, Winters. This is why I put you in charge of the team."

Connor watched as Team Alpha began an orderly withdrawal from the ryklars. Winters and two others retreated, then provided covering fire for the others' retreat. The ryklars pressed forward. Several climbed the trees and jumped to the next tree, using their claws to propel them along at incredible speeds. Connor saw a ryklar get hit, but it hardly slowed down. He couldn't tell whether the shot had penetrated the skin.

Connor stayed parallel with his recruits, anticipating that the ryklars' hunting instincts would drive them to push forward. Connor clutched the AR-71 and readied the grenade launcher. He glanced at Team Alpha's progress and saw that they were nearing the rock wall.

The pack of ryklars roared as they pushed forward. A small group broke away and tried to circle around the retreating recruits. Connor fired two grenades at the main pack and then another at the smaller group. The grenades landed right in the middle of the creatures and detonated. A small explosion killed the ryklars closest to the grenades and wounded several others. The remaining creatures scrambled back and Connor opened fire. Incendiary rounds streaked into the ryklars, penetrating their toughened skin. The remaining creatures dove for cover, using the base of trees. The recruits also fired their weapons, pinning the ryklars down.

"Good, now run away," Connor muttered.

He moved closer to the recruits and came to the rock wall. The ryklars hadn't come out of cover, and the recruits began scaling the wall, each taking a turn to watch for an attack.

Connor heard rapid foot stomps behind him a split second before he was slammed into the wall. He struggled to regain his feet and then dove to the side. A ryklar slammed into the wall and spun around to face him. The creature's heavy breathing was a mix of grating growls. It held all four of its arms wide, and the clawed, elongated fingers were curled menacingly. The creature charged and Connor swung the butt of his rifle up, catching it in the face. The ryklar shook its head. Connor fired his rifle and the incendiary rounds burned a hole right through the creature's chest.

Another ryklar started to charge, but a loud shot from the M-Viper sniper rifle snapped the creature's powerful head back. Connor engaged the combat suit's jets and jumped ten feet into the air. His armored hands gripped the rock wall and he began to climb. The recruits were near the top, and Winters was providing covering fire. Connor quickly caught up to the recruits and crested the ridge. He spun around and fired his weapon at any ryklar that dared approach the wall. The rest of the recruits reached the top.

"Extraction point is this way," Connor said.

The weeks of conditioning kicked in as the recruits followed his orders and moved away from the edge. Compton stayed by his side.

"It's good to see you, sir," the big man said, keeping his weapon aimed at the cliff's edge.

The area near the cliff was open. Connor activated his IR tag, and the recruits did the same. A few ryklars attempted to come over the cliff, and they fired their weapons at them, convincing them of the futility of that approach.

The Hellcat streaked across the sky and quickly came to their position. Diaz swung the nose of the ship around so the rear doors were closer to them and the doors opened. Team Bravo helped them climb aboard, Connor getting in last. He turned around and faced the edge of the cliff where a lone ryklar stood with its arms hanging loosely. The creature cocked its head to the side.

Compton aimed his weapon.

"Lower that weapon," Connor said.

"But, sir, it's right there," Compton said and lowered his weapon.

More ryklars climbed over the edge, but they didn't charge. Several of them cocked their heads to the side and turned away from the Hellcat. The creatures then began running toward the west with hardly a backwards glance.

Connor frowned and brought up the sonic detector interface for his combat suit. He scanned the higher frequencies.

"I don't understand those creatures," Compton said.

"Sir, any idea why they attacked us?" Winters asked.

"I'm not sure, but check this out," Connor said. He sent the data feed to the nearby wallscreen in the Hellcat.

Diaz set the Hellcat to auto-hover and joined them.

"What are we looking at?" Diaz asked.

"I don't know. It's some kind of high-frequency signal," Connor said.

"Sir, this is beyond human hearing, but perhaps those creatures can hear it," Deacon said.

"That's crazy," Compton said.

"Not necessarily," Blake said. "Their skull is pretty big,

particularly near their ears. I bet they can detect this frequency. Think of it as a dog whistle."

"Who's blowing the whistle?" Connor asked.

The more they learned about the ryklars, the stranger those creatures became.

"Were you guys attacked too?" Compton asked.

"They tried to ambush us," Randle said. "We were fighting them off when Sergeant Diaz came and picked us up."

Connor did a quick headcount and all recruits were accounted for. "Sergeant, get us back to camp."

Diaz headed for the cockpit. The rest of the recruits sat down, but they were all looking at Connor, waiting for some kind of explanation.

"They attacked the Hellcat, too, and disabled our communications. That, and two of the surveillance drones are offline. My guess is that the ryklars somehow coordinated this attack," Connor said.

The recruits took a moment to absorb this information. No one wanted to talk about it anymore, but the questions kept coming to Connor. He'd never heard of any creature besides humans launching such a wide-scale attack.

"We'll debrief when we get back to camp," Connor said.

The recruits settled back into their seats.

"You guys did well today," Connor said.

"But we didn't make the extraction point," Deacon said.

"The exercise was a test of your search and rescue capabilities, as well as your abilities to adapt to new situations. For the record, you all passed this exercise," Connor said.

The recruits let out a hearty cheer except for Randle and other members of Team Bravo.

"Sir, we didn't successfully rescue our targets. Two people were dead," Randle said.

"I'm aware of that, but you did manage to save two of them.

Things are going to happen. Things like that storm—that's going to impact any operation. There are times to take risks and there are times to hunker down. It's the mark of a good leader to know when to do which," Connor said.

"Yes, sir," Randle said. He leaned back, rested his head against the seat cushion, and closed his eyes.

21

THEY RETURNED to camp and Connor had the recruits get checked out by Deacon and Allison. The two medics made quick work of assessing any injuries. Blake approached Connor with all the authority of the ranking medical officer and told him in no uncertain terms that he couldn't simply order her away by insisting he was fine. But except for a few bumps and bruises, Connor *was* fine. The combat suit armor had held up well against the ryklar attacks.

Connor stood outside the Hellcat. The recruits were getting cleaned up and hitting the showers. He had Sean Quinn manning the monitoring station.

"Commander, you should see this," Diaz called down from the roof of the Hellcat.

Connor stepped back inside the ship and climbed the ladder to the roof. Diaz and Compton stood over a jagged hole where the ship's communications array had been housed.

"Those things are freaking strong. It's as if the bunch of us bashed the crap out of this thing with pry bars, except the ryklars did it with their bare hands," Diaz said.

Connor squatted down and took a closer look. "We just need to patch it up until we get back to the compound for repairs."

"You think we'll be recalled?" Diaz asked.

Connor glanced at Compton. "Why don't you go get cleaned up."

Compton left them.

"How long do you think it will be before you'll have this ready?" Connor asked.

"It's just a patch job, so not long at all," Diaz said.

Connor nodded. "To answer your question . . ."

Sean Quinn shouted for Connor from the command tent.

"I think that answers your question. I need to go report this. I'll send Owens up here to help you," Connor said.

He entered the command tent and saw Franklin Mallory's face on the main holoscreen.

"Hello, Franklin, we've got some new intel on the ryklars," Connor said and proceeded to bring Mallory up to speed.

Franklin took a sip from his black coffee mug. "Sounds like you trained them well."

"Considering what they were up against, they've more than satisfied the requirements to graduate to the next level of training. I'd say they've been field-tested and are ready to be put to use," Connor said.

"Good, then it's not a surprise that you're being recalled to the compound. In preparation for this, we've designated part of Field Ops Headquarters for your use, as well as a permanent parking space on the airfield. You'll even have designated barracks while on duty," Franklin said, his eyes gleaming.

"A permanent parking spot. I bet Mills loved that. We'll start breaking down the camp then," Connor said.

"Just make sure the equipment is secure and stowed for now. I'm sure it's only a matter of time before the next class of recruits will start the training. We'll see you tomorrow," Franklin said.

The comlink closed.

News of their imminent departure soon spread among the recruits, which added a spring to their steps. The recruits spent the remainder of the day packing up all the equipment that needed to be secured. Connor had to write up a report of the events that had transpired during the exercise. He recalled many of his fellow officers complaining about the endless reports they had to file, but Connor had never minded all that much. He looked forward to the quiet time to reflect on the performance of his team—the objectives they'd achieved, or failed to achieve. It was how they improved.

The next morning, the first Search and Rescue team of New Earth boarded the Hellcat. Utility bags were stuffed with personal belongings. Weapons crates and ammunition were stored as well. Connor took one last look at the camp and then closed the rear doors, joining Diaz in the cockpit.

Connor engaged the flight controls and the Hellcat rose into the air. Less than thirty minutes later they were landing at the main compound.

"Civilization," Diaz said.

The recruits lined up just outside the Hellcat.

"There will be a graduation ceremony later today. Fresh uniforms are located in the barracks. Report to Field Operations Headquarters in two hours. Dismissed," Connor said.

The recruits snapped a salute and then headed off the airfield. Diaz also left him, and Connor waited for the maintenance crew to arrive. He hadn't spent that much time at the compound, and the training camp felt more like home to him than this did. He noticed a team of Field Operations personnel equipped for an excursion beyond the confines of the compound across the airfield.

Damon Mills was with the team, and Connor walked over.

Mills was issuing orders to his team and they climbed aboard the troop carrier ship.

"I heard you were coming back into town," Mills said.

His tone was neutral, borderline professional, which was enough to pique Connor's curiosity.

"Where you heading?" Connor asked.

"One of the FORBs went dark last night. We're heading out there to see what their status is," Mills said.

"Have there been a lot of problems with the research bases?"

"Can't afford to take chances. Since you showed up, Mallory has had me updating our protocols, which includes that if a FORB goes dark for six hours or more, we have to go investigate," Mills said. There was still some bitterness in his tone but none of the hatred that had been there before.

"I'm not your enemy, Mills."

Mills snorted. "No, you're just a pain in my ass," he said and frowned. "But some of your suggestions did help. I better get to it."

Connor walked back to the Hellcat. There were times when he wanted to choke the life out of Damon Mills and other times when the man wasn't too bad to be around. Connor had no illusions that they'd ever be friends, but it would help if they could work together.

THE GRADUATION CEREMONY was a small affair attended by friends and family of the former Search and Rescue recruits. There were no dress uniforms for any division of Field Operations and Security, so they wore the green jumpsuit with the golden sunburst patch on one shoulder and a white shield with a black lightning bolt across the middle on the other.

Connor stood at a podium, delivering a commencement address to the new Search and Rescue Squad.

"You're the very first class to graduate from the new Search and Rescue Division of Field Operations. I can confidently say that you've set the bar high for the next class," Connor said.

The squad of former recruits rose to their feet and snapped a crisp salute, each with a hungry, confident gleam in their eyes. Connor brought his heels together and returned the salute. His gaze lingered on each of them.

Juan Diaz stepped forward, shoulders back and chest puffed out. "Lightning Platoon, dismissed."

There were cheers from those in attendance. Connor glanced over at Tobias and Ashley Quinn, each of whom wore proud expressions for their son. Allison Blake was alone, and she walked over to Connor.

"We're missing Noah," Blake said.

"Agreed. No one here at the compound for you?" Connor asked.

Allison shook her head. "My brother is still on the Ark."

"Oh, I had no idea," Connor said.

Nate Poe came over and asked if he could borrow Blake for a few minutes, so Connor was left standing alone. He saw Diaz was with his on-again-off-again girlfriend, Victoria. Connor never knew what to do with himself at these types of formal functions. He'd stay here for his new team because they deserved that much, but he wouldn't like it. He'd been on the colony for just over two months and he still felt completely out of place.

Ashley Quinn spotted him and came over. "Boy, if you don't look like a fish out of water, I don't know who does."

"Have you heard from Noah?" Connor asked.

Ashley shook her head. "He's still at Lenora's research base. So what are you going to do now?"

"Do you have a job for me already?"

"Not my department. Speaking of which," Ashley said as Franklin Mallory joined them.

"The man of the hour," Mallory said.

"Not me. Them. Have you reviewed the mission report for their final exercise?" Connor asked.

"Yes, and I've circulated your comments about the ryklars to our field biologists. They're very excited," Mallory said.

"I wouldn't get too excited. Those things are dangerous and hellish to put down if they attack," Connor said.

"Toughened skin that's resistant to the standard round and the ability to conceal their body heat," Mallory said.

Connor pressed his lips together. "They want to study them?"

"Of course," Mallory said.

Connor glanced at Ashley. "I understand wanting to learn about them, but where are the ethical lines here? This is a highly advanced species with almost humanlike intelligence."

"Calm down, Connor. We're not going to start bagging and tagging them. We did, however, retrieve a few of the deceased specimens to study," Ashley said.

"They respond to a high-frequency sound, and I wonder if we can trace it to the source. When is Noah getting back?" Connor asked.

Mallory frowned. "I thought you knew. Forward Operating Research Base number 97 has gone offline. I sent Damon out there this morning. They should be arriving at the base soon."

"Mills mentioned going to investigate an offline base, but I didn't know it was that one," Connor said.

He kept thinking that the coordinated attacks by the ryklars and their abrupt withdraw from the area were connected somehow.

"What's the matter?" Mallory asked.

"Something doesn't seem right to me. I'm suspicious that the attacks and now this offline research base are connected somehow," Connor said.

"That base is over two hundred kilometers from your camp.

That would be a fair distance for any animal on foot, even a quadruped," Mallory said.

"They hunt those landrunners and they're fast. I need to check into this," Connor said.

"It's okay to take a day off," Ashley said. "There's a team already en route to the base."

"There *are* no days off. You know that," Connor said.

Mallory sighed. "Alright, let's head to the command center and see what we can find out."

Connor and Franklin slipped away from the celebration and entered the command center, where the watch commander greeted them.

"I just need to borrow one of your techs," Connor said.

"Of course. Use Bailey," the watch commander said.

Bailey sat at a workstation nearby and Connor headed over to him. Bailey had a pouch gut and long shaggy hair. He saw Connor and Franklin and immediately straightened up.

"What can I do for you, sir?"

"I want you to scan for this frequency," Connor said and used his implants to upload the data to Bailey's terminal.

Bailey examined the data dump. "Ultra-high-frequency sound. Hmm . . . Okay, let's task some of our drones on this," he said.

The tech worked through the options for the drone-control network.

"Now we just need to amplify the signal and . . . Here we go," Bailey said.

The graphic output appeared on the screen.

"Can you trace it to the source?" Connor asked.

Bailey frowned. "Not right now. I'd need to task ten percent of our drones for this, but they're needed to support the teams we have in the field. I can, however, tell you which direction the signal gets stronger."

"What good will that do?" Franklin asked.

"We can map out the path of the signal and see what's in its path," Connor said.

Bailey nodded. "Exactly. One sec and I'll put it on the main screen."

Connor looked up from Bailey's workstation and faced the main wallscreen. A map of the area had a quadrant overlay superimposed over the main compound. The signal for the high-frequency sound became stronger in a westerly direction.

"Show the research bases along that path," Connor said.

The doors to the command center opened and Tobias Quinn walked in. He headed over to them.

"What's going on?" Tobias asked.

"Chasing a hunch," Franklin said.

Connor hadn't spoken to the governor since his son had joined Search and Rescue. Franklin quickly filled Tobias in on what they were doing.

"Bailey," Connor said, "show the research bases on the map."

"Sorry," Bailey said and tapped a few commands into the interface.

The output on the map updated.

"There!" Connor said.

Forward Operating Research Base number 97 was a short distance off from the line.

"This doesn't prove anything. We don't have a location for the source of the signal. We just know the general direction, and that happens to be in the direction of the base," Tobias said.

"You're right," Connor said, "but we should investigate. Has Mills checked in?"

Tobias frowned. "Franklin," the governor said and conveyed his opinion on the matter.

"Connor, 97 has had communications issues at least a half a dozen times. It's one of the things Noah keeps having to fix," Mallory said.

Every instinct in Connor's gut shouted that there was trouble at that base. "Lenora said they'd found more alien ruins near the base. What if the signal is from something they've found?"

"That's a hell of a leap, even for you," Tobias said.

"You didn't see how the ryklars reacted to the signal," Connor said.

"How do you know they reacted to the signal at all? We don't know when it began," Tobias said.

"Let me take my team and go investigate," Connor said.

Tobias's eyes widened.

"Mills took a team out there to assess the situation. If they have an issue or observe any ryklars in the area, he'll report it," Franklin said.

Connor glanced at the two men. Neither looked as if they were inclined to listen to him. "Can you at least send a warning to Mills?"

"I know you and Damon got off on the wrong foot, but he's really quite capable. I'll have the watch commander send him a message," Franklin said.

The Director of Fields Ops walked away, and Tobias regarded Connor for a moment.

"I was against Sean joining Search and Rescue, but I've seen some real changes in him. I need to level with you. Sean is meant for more than a glorified soldier. I hope you realize that," Tobias said.

"You should speak to your son about what he wants instead of telling me about your plans for him," Connor said.

Tobias's nostrils flared as he tried to control his temper. Connor left the governor and took a closer look at the information on the main wallscreen.

Franklin met up with Connor. "The watch commander will keep us apprised of the situation," he said and guided Connor from the command center.

Connor felt that they were making a mistake, but his arguments for sending his team had fallen short. Even he acknowledged that his reasoning had a number of flaws to it and that any chain of command would have done as Franklin Mallory was doing right now. Connor established a network connection to the command center so he'd have a firsthand look at any new developments. If Mills missed a check-in, he'd take his own squad to investigate, with or without permission.

22

CONNOR SPENT the rest of the day noting equipment locations and visiting the munitions depot to confirm that his access still worked. He didn't have reason to believe otherwise, but it didn't hurt to check. While there, he put in a requisition for a shipment of high-density nano-robotic ammunition to be delivered to the Hellcat. The desk sergeant reviewed the requisition and gave Connor a hard look.

"This is for that new squad?"

Connor nodded. "That's right. Is there a problem?"

The desk sergeant shook his head. "Not at all, Colonel. My name is Williams, sir, and I just wanted you to know that I appreciate everything you've done for Field Ops."

Williams stuck his hand out and Connor shook it.

"Have we met?" Connor asked.

"Not exactly, sir, but my wife was with the security detail you assisted a few months ago. I'll have the boys deliver this to your ship right away. Regarding your ship . . ." Williams said.

"What about it?"

"I noticed the Hellcat isn't outfitted with the main gun."

"That's right. It was supposed to follow in a different container," Connor replied.

Williams nodded. "We've got it here. Just say the word and I can have it mounted."

Connor's eyes widened. "That would be great. If I had any, I'd give you a bottle of Kentucky's finest bourbon."

Williams held up his hand and shook his head. "No need. I'm a scotch man myself and a group of us have a batch of Canadian whiskey that'll be ready soon. You join us for a drink some time and we'll call it even."

Connor said he would and left the munitions depot, heading for the armory. He spotted Sean Quinn following him and waved him over.

"Shouldn't you be out celebrating?" Connor asked.

"I was, but a friend of mine overheard you in the command center. Do you think there's trouble in one of the research bases, sir?" Sean asked.

Connor glanced around to be sure they weren't being overheard. "Who talked?"

"Sir?"

Connor gave him a hard look and the denial fled Sean's face.

"Lars Mallory told me," Sean said.

Connor nodded, remembering that Lars, Sean, and Noah were all friends.

"It could be nothing. Mills took a team out to a research base that went offline," Connor said.

Sean looked unconvinced. "Permission to speak freely, sir."

"Go ahead."

"Respectfully, sir, that's a load of garbage. If you really thought there wasn't going to be any trouble, you wouldn't be moving supplies to the Hellcat. 'Hope for the best but prepare for the worst' is how you put it, sir," Sean said.

Connor met the kid's challenging stare. "You're right. I think there's a problem at the research base."

"Are we going on a mission?" Sean asked excitedly.

"Keep your voice down," Connor said.

"Sorry, sir. Which base is it? Where is it?"

Connor walked away from the armory doors and Sean followed him. "It's 97."

Sean frowned and then his eyes lit with sudden comprehension. "Oh my god! Noah's there!"

"I know," Connor said.

"We need to do something! We should take the Hellcat and go right now," Sean said.

"We need to do nothing. You should be on your way. If it comes time that Lightning Platoon is needed, you'll be alerted with the rest," Connor said.

"But, sir—" Sean began.

"That's an order, Private. Now get out of here."

Sean's lips became thin. "Yes, sir," he said and turned around.

Connor started heading toward the Armory door.

"Sir, if you plan to acquire something along the lines of Field Ops combat suits, you might be in for a surprise," Sean said.

Connor's shoulders stiffened and he turned around.

"The desk sergeant is a real hard-ass and is loyal to Damon Mills," Sean said and shrugged.

"Shouldn't matter," Connor said and turned toward the door.

"You're right, it shouldn't, but he could bury your request in red tape, and if something really *is* wrong at 97, we'd be delayed getting there," Sean said.

Connor clenched his teeth together, considering.

"And you think you can help out with that," Connor said.

Sean smiled and nodded. "Governor's son."

Connor knew he shouldn't encourage this sort of ploy, but he didn't have time to wait for a desk jockey on a power trip to thwart his efforts. Connor jerked his head toward the door, and Sean entered first.

Sean Quinn stuck by Connor's side after that and made himself useful. Once they were back at the Hellcat, they checked that the communications systems had been properly repaired and that Williams' team had mounted the main gun below the nose of the ship.

"What kind of gun is that?" Sean asked.

"It's not a gun. It's an M-180 gauss cannon and can shoot projectiles up to thirty millimeters in size," Connor said.

Sean's mouth rounded in surprise. "Too bad we couldn't mount something like that to the armored ATV we've got in the Hellcat's cargo area."

"Could never handle the recoil. This cannon is bolted into the Hellcat's frame," Connor said.

"What are we going to do now, sir?" Sean asked.

"Nothing. We've done everything we can for now," Connor replied.

Night had settled over the compound, and they hadn't heard from Damon Mills' team since they were at the halfway point to the research base.

"Shouldn't we recall the others? You know, to be on standby?" Sean asked.

Connor shut down the diagnostics he was running using the Hellcat's computer systems. Everything checked out.

"No," Connor said. "There're protocols in place for a reason. Damon still has time to check in before they're overdue. I'll send out an update and recall the team if something develops. Otherwise, you're dismissed."

Sean looked as if he wanted to make another argument but let it go. "Yes, sir."

Sean left him, and Connor went to the barracks that were set aside for Search and Rescue. He opened the metallic door and walked inside. Elyse Winters was lying on one of the beds and Wayne Randle was on another.

"I thought you guys would be with your significant others," Connor said.

They both sat up.

"Sean contacted us earlier, so we thought we'd stick around," Winters said.

"Guys, I appreciate it, but you can go home. I'll call you if I need you," Connor said.

"If it's all the same to you, we'll stay here," Randle said.

"Suit yourselves," Connor said and headed for the officer's quarters. He couldn't help but feel a little bit of pride in their dedication.

There were two officers' quarters in these barracks, and Juan Diaz slept inside one of them. Deciding not to wake his second in command, Connor went inside his own quarters and lay down. He had every intention of sleeping for the little bit his body required, but he couldn't seem to get settled. After half an hour he gave it up, got out of bed, and activated the terminal in his room. A large holoscreen flickered on. He brought up a map of the quadrant they were in and then put in a flight path to FORB 97. A fully loaded Hellcat would make the journey in about three hours. He checked his connection to the command center at Field Operations Headquarters. There still hadn't been a check-in from FORB 97 or Damon Mills.

Connor went over to the sink and splashed some cold water on his face, looking at himself in the mirror.

"It's *not* nothing," he said and strode to the door.

Once outside, he heard Diaz shuffle to his feet from the other room and hastily opened the door.

Connor looked toward the bunks and Lightning Platoon was on their feet, waiting for him.

"What the hell?" Connor said.

Diaz cleared his throat. "We know you, sir. If you think there's something wrong at that base, we're with you."

Connor walked toward the bunks with Diaz at his side. All of Lightning Platoon stood at attention.

"Alright," Connor said. "Let's get to it. Be on the Hellcat in five minutes."

Diaz clapped his hands together. "Yeah, let's go get her."

Connor looked at Diaz and frowned.

"Lenora. 97 is her base," Diaz said.

Connor shook his head. 'There is no . . . There are lives at stake."

"I know," Diaz said quickly. "And Lenora's there," he said and grinned.

Connor's brows pushed forward. "Just get on the damn Hellcat, will you?"

It was still the middle of the night, so the airfield was quiet. Connor and the others made it to the Hellcat without being seen. They opened the doors and Connor called Amy Owens to the cockpit.

"We might need your help with something," Connor said.

"What do you need, sir?" Owens asked.

"I need you to block our transponder for the next hour. Until then, they can lock us out of the ship," Connor said.

"No problem," Owens said and returned to the back.

Connor went through the preflight checks while Diaz did his own checks.

"At some point we're going to need a pilot of our own," Diaz said.

"I'll place an order at the pilot store," Connor replied.

They were green across the board and Connor engaged the engines. The Hellcat was located on one of the secondary fields for smaller ships used by Field Operations and Connor had noted the hole in security for this field. He ran a quick sweep with his scanners and there were no drones and no Field Ops security in the area. That would probably change after today. He raised the thrusters and they left the compound behind.

Connor had Owens activate their transponder, which would automatically check in at the compound command center. It was a half hour later that Franklin Mallory raised them on a comlink channel.

"This is Gates," Connor said.

He activated the holoscreen and Mallory's face appeared. His gunmetal hair was ruffled as if he'd just gotten out of bed.

"I should have known you were going to be a thorn in my side," Franklin said.

"It's not intentional," Connor replied and checked their heading.

They'd been scanning for any comlink signals from FORB 97 or distress calls from Mills' team and had come up empty.

"I know what you're going to say and I know Tobias is going to have a fit about this. Worst-case scenario, we waste a trip out there," Connor said.

Franklin shook his head and bit his lower lip. "That's not the worst-case scenario. If you're wrong, it's both our asses on the line. I stuck my neck out for you."

"I'll tell him it was all me," Connor said.

"And that you ordered your team without authorization—" Franklin began.

"Cut the crap. Tobias is a governor. He's not an overlord. We started down this path because of what was happening near the compound. We're Search and Rescue. Let us do our jobs," Connor said.

"Okay, we'll do this your way, but I want regular check-ins," Franklin said.

"Will do. I have one more request," Connor said.

"When don't you?"

"Stop worrying. This is the price we pay for being able to live with ourselves," Connor said.

The comlink closed and Diaz shook his head. "Did you bump heads with your superiors back home?"

"Sometimes, but we had a lot of latitude because we conducted operations out of contact with COMCENT," Connor said.

He tried not to think about the last time he'd trusted his gut in his hunt for the Syndicate on Chronos Station. Millions of people had died. He'd spent a lot of nights thinking about it since he'd awakened aboard the Ark, about what he could have done differently.

He brushed those thoughts aside. He was on a planet that was over sixty light-years from Earth. As strange and somewhat familiar as this planet was, it was a place for new beginnings, and he'd committed himself to being a shield for these colonists. Part of him hoped he was wrong and the research station was just experiencing communication issues. If so, Mills would lord it over him for a while. But if Connor was right, at least what they were doing now would count for something.

23

CONNOR LEFT Diaz in the cockpit and went to check on the squad. Their gray metallic combat suits gleamed under the overhead lights. Their helmets were on, but the visors weren't engaged, so he could see all of their faces. Most were armed with the AR-71s, but Winters had an M-Viper sniper rifle and the M11-Hornet SMG holstered on her side. Connor glanced over at Sean Quinn and saw that he had the same equipment. He moved on and stood in the middle of the squad.

"We've had no reply from the research base, so we'll assume the worst. We'll be doing a flyover of the base to assess the situation. Be prepared for a low altitude combat drop deployment," Connor said.

He looked at each of them and they all acknowledged his command. "We'll break out as we did before for your final exercise —same teams as before except either Sergeant Diaz or myself will be with you. Winters and Randle, you'll be our seconds. Is that clear?"

"Yes, sir," the squad said.

"Remember your training. Stay focused," Connor said.

He headed back up to the cockpit and glanced at the broadcast signal. Connor took back control of the Hellcat and sent a canned check-in message to the compound.

The research base was nestled in the foothills of a vast mountain range. Connor had the scanner array activated, but there were no signals of any kind being detected.

"Not the best sign," Diaz said.

Connor focused on the heads-up display as the Hellcat sped along. He'd kept their approach at an elevated altitude so they'd have a bird's-eye view of the research base, and he finally caught a glimpse of a glistening metallic structure in the distance. They were flying over thick forests, so they didn't have a clear view of the ground. Connor switched on the ultrasonic high-frequency detector and the signal was orders of magnitude stronger than back at the compound.

"The source of that signal has to be close by," Connor said.

They closed in on the research base and the scanners detected an energy signature.

"At least the lights are on," Diaz said.

As the Hellcat sped closer, the grounds near the research base appeared to be moving. Connor tightened his grip on the thruster controls.

"They're under attack," Connor said.

There was a large perimeter fence surrounding the standard prefab habitat structures, and there were bright flashes of light all along the fence. Connor magnified the view and saw hordes of ryklars storming the base.

"Look," Connor said, "there are survivors."

They saw weapons being fired into the ryklars, but more kept coming. Connor knew the electrified fence was meant to be a deterrent but couldn't sustain an ongoing assault.

Diaz peered at the screen intensely. "They're only armed with CAR-74s."

"You'd better get back with the others," Connor said.

Diaz pulled himself out of the copilot's seat. "And here I thought I was going to have to talk you into staying," he said and gave his armor a quick check. "You're the better pilot."

Connor glanced at the heads-up display. There were hundreds of ryklars scrambling around and some were making a run on the base. He saw a few make it over the fence.

"Use the incendiary rounds. And scrounge up every weapon we've got on the ship and take them down with you. I'll make passes, cutting into their lines with the main gun. Conserve your ammo as much as you can," Connor said.

"I'll see you down there, sir," Diaz said and left.

Connor glanced at the door to the rear of the ship. He wanted to be on the ground with his team. He was almost of a mind to call Diaz back in so he could fight with the group, but the sergeant was right. Connor was the better pilot, and with the main cannon he could do much more damage from the Hellcat.

The Hellcat flew toward the besieged research base, which was just a collection of standard habitat buildings arranged like a small compound. ATV tracks had worn dirt paths leading away from two gates in the perimeter fence. Connor flew to the FORBs interior and pressed the button that changed the jump indicator in the back of the ship to green. The onboard video feed showed Lightning Platoon in two lines, dropping twenty meters down to the ground. Diaz and Compton pushed an armored, high-impact storage crate out of the back of the ship and then followed.

Connor closed the rear doors and pushed the accelerator. The Hellcat lurched forward and Connor gained some altitude. He armed the main cannon and set it to full auto, then leveled off his approach. The ryklars were concentrating their efforts at the two main gates. They had the research base surrounded, but they moved around so fast that it was hard to get an accurate count. Connor swooped down to make his first attack run, grabbing the stick and squeezing the trigger. The Hellcat's main gun unleashed the M-180 gauss cannon in an onslaught of thirty-millimeter projectiles. The slugs tore a line through the ryklars, cutting them to pieces.

Connor made another pass and this time he saw the red blaze of AR-71 assault rifles cutting into the ryklars from the observation platforms around the research base.

Connor swung the Hellcat around and continued to mow down the ryklars, but they kept trying to get into the base. He made three more passes before the ryklars retreated into the forest, leaving the land outside the base covered with their dead. Connor circled around the base and saw that there were quite a few dead ryklars inside the perimeter fence as well.

He hovered in the air, running a scan of the area. The ryklars must have retreated deep into the forest. He couldn't detect them at all, and the Hellcat's engines were too loud for any kind of sonic detection. Connor made one more pass, circling the perimeter of the research base. He saw the troop carrier Mills had taken from the compound the day before. It looked charred, as if it had been in a battle. There were large gouges in the hull.

Connor brought the Hellcat in for a landing in the middle of the research base, cut the engines, and left the cockpit, taking his rifle with him. The cargo bay doors opened and Connor walked down the ramp, hearing the cries of the wounded. There were research base personnel running around, most looking haggard and scared. They looked at him as if they couldn't quite believe he was really there.

There were two women clutching each other in a firm embrace. One of the women gave him a determined look.

"Where's Damon Mills?" Connor asked.

"We need to get out of here. They're gonna come back. They always come back," one of the women said.

The more levelheaded of the two held the other closer. "Shhh, we're going to get out of here now. The ships from the compound will be here any minute now, you'll see."

Connor's mouth went dry. They thought they were being evacuated.

"This is Carol. She's just scared. I'm Lori."

"I know you've been through a lot, but can you tell me where Damon Mills is? He came on that troop carrier yesterday," Connor said.

"We can't all fit on that ship," Carol said, her gaze fixed on the Hellcat.

"If he's still alive, he was at the gate where the fighting was worst," Lori said.

Connor nodded. "We're going to get you out. Are you alright here?"

Lori sucked in her bottom lip and nodded.

Connor left them and walked toward the front gates. There were several Field Ops personnel gathered around a man who was lying on the ground. Blake hovered over him. Connor went closer and saw that the man was Damon Mills. He had a deep gash down his thigh from a ryklar claw, and Blake was treating the wound with medipaste to bind it.

Damon Mills looked up at him with bloodshot eyes. "Never thought I'd be happy to see you."

"What happened here?" Connor asked.

Damon winced as Blake prodded the wound, and he sucked in a shaky breath. "Where are the other ships?"

"There are no other ships. It's just us," Connor said.

Mills gritted his teeth and tried to get to his feet. Blake tried to stop him and he scowled at her.

"Somebody, help me up," Mills said and looked back at Blake. "Go help someone who needs it."

Blake glanced at Connor and he nodded for her to go.

"I called in an evacuation shortly after we arrived yesterday.

Are you saying the compound has no idea we're in trouble?" Mills asked.

Connor glanced around at the people at the base. They looked exhausted and almost dead on their feet. They kept looking past the perimeter fences as if the ryklars would return at any moment. "Mallory has no idea."

24

Mills sagged on his feet and Connor helped him down to a sitting position.

"Just rest for a second," Connor said and opened up a comlink to Diaz. "What's your status?"

"We've got a lot of wounded people here. Deacon is helping. I had Blake on the other side of the base. The fence is in really bad shape. I don't know how it's still standing," Diaz said.

"Have Randle secure that area. Get Ramirez to assess the fence and then meet me at the Control Center," Connor said.

One of Mills' team members helped the commander to his feet.

"What happened to your ship?" Connor asked.

"Those damn creatures happened. The landing zone for this base is outside the fence. They attacked it sometime yesterday. We cut a path to the ship and managed to move it over there, but it's taken heavy damage. It can't fly," Mills said.

Winters headed toward them with Owens, Poe, Jackson, and Compton.

Connor waved them over. "Compton and Jackson, I want eyes

on this gate at all times. If the ryklars so much as poke a claw beyond the forest line, I want to know about it. Poe, I want you up in the observation tower right there."

The three men left for their assignments.

"Winters and Owens, I need you to get the troop carrier flight-ready if you can," Connor ordered.

They left, and Connor followed Mills as he limped to the command center.

The holoscreens inside showed systems offline and multiple errors.

"Charlie," Mills said, "we need that power generator online."

Charlie wore a dirty blue jumpsuit and looked as if he hadn't slept in days.

"We took it offline to make repairs to the fence," Charlie said.

Mills turned toward Connor. "How many people can you fit on that ship of yours?"

Connor glanced around. "Not enough. Why are communications down?"

"Some kind of interference. That kid Noah was working on it," Mills said.

"Where is he?" Connor asked.

"He was with the archaeological team that went to the ruins yesterday, led by Dr. Bishop. They left before we got out here," Mills said.

Connor's insides went cold. "Yesterday? Did you send anyone to look for them?"

"The ryklars started gathering shortly after they left and stayed in the area, with more coming all the time. They started attacking the fences last night. There was no way we could get anyone through. The team took the only armored ATV," Mills said and gave Connor a sympathetic look. "There's no way they could have held out this long. I'm sorry. They're dead."

An image of Noah joking with him at the training camp's

command center immediately came to mind and was quickly followed by a vision of Lenora with her quick wit and long auburn hair. He remembered the brush of her lips on his cheek.

"I'm not abandoning them," Connor said.

"What about the people here?" Mills asked. "They need your help too."

"I have an armored ATV in the Hellcat. I'll take a small team to assess the status of the archaeological group," Connor said.

Mills limped over to him. "Connor, there's no way they survived the night."

Connor glared at him. "Some would call it a miracle that *you* survived the night here. With comlink signals severely limited, I'm not counting anyone out. On the off chance that they *did* survive, they'll need help. They'll never make it here on foot with all the ryklars in the area."

"We need to contact the compound." Mills frowned in thought and checked the wall clock. "You're early. We're not considered overdue until right now."

"I had my suspicions that something was wrong when you failed to check in," Connor said.

Mills shook his head. "Shit, knowing you, I bet you disobeyed orders to be here," he said and sighed. "I guess I owe you my life, but I still think you're a pain in the ass."

"Likewise," Connor said. "We had communications with the compound until we were within fifty kilometers of this base. I'm going to leave some of my team here to assist in the base's defense. We'll also take the Hellcat out of range of the interference and let the compound know we need a base-wide evacuation."

"Going to the archaeological site is suicide," Mills said.

"Then you can return the favor and come rescue us," Connor said and started walking toward the exit. "Oh, one more thing. My team is very good at their jobs. If they have a suggestion, I strongly urge you to listen to them."

Connor left the command center and recalled his team to the Hellcat. Diaz had armed the surviving Field Operations security detail with the weapons they'd brought. They were now standing watch.

The team assembled outside the Hellcat, with the exception of Deacon and Blake, who were still attending the wounded, and Winters and Owens, who were working to get the troop carrier ship flight-ready.

Connor explained the situation to his team. "Diaz, I want you to take the Hellcat out about fifty kilometers and send an emergency broadcast back to the compound and the other research bases. If there're Field Ops people there with a ship, they're to come here and help evacuate this base on my authority."

"Yes, sir. Where will you be, sir?" Diaz asked.

"There's an archaeological team unaccounted for. They left before the attack yesterday. The last drone surveillance had ryklars heading toward the site," Connor said.

"Is Noah with them, sir?" Sean Quinn asked, his brows drawn up in concern.

Connor nodded. "Listen up. This base needs to be defended. If the ryklars are anything, they're determined to get in here. My guess is they're regrouping for another attack."

"Regrouping," Donna Marten said. "Sir, animals don't regroup like a fighting force."

"The ryklars are smarter than your average predator," Connor said.

"What about the research team, sir?" Sean asked.

"I'm going to take the armored ATV to investigate what happened to them," Connor said. Several people started to speak, and Connor held up his hand so they'd quiet down. "I'll take three volunteers with me, but I won't order any of you to come. None of you have to go, but we're the only chance they have."

"I volunteer, sir," Sean said without hesitation. "We're Search and Rescue, sir. We go where no one else will go."

Sean was echoed by all the rest. All of them were willing to put their lives on the line for this. Connor had trained many soldiers in his career, but all the training in the world couldn't predict how a person would react when they found themselves in the thick of it.

"This sucks," Diaz said, drawing the team's gazes toward him. "I can't volunteer because no one else can fly the Hellcat," he said and glared at Connor. "I told you we needed a damn pilot."

"I have one on order for when we get back," Connor said and looked at the rest of the team. "Thank you. All of you. I'm sure if the others were here, they'd do the very same thing. I've only seen that kind of courage in one other team I've worked with, and they were the best."

The Lightning Platoon's faces gleamed with pride. Connor had told them of the Ghosts on more than one occasion—how they were the most effective team he'd ever served with. He still wished they were here with him, but looking at his new squad, he saw echoes of what the Ghosts had been in each one of them, and it made Connor proud to be their commander.

"Compton and Jackson, you're with me," Connor said.

Sean Quinn gave him a hard look and Connor regarded him for a moment.

"I'm coming with you, sir," Sean said in a determined voice that was reminiscent of his mother.

Maybe it was the fact that Connor had once had a son named Sean, or perhaps it was the fact that Ashley Quinn had been one of the first people on the Ark to be kind to him—a mother figure for all—but he felt responsible for Sean Quinn. He'd even bumped heads with Tobias about Sean and the man he was becoming. But Connor couldn't allow himself to view Sean as a boy anymore. It just wasn't fair.

"Alright, you can come," Connor said.

Compton's deep voice let out a hungry laugh. "You're running with the big boys now, Bling," he said.

Sean smiled widely for a moment and then was back to business.

"You all have your assignments. Protect this base until help arrives. Stay focused. The ryklars like to try to overwhelm their prey. Marten and Poe, you can do more damage up high with your rifles than fighting in the thick of it," Connor said.

Diaz ran to the Hellcat and returned with a small black case, handing it to Sean. "Flare gun. Fire it into the air and I'll come get you with the Hellcat."

"Excellent work, Sergeant," Connor said.

There was still an angry glint to Diaz's gaze, and Connor knew he hated that he couldn't go with him.

"These people need you here. Keep them safe," Connor said.

Diaz snapped a salute and headed back to the ship, muttering about pilots.

Connor glanced at Compton. "Let's get this ATV offloaded."

25

THE ARMORED ATV left the research base at sixteen hundred hours. Connor saw an unnamed mountain range in the distance, its high peaks wreathed in clouds. Jackson drove and kept them moving at a steady pace. He kept a sharp lookout ahead as he drove down the worn path. Compton held his weapon and kept a close watch out of one side of the ATV while Sean Quinn kept watch out of the other side. Connor wished there were a turret on the roof. It would have given them a good view of everything around them.

Connor tried to open a comlink to the archaeological team, but there was no reply. The ultra-high-frequency sonic detector still showed a strong signal up ahead, and Connor was certain the alien ruins were tied to the ryklar attack. What he didn't understand was why the ryklars were so focused on the base.

The forest was quiet but for the steady grind of the ATV's tires on the ground.

Connor ordered Jackson to go faster and looked at Compton. "Standard protocol for remote security is a two-person Field Ops team as escorts?"

"Affirmative, unless there were predators spotted in the area. Then they might have taken two more with them. They'll only be armed with the CAR-74s, and the others will only have sonic hand blasters," Compton said.

"Noah would have brought his own rifle with him," Connor said.

Compton nodded. "I'd forgotten about that."

Connor glanced over at Sean. He cradled his M-Viper with one hand and had his other hand on his SMG. He peered out the window of the ATV, keeping careful watch outside.

"Sir, we're picking up another vehicle's beacon ahead. It's really close," Jackson said.

Connor returned to the front of the ATV and looked at the small heads-up display that appeared over the dashboard. The other ATV was less than half a kilometer away. If the ryklars had broken off from the main group, would the team be holed up in the ATV, or would they have gone somewhere else? He should have asked someone at the base what they knew about the ruins. Any information would have given them an advantage. Instead, they were blazing their own trail. Hopefully, Lenora and her team left enough evidence that they could follow them.

Ahead of them the ground sloped upward, and as they drove over the edge, Connor caught a glimpse of the other ATV. The heavy vehicle was turned over on its side. One of the tan doors was bent outward as if something had used brute strength to tear it open. Jackson slowed down and pulled the vehicle over to the side of the path.

Sean Quinn made a move to open the side door.

"Wait a minute," Connor said.

They waited a full two minutes before Connor opened the door and exited the vehicle. He switched his helmet view to infrared, and the overturned ATV appeared in cool blues, the only warm spots being where the sunlight hit the vehicle. Connor circled around and saw that the windshield had been kicked out. The interior was shredded, but there wasn't any blood.

"I don't think anyone was inside when this damage was done," Sean said, looking relieved.

Connor engaged the sonic detectors and scanned the immediate area. No ryklars were detected. He switched his helmet back to normal combat-assist view, which had a HUD overlay. His suit computer would help identify any threats that came into view.

"Let's follow the path. Compton, I want you to bring up the rear," Connor said.

"You got it, sir," the big man said.

Connor took point with Sean right behind him. Jackson and Compton followed. The path took them through the brush to a large fissure in the ground. Connor glanced up and saw a bright blue sky overhead, but this place would be hard to detect if they were flying. Connor walked to the edge and saw a fifty-foot drop to the bottom. Thick vines with wide, pale yellow leaves grew across the narrow fissure, and Connor could only just make out the bottom.

"There's an elevator," Sean said.

Connor saw the winch system with cables that went over the edge. "See if you can raise the platform."

Sean went over to the winch and pressed one of the buttons. The winch motors started retracting the cables, and Compton and Jackson kept their AR-71s aimed at the area where the platform would appear.

There was a loud snapping sound and then the top of the platform appeared. Connor peered over the edge and then stepped onto the platform. The others joined him and Connor pressed the button to descend.

They moved downward at a steady pace, all of them keeping a watchful eye on the surrounding area.

"I've got nothing in IR," Compton said.

"I'm not tracking any movement either," Jackson said.

Connor tried to reach Noah with the comlink, but there was no answer to his broadcast signal.

They reached the bottom, where a shallow stream trickled by. Piles of dark stone and dirt were off to the side. A flickering light lit the tunnel across from them. Connor gestured for the team to be quiet as they headed toward the tunnel. The rounded entrance was eight feet across and gave them more than enough headroom. Overturned lights littered the ground, but the few that were still working cast a soft yellow light. Connor's helmet display automatically compensated for the dim lighting. The smooth walls had uniform scuff marks from an industrial digger. Connor's heads-up display registered the end of the tunnel at twenty-five feet, and they cautiously approached to find that it opened into an enormous underground cavern. They emerged onto a ledge that overlooked a small underground city. Over a hundred light-stands were positioned on the rooftops throughout the cavern, which gave it an artificial glow. Flat square rooftops stretched out before them with deep shadows down below the rooflines. Faint glowing lines surrounded some of the rooftops, adding more light to the dim cavern.

"I knew they'd found ruins, but this is amazing," Sean whispered.

They were high up above the grounds, and Connor glanced around, looking for a way down.

"Contact!" Sean hissed. He brought up his M-Viper sniper rifle and peered through the scope.

"Easy," Connor said. "Tell me what you see."

"Twelve hundred meters that way," Sean said and gestured toward the left side of the cavern.

Connor looked in that direction and enhanced the view so he could see better. Scurrying from rooftop to rooftop was the spotted back of a ryklar. Connor panned his view but didn't see any more in the area.

"Should I take the shot?" Sean asked.

"No," Connor said.

Sean looked up from his scope. "I can get him."

"I know you can, but I don't want the other ryklars in the area to know we're here," Connor said.

Sean nodded. "Understood, sir."

Connor continued looking for a way to get down and saw a few anchor bolts drilled into the rock wall with a nylon rope attached. They used the rope to lower themselves from the outcropping, and Connor found himself wondering how Lenora had discovered all this in the first place.

They ended up on top of a flat roof that butted against the cavern wall. There were small metallic bridges that connected the buildings, and Connor squatted down to feel the smooth surface. Certain parts of the substance glistened in the light from his combat suit.

Connor led them toward the middle of the cavern. The buildings had octagonal shapes carved into them and he wasn't sure whether they were doors or windows. They were much larger than any standardized door he'd ever seen. Connor opened a comlink and set it to broadcast.

"Archaeological team, this is Connor Gates from Search and Rescue. Acknowledge."

Connor waited fifteen seconds before repeating himself.

The comlink status on his helmet display showed a red circle with a line drawn through it, and Connor was about to repeat himself when the status changed to green.

"Commander, this is Noah Barker. Thank god you're here. We read your signal."

"Good to hear your voice, Noah. What's your status?" Connor asked.

"The ryklars tracked us in here and we lost some people when they attacked. We tried to reach the base, but our signal couldn't get through," Noah said.

Connor could hear the tension in Noah's voice. "How many people are with you?"

"There are seven of us now. We came here with ten, sir."

"Understood. We came in through the tunnel and are near the middle of the cavern. Can you tell me your location?" Connor asked.

He heard Noah repeat the question and it sounded like the comlink was handed off to someone else.

"Connor, Lenora here. Noah said you were in the middle of the cavern. We're—"

A loud screech echoed through the cavern, making Connor jump. He spun around, checking the area. The others were doing the same.

"We've been made, sir," Compton said, pointing his rifle.

Standing on the rooftop a hundred meters away was a ryklar, each of its four arms held out, its muscular chest heaving as it drew breath. Another one climbed up next to it and let out an ear-piercing cry. Several more ryklars climbed on top of nearby buildings within a hundred meters of their position.

"Could really use that location," Connor said.

They slowly moved off the roof they were on and retreated from the ryklars.

Jackson cursed and brought up his weapon. Before Connor could tell him to hold his fire, an incendiary round burst forth from the chamber and streaked a line of red, taking a ryklar in the chest.

The ryklars charged.

"Don't shoot them! We weren't attacked until we fired the first shot," Lenora said.

Connor fired his weapon as they retreated to the next rooftop.

"A little late for that. Where are you?" Connor asked.

Compton and Jackson provided covering fire while Connor and Sean moved to the adjacent building. Sean aimed his rifle, and the M-Viper unleashed with such force that the projectile took out two ryklars that were charging toward them.

"We're inside one of the buildings. Noah said he's painting our location for you," Lenora said.

Connor scanned the area and saw an IR laser moving in side-to-side motions.

"I've got 'em. Fall back," Connor said.

They made steady progress toward Noah's IR signal. The ryklars weren't charging them in a blind rage like they had been at the research base, but there were more coming and the cavern echoed with the sounds of their calls. Connor and the others dropped off the roof and sprinted toward Noah's signal. When they reached the building, a thick octagonal door opened and they rushed inside. It took all of them to push it closed. Connor listened by the door and heard several ryklars growling as they ran by.

Connor blew out a breath and pressed his hand against the door. The smooth cold surface seemed sturdy enough, but he couldn't be sure it would withstand ryklar claws.

"It's made out of some kind of alloy," Noah said.

Connor patted him on the back. "Thanks for showing us the way. I'm glad you're alright," he said and looked at the others in the room.

"Any injuries?" Connor asked.

Lenora stood with her arms crossed and her eyes blazing with anger. "The ryklars had just settled down enough that we were going to try to get out of here, but now we'll have to wait even longer, thanks to you."

Connor frowned. "My team risked their lives to get here. A little appreciation would go a long way."

278   KEN LOZITO

"I'm sorry if you're feeling underappreciated, but the creatures were scattered until you barged in. I was trying to tell you not to shoot them. What is it with you soldier types? You think the only way to solve problems is with a gun in your hands," Lenora said.

"They were closing in on us," Compton said and clenched his teeth.

"Yeah, and you panicked," Lenora said.

"Compton," Connor said, "stay on that door."

Compton blew out a frustrated breath and walked over to the door. Connor regarded Lenora for a moment, and underneath her show of anger was fear. They were all shaken up and lashing out.

"Let's just calm down for a minute. We've got some field rations and water. When was the last time any of you ate?" Connor asked.

At the mention of food and water, the archaeological team perked up and came over. A man in a blue Field Ops uniform approached him. He had blond hair that was shaved on the sides.

"I'm James Brennan, sir. Me and my partner, Craig, are the security detail for this group. I just wanted to say that if your man Noah hadn't been with us, there would be even fewer of us left," Brennan said.

Connor glanced over at Noah, who was off to the side speaking with Sean.

"I'm glad he could help," Connor said.

"Emmerson, Craig, sir," said a man who looked barely eighteen years of age. "Brennan and I would like to join your platoon," Emmerson said and looked away. "If we make it out of here."

"We'll talk about it *when* we get out of here. Just stay focused and be smart, and we'll all get out of here." Connor glanced at Lenora and she looked away. "Give me a moment. Go check in with Compton."

The two Field Ops agents nodded and went toward the door, where Compton leaned against the wall.

Connor stepped closer to Lenora. "Team here looks kind of young."

Lenora shook her head and sighed. "I'm sorry about before. It's just that we've been running around here for over a day and those two won't listen to me," she said, nodding toward the two Field Ops guys. "The ryklars showed up and they just fired their weapons at them. Then the ryklars attacked and two of us were down almost before we had a chance to react. We lost Ellena this morning." There was a catch in her throat. "She was—damn it—" Lenora looked away, her shoulders shaking. Connor reached out and rubbed her shoulders soothingly.

"Sounds like you've been through a lot. It's okay to take a moment," Connor said.

Lenora jerked away and her blue-eyed gaze became stormy. "Don't you try that psychological crap with me, Gates."

"Okay, I won't," Connor said and held up his hands in front of his chest. He then reached inside his pack and pulled out a container of water, offering it to her.

Lenora's gaze softened. "Thanks," she said and drank from the container.

"The ryklars have attacked the research base. Hundreds of them. They even attacked my team back at our camp a few days ago, which is hundreds of kilometers away. I can assure you it was unprovoked."

"The base? Is it . . . Is everyone okay?" Lenora asked.

"There are a lot of people hurt. Mills and his team were defending the base until we showed up. Most of my team is back there helping. They've called for an evacuation by now," Connor said.

"We can't leave here now."

Connor frowned. "It's too dangerous to stay. We've got to focus on getting out of here and figure out why communications are blocked. It's going to be dangerous out there. The ryklars were moments from attacking us, and I won't fault Jackson for defending himself."

Lenora sighed. "How would we even know what provokes them? Our presence here could be enough of a provocation. You react with violence and you'll receive the same in kind. Before the attack they seemed agitated, but I'm not sure by what," Lenora said.

"You want to make friends with them?" Connor said and immediately wished he hadn't.

Lenora thrust the container back at him. "What is it with you? Not everything is black and white, friend or foe. We need to figure out why they're attacking in the first place."

"We need to get out of here, alive. That's my first priority, not doing a study on a creature that wants to kill us," Connor said.

"You don't realize what we've found here. An alien civilization built this place," Lenora said.

"Where did they all go then?" Connor asked.

"Haven't figured that out yet," Lenora said.

Connor glanced toward the door, his gaze taking in the octagonal shape. "You're not going to say the ryklars built all this?"

Lenora shook her head and laughed. "No. De-evolution is the most absurd theory there is. An intelligent species will not suddenly become stupid because of evolution. Cultures and societal practices lead to the downfall of intelligent species, not evolution."

"Okay, so not the ryklars," Connor said.

"Also, we found several statue fragments and none of them look like a ryklar," Lenora said.

Connor pressed his lips together. "So that whole speech about evolution . . ."

"Was just so I could impress you, and it helps me calm down," Lenora said.

Connor felt the edges of his lips pulling upward. "How much of this place have you explored?"

He took a quick glance at the others in the room and tried to gauge their chances of going out the way they'd come in—navigating the cavern and climbing the ropes with the ryklars dogging their every step. Their chances weren't very good.

"We were in here quite a long time before the ryklars showed up. We first discovered this place about a week ago, came across some technology here, and sent for Noah to come help with the analysis," Lenora said.

Connor looked at the sparse room. While it served their purposes, he couldn't figure out what it was originally meant for. "What kind of technology are we talking about here? Advanced tech like what we have? Better? Worse? The same?"

Lenora's brows drew up together in thought. "Not more advanced than us, at least not that I can tell. We didn't find any spaceships or anything like that. We need more time to study this place. Take the material this building is made of—some type of alloy. We need a chemical analysis of its composition, but there are things we can learn from this place that will help with the colony."

"Like a new element. Could be useful."

"Not my area. We've been making new alloys from the elements on Earth for thousands of years. Perhaps this species has a new compound or way of mixing things together. Stuff like that," Lenora said.

Connor nodded. "I understand that this find is important, but my first priority is to get everyone here to safety. I can't do that if we stay in this building. Do you know of another way out?"

Lenora regarded him for a moment. "There's the main entrance."

"Good, let's go there and get out of here. We can make a path and keep the ryklars at bay while we escape. We have an armored ATV that we can squeeze everyone into," Connor said.

Lenora shook her head. "The ryklars are at the main entrance."

"How do you know?"

"I had a small surveillance drone mapping the cavern. The last video feed I saw from it showed the entrance with a lot of ryklars already there," Lenora said.

"What were they doing?"

"I'm not sure. Looked like they were guarding it. They'd go to the interior and then return to the entrance."

"Is it still online? I scanned the area and didn't detect any drones," Connor said.

Lenora shook her head. "No, we lost contact when we entered a chamber deeper inside the cavern."

Noah walked over. "We didn't touch anything. Things just sorta turned on by themselves when we came inside this place."

"What was inside?" Connor asked.

Noah glanced at Lenora for a moment. "It was like a double pyramid. You know, like someone stuck the bottoms of two pyramids together. The middle of it started glowing. That's when the comms went out."

"By the next day, the ryklars started showing up," Lenora said.

"When did this happen?"

"Two days ago," Lenora answered.

"Did anything else start coming on when you guys started poking around down here?"

"Several places had power to them, which I thought was interesting. Why do you ask?"

"Because during a training exercise, my team was attacked by three packs of ryklars that seemed to be coordinating with each other. Then they suddenly ran off and we detected an ultra-high-frequency transmission. The source of it wasn't far from where we're standing," Connor said.

Lenora glanced at the others excitedly. "Some of us thought that perhaps the ryklars were some kind of guard dog for this place. If what you say is true, a lot more of them are heading this way."

Connor's mind raced but kept coming back to the same thing. "We need to get out of here. We can't wait for them to calm down."

"The main entrance is guarded, but there might be a back door if we go deeper into the ruins," Lenora said.

Compton turned around. "Did someone say go deeper into the ruins?"

Connor nodded. "It might be our only way out of here."

"Great," Compton said dejectedly.

"That's why you have the biggest gun," Connor said and then ran his hands over his face. "Okay, we can't stay here. I need to know who's armed and any supplies or equipment you have with you—anything we can use to help us stay alive."

26

For the next twenty minutes, Connor spoke with Lenora's team about the layout of the ruins here. The one thing they had going for them was that the alien race that built this place planned it out like a large grid and used all the space. All the buildings were square, and even the walkways between them had a consistency in measurement that was equal to any of the planned cities back on Earth. If the ryklars hadn't been out there waiting to kill them, Connor could have appreciated that. As it was, he had to pull the useful information he needed from them while asking that they keep their conjecture to a minimum. But these were scientists, a breed of humans that was conditioned to being long-winded.

Connor went to the door. He would be taking point. There weren't enough guns for everyone. Sean had handed Lenora his SMG and she assured Connor that she knew how to use it. Lenora was standing behind him, and at first, Connor had been worried she'd shoot him in the back. Accidentally, of course. But whenever he looked back, she was holding the SMG as if she'd been handling firearms her whole life.

Noah came over to his side. "I just wanted to let you know that I've made some progress with that other project."

"You were finally able to decode it?" Connor asked.

Noah shrugged. "I had some help. I stored my findings so far on my personal data storage device. You're gonna wanna see it. There's been a lot more going on back home than anyone realizes."

"Some people already know," Connor said.

Noah bobbed his head. "Yeah, some people."

Connor had been extremely curious about Noah's side project decoding the data burst from the deep space buoys that bolstered data communication signals from Earth, but he needed to push all that aside.

The two teams were clustered near the door. Connor had assigned them their places and interspersed his squad among them while having Compton cover their six.

"Once we're outside this room, we need to be as quiet as possible. If you spot something, don't shout or scream. Instead, inform the nearest member of my squad or Field Ops security. No one will fire their weapon without my say so unless a ryklar is bearing down on you. We want to avoid a confrontation with them. Is that understood?"

Everyone acknowledged their understanding.

"Lenora and Noah, you're with me at the front," Connor said.

They opened the octagonal door. While the door was heavier than it looked, it made hardly any noise. Connor took a quick look outside and there were no ryklars in sight, so he stepped out and stayed near the wall of the building. He glanced above and didn't see any creatures. Connor frowned, not trusting that the ryklars had just given up on them.

He waved over to the others and they quietly left the building. Connor peeked around the corner of the building and saw that the way was clear. Lightning Platoon's helmets enabled them to see well in the low-light conditions, but the archaeological team didn't have that luxury and had to stick close to the people who could see.

They made steady progress deeper into the cavern. Several ryklars screeched a call that sounded as if they were on the other side of the cavern, but because of the echoes Connor couldn't be sure. They reached the end of the cavern and there was a clear path that went off in either direction. Connor glanced at Lenora, who gestured toward the right. There were rows of squat buildings and the cavern ceiling was lower there.

Noah whispered Connor's name and he looked back. Down the line of people, Compton gestured with his rifle up toward one of the buildings. Connor nodded and held his finger up to the face of his helmet. He brought his rifle up and waited.

Don't be there.

Connor gestured to the others to stay where they were and pointed at Noah to follow him. They crossed the narrow pathway and circled around one of the buildings, then Connor stopped and listened for a moment. He heard the sounds of a clawed foot scuffling nearby, then a blast of the breath sounds the ryklars made. Connor craned his neck around the corner of the building and saw a group of ryklars in the distance, heading toward them. He stepped back into cover and he and Noah went back to the others. Connor gestured to his team that the ryklars were closing in on them. Compton bobbed his head that he understood and focused his attention behind them.

Connor motioned for the others to follow and he set off at a quicker pace than before. The cavern floor became uneven and sloped toward the wall, but the wall curved around to a passageway that led them away from the cavern. He glanced back at Lenora and she gave him an encouraging nod. There was a light toward the end of the tunnel, and as they got closer, Connor realized it came from outside. They jogged the rest of the way to the end of the tunnel and stopped. To the right, the sounds of rushing water came from a nearby waterfall. They left the tunnel and emerged into a forested valley that was surrounded by mountains. Amidst the trees were alien ruins that closely resembled what they'd seen inside. The pathways were carved from a pale stone, which was also used to form the base of the buildings. In the middle of the valley was a tall spire.

"They're in the tunnel," Compton said, trying to keep his voice down.

Connor looked at Lenora. "Have you been here before?"

"Only briefly."

"We need higher ground so we can see where we are," Connor said.

He tried to open a comlink back to the research base, but there was no response. That would have been too easy.

The tallest thing in the valley was the spire, and Connor led them toward it.

Lenora grabbed his arm. "Not directly toward it. The ryklars like to occupy the middle. We should circle around and then go inwards."

Connor changed direction and they skirted the edges of the ruins. The forest had swallowed up some areas of the city. A loud screech pierced the air, echoing off the mountains, and more ryklars responded from inside the valley. Connor quickened the pace, taking the group along the edge. He caught a few glimpses of the interior of the ruins and the spotted backs of the ryklars. They were hunting for them, and Connor quickly started looking for a place they could use to hide.

There were several more screeches, followed by snarling. Connor looked back toward where he'd seen the ryklars and saw two groups of them fighting. They'd charge each other, attacking with their claws, and then they'd break apart.

"Commander," Noah said in a low voice. "I've detected the

source of the ultra-high-frequency waves coming from that tower. If we—"

Noah was cut off as gunfire erupted from the end of the line, and Connor's attention snapped toward the sound. There were three ryklars charging toward them. Compton and Jackson fired their weapons with precision. Sean Quinn aimed his M-Viper and took out the third ryklar with a shot to the chest. Connor called for them to follow him. Abandoning all pretense of sneaking around, Connor led them from the trees into the ruins.

They ran near the remnant buildings and Connor looked at Noah. "If I can get you into that spire, do you think you can shut down the signal?" Connor asked.

Noah's eyes widened. "I'll do my best, sir."

Lenora's mouth slackened. "The two of you can't go off by yourselves."

Connor gestured for the others to come closer. The ryklars were searching the forest but hadn't detected them in the ruins yet.

"We're going to split up," Connor said. "Compton, I want you, Jackson, and Quinn to take these people and hide in that building over there. Noah and I are going to take out the signal coming from that spire. Once it's down, call for backup."

"Sir, you need more than just the two of you if you're going up to the spire," Sean said.

"I'm going with you," Lenora said. "I'm the most familiar with the ruins."

"Bling is right, sir," Compton said. "Take him with you."

Connor didn't like it, but he knew they were right. Their odds of success were higher if they had a few more people with them.

"I hope you guys can run fast," Connor said. "We'll draw the ryklars away."

Connor sprinted away, with Noah, Sean, and Lenora following close behind. He screamed and fired a few shots into the air. The ryklars responded almost immediately, as howling and snarling sounded nearby. Connor weaved his way through the ruins, pushing toward the spire. He glanced behind him and saw a ryklar galloping on all fours, closing in on Sean Quinn. Connor raised his weapon and Sean darted to the side. Connor squeezed the trigger and an incendiary round shot out, hitting the creature in the chest. The ryklar roared and kept coming. Connor shot several more times before it stumbled and fell.

Noah and Lenora passed him, and Sean thanked him when he caught up.

They had reached the bottom of the bronze-colored spire, and Connor saw glowing lights on the inside. He glanced behind him and saw more ryklars running toward them in a frenzy.

"Go on. We'll hold them off," Connor said.

An octagonal entrance lay open before them, and Noah and Lenora ran inside while he and Sean positioned themselves on either side of the entrance. Connor squatted down, using the wall for cover, and Sean did the same thing. A horde of ryklars came toward them down the main thoroughfare. Connor applied the high-density nano-robotic ammunition to his grenade launcher and fired grenades one after another into the horde. As the grenade timers expired, he and Sean took cover. Several loud explosions shook the ground at his feet. Connor came out from cover and ryklar corpses littered the road. Some ryklars crawled away, their roars becoming whimpers. Ryklars beyond the blast radius shifted their clawed feet, rocking from side to side. Some of the ryklars started shoving others, and a vicious battle broke out among them.

Connor heard Sean load a high-density ammo pack into his M-Viper. More ryklars showed up and Connor noted that several large alphas were driving the others forward. The ryklars' growls came from within their mass of thick red tentacles, and with so many of them, Connor felt that he was looking at a horde of bloody beards bringing the promise of death.

Connor heard shots being fired from somewhere within the spire.

"The others are in trouble," Connor said.

He looked for a way to barricade the doorway, but there was nothing. What he wouldn't give for some heavy explosives.

"Fall back into the spire," Connor said.

They left the entrance and headed into the spire's interior. The inside of the spire was an empty space with a hollow shaft running toward the top. There weren't any stairs, but a wide ramp ran along the wall. Connor glanced up and saw that a platform extended from the wall about fifty feet above them.

Connor and Sean ran toward the ramp. They'd just completed their third time around when Connor heard more shots being fired, but he couldn't see what the others were shooting at. He glanced downward, expecting ryklars to come inside at any moment.

Sean Quinn had turned out to be among the strongest of all the recruits, and it was no surprise to Connor that he could keep up with him. They quickly closed in on the platform. There was a pedestal in the middle, and hovering above it was a twin-sided pyramid with a glowing light emanating from the two bottoms. The bottom point of the pyramid hovered between two small columns. There were workstation panels near the pedestal, and one of them glowed red. Five ryklars dropped down from above. Connor brought his rifle up to shoot but waited to see if the ryklars would attack. They seemed enthralled by the twin pyramids. Connor heard a strange hum and the floor began to vibrate. The ryklars turned toward Connor and Sean, then charged. They fired their weapons, tearing the ryklars apart at such a short range. Even in the creatures' final death throes, they tried to claw their way toward them. It was as if they were hyped up on some kind of stimulant.

Connor and Sean ran over to the others. Noah was hunched over the wide glowing panel, which was made out of a curved translucent material.

"Is this the source of the signal?" Connor asked.

"It is, but I can't figure out how to turn it off. I don't know what any of these symbols mean," Noah said.

Connor looked for some kind of power source but couldn't find anything.

"It's held up there by a magnetic field," Lenora said.

The sound of ryklar screeches came from the bottom of the spire. Noah slammed his fist down and growled, then looked back at Connor and held up his hands in silent resignation.

"Stand back," Connor said.

Noah glanced at him and then pulled Lenora away. Connor raised his weapon and fired it at the floating pyramid, but the high-grade incendiary ammunition ricocheted off, making a loud gong-like noise that reverberated off the walls. The ryklars howled in response, almost as if they were in agony. Seeing that his shots had no effect, Connor stopped shooting.

He had another grenade but didn't want to waste it. The ryklars resumed their snarling, which became louder as they got closer to the platform. Sean went to the other side and knelt down. He aimed his weapon and started shooting.

"There's nothing I can do. I'm going to go help him out," Noah said.

Connor looked at Lenora. "Any bright ideas?"

"Well, shooting it was a waste of time," Lenora said and started circling around it. "The ryklars are clearly conditioned to have a response to this thing, and they don't want anyone . . ."

Lenora's voice trailed off. She walked over to the pedestal where the bottom point of the twin pyramid hovered about a foot above the top. She looked back at Connor and belted out a loud whoop. Lenora's voice echoed off the walls of the spire.

Her eyes widened. "Come here!" she said, waving him over.

Connor rushed to her side.

"Does your helmet have a speaker? Can it amplify the sound of your voice?" Lenora asked.

"Yeah, but what good is that gonna do us?"

Lenora whipped out her PDA and brought up the small holodisplay. "This place is one big acoustic resonance chamber. It's designed to amplify sound waves. If we can match the frequency coming from this thing, the acoustics in this chamber will amplify it and cancel out the original signal."

Connor's heart raced. "What do you need from me?"

"Just leave your helmet here," Lenora said and glanced over at Sean and Noah. "And get their helmets and place them on two opposite sides of the platform."

Connor ran over to the others. The ryklars were quickly coming up toward them. He brought his weapon up and fired his last grenade into the ryklars storming up the ramp. Connor ducked down, and Sean and Noah did the same.

Boom!

Connor winced at the sound, the brunt of which he bore without the protection of his helmet.

"I need your helmets," Connor said.

Sean and Noah snatched off their helmets and handed them to him. "Keep slowing them down. Lenora might have a way to stop them."

Connor ran and placed the helmets on opposite ends of the platform and used his implants to connect the output from his helmet to the other two helmets.

He went back to Lenora, who was busy working.

"How long is this going to take?" Connor asked.

Lenora glanced up at him. "I need to record one complete

sequence of the original frequency. Then we'll see. Should only be a few minutes."

The ryklars were getting closer.

"We may not have a few minutes. Do we have to stay in here to transmit the broadcast?"

Lenora jumped at the sound of the ryklars. "No. No, we don't."

Connor grabbed her arm and pulled her along with him. He called for the others and they went back out onto the ramp. They headed upward, and as they curved around the spire, they saw the ryklars from across the way.

Connor glanced at Lenora and she shook her head. The ryklars noticed them and quickened their pace up the ramp.

"Getting low on ammo," Noah said.

Sean echoed the same.

Connor already knew he was low. "Hold your fire. We just need to keep them from doing an all-out charge."

The ramp came to an end and the top of the spire was still high above them. The ryklars came around the ramp. The redness of their stubby tentacles extended upward so their entire faces looked inflamed. There were hundreds of them on the ramp.

"I've got it. Signal broadcasting!" Lenora said.

Connor glanced around, looking for something to happen. The ryklars came to a stop, their heads making jerking movements.

Connor and the others bunched together at the end of the ramp. The ryklars' growling gave way to a high-pitched whining, and the reddish color of their tentacles began to fade. One creature pushed its way through the others and let out a vicious roar.

Connor took a few steps away from the others and howled in response. The ryklar beat its claws on the ground and came closer.

Connor strode forward. "Is that all you've got?"

He heard Lenora say something and Noah urged her to stay back. "The commander knows what he's doing," Noah said.

Connor hoped he knew what he was doing. He glanced down at his AR-71 and the ammo meter showed that he was nearly empty.

When the ryklars reared up, they were easily six feet tall and thickly muscled, but they spent most of their time hunched over.

Connor watched as the ryklar's claws twitched, and he ventured even closer, screaming and waving his weapon back and forth. The ryklar jerked its head to the side and looked as if it were wincing in pain. Then it collapsed to the ground. Other ryklars did the same, but there were still hundreds of ryklars between them and the exit.

"It's working," Lenora said.

Connor slowly moved back toward the others. With the ryklars quieting down, Connor was able to hear the loud groans of metallic supports protesting under too much weight.

Shit.

The others looked around in alarm. The floor shook beneath their feet and there was a loud crashing sound beneath them.

Connor grabbed hold of Lenora. "Hold on to me," he said and pulled her into a firm embrace.

"We've got to get down. Use your suit jets to slow down your descent," Connor said.

"I'm almost out of propellant," Noah said, his eyes wide with terror. "I had to use some—"

"I've got you," Sean said. "And if you tell anyone about this, I'll kick your ass."

The loud snap of a cable ripping echoed throughout the spire.

"No time," Connor said.

Holding on to Lenora, he leaped away from the ramp, using a burst from his suit jets to push them out into the middle of the shaft. They quickly closed in on the central platform. The twin pyramids tumbled to the side, falling off the pedestal, and then the platform crashed down to the side. Lenora cried out. They were free-falling down the spire. Connor gritted his teeth. Without his helmet, he had no readout that told him how far away the ground was, so he had to judge based on what he saw. He fired his suit jets in a long burst. Holding on to Lenora threw off his center of gravity, and they sailed toward a ramp filled with ryklars, but the creatures hardly noticed them. They were still disoriented from the signal going offline. Connor leaned toward the left, angling the suit jets, and they moved away from the ramp.

Sean and Noah flew past them. Connor saw that Sean was trying to slow down using his jets, but the two of them weren't aligned. There was nothing Connor could do. He could hardly keep himself and Lenora stable as they barreled toward the ground. He saw the two young men slam against the side of the ramp and bounce off, hitting the ground hard.

Connor fired his suit jets at full blast and they landed roughly. He clutched Lenora's body to him while holding her head to his armored chest. His feet got tangled and they both went down. Above them the ramp supports were coming apart faster and soon the whole thing was going to come crashing down. Connor quickly regained his feet and helped Lenora up.

"I'm fine. Go check on the others," Lenora said.

Noah and Sean were sprawled nearby, and neither of them was moving. Connor ran over to them. Without bothering to check whether Noah and Sean were alive or dead, he grabbed hold of each of them and started pulling them toward the exit. Lenora came to his side to help. Connor heaved and pulled, and they dragged the two boys through the exit.

Sean Quinn cried out in pain. There was blood coming through the arm of his combat suit. Connor could hardly breathe as he kept pulling, and he heard Lenora gasping as she did the same. He glanced up at the spire towering above them, and it looked as if it were swaying.

"Come on, damn it," Connor said through gritted teeth.

He wasn't going to let those two boys die here. He made his burning muscles move through sheer force of will, and Lenora grunted with effort. Connor's foot slipped and he fell back. Then he heard the pounding boots of people approaching from behind.

"We've got this, sir," Compton said.

Connor looked up in surprise. Compton and Jackson, along with the two other Field Ops agents, picked up Noah and Sean.

Connor pushed himself to his feet and helped Lenora get up.

"Sir, we have to move," Compton said.

"Don't wait for me," Connor said.

Lenora stumbled, favoring one foot. The spire started coming down. Connor scooped Lenora up and ran.

"To the side!" Lenora said.

Connor bolted to the side, following the others into the forest. Loud cracking sounds came from behind him, and a blast of air pushed him onward. Connor tried to go faster, but he had almost no strength left. Lenora told him to put her down. Connor glanced behind them as the spire crashed down right where they had been.

Connor gasped for breath. "How are they?"

Sean and Noah had been placed on the ground. Sean was awake, wincing if he tried to move, and Noah was unconscious.

"This one has a broken arm and the suit computer says a few cracked ribs," Compton said, gesturing toward Sean Quinn. "I'm not sure about Noah. He got banged up pretty bad."

Lenora hobbled over to Noah and began assessing his injuries.

Connor glanced around. "Where are the ryklars?"

"They hardly chased us. Most of them followed you into the spire. There're still some in the ruins, but they're acting strange," Compton said.

"Sir," Sean said, his voice hitched higher in pain.

Connor went over to him. "Just lay there."

"In my pack . . . flares, sir," Sean said.

Connor rooted through Sean's pack and found the flare gun just as a comlink registered with Connor's suit computer. With the spire down, communications had been restored. Time enough to figure that piece out later.

"This is Search and Rescue," Connor said.

"Search and Rescue team, this is the Hellcat. What's your position? Over," Diaz's voice said over the link.

Connor held the flare gun above his head and fired. He waited a few moments and fired again.

"I have your position. Will be there in a few minutes. Hellcat out," Diaz said.

Connor sat down because he couldn't stand up anymore. He was spent. Compton told him that he'd found a safe place for the archaeological team to stay while they made their way to the spire. Compton offered him some water and Connor drank it. Not wanting to get too stiff to move, he got back on his feet and looked out toward the ruins. The ryklars swayed on their feet as if they were too exhausted even to stand. Some of them collapsed to the ground. A few of the creatures glanced toward them when Diaz came with the Hellcat, but none came any closer. They carried Sean and Noah on board.

"Evacuation of the base has started," Diaz said and paused to take a good look at him. "What the hell did you do in there?"

Connor coughed and felt a sharp pain in his side, which made him wonder if he'd broken a few ribs, too. "Oh, you know. Jumped down off a tall building after Lenora fixed our communications problem and saved our asses."

Lenora glanced over at him. She'd just secured Noah to the stretcher in the Hellcat. "You need to sit down. Diaz, make him sit down. He's got injuries. I know it."

"So do you," Connor replied.

Diaz shook his head. "You guys are a pair, I tell you," he snorted.

They finished getting everyone on board and Diaz flew the Hellcat out of the alien ruins. Connor sat down and leaned his head back, took a deep breath and blew it out. He'd thought colony living was supposed to be easier than this. He hadn't been this exhausted in a long time.

He activated the wallscreen nearby. There were hundreds of ryklars among the ruins, but they were hardly moving at all.

"I don't think I've ever seen them so calm," Connor said.

Lenora watched the wallscreen. "Are you recording this?"

"I am now," Connor replied.

He looked over at Sean and Noah. Both were strapped to a stretcher. They'd be at the research base in a few minutes. Connor closed his eyes.

27

CONNOR WAS JERKED awake by the Hellcat's rough landing. He looked around the cargo area as the others were jostled from their thoughts. Connor sucked in a deep breath and rubbed his face with his hands. His nanites gave him a distinct advantage over others in that he needed less rest to fully recover his strength, but the fifteen minutes it had taken to fly from the ruins back to the research base hadn't been enough.

The rear cargo doors opened and Allison Blake ran up the ramp, heading directly to the two stretchers where Noah and Sean lay. She knelt down and immediately started assessing their injuries.

Connor walked down the ramp and saw Damon Mills in the distance, coming toward the ship. He walked with a limp and was using a stick as a makeshift crutch. There were multiple troop carrier ships setting down and lifting off as the base was evacuated. Lenora came out of the Hellcat and stood by Connor's side. She glanced at all the damage—from the ruined perimeter fences to ryklar bodies outside the fence and inside the base.

Mills stopped in his tracks when he saw Lenora and the rest of the archaeological team step out of the Hellcat, and Lenora asked Connor what was wrong.

"He thought your team was all dead," Connor said.

Lenora frowned. "Given the state of this place, I can hardly blame him, but I'm glad you didn't share his opinion," she said and looked back at her team. "Looks like we're evacuating. Take a few minutes to gather your personal belongings and come back here."

Diaz came out of the Hellcat. "Sir, Blake reports that Noah and Sean are stable, but we need to get them back to the main compound for treatment."

"Understood," Connor said.

Lenora glanced at Connor. "I assumed that since you've gotten us this far we'd catch a ride with you back to the compound."

"I wasn't going to just up and leave you by the side of the road. I'm not that heartless. I'd at least make sure you had a ride home first," Connor said.

Lenora's mouth rounded in surprise and then she narrowed her gaze. "If you leave without me, I'll hunt you down."

Connor laughed.

"Dr. Bishop," Mills said as he approached. "I'm happy to see that you and your team are alive. We've initiated the system shutdown of the research base, and the data backups are already en route to the compound."

Lenora thanked him and then headed over to the command center.

Mills walked over to Connor. "You have this habit of proving me wrong. I'm thankful you and your team were here. They were critical to our survival even after you left."

"How bad was the attack?" Connor asked.

"They came at us hard like they did before. Thanks to Diaz in the Hellcat and the weapons you brought, we managed to hold them off. There were some casualties. It seemed that the ryklars became even more ferocious before they suddenly broke off their attack and headed your way," Mills said.

"We might have had something to do with that," Connor said.

"Judging by how you look, it must have been quite an ordeal. There'll be more of a debriefing when we get back. I wanted you to know that you're still a pain in the ass, but if you ever need anything . . . let's just say I owe you a few," Mills said.

"I'll hold you to that. And one more thing before we get out of here. I know there's something going on with the colony and how we came to be here, and I'm not the only one. I know you and Mallory probably know more about our situation here than most," Connor said.

The frown on Mills' face became grim. "You're right. We'll talk more when we get back," he said and walked away.

Connor watched him go. Mills hadn't even tried to deny it, which bothered Connor more than he cared to admit. The rest of Lightning Platoon returned to the Hellcat, and Connor greeted them. He was relieved they'd all made it, although not entirely unscathed. Some of them had a few wounds requiring treatment.

Diaz shook his head. "You never let up. No sooner does one crisis end than you want to jump into the next one."

"I understand the need for secrecy, but if what Noah found is really as bad as it sounds, everyone has a right to know," Connor said.

"Right to know what?" Lenora asked. She carried a large backpack stuffed to the max.

"I'll ready the Hellcat for takeoff, sir," Diaz said and fled.

They went back to the ship. "One of Noah's side projects. Something we were working on together," Connor said.

Lenora arched an eyebrow. "Oh, you're the other person. I knew he was working on something, but he wouldn't say what it was."

She stored her pack in one of the compartments, and Connor glanced at the cockpit.

"We've got a few hours' flight back to the compound. You can fill me in on the way," Lenora said.

She leveled her gaze at him as if daring him to tell her that he couldn't talk about it.

"Why don't you join us up front and we can talk," Connor said.

"Oh boy, I get to sit up front with the big boys," Lenora joked.

28

It had been barely two days since the evacuation of Forward Operating Research Base number 97. Connor had shared the information Noah had found with Lenora, and she was as perplexed as the rest of them despite her close friendship with Ashley Quinn. She advised him to take his concerns directly to Franklin Mallory and Tobias Quinn. There would be a debriefing at Field Ops and he'd use that opportunity to kick over some rocks and see what turned up.

Since Connor still didn't have a permanent residence at the compound, he stayed at the barracks near Field Ops where he'd just returned to get cleaned up. There was hardly anywhere he could go in Field Ops without someone expressing an interest in joining Search and Rescue. Between answering questions about ryklar behavior for representatives from the field biologists' office and checking on Sean and Noah at the hospital, Connor had very little time to himself. Sean and Noah had suffered some broken bones and Noah had a concussion, but otherwise they would make a full recovery. Quick healing treatments would have them back on their feet in no time. He'd also met with the rest of his platoon to go over the events that had transpired at the research base. They would be returning to the alien ruins to retrieve the armored ATV they'd left behind.

There was a knock on his door.

Connor had just finished dressing in a Field Ops green jumpsuit with the Search and Rescue shield on his arm. He opened the door to Sean and Noah.

"Shouldn't you two still be at the hospital?" Connor asked.

"My leg has healing strips around it and I can walk on it now," Sean said.

Connor looked at Noah with a raised brow. "You had a head injury. I know you're not cleared to be here."

"Oh come on, you don't think I'm going to stay in bed while you confront Tobias and the others alone," Noah said.

Connor considered having Noah escorted back to the hospital.

"Sir, I checked the readouts for the halo Noah's been wearing. The numbers over the last twenty-four hours show that the swelling has gone down almost all the way," Sean said.

"So you're a doctor now?" Connor replied.

"No, sir, but you know my mother. Some of that stuff rubs off, and I've worked a rotation through the hospital."

Connor speared a look at Noah. "Alright, but if you feel the slightest headache, dizzy spell, or anything like that, I want your word that you'll speak up."

"Yes, sir," Noah said, his eyes shining with excitement.

They left the barracks.

"Haven't they given you a permanent apartment yet?" Noah asked.

"I'm holding out for a place with a waterfront view and a boat," Connor replied.

They walked to Field Ops Headquarters and headed to the

upper levels. Diaz met them along the way and had Lenora with him.

"They moved the meeting to the conference room across from the command center," Diaz said.

"Any idea why?" Connor asked.

"Above my pay grade."

Connor smiled a greeting at Lenora.

"I figured I'd be here too, since you told me about Noah's side project," Lenora said and looked at Noah. "Shouldn't you be resting?"

"I already told him," Connor said.

They walked past Franklin Mallory's office, and his son, Lars, was just coming out of the command center.

Lars' eyebrows rose. "What's going on?"

"Time to get some information about that thing I told you about," Noah said.

Connor heard Lenora snort. "So much for secrets," she murmured.

Diaz opened the doors to the conference room and they walked in.

Tobias and Ashley Quinn sat at the far end of the table with Franklin Mallory and Damon Mills. There were a couple of other people Connor didn't recognize.

Ashley stood up and stared pointedly at her son. "I don't recall inviting the two of you to this meeting. Or you, Lars."

"They already know pieces of it, so whether they find out the complete picture now or I tell them later is up to you," Connor said.

Tobias narrowed his gaze. "I'm surprised. I would have thought you of all people would be familiar with the concept of the need to know."

"There's a time and place for it," Connor said. "I can vouch for

Sean and Noah's character since I've worked with them. And if Lars is anything like his father, that's good enough for me. It's not that far of a stretch that Noah discovered something he didn't completely understand and asked his two closest friends for advice on how to handle it."

"Indeed, the three of them are inseparable at times," Tobias said and looked at the young men, considering.

"I suggest we let them put that youthful energy into something constructive," Connor said.

Tobias glanced at his wife.

"Oh for heaven's sake, sit down then," Ashley said. "But fair warning to you three. You may wish you only knew the half of it by the time we're done here."

Connor sat down in the nearest chair, and Lenora sat next to him. Noah and the others filled the seats nearby.

Tobias cleared his throat. "I guess we'll begin. To my right is Dr. Eric Zabat, astrophysicist, and next to him is Dr. Marie Parks, planetary scientist."

Dr. Zabat was a small man whose facial features looked to have Asian ancestry. His beady eyes showed an active intelligence that Connor had come to recognize in the colonists. Parks was a plump woman who gave Connor and the others a friendly smile in greeting.

"Why don't you tell us what you know first, and then we'll fill in the gaps as we go," Tobias said.

"Sounds fair," Connor said. "While at the training camp, Noah reached out to me about a data burst he'd stumbled upon from the deep space buoy network. I thought he was trying to play a joke on me at first, but the more he showed me, the more interested I became. Noah, why don't you put what you found on the holoscreen so everyone can see."

Noah used his PDA to activate the holoscreen in the middle of the conference table. Two holoscreens appeared so everyone around the table could see the data.

"The data header had this reference: EOD-Extinction Critical Alpha. What followed was a set of programming instructions for the Ark. There was also mention of M. Wilkinson, but I'm not sure who he is," Noah said.

Connor's gaze slid to Tobias. "Admiral Mitch Wilkinson, flag officer of the Battleship Carrier *Indianapolis*. I'd say that's one hell of a coincidence."

Tobias met his gaze and nodded.

"Before the attack on the research base," Noah continued, "I was able to decode the remaining parts of the partial data fragment."

"That's a bold claim," Dr. Zabat said. "How did you decode the message?"

"I had help," Noah said.

Zabat looked over at Tobias.

Connor looked at Noah and pressed his lips together. "He had help from someone on the Ark. Now he's got the entire thing decoded and I'm pretty sure he can find the rest of it. Now tell us what's going on. Why was the Ark mission changed and what happened on Earth?"

Tobias sighed. "Why didn't you come to us when you found the data burst?"

Noah stiffened. "I don't know."

Tobias regarded him for a moment and then looked at Connor. "Only the first group of us who were awakened know what I'm about to tell you. This won't be easy for you to hear."

Connor leaned forward and clasped his hands in front of him.

"When we first woke up we discovered that we were sixty light-years from Earth, according to the Ark's nav computer. The journey had taken us over two hundred years. We only had fragmented records from Earth, which I'll go into shortly. We knew that a Dr. Lucia Stone headed up the effort to override the Ark mission and that she was working with your friend, Admiral Wilkinson. You see, they'd found something in Earth's oceans, some type of parasitic organism or virus. Marie, you're better at explaining this than I am," Tobias said.

"Of course," Dr. Marie Parks said. "Dr. Stone doesn't go into a lot of details about the origins of the virus other than to say that it came from the oceans and eventually spread to humans."

"There has to be more than that. What does this virus do, exactly?" Connor asked.

"It's hard to explain because in some respects it behaves like a virus and in others like a living entity. For example, viruses rarely cross from one species to another. This one does and on a wide scale, particularly among mammals. This virus can affect the DNA of the infected host and causes dormant genes within our genetic makeup to express themselves. This causes the infected hosts to die. Dr. Stone said there were theories that the virus was going through a growth stage as it perfected itself. Nothing was immune to it. They tried to find a cure using every means at their disposal, but the virus had found a rich genetic diversity in one of the most populous species on Earth," Parks said.

"Humans," Connor said, his voice sounding grim.

"Exactly. Scientists attempted to alter the virus since it couldn't be cured," Parks said.

"What'd they do?" Connor asked.

"We're not exactly sure, but Dr. Stone said they made it worse. Instead of weakening the virus, they made it stronger somehow. This was all in the summary, which includes references for more detailed information, but the data is gone. Even parts of the summary don't make sense," Parks said.

Connor glanced at Tobias. "What do you mean the information is gone? Where is it?"

"Oh my God," Noah said.

Connor looked at Noah, but he was watching Tobias, waiting for the governor to confirm what he was thinking.

"The deep space buoy network was designed to transfer data transmissions from Earth to our ship. The buoys bolstered the signal, among other things," Tobias said.

"Right, so why don't we have all the data this Dr. Stone sent?" Connor asked.

"The Ark didn't arrive here entirely free from damage. We've had some system failures. The data was expunged by the Ark's maintenance systems for managing data storage," Tobias said.

Connor scratched the stubble of his beard and his eyes widened. "Are you saying some data janitor program deleted the transmissions from Earth?"

Tobias's eyebrows pulled together. "Yes. There's a fixed amount of data storage available. The updated mission program that included our amended destination took up a significant amount of space. The Ark's systems rightfully determined that the lives of three hundred thousand colonists outweighed the updated information from Earth. The system had been designed for an eighty-five-year journey."

Connor glanced at Lenora, and her mouth was hanging open in shock.

"Can't we contact Earth to find out what happened?" Connor asked.

Tobias slumped in his chair. "We sent a response back, but you must remember that a small data burst will take over sixty years just to reach Earth and then we'd have to wait just as long for a response."

Connor's heart sank. "Can't we recover the data somehow?"

"All attempts have yielded only fragments," Tobias said.

Dr. Zabat cleared his throat. "We're limited to the speed of light, but we don't need to wait that long to see what happened to Earth."

"Show them the model," Tobias said.

Dr. Zabat opened the holoscreens, which showed a distant image of a star with nine planetary bodies highlighted.

"This was our home. The telescopes on the Ark took pictures of our solar system during the first leg of its journey. Here's the image from farther away. I'm going to speed up the orbits of the planets and the simulation is going to emphasize the wobble in the light coming from our sun. This is normal," Dr. Zabat said.

The image moved to the side so it only took up half the space. "This is the current image of Earth's solar system. And remember, anything we see now is from sixty years ago."

Connor watched as a secondary distant image of the solar system appeared on the second holoscreen. The image was from much farther away, but the wobble occurred more often than on the other screen.

"We think the increased wobble is from a massive debris field," Dr. Zabat said.

Connor's mind raced as he tried to think of all the space stations that had been built over hundreds of years—colonies established at places like Mars and Ganymede Station.

"Destruction on an unimaginable scale," Tobias said.

Bile crept up Connor's throat and he forced it back down. "This has to be some sort of mistake. What you're saying doesn't make any sense. How did the virus lead to that?" Connor rose from the chair and started pacing. His thoughts were scattering to oblivion and he kept shaking his head.

"There are references in the data we received that talk about a massive war fought between Earth and the colonies. The virus altered human beings, making them into something else. There was more from Wilkinson. He was adamant about an unstoppable fleet," Tobias said.

Connor wanted to hit something, anything, to distract him from what he was hearing.

"Connor," Lenora called out to him.

Connor looked at her, not knowing what to say. Noah and the others had somber and pale expressions.

"This is a lot to take in. We'll make all the data available for you to look at," Ashley said.

"What was that about a fleet? Is this why they changed where the Ark was going?" Connor asked.

"That's what we think. Now we have a decision to make. This is something those of us in the room have been struggling with ever since we arrived on this planet," Tobias said.

Connor's hands came to rest on his hips.

"We have to decide whether to abandon this world," Tobias said.

Leave! Where could they go?

"Are you crazy?" Lenora said and looked at Ashley. "Please tell me this isn't true."

"Why would we have to leave?" Noah asked.

Tobias cleared his throat. "We think there's a fleet of these things heading here right now."

Connor's hands dropped to his sides.

"We didn't have credible evidence of it until recently," Tobias said.

"Help me understand something," Connor said. "The Ark program took the combined resources of the solar system to build and equip the ship for an interstellar journey. It was the only one of its kind. So how could a fleet of ships that aren't even designed for interstellar travel be coming here?" Connor asked.

Tobias shrugged. "I have no idea how, but the technology is there and we have evidence of something coming."

Connor sucked in a deep breath and looked at the others in the room. "What have you found?"

"Dr. Zabat, if you please," Tobias said.

"The buoys in the deep space buoy network can operate with a bit of autonomy, but they only keep track of the nearest buoys. They report the locations of each buoy in the chain to be sure it remains intact," Zabat said and began updating the image on the holoscreen. "Based on the reports from the *Galileo*, there were thousands of buoys deposited on our way here from Earth. Are you with me?" Dr. Zabat asked.

Connor and the others nodded.

"We would expect to find a number close to the number of buoys deployed when the nearest one checks in, but the number of buoys remaining is less than a few hundred," Zabat said.

Connor frowned in thought. "You think something is using the buoys to find out where we are?"

Tobias regarded him for a moment. "You have good instincts for gauging a situation. Given the evidence, what do you think?"

Connor looked away as he searched for some reasonable explanation that could account for what Tobias and the others were saying.

"You know what? Take a few minutes to consider it," Tobias said.

The governor got up and left the conference room with Mallory and the two scientists. Ashley stayed behind and went over to her son.

"You knew about this?" Sean asked.

Ashley nodded. "We didn't know how to tell you."

Connor glanced at Noah, who looked extremely pale.

Noah noticed him watching. "I'd hoped it had all been a mistake, some misunderstanding. What do you think?"

"I don't know what to think," Connor said.

"We look at the evidence," Lenora said. "We look at the data they have and validate the claim."

"What if they're right? Let's assume for a moment that it's just as they say and we are the last . . ." Noah's voice trailed off.

Connor's shoulders slumped and he used the chair to hold himself up. "Damn it!" he cried and pulled the chair away from the table, flinging it into the wall. He began pacing and shaking his head, then looked at Ashley for a moment and turned back around.

Lenora stood up and looked at him with concern.

Connor spun around. "You know, when you first pulled me out of that stasis pod and I got down here, I told myself that he'd had a good life. Wilkinson was a man of his word and would look after him." Sorrow closed Connor's throat and he swallowed hard. "It was the only saving grace for coming to terms with the fact that I would never see my son again, and now that's been taken away."

"Oh, Connor, I'm so sorry," Lenora said.

All the assumptions he'd had about his son having a good life melted away and the inside of his eyelids felt hot. Instead, he was filled with the certainty that his son had died a horrible death along with everyone else he'd ever known. He took several deep breaths to steady himself and something cold took over inside him —that part of him that showed up when he'd fought battles with his old platoon. It swept the pain to the side so he could think and function. He had no other choice. To give in to everything he felt would unravel him, and that was something he couldn't do. Not now.

Tobias and the others returned to the conference room. Damon Mills looked at Connor and gave him an understanding nod.

Lenora came over to him and placed her hand on his arm. Her touch was soothing. "Are you alright?" she asked softly.

Connor shook his head. "No, but I'd rather know the truth than believe a lie."

He bent over and righted the overturned chair, bringing it back to the table. Tobias sat down and waited.

"We'll want to see the data, but given the loss of so many buoys . . . In any other circumstance, I'd say it was a hostile force following a trail of breadcrumbs right to our door," Connor said.

"You mentioned before that you were considering whether we should leave?" Lenora asked.

"This isn't my decision to make," Tobias said. "But it might be our best option."

Connor shook his head. "No, it's not."

"We've deployed a few telescopes and have them mapping the nearby stars for habitable worlds. We could pack everyone here back on the Ark and head to one of those worlds," Tobias said.

"That's a terrible idea," Connor said.

Tobias frowned. "We've had months to consider this and you've only just found out. You should know that there are more than a few of us who think this might be the best option."

"Well then, I'd tell them the same thing I'm telling you. Leaving is the last thing we should do," Connor said.

"Why don't you tell us what you're thinking?" Ashley interjected before her husband could reply.

"You've worked hard to build a colony here. There are things in this world we simply didn't have back home," Connor said.

"You mean the alien civilization that died out here?" Tobias said.

"For one. Lenora says there's a lot we can learn from them. Perhaps there's something we can use. If we pack everything up and try to run to some other star, there's no way to know what we'll encounter once we get there. And there's also no guarantee that whatever is on its way here wouldn't find us wherever we go," Connor said.

"Statistically, we have a much better chance of survival if we were to move the colony to another place without leaving a trail of breadcrumbs for those things to follow," Zabat said.

"Oh, really? Tell me, how fast are they coming? Do you know when they'll get here?" Connor asked.

"It's hard to say. We don't have an accurate date for the last transmission from Earth. It could be ten months from now or ten years," Zabat said.

"Do we really want to risk our lives on another few hundred years' journey on a ship that's already out of design specifications and hope for the best?" Connor asked.

"When you put it in those terms, no, but we've been checking the Ark, system by system," Tobias said.

"We can dig in right here. Make this place our home. We've already expended a tremendous amount of resources to set up what we have here," Connor said.

"How can we succeed where billions of people have failed?" Tobias said.

"I don't know," Connor said.

"We know hardly anything about them. We don't know how many there are, whether it's one big ship or a fleet, not to mention the specifics of the virus," Tobias said.

"We know they're coming, which is more than the people of Earth knew. That's what this Dr. Stone gave us: a warning. Not to mention three hundred thousand of humanity's best who are still asleep on the Ark. We have intelligence and a new world. Let's leverage our assets. I, for one, would rather spend the next few years preparing to face an enemy I know is coming than take my chances on another journey where I have no control over my own fate," Connor said.

Tobias leaned back in his chair and breathed deeply.

"I agree with him," Mills said, speaking up for the first time.

"Really? *You* agree with him. I think you're feeling appreciative that he saved your life," Tobias said.

"Maybe, but Connor has demonstrated skill sets we're lacking," Mills said.

"Tobias," Connor said, "I know you and the others conceived this whole idea of a colony with the intention of distancing yourself from people like me—the military, that is. Your instincts are telling you to run. Mine are telling me that we stay and fight. Most of you left Earth for your own reasons—the sense of adventure, pioneering to the unknown, a fresh start. I bet not one of you expected to be the last humans in the universe. But we may have to accept the fact that everyone and everything we left behind is gone, killed by an enemy we can't even begin to understand. The mission was altered for a purpose, and that purpose was to give us a fighting chance.

"Someone back home kept sending us messages about the enemy because they thought we would need it, that we'd be here to receive them. We owe it to those brave souls to make a stand here. You said we couldn't make this decision on our own. Then let's wake everyone else up and decide. Perhaps there's someone who'll have some key piece of knowledge we'll need."

Tobias rubbed his forehead in thought.

"I agree with Connor," Franklin Mallory said.

Lenora did the same.

"I do as well," Ashley said.

Tobias glanced at his wife with his mouth open wide.

"You're the smartest man I know and you've done a great job getting this colony started, but in this, Connor's right," Ashley said.

"Once we wake everyone up, there's no going back onto the Ark," Tobias said.

Ashley nodded. "I know," she said.

Tobias sighed and swung his gaze to Connor. "You know, when you first showed up I didn't know what to expect from you, but it definitely wasn't something like this. Even if I was against waking everyone up, I'd be outnumbered by the votes of those already awake."

Connor nodded, not feeling the slightest bit satisfied. He'd already moved on to the next task. A small part of him demanded that the grief he was locking up inside must have its due, but he wouldn't let it. He'd spent more years as a soldier than not, and those instincts drove him onward. This colony was only just beginning, and he would see to it that they had a fighting chance to survive.

29
———

SEVERAL DAYS after learning about the fate of Earth, Connor found himself on the Ark once again. He hadn't even thought of returning to the behemoth-sized ship that had carried all the colonists to this planet, but Ashley Quinn had been insistent that he come at once. He'd brought Sean with him on the shuttle.

"Your mother can be . . ." Connor said.

"You have no idea," Sean said.

They docked the shuttle and left the hangar bay. Ashley had given them instructions to come straight to the medical wing. It was a bit strange for Connor to be back there. The last time he was there, he'd thought he'd been taken prisoner by the Syndicate and this was some elaborate way to test out their interrogation techniques. Boy, was he way off the mark on that one.

Sean knew the interior of the ship better than Connor, so he led the way. They went to the medical wing where he remembered first coming awake. They passed Dr. Baker, who did a double take when he saw Connor and then scowled. Connor ignored the doctor and headed to the administration area. A duty nurse was sitting at the desk. She looked up and smiled, recognizing Sean.

"Oh good, you're here. She's been expecting you. She's down the hall in room twenty-three," the nurse said.

Sean thanked her and led Connor down the hall. They reached room twenty-three and knocked on the door.

Ashley Quinn opened the door and smiled at both of them. "You brought my son with you. What a nice surprise."

"I had a mother once, too. I know what you guys like," Connor replied.

Ashley gave her son a quick hug and then beckoned them inside the room.

There were two stasis pods across the room and Connor glanced at Ashley. "What's this about?"

Ashley walked over and stood between the two pods. "Remember when you wanted to know if there was anyone else here we weren't expecting? Well, take a look for yourself."

Connor walked over and peered inside the pods. A wide grin escaped his lips and his eyes gleamed.

Sean walked over and looked inside. "Who are they?"

Connor put his hand on one of the pods. "This is Major Kasey Douglass and that is Wil Reisman. They were part of the Ghosts."

Sean's eyes widened. After hearing Connor talk so much about his old platoon, they'd become legends among Search and Rescue.

"We're not finished going through everyone yet, but if this Admiral Wilkinson got the three of you on board the Ark, there's a good chance he got the rest of you on as well," Ashley said.

Connor laughed and couldn't keep the smile from his face. Finding the Ghosts would help immeasurably with training more troops. He narrowed his gaze at Ashley playfully. "You brought me here to help wake them up."

"Of course. Can't have another one of you military types running around the ship, acting crazy. Sit tight. This is where things get interesting," Ashley said.

Connor kept looking at the stasis pods as if he wasn't quite sure whether this was a dream. He'd wondered what the admiral had done with the other Ghosts. It would be tough on them, but at least they would have their unit to support them. It was a cold comfort, but sometimes the men and women who served with you were what got you through the day.

———————

THANK you for reading *First Colony - Genesis.*

IF YOU LOVED THIS BOOK, please consider leaving a **review**.

Comments and reviews allow readers to discover authors, so if you'd like others to enjoy *First Colony - Genesis* as you have, please leave a short note.

The First Colony series continues with the next book, but before you grab the sequel, I'd like to offer you a free science fiction story I wrote. If you join my mailing list, I'll send you a free copy of **Crash Landing**, a story that features Kladomaor and the earliest events in the Xiiginn uprising that plunged the Boxans into an interstellar war. You can read Crash Landing for free by signing up by clicking the link below.

Click Here to download your FREE copy of Crash Landing

The First Colony series continues with the 2nd book - **First Colony - Nemesis**

ABOUT THE AUTHOR

I've written multiple science fiction and fantasy series. Books have been my way to escape everyday life since I was a teenager to my current ripe old(?) age. What started out as a love of stories has turned into a full-blown passion for writing them.

Overall, I'm just a fan of really good stories regardless of genre. I love the heroic tales, redemption stories, the last stand, or just a good old fashion adventure. Those are the types of stories I like to write. Stories with rich and interesting characters and then I put them into dangerous and sometimes morally gray situations.

My ultimate intent for writing stories is to provide fun escapism for readers. I write stories that I would like to read, and I hope you enjoy them as well.

If you have questions or comments about any of my works I would love to hear from you, even if it's only to drop by to say hello at
KenLozito.com

Thanks again for reading *First Colony - Genesis*.

Don't be shy about emails, I love getting them, and try to respond to everyone.

Connect with me at the following:
www.kenlozito.com
ken@kenlozito.com

ALSO BY KEN LOZITO

SPACE RAIDERS - FORGOTTEN EMPIRE

SPACE RAIDERS - DARK MENACE

ASCENSION SERIES

STAR SHROUD

STAR DIVIDE

STAR ALLIANCE

INFINITY'S EDGE

RISING FORCE

ASCENSION

SAFANARION ORDER SERIES

ROAD TO SHANDARA

ECHOES OF A GLORIED PAST

AMIDST THE RISING SHADOWS

HEIR OF SHANDARA

IF YOU WOULD LIKE TO BE NOTIFIED WHEN MY NEXT BOOK IS RELEASED VISIT
KENLOZITO.COM